NICK SMITH is a bestselling a··· ꞌ   ꞌ
Charleston, SC. His previous
Killer Cult, *Scriptwriting*: *The*
writer and producer on movies, ꞌ
He founded and ran Scotland's   ᵤne
Writers' Studio in England for tw

Since moving to the USA in 2c   ꞏᵢₖed with the Actors'
Theatre of South Carolina and othe. ꞏᵢₑatre companies, as well as the
Charleston City Paper (writing a regular visual arts column), the *Post
& Courier*, *Charleston Magazine* and *The Scotsman*. He recently
directed *For Liberty*, a feature film set during the American
Revolution.

Undead on Arrival

NICK SMITH

Luath Press Limited

EDINBURGH

www.luath.co.uk

This novel is a work of fiction. Any references to historical events; to real people, living or dead; or to real locales are intended only to give the fiction a sense of reality and authenticity. Names, characters, places and incidents are either the product of the author's imagination or are used fictitiously, and their resemblance, if any, to real-life counterparts is entirely coincidental.

First Published 2007

ISBN (10): 1-905222-49-1
ISBN (13): 978-1-9-05222-49-0

The author's right to be identified as author of this book under the Copyright, Designs and Patents Act 1988 has been asserted.

The paper used in this book is recyclable. It is made from low chlorine pulps produced in a low energy, low emission manner from renewable forests.

Printed and bound by
Bell & Bain Ltd., Glasgow.

Typeset in 10.5 point Sabon by
3btype.com

Thanks to the following friends for their unstinting Southern hospitality:

Chris & Clarence, Boo & Macon, Borys & Valerie, Sharon & Rodney, Michael & Eileen, Dennis & Pamela, Stef, Patrick, Charles, Curtis, Trev, Nitin, David, J.C., John, Mark, Jamie, Philip, Christie & Hutch.

Special thanks to my editor Tim West for wading through six years' worth of rewrites to lick *UoA* into shape.

'That Time I Called You Ugly' by Sir Funk, reproduced by permission of Remote Music Publications. 'We Are Naughty Ladies' by The Naughty Ladies, by permission of Naughty Ladies Corp. 'Crashin' Those Gates,' 'Dead Or Alive,' '(Dead Men) Tell No Tales,' copyright 2006 Tewkie Shephard, by permission of Lambchop Cuts. 'Dead End,' 'Philanthropy' by Reuben Whitley, The Estate of Reuben Whitley, by kind permission of Candid Publishing, Lincs.

A short film adaptation of *Snap Judgement* premiered at the Folly Felder Film Festival, South Carolina in 2004. It was directed by Trevor Erickson.

Video People

I feel no pain dear mother now,
But oh, I am so dry!
O take me to a brewery,
And leave me there to die.

Anon, 19th century

More than one man has gone to sleep calmly in the evening not to wake up again in the morning.

Ferdinand Hodler, Inscription, *Night* 1889–90

For some people, living with the consequences of their actions is worse than death.

John Dance, *Top Priority*

CHAPTER I

Heroes and Villains

GLEN GLASS WISHED HE was dead. The deceased have no responsibilities, they have nothing to fear, they don't lie awake at night worrying about their utility bills. Their relatives are left to pick up the tab and deal with any bureaucratic nonsense. Best of all, the dead don't have hangovers. In Glen's experience there was nothing worse than having to come to work after a night of heavy drinking.

He blamed his friend Mark for dragging him out at the last minute. It hadn't been Glen's idea to stay out so late, especially on a Thursday. But the bright lights of Broughton Street can beguile the most abstinent of men, and Glen was fond of a pitcher or two at the weekend.

He sat at the staff room table, his left elbow soaking up a pool of spilled coffee. His round face and wide green eyes were dull, his shoulders slouched. His hairline receded slightly and he didn't always bother to shave. He had his favorite jacket on, which was comfortable but overworn. He didn't like his clothes to look too new, like he was some showoff wetback just out of the mall, 'look at me in my fine straight-off-the-counter clothes' – he preferred comfort to keeping up with the clothes horse Joneses.

He wore trainers, and jeans with grass stains from coffee break kickabouts on the lawn behind the shop. There was a low drone between his ears that wouldn't stop. Trying to shake the dogbite buzz he focused on twisting his wedding ring round his finger, back and forth, watching the fluorescent light catch the gold plate.

Glen's wedding ring wasn't much to speak of. It was cheap and lightweight, paid for by his in-laws back when he'd been the dark half of a penniless young couple. It was a simple band with an inscription on the inside: *Misbah*. The ring felt heavy to him – in fact, it seemed that he'd never carried anything heavier.

Glen had read stories of convicts who were branded by their jailers. He didn't carry a mark, but to him the engraving on his ring was the modern equivalent. His wife owned him, told him where to go and what to do, frowned or scolded when he didn't act as expected. In return for a quiet life, Glen kept his head low and kept wearing the ring.

Misbah was no ogre; she was petite, shorter and slimmer than her husband, and more serious as well, her black hair always tied back in a severe bun. She would brook no nonsense and spoke her mind whenever she got the chance. With her deep brown eyes and thin lips she lulled a lot of people into underestimating her, but she liked a good argument and won every one that she started. She loved Glen and was prepared to do anything for him, sacrificing a career to help him raise two kids, but that didn't mean that she'd put up with any old nonsense.

Glen's workplace, a modest independent store called Video People, often became a refuge. He could do what he liked there (boss and customers permitting) without his wife breathing down his neck. She probably felt the same way when she escaped to her office, a small insurance company on Queen Street. The couple would occasionally meet for lunch – Glen's store was five minutes' walk away from Misbah's building – but lunch hours are supposed to be relaxing, so more often than not they would stay in their respective staff rooms with a sandwich instead.

Today Glen sat on his own, hunched over a Soup in a Box, inhaling its spicy beef musk. His sinuses were blocked up and he felt tired most of the time – a result of too many late nights out boozing with his pal. For some twisted reason, his exhaustion was the source of much amusement for his colleagues. They all knew that Glen was hungover, and although nobody said anything about it they tried to make as much noise as possible, and Tony gave him all the heavy work to do.

Tony Atone was the boss. He had little interest in movies and less in the business side of the store. He'd set up the enterprise with some money left to him by his late mother-in-law. He enjoyed meeting the public, having long-term membership of the Chamber of Commerce and best of all, telling people what to do. His underlings lived in the constant fear that he'd lose interest and close up overnight. Tony feigned a playboy existence, complete with yacht club jacket and well-groomed moustache. He was a menace who gummed up the work whenever he was in the store.

To beat the workhorse blues there were Glen's colleagues – his band of brothers, fellow sufferers, the angels on his shoulder. Or so he liked to dream. If his colleagues had really been angels, they would have been of the biker variety. Alan Hayes (long limbs, short hair, long face) was in charge of snacks, memorabilia and other useless tosh. He'd enjoyed a sedate time until Pokémon hit big, when his counter became besieged by snotty kids who'd do anything to get particular cards. And what do you do with a ten-year-old schoolgirl who attempts to shoplift a Mewtwo power card? Slam her in the local nick and throw away the key? Alan hadn't liked children very much before they became obsessed with Japanese trading cards. He liked them even less now.

Dour old Russ Coyle was the curly-haired chief buyer, up to date on all the top-selling items from Europe and the Orient. At the moment, along with the usual blockbuster titles, he was hawking action figures tied in with various films. Tod McFarlane's *Spawn* toys always sold well – they were imaginative and highly detailed. Like the strips and cartoons they stepped from, these creations were lurid, glossily packaged and overpriced. Tony thought that £12 for a six-inch toy was about right. Glen found it a little steep.

The breadth of merchandise available these days was astounding. The figures were lifelike in the way they looked and moved. There were movie spin-offs and accessories to die for, not to mention robotic gadgets and shelfloads of junk with a horny plastic stink.

If Glen had been younger, the right age to collect such tat, he would have been in heaven, acting out stories featuring his favorite characters from those all-time great films and shows: *X-Men*, *Yellow Submarine*, *Scooby Doo*. You could even get tie-in statuettes of Eminem and the Muppets, or Kubrick versions of the *Pulp Fiction* gang. They cost twenty pounds a piece, but with these lumps of rubber and plastic in your hands *you* could control the adventures of your idols – not some Hollywood producer or jumped-up band manager.

Glen had to settle for buying a product for his son, watching the boy playing with it for a couple of days – Dad wasn't invited – then chucking it in the cupboard and ignoring it. Until, that is, Glen found it, started fiddling with it. Then Paul would snatch it away, claim it as his, run out into the garden. The toy would end up in the bin, left in a Burger King or swapped for a WWF doll. Nothing was sacred in Glen's house, not even a father's heartfelt present to his son.

Despite Glen's mopes, the store was a cool place to work. The stock changed weekly, ensuring a shifting array of colour all around the premises – sleeves, posters, mysterious cartoons from the Far East. Glen liked to see punters' faces light up as they spied a rare release they were looking for, or noticed that a new historical epic had arrived. He would listen to the excited talk of browsing schoolchildren, arguing over who would win in a fight between Batman and the Crow, and didn't mind helping people to find a tape that they couldn't quite remember the title of – like, you know, the one where Hugh Jackman plays a time-travelling Englishman?

Most of all, he loved his wage packet – Tony handed it to him on the last day of every month. It always contained a different amount, depending on how much overtime Glen had racked up. He would hold the small white envelope up to his ear, rustling it between finger and thumb, trying to guess whether there was a bonus inside. The kind of release that made *his* face light up.

On this grey day, with his paycheck long spent, determined to live up to his motto 'I put off till tomorrow what I don't want to do today,' Glen hadn't moved for the past half-hour. He had that dead man feeling, as if his body was on automatic, a flesh machine serving no intrinsic function. His lunchtime ended swiftly and he dragged his aching body behind the counter. In his hand he held the spicy beef soup, now stone cold, and he plonked the murky mug on the counter with a splash. The surface was covered with a Spaghetti Junction of coffee rings and dirty coasters, which the sales team enjoyed expanding each day.

Sipping his soup, Glen saw his ghoulish reflection in the bottom of the mug. *This is what I'll look like when my life is over,* he thought. *Sometimes it feels like my life is over already.*

One of his regulars entered the shop, a big-boned guy with bald-patched hair and a dark brown beard – his eyebrows had just started to grey. His name was Vian Lucas. He worked in the political arena, had a wife and a dog, but his first love was John Dance.

Dance was a movie character with a franchise that spanned the past couple of decades and an appeal that crossed to Asia, the Middle East, and even parts of Galashiels. His premise was simple – he was a spy psychologist, always in the thick of action despite his own reluctance, helping mentally unstable secret agents overcome their problems and dissuading evil maniacs from conquering the world.

Vian had been raised on Dance's family-friendly, action-packed extravaganzas. Although Glen didn't like Vian all that much, the two men had the special bond that only fandom can bring. They spoke a secret language, with the talent to quote dialogue verbatim from Dance's epics; they had shared memories of the hero's loves, losses and outré gun battles.

Right now though, that bond was on the point of breaking thanks to a car boot sale dispute. Glen liked to visit jumble sales and second hand stores, looking for Dance items to add to his collection, hoping to find some rare gem amidst the piles of old books and unwanted tapes. On one of his Sunday morning trips to Pilton, he'd found an old film can with an intriguing label.

The can was marked *Peter Foothill*, and as any fan knew, this was the name of the director of the first ever full-length John Dance movie, *Spyland*. Foothill was said to have defined the celluloid hero just as Sam Robbins had defined the version of literature, incorporating his own dress sense and cultured tics into the character.

Trying to contain his excitement, Glen asked the seller for a price.

'That tat?' The man shrugged. 'A quid?'

Glen had reached for his wallet, not daring to say anything in case the man heard a tremor in his voice and realised that the can might actually be worth something. But before he could pull out some change, a voice said, 'I'll give you ten.'

Glen didn't know how long Vian had been standing behind him. Turning, he looked his fellow fan dead in the eye, trying to decide how stubborn he could be. 'That's a tempting offer,' Glen eventually said, 'we could all do with a few more bob in our pockets. But this man,' he looked directly at the car-booter, 'obviously has integrity. Everyone heard him agree to sell me that old thing for a pound.' In actual fact, no one was interested in the transaction apart from the two fans and the seller, who looked embarrassed. 'He couldn't possibly go back on his word. Could you?'

After a brief hesitation, the man shook his head and took the money. Heading out of the car park with his booty, Glen was stopped by Vian.

'Wanna take a look in this thing?' Glen asked. Vian nodded in a slow, sullen way. 'It's probably nothing,' Glen continued, prying off the lid with frost-numbed fingers.

'You're right,' Vian giggled, 'it is nothing.' The film within was unmarked and skinny. As Glen held a few frames up in the harsh morning light, they saw blotchy images that had no place in a John Dance film. 'Looks like you saved me a tenner.'

'The can's still a nice collectible.' Glen had to have the last word, leaving Vian to feel hard done by, but he didn't feel smug for long. Misbah was always telling him off for wasting money on rubbish; the rusty old can under his arm looked less attractive than his usual finds. He also felt guilty for stiffing the seller, but hey, it was just junk.

Now Vian had returned to the video store for the first time since the sale. He didn't need to ask about the film strip. As soon as he stepped up to the counter, Glen told him that he hadn't been able to watch it.

'I took the damn thing home, held it up to the window to see what was on it – the frames were full of blotches. Tried to find a projector to run it on, but those things are pretty much obsolete.'

'You could get it transferred onto tape,' Vian suggested, his eyes burning bright with curiosity.

'I'm not gonna fork out twenty quid for a bunch of blotches. I was robbed.'

'Can you lend it to me? I'd like to take a look at it.'

'I don't think so.' This was a tricky moment. Glen had lent stuff to Vian before and he'd never seen it again. 'I'll hold onto it for the time being.' He folded his arms and tried to look stern. The can was stashed under the counter, wrapped in a carrier bag. As far as Glen was concerned it would stay there until Vian left the store.

Unable to look Glen in the eye, Vian turned to a shelf packed with movie memorabilia, caught sight of an action figure and waved it under Tony's nose.

'This Agent Erickson figure looks nothin' like him,' Vian moped. 'His arms're too short.'

Tony gave him the time of day and not much more. Only Glen paid any real attention to Vian, engaging him in lengthy conversations – anything to avoid working in the stockroom. These discussions were often heated, along the lines of what should be done with the John Dance franchise, the best writers and directors, reminiscences about the strengths of the series: in Glen's opinion, the stories and characters; for Vian, the special effects. While Glen tended to ignore the finer points of the movies' behind-the-scenes technical work, Vian revelled in them, soaking up facts like a hairy bath sponge.

When Vian saw Glen's eyes glaze over, or had shot his bolt of nerdy facts for the day, he would break off the discussion and amble out of the shop. Glen had got used to this pretty quick, but whenVian tried on this occasion he saw no reason to be polite.

'Where d'you think you're going, chum?'

Vian halted mid-shamble. He wasn't used to this kind of treatment. 'I've, um, got to run. I'm late.' Glen knew that he had nowhere to rush to. Vian disappeared anyway, and Glen shook his head in bewilderment. Fanboys were a species unto themselves.

The shop was quiet that afternoon, thank God. Glen wasn't interrupted as he unravelled a few feet of the film, holding it up to the light so that he could see the frames again. He couldn't make much out – a few lines and blobs, plus the image of a man in spectacles – but he marvelled as sunlight shone through the flimsy strip of celluloid. He knew that a movie was an illusion, still pictures running past a bright light, tricking his brain into believing that the movement on screen was fluid. Still, he felt there was something magical about the whole process. There didn't seem to be much that was magical about his car boot find, however. Glen rolled the film up in annoyance and put it back in the carrier bag, leaving the empty can out so that he could admire it.

Returning to his duties at the counter, he watched a gorgeous girl in her early twenties, her straw-yellow hair tucked under a baseball cap with a few strands keeking out as she prowled the aisles. He wondered if she liked action movies, and his heart soared when she perused a copy of *Cyberkill*, one of the best John Dance films. He walked up to her, swallowed hard, and asked if he could help. He tucked his left hand into his pocket so she wouldn't see his ring.

'Is this a remake?' she wanted to know. Her voice was husky; she reminded Glen of Demi Moore. He knew that the movie she held was full of classic scenes, that the film started mid-story (it was the second part of a trilogy-within-the-series) and that you could see the scriptwriter's abilities improve as the tale progressed. This was one of his favourite stories, from a halcyon age of Hollywood yarn spinning. All this information sat in his head and stayed put.

'Yeah,' he replied. 'They changed the locales and the name of the villain, but essentially it's a remake of an earlier Dance movie. Really good.' He kept his explanation as short as he could. He didn't want to seem like a nerdy showoff.

The girl dumped the box back on its shelf. 'Don't like remakes,' she moaned. Glen rolled his eyes. How could someone so bright be so ignorant? He was about to correct her mistake when two men entered the shop, both wearing black leathers and motorcycle helmets. Unlike some of the shifty grown-ups who sulked round the store, these guys were very sure of themselves. They knew exactly what they wanted and aimed straight for it.

The film can sat on the counter for all to see. One of the bikers snatched it up in a gloved fist, raising his visor in salute to his booty, bright blue eyes checking that it was kosher.

Glen left his star customer and went to challenge the thief, but retraced his steps as the second biker produced a handgun and pointed it at Tony. The shop owner's yelp of dismay alerted the rest of the staff.

'What do you think you're doing?' asked Alan, amazed.

'You're scaring my customers,' complained Tony. The vibrato in his voice indicated that he was feared as well.

'I can see you're professional guys,' Alan said in a soothing tone. 'I'm impressed. Now put it away.' As Alan moved within an arm's length of the biker, he was pushed away, landing on his back, winded.

Russ looked down at his colleague. He wanted to get to the door but one twitch of the gun changed his mind and he stayed put. Tony began to whimper.

'Dave, is that you?' Glen recognised the blue-eyed intruder and started to relax. 'Is this some kind of prank?'

'No prank, just business. Stay back, mate.' Dave's companion wasn't so talkative. He swiped at Glen with the butt of his gun, catching him in the face. Glen joined his colleague on the floor.

The strip lights crackled above Glen's head, dimming the room for an instant and giving the thieves an eerie aura. Dave motioned everybody in the shop to lie face down, picking up the film can while the gunman raided the till. Glen looked at the can, which seemed tiny in the thief's black-gloved hand; his hangover evaporated and he turned to look at the girl in the baseball cap. She was terrified.

This was his chance to be an action hero, to get his name in the papers, impress his friends and maybe even get the girl. He started to raise himself slowly upwards, inch by inch so that no one would notice. He looked at the gun and reminded himself that he wasn't on tip top form, that he'd had a lot to drink the night before. What if his reactions were a fraction more sluggish than usual? What if this was a prank being played by Dave – his next door neighbour – that had got out of control? And what if he was shot in the head, or worse? He moved one hand down to guard his groin. He couldn't do it. He couldn't take the risk.

The thieves backed out of the store. This was his last chance to become a have-a-go hero. He dared to raise his head, look the gunman in the face – but he had that dead man feeling again. Rawer this time, as if he was one gunshot from the grave. So he did nothing.

Glen heard the customary beep that sounded whenever the door opened or closed. 'Thanks for staying so calm, crew,' said Tony as the customers fled the shop. He was already reaching for the phone. He'd call the insurance people first, then the police. 'No damage done.'

'My nerves are shred to ribbons,' Russ complained.

'Yeah,' Alan said as he nursed his bruised back, 'we want the rest of the day off.'

Tony frowned. 'If you all want to leave early today, I suppose I can't stop you. Glen?'

Everybody looked at Glen expectantly.

'Can't argue with the majority,' he shrugged. He knew that Tony wouldn't pay him for hours that he didn't work, especially when money was missing from the till.

'Thanks Glen,' said Russ, still in shock.

'I need a cup of coffee,' Alan mumbled, 'calm myself, like.' He headed for the café next door, Russ in tow. Glen took one last sip of his cold soup and spat it back in the mug. He hated Fridays.

CHAPTER 2

Rewind Life

'So this is what it feels like,' said Hernimann, his eyes squeezed shut, fists clenched; 'after all the dirty ops, the secret coups, the lives I've ended. I never looked straight at them. Didn't want them staring at me, accusing me, and I sure didn't want to see the light leave their eyes. Big bad Hernimann, the ruthless butcher, too afraid to look up as I finished the job. That's why I was always so meticulous.' Hernimann coughed and spluttered. 'They gave me a commendation for being good at my job.'

'I know,' Dance said softly.

'Now it's my turn to glare. And there's no enemy insurgent to accuse.'

'Then who did this to you?'

'The worst, most malevolent badass exterminator you could possibly think of. Yeah, me. I knew no one could kill me and I was sick of waiting for 'em to try. So I did it.'

Dance, trying to hide his astonishment, looked at the knife wound in Hernimann's navel. Too much blood had leaked out and the pain must have been almost impossible to bear.

He looked up at Hernimann's face, his eyes. For a moment there was recognition, the assassin channeling his anger into one last anguished look before the light was gone.

From Cold Soldiers *by Sam Robbins*

'WHAT HAPPENS TO US when we die, Dad?'

'Our bodies are buried, or cremated,' Glen replied, disconcerted by the question. He was sitting with his son on their paisley patterned sofa, watching Ricky Diener on TV. 'Some rich poombahs get themselves frozen, to be thawed out in a hundred years' time when there's a cure for their fatal illness.'

'I mean, what happens to me? My mind, what I think?' Paul's chin was tilted upwards, his smooth round face hued blue by the TV's cathode rays. The fair-haired child had aquamarine eyes, short thick fingers and big feet.

'Nothing. Blackness.' Glen wiped at an old pizza stain on the arm of the sofa. It wasn't going to come off in a hurry. 'Nobody knows for sure. Priests reckon we have a soul, which goes to heaven if we're good and hell if we're bad. It's what God-fearing people have decided over the years.'

'I know that.' Paul picked his nose thoughtfully. 'But is it true, Dad?'

'There's a Gullah legend of a coachman who takes folk to the afterlife. He doesn't judge them – he's just a coachman. He holds a whip in one hand and a whipped cream pie in the other. The whip symbolises what's going to happen to you if you've been naughty, and the pie –'

'Means you're going to have a party?'

'Yeah, the whipped cream pie is for a party.'

'Do you believe all that gumbo jumbo, Dad?'

'All I know is, as you get older, tired, it's nice to know there'll be an end to it all. You can shut yer eyes and rest, no more drudgery or worries or responsibilities. Peace. What's got you asking such morbid stuff? Is it him?' Glen pointed at Ricky Diener. The pop oik was shambling around on the telly like an extra from Michael Jackson's *Thriller*.

'Naw. Kelly Cornish at school's always going on about stuff like that. She's a goth, black nails, a bit skinny.'

'You like this Kelly chick?'

'She's weird. I used to hang out with her but my friends made fun so –'

'Don't let your pals dictate your life. You do what your gut tells you, don't worry about what other people think. Start caring about that and you'll never get anything done. Is *Cold Case* on yet?'

Paul flicked channels like a pro.

'Just started.'

'Then get yer scabby feet off the sofa and let's watch it.' Glen froze as soon as he heard himself say those words. *I'm turning into my Dad*, he thought with horror. The unfortunate fate of all sons. *I'm the spawn of Jolly Jack Glass*. And what had been so bad about Glen's parents? They'd ignored him, earning money and having fun instead of spending time with their son. Oh, what a chore that would have been! Helping him with homework, teaching him to ride his bike, giving him the full gen on the bees and the birds. All that had been left to fate, he'd been a latchkey kid and he didn't want to see his own sprogs go the same way.

He spent his free time with Paul and Lucy instead of wasting it on his parents. He didn't return their calls or reply to their letters. He e-mailed them cards at Christmas, Easter and on birthdays, his gift token effort four times a year. Funnily enough, the less they saw Glen, the more they loved and missed him – that idealised version of their son that lurks in the head of every mother and father.

On those rare occasions when the prodigal returned, Glen dreamed of holding a sophisticated, mature conversation with his Dad, chewing over their lives from a healthy, thoughtful perspective. But he knew that it would only take a few hours for the family to fall back into the old rut of emotions that they'd gouged while Glen still lived at home. The father jealous of his son's freedom, friends (more generous) and lovers (younger and more numerous – in the years before Misbah, of course).

Jack wasn't one to bear a grudge. But although he saw little of his thirty-four-year-old son, he still pined for the love Anna had held for him before they'd heard the patter of sweaty little feet.

Glen and Misbah's relationship wasn't perfect either. On the rare occasions when they got out of the house together, they were always out of synch. One of them would be in a bad mood, overtired, with a mind full of troubles or a plain old headache. They weren't experiencing life to the full, enjoying the movies that they saw and the meals that they ate. Above all, they couldn't appreciate each other. What an irony – to spend every day with the love of your life and be too sick and tired to savour the moments.

An example: when Misbah got home late from work that evening, she found Paul and Glen lounging on the sofa, the living room in a state, and a stale sock smell in the air.

'Awright hen,' said Glen absently. 'I was held up at gunpoint this morning. How was your day?'

'I don't believe this. You'd live in a sty if you had the choice, wouldn't you?'

'As long as they had cable,' Paul smiled.

'Where's Lucy?' Misbah asked. She sounded deadly serious.

'Upstairs, doing her homework,' Glen reassured her. His right big toe stuck through a hole in his sock. He wiggled it idly.

'No she isn't. She's playing with my make-up and talking to her friend on the telephone.'

'So why did you ask where she was if you knew already?'

Misbah didn't reply. She stomped up the stairs to vent her frustrations at her daughter. Glen left his son transfixed by the television and snuck into the kitchen.

I'm a thief and I'm going to hell. Not a thief in a bad way – no one's been hurt because of my thoughtless actions, unless you count being hungry as hurt – but naughty enough to face the pits of Hades all the same. I'm eating my wife's Caribbean Crunch.

He hadn't planned on eating the whole packet. He'd got peckish one morning and grabbed a few kernels of wholesome goodness. They'd tasted so good. Forbidden pineapple, raisins – and dried banana, too. He'd had a whole bowl one evening on one of those rare occasions when he was home alone. He'd known she wouldn't realise. But now, weeks later, after much sneaking around the breakfast bar and quiet, frenzied mastication, the box was almost empty and there would be hell to pay. Glen was an unmitigated hypocrite. If she used his Fab Dad mug, he'd throw a completely unacceptable tantrum. Yet he expected her to take such invasions of her privacy like – well, like a man. Glen should have stood his ground and faced her. Instead he buried the cereal packet in the nether reaches of the bin and nipped out for a pint.

It was difficult to get out sometimes. Like a snare, his favourite channel trapped him every Friday night. Cable's Fake TV covered historical events, topical news and the like with a twist – all the coverage was untrue, spoofed or played-for-dead-serious, convincing dull witted viewers that Colorado was flat or that William Wallace was born in Australia. A trip to the cinema, a nice meal at the local Indian, was easily scuppered by one glance at TV Times. Glen knew how to operate a VCR – he had two, a fancy modern one and a creaking top loader – but there was nothing quite like watching a funny show 'live,' as it was transmitted. Glen could laugh with the unseen audiences, watching in surprised amusement as Ray Romano took everything the world threw at him.

Tonight though, Glen had arranged to meet a friend at the local bowling alley opposite his house. He wasn't a member of the club – more of a watcher than a player – but they let normal people in after six. The drinks were cheap, that's what really counted.

The interior was dingy, with a dark brown décor fashionable sometime never. Two large windows looked out onto the street, so that patrons could enjoy a drink and watch passing traffic at the same time. In the centre of the club were two pool tables, the felt faded and thin at the edges. The cues were proudly lined up together like pikestaffs displayed in a rack. The tables were idle and the bar was about half full. Nobody smiled.

As Glen entered he spied Mark O'Murchu, a slim Irishman in designer specs, standing at the bar. Mark moved his body to and fro, out of synch with the jukebox tune – some pop idol pompery.

He was trying to charm a scowling barmaid, asking about her background, taking an interest in her life. The droplet of drool listing on his chin put her off, no matter how many sweet nothings he came up with. So Glen didn't interrupt very much when he leaned in and ordered himself a pint.

'I'll get 'em,' Mark smiled, fluorescent light glinting his dribble. 'Two Buds and a pickled egg please Carol.'

'Charlene,' the barmaid moaned. 'I thought you Paddies only drank Guinness.'

'I've been brainwashed,' Mark told her, 'here too long.' He introduced Glen as a long-term pal, a good for nothing and a John Dance fan, in that order. Glen rolled his eyes on cue.

'Aren't you a little old for John Dance films?' Charlene asked as she served the drinks and took Mark's cash.

'All men are big kids at heart, you know that.' Glen's standard reply.

'Some are bigger than others.' Charlene gave Mark one last look of disdain as she handed his change over. She glided away to darken someone else's day.

'You and your chat-up lines!' Glen declared. 'You couldn't pull a flush.'

'Egg?' Mark proffered the offending object, his fingers slick with vinegar. He scrutinised his fellow patrons. 'They're all wearing the same shoes,' he whispered as Glen ordered two more beers. Mark grabbed a pool cue, put 50p into the coin slot in the nearest table, and set the balls up for a game. One of the bowlers approached, pointing at a blackboard on the far wall. Several indecipherable names had been scrawled there.

'Must've booked a game,' Glen said, leading his friend to a window seat. The bar was beginning to fill up nicely.

'But nobody's playing...' Mark complained quietly.

'These guys are my neighbours.'

'You still coming to Glasgow Tuesday?'

'Course,' Glen sniffed. 'Lost the tickets yet?'

'Give me a chance. Maybe on the night.' Mark had tickets for the Hogmanay street party, arranged by Glasgow City Council and Radio One. A big party traditionally took place in George Square, but there was a lot more going on in the High Street car park. Mark always like to be where the action was, and had invited Glen to join him back in August. With fond memories of the Millennium celebrations, Glen had happily agreed. The tickets were free if you applied in advance; three months had swung it for Mark.

'I interviewed that Ricky Diener the other day,' Mark smirked. His job as a reporter for the *Evening News* occasionally gave him the chance to meet celebs. 'His new single's in the top ten.'

'Lucky git,' Glen muttered into his pint. The club was getting busier and a pair of bowlers racked up the balls on the pool table.

'Who, me or Ricky?'

'Your new celebrity friend. Appearing on *Top of the Pops*, gaggles of girls screaming after him...' It was no coincidence that he'd seen Ricky on TV so recently; the star was engaged in one of those annoying media blitzes so beloved of British personalities – not that Ricky had one.

'I think he deserves a bit of luck after all he's been through.'

'You didn't fall for his marketing gimmick, did you? I thought you were the original Mr Cynic.'

'Oh, it's no gimmick,' Mark replied, eyeing up the jar of pickled eggs. 'He's true blue.'

'He stinks.'

'Well, you got that right. A bit overexposed, maybe.'

'So your full-page interview'll really help with that, won't it?'

'Three pages,' Mark retorted, detecting a hint of jealousy in his friend's voice, 'including a half-page pic. How's your best beloved?'

'She ain't happy, just for a change.' Glen was ready to go... but he felt relaxed and he lived so close – it wouldn't take long to get home. 'Your round, mate.'

Sir Funk were playing on the jukebox now, their usual pub rock frolic:

That time I called you ugly
It was only for a joke
Your sense of humour leaves you
When you're acting the old soak.

I don't mean to be unkind
I'm not the sort that's mean
But there's merry and there's plastered
Rarely somewhere in between.

Mark did his duty while Glen sat, twisting his wedding ring round his finger again. He wanted to tell the reporter how difficult home life was, how Misbah had changed since they'd married and had kids, how he felt trapped and strangely lonely. His wife earned more than him and worked harder, leaving him holding the babies... but Glen and Mark didn't talk about stuff like that. Oh, there were tribal gatherings down the pub for a big game or a few beers, but that kind of camaraderie had a falseness to it, a fake booze-has-brought-us-brothers-together taint. A quick blether over noisy jukebox tunes was totally different from forming a long, deep-meaning friendship with a member of the same sex. Why put yourself out for a chum when you could make do with a brief e-mail instead?

These days people didn't have forever friends; they had electronic pen pals instead. There was a lot to learn about the world from distant relations, but folks knew less now – they realised less – about their own nearest and dearest, their home environment.

Mark and Glen talked cadswallop instead.

'If only we could rewind our lives like videotapes,' Glen mused as Mark returned from the bar. 'We'd be able to take a step back, prepare, tape over the embarrassing bits or dub on a funkier soundtrack. We can edit our memories, recall the highlights and cancel out the crap. But there's always a wee voice inside your head saying "you messed up. On several occasions. You've failed in the past and you'll lose out in the future. I'm not going to let you forget it."'

'Get that down ya,' Mark chuckled. 'There's a special on the Tennents. She could have told me that before.'

'I think Charlene was too busy resisting your animal magnetism.'

'She's called Carol. I told her that the essential interconnectedness of the universe is such that no one individual can ever truly be alone. She's still mulling over that one.'

'Are you feeling alright?'

'Some would argue that remembering your mistakes is a good. We can learn from all our balls-ups.'

'Not true. You only need to look at history, from military campaigns to legal losses, to see that human beings don't get the message after the event. Historical mistakes are repeated after hundreds of years of lesson learning. What chance have I got, me, one person with maybe eight decades to play with?'

'Sure you don't want an egg?' Mark gave a toothy grin, yolk squished between his incisors.

'We toddle on, making more mess the further we step from our homes.' Glen hadn't finished his tirade. 'The only thing I've learned is that if you stay in bed as much as possible, you can avoid a lot of life's problems. No possibility of getting run over by a motorbike, drowning in a vat of oil, choking on a restaurant starter or getting arrested for smuggling. The world would be a better place if people spent more time in bed. I think John Lennon said it better than me.'

Mark shuffled nervously on his wooden stool. One of the bowlers was looking at him funny.

'I want to fast forward my life,' Glen concluded. 'Not all of it, the boring bits. Waiting for a bus, queuing to get into a movie. Any queue in fact. Boiling a kettle, toasting bagels...'

'I'm sick of local court reports. I got some freelance work the other day for this new magazine devoted to horoscopes, *Bits & Pisces*.

Helps pay the bills but it's not what I'm after. I'd like to do more crime stories. Y'know, big-hitting stuff. I could be the next Sam Fuller.'

'Dear Deirdre, more like.' While Mark sucked on his eggs, Glen took the opportunity to tell him about the store hold-up. 'I'm pretty sure it was Dave.'

'Have you had a go at him yet?'

'Confronted him about it? Nah. Wouldn't know what to say to him.'

'He terrorised your store. He should be locked up.'

'He's an old mate. And what would happen if he did get arrested? Some of his heavier acquaintances would come see me and do me over, just for shits and giggles.'

'All you have to do is knock on his door, say hi, then tell him what you think of his pranks. Kick him in the pills if you think it would make you feel better.'

'Would the hold-up make a good story for the paper? Maybe I could threaten him with that.'

'It would've made the front page if someone'd tackled them. Why didn't you do anything?'

A good question. As a boy, Glen had wanted to be John Dance. The character was brave, with a snappy answer to every question. He had experience, intuition and confidence – all the things that Glen lacked.

By the time his own rugrats had arrived, Glen had realised that he would never be hired by the Secret Service for a dangerous field mission. There were, however, more down-to-earth ways to be a hero. He could be a good husband and father. Helping his wife, listening to her, trying not to take her for granted even though every passing day made this more difficult. Empathising with his children, spending time with them but giving them freedom, loving them yet always preparing to lose them. Real heroics. Real life.

Glen had tried this for a while. When his wife interfered – told him he had the ironing board the wrong way round, or wasn't raising

Paul right – he took her comments into account, behaved himself. He brought her breakfast in bed and drove her to work and back. Like a New Year's resolution with a built in timer mechanism, his goodwill had only ever lasted two months. Then they were back to bickering, point-scoring, petty threats.

The kids didn't fare so well. Bringing them up was tough; Glen's feelings for them changed from day to day, love and hate always battling against each other. Paul was a chore and a cherub, Lucy a haloed waif and harpy by turns. Glen had already started saving for her wedding.

The children were miniature money pits, gross generators of snot, bright yellow vomit, tears and selfish tirades. They ruled his routine and killed a lot of the fun in his life. They also gave him satisfaction, a sense of purpose, a reason to exist. Deep down he knew there could be nothing more important. Any other concerns – about his fitness, his back, his mental state – were selfish. There was enough self-concern in the world without him adding to it. So he gave himself wholeheartedly to his kids whenever the thought occurred to him and his ego allowed.

They would drag him out on walks, not telling him where he was going. Always somewhere damp and mucky. Glen didn't mind; it made a change. He was used to making all the decisions, devising activities to suit a whole family. The walks didn't last long – half an hour or so – but life seemed to slow down in the interim. The participants noticed real things, rotten leaves, trampled worms, discarded tea bags and puppy crap. When they returned to their cosy living room with its TV and video games, they appreciated that fantasy world even more. It was safe, supportive, the climate was controllable and the air didn't smell too bad.

'Guess I'm not hero material,' he told his friend, but Charlene distracted Mark again. Glen knocked back the rest of pint number three and stood up unsteadily. He didn't like to drink on an empty stomach – it gave him hiccups – but Mark's egg fad had put him off his dinner. It was time to go home nevertheless. With any luck, Misbah would be asleep (exhausted from work) and the kids would be quiet. He wanted to give Mark a manly hug but worried that this would be deemed inappropriate in a bowlers' club. So he half-raised his hand in farewell instead, and left Mark to watch the hypnotic sway of the barmaid's bosom.

Glen crossed the street with purposeful strides. Round the back of Number Seven, fiddling under the bonnet of a BMW, was Dave Barr. He was a tall, imposing ex-boxer with bright eyes and outrageous sideburns.

'How you doin'?' Dave asked in a mock New York brogue.

'I ain't got nothing for ya,' Glen replied. It wasn't much of a trademark greeting and it didn't mean anything in particular, but it was theirs. 'What the hell were you playing at today, Dave? Where's my film can?'

The thief said nothing for a moment, wiping his oil-stained hands on a green rag. He looked at Glen with caution. 'It wasn't my idea, mate.'

'Whose was it? Y'know, stunts like that put customers off from coming into the shop. If we aren't busy then Tony will start sacking people.'

'Tony's insured, you got nothing to worry about.' Dave wiped his oily hands on his leather jacket. 'I can't say who put me up to it. Sorry.'

Glen looked at Dave's shed, its felt roof loose and flapping in a slight wind. He leaned against a grubby yellow gate, trampling a healthy crop of weeds. 'I'll tell your Mum.'

'No, no, you don't have to do that.' Dave stood up straight. 'I never met the guy who hired us. My partner did.'

'Your extremely violent partner?' Glen frowned. Dave usually worked alone.

'Yeah, apologies for that, man. He got excited. I didn't know he had a gun, not a loaded one anyway.'

'You let him wave a loaded weapon at us? You know us, Dave.

We've lived in the same street for years. You drank all the brandy at our Christmas party...'

'I couldn't control him. He's a nutter.'

'What's he called? Where is he?'

'Leave it, mate.' Dave closed the bonnet of his BMW. 'He's not a pussycat like me.'

'You got the pussy part right.' Glen took his cellphone from its holster. 'What's your Mum's number again? I'm sure she'd like to know you're up to your old tricks.'

'Ash. His name's Ash.'

'Where can I find him?'

'He finds me when he wants something,' Dave sighed. 'He's not too polite about it either – he's the kinda guy you don't say no to, know what I mean? You're into all that spy stuff. You'll get hold of him if you look around hard enough.'

'Some help you are.' Glen ran an admiring hand along the roof of the BMW. 'Another new car, Dave?'

'Yeah, got bored with the old one.' Glen's neighbour was a nice person as thieves went. He trusted Glen. Otherwise he wouldn't have shown off his hot property so blatantly. Every week a new electrical appliance, fancy ornament or small item of furniture. Garden chairs were a speciality – they were seldom locked up or bolted down by their rightful owners. Dave stockpiled them, hocking them off to a lanky guy in Longniddry. This month he was into cars.

'You're not gonna leave that there, are you?'

'Some guy's picking it up in an hour. Just wanted to make sure it was ticking over nicely before I tucked it round the back.' Glen was always in awe of the man's brazen cheek. While he cowered in his home, Dave was out having a wild time, making up his own rules. Glen had never stolen property in his life (not counting Misbah's breakfast cereals), although he didn't mind the odd hand-out from his neighbour.

Dave kept talking, acting as if he'd never held up Glen's store.

Glen was too bemused to argue. 'Doing anything special to see in the new year?'

'I'm supposed to be going out with Mark, to Glasgow – I haven't told Misbah yet.'

'How do you think she'll take it?'

'About as well as anything else I put off telling her, or lie to her about.'

'It's not long off,' said Dave, incredulous. He tinkered some more, deep in thought. 'You should take her out. Butter her up, then break the news to her gently. Take her to Chez Andres. I'll look after the kids. I've not got anything planned this weekend.' He threw the rag and it struck Glen in the chest with an oily slap. 'Ash gave me this, told me to get rid of it pronto. If he finds out what I'm doing...' He shook his head and Glen held the rag tight in his hand, feared that Dave would snatch it back.

'I'd thank you, but after your behaviour this morning –'

Dave didn't hear Glen. He'd already hopped into his car and was revving the engine. 'Sweet as a peach. Give us a shout when you've fixed it with your wife.'

By the time Glen had hicced his way into the house, his family had vanished. The place was tidy, the dishes washed and the beds made – a whirlwind effort from Misbah, no doubt. A scribbled note by the phone told Glen that his wife and kids had gone for dinner at the nearest Pizza Hut.

How unfair! Misbah knew how much Glen loved the Hut's all-you-can-eat deals, loved piling his plate high with goodies from the buffet and hotplates. Or the Treat for Two, where he would order a massive pizza knowing that his wife wouldn't be able to eat half, leaving all the more for him. *To the lion belongs whatever it has seized*, he would tell himself. And the coke refills – imbibing as much as he could because each fresh glass of the syrupy drink was free.

Dave's rag still clutched in his hand, Glen sat in his saggy old armchair, carefully positioned for optimum view of the telly. He felt betrayed for a while, petulant even. He watched a bit of *Cyberkill* to cheer himself up, then suddenly understood. His wife was doing him a good deed. He needed to lose weight.

At twenty-five, Glen had been laughing, lean as a rake and twice as sharp. He'd heard that from that age you would become what you ate, your muscles turning to blubber, wrinkles vying for attention across your face. He managed to stay stick-thin, eating what he liked until his first kid arrived. Then in true Homer Simpson style his belly had sagged and his hair had thinned.

Maybe it was all the leftover baby food he gobbled, or those comforting packs of marshmallows, but by the time his second child appeared he had a second belly to match. He could still see his toes when he went to the bathroom in the morning, but his member was a long distant memory.

All the treats had had to go. No more chocolates, sherbet dips, pork scratchings or the holiest of holies, barbecue beef flavour crisps (which didn't taste like beef at all, but were morish all the same). Still he kept piling on the pudding. No matter what Glen didn't eat, by the time he was thirty he was fighting a losing battle against food, 365 days a year and no knockouts, never hungry but always starving. This would have been a poor sob story for any-one who'd really gone hungry, but it had meant a great deal to Glen – so he'd considered taking some healthy exercise.

As an eager teen, he'd indulged in a smattering of weight training with his Dad in the YMCA. Dad could lift ten times as much as Glen, stretch further, grunt louder. Jack was a man and his son was a squeaking pip. All the same, Glen had enjoyed the manly pursuit, though he'd been embarrassed in the showers (Jack's bits were so big and Glen's were so pitifully small). Now the city was full of high-powered gyms and health clubs, all eager to suck Glen's wallet dry. While he chose which club to join he subscribed to the theory that thinking about physical exercise actually burnt off some calories.

If you could convince your body that you were sprinting or cycling through the force of your imagination, it would be fooled in small, miraculous doses.

Worth a try. Glen stretched back in his chair and imagined that he was the dashing Agent Erickson, North Dakota's finest superspy, brawling with Chinese mastermind Chen Sung and assorted minions, performing death-defying leaps and fisticuff stunts. Glen was a doyen of daydreamers, his brain working overtime on the challenge. By the time he'd defeated Chen Sung he was so exhausted that he needed a king-size chocolate bar to pep himself up.

Stripping off for bed, Glen admired himself in the bathroom mirror. He didn't seem so bad – his paunch was practically nonexistent if he sucked it in and looked at himself at the right angle. His hair was still dark brown, with no silver strands as yet; his bright green eyes glittered with a subdued intelligence and his nose was only crooked in two places. As he tucked himself up in bed, he closed his eyes and a vision of the shop thieves filled his head. He would dream of saving his colleagues that night, leading them to a free and bountiful tropical land where they'd never have to work for Tony again.

CHAPTER 3

The Parent Trap

THE ALARM RANG EARLY next morning and Glen sat up with a jolt. He could still taste the chocolate residue of the Mars bar on his teeth. *My diet starts tomorrow*, he told himself.

'What's going on?' he asked Misbah groggily. 'It's Saturday, innit?'

'You promised to help your Dad with that thing, remember?' his wife replied matter-of-factly. It was all Greek to Glen. He couldn't recall what the thing was, what any of his plans had been for the weekend, or what the date was. His mind could not wake up properly until it had had its morning fix of coffee.

'Caffeine. I need caffeine.' He half expected Misbah to leave him to fend for himself, but she surprised him with a bedside cup of Nescafé. He was forgiven, apparently.

'Where's – there was a piece of cloth –' Glen drawled.

'That dirty thing? I threw it out.'

Glen leaped out of bed and bounded downstairs, digging his arms elbow deep into the kitchen bin. In amongst the eggshells and lettuce leaves was the rag, which he rinsed under the tap. It was a tunic, the kind that Dave and Ash had worn during their robbery. The only clue Glen could find was a label marked RHS.

Not taking the time to shower or brush his teeth, he got dressed and grabbed his keys. 'Oh no you don't,' said Misbah, blocking the front door with arms folded. 'We're due at your parents' in half an hour.'

'But I have to find the guy who stole my can.'

'You can play your spy games after you've done your familial duty. You think I'm going to suffer without you?'

Paul and Lucy didn't mind visiting their grandparents – they always got sweets and pocket money – but Glen was reluctant. He had a villain to track down and besides, he didn't think he had much in common with his Mum and Dad. *My parents are disembodied voices on the other side of the* VHS-C, he sulked as he took the A90 to Denny. *I can't make the link between those fresh, naïve faces on the video and my haggard, disillusioned parents of now.*

Most of the roads in Stirlingshire looked the same. So did many of the houses. Jack and Anna lived on a housing estate, their street a brick blot on a grassy green expanse of land. The house was tarnished but tidy, with netties, mossed roof tiles and a white porch; there was a water feature in the front garden complete with attendant fishergnome and miniature wheelbarrow. Inside, the décor was as tasteful and inoffensive as that of any other interior to be found in the area.

Once inside, Glen sat in his Dad's favourite chair. The man of the house huffed, and puffed on a cheap cigar. Anna glowered at him but said nothing. Paul breathed in the fumes, nostrils wide; Lucy's eyes watered. No one dared to comment.

'Typical,' Jack glowered, rummaging through his newspaper with hands gnarled as an elephant's hide. 'Nothing on the boob tube. Same every winter.'

Nothing on TV? *Was he mad?* There was always something on. Twenty years ago, before Jerry Springer, Dr Phil and trash TV, you had to make do with children's programmes during the day and a thumping good novelisation at night. Now there were lunchtime shows, breakfast broadcasts, low budget late night fillers for terminal insomniacs. The preschool kids' stuff was far more intelligent than Richard and Judy. Barney could beat Oprah in a live televised debate any day.

Glen didn't lodge a vocal complaint. He gazed through the window, watching two tractors rumble up and down a mottled field. He kept quiet while Misbah made small talk with his mother; they got on well together, despite their dissimilar personalities –

Misbah small and assertive, Anna large and assertive. Glen got his Quiet Man act from Jack, who didn't believe in speaking unless there was something important that needed to be said. He left the chitchat to the 'jabbering women.' Jack was an old school Dad who brooked no nonsense and would never be shaken from his position as King of the Household.

'Can I have a suck on your cigar, Gramps?' Paul grinned.

'Cheeky.' Jack swiped at Paul with his newspaper, clipping the boy's ear with the corner of page twenty-two. That was the funniest thing that had happened all day.

'We haven't seen you for so long, Glen,' Anna said, trying to draw her son into the family conversation. 'We've seen Misbah and the kids a couple of times this month, but you're always so busy.'

Do you miss me? Glen wanted to ask, but he was afraid of the response. 'Busy,' he decided, 'with work and that.'

'That's a shame, darling.' Anna's hair was permed and she was fully made up. She liked to look nice for visitors. Now that she and Jack had retired, they both looked forward to company, especially when Paul and Lucy came around. Jack would never have admitted this, of course. 'Who's for a nice glass of juice?'

'Well, we don't want a horrible glass of juice,' Glen ventured, but no one got the joke. As Anna swanned off into the kitchen, Misbah gave Glen a look. This split-second glance signified that he should attempt to engage his father in conversation.

'The shop was robbed yesterday, Dad.'

'I was robbed once. Bank robbers with sawn-offs. Or machine guns, I forget which.' Typical Jack. He would always go one better than Glen – if his son had a cold, Jack had the flu; if Glen got a flat tyre, Jack would reel out some story about the time his engine exploded. This Tetley-drinking tyrant was impossible to impress.

'Where was that, Jack?' Misbah asked with an interest that had been completely nonexistent when Glen had shared similar news.

'South America. On holiday. I gave one of the beggars what for.

They weren't expecting that – most blokes with guns are nancies, hiding behind their peashooters. The others got away,' he concluded sadly, as if wishing that he'd had the chance to wrestle the entire gang into submission.

'Shame you couldn't have got a good punch in,' Misbah said to Glen. She was joking but he took it badly.

'I've seen this boy box at school,' said Jack with the chortle of a nut cracked between two pebbles. 'He couldn't batter a fairy cake.' Paul and Lucy joined in the laughter. Anna asked what the cause of all the hilarity was as she rattled into the living room with a tray full of sweet things. She began her traditional, good-natured argument with Misbah over who would do the washing up, and Glen sank into the armchair and closed his eyes. Roll on Monday.

'I've got a question for you, Dad,' he said, his eyes still shut.

'A question, eh? And there was me thinkin' you knew everything.'

'Just because he's a know-it-all,' Misbah smiled, 'does not mean he's got any brains.'

'Okay, okay. Does anyone know what RHS stands for?'

'That's easy,' Lucy giggled. 'Royal Hospital of Scotland.'

'There speaks a wise young lady,' said Jolly Jack, patting Lucy on the head.

'About that thing you wanted Glen to help you with,' Misbah said, and Glen's lids snapped open again. Was he not allowed even a moment's peace?

'Oh aye, the thing. C'mon son.' Jack stood up with a nasty creak and Glen followed meekly behind. 'It's your Mum's vegetarian diet. The sweetcorn and whatnot blocks up the drain. I'd get down there and scoop it out, but what with the metal pin in my hip…'

Glen was led into the back garden, where a small drain was clogged with dark gray matter. He was the kind of guy who would assess a maintenance problem, have a look round the house for tools, then call a plumber. But he could tell that if he didn't unblock the drain there and then, he'd regret it later. It wasn't worth arguing about or putting off any longer, so he fetched a pair of pink marigolds from the kitchen and got down on his hunkers, probing the murk with rubber fingers.

'No, you've got to get stuck into it, lad!' Jack barked, supervising. 'Scoop it out.' Glen hated it when his Dad called him 'lad.' And his nice glass of juice was getting warm. As he began to lose his temper he found new energy, digging the drain clean and placing the residue in a Tesco bag. He wanted to retch but he had to prove that he was a man, even if he was wearing pink rubber gloves. So he scraped the drain and attendant pipe clean until Jack was satisfied.

'Well done, lad.' Glen was sure that his Dad referred to him that way just to annoy him. 'Time for your juice.' The muckraker removed his gloves – and here was the tricky part: it was impossible to take the second one off without touching some of the sewage with his fingertips – then placed them in the seeping bag. That was it, Mission Impossible accomplished. The ice in his juice had melted, diluting the drink, although Anna did offer to top it up.

'I've made a nice veggie casserole for lunch,' she smiled. Glen felt quite ill.

On the way back to Edinburgh, Glen made a deal with his wife. In exchange for a couple of hours of 'spy time,' he'd take her out for dinner. Glen would track down his quarry, Misbah would get a change of scene and the kids would get a night off from their parents. Everyone would be happy.

After he'd dropped Misbah and the kids off at home, Glen got a tankful of petrol and hurried to the hospital. For once he broke the speed limit, even though he knew he'd probably get stopped by the police. Some people went through life flaunting rules and getting away with it; he'd always been the type to get caught if ever he got his nose dirty. One dram over the limit and he'd end up in court for drunk driving. Lose a tax form and he'd get a hefty fine from the Inland Revenue. But right now he felt different. John

Dance didn't get speeding tickets or miss payments. He was too busy saving the world to worry about such things.

Fortified by his fantasies, Glen made it to the new Royal Hospital without a hitch. It was quiet for a Saturday afternoon and he found a parking space close to the main entrance. Getting out of his car, he put on his sunglasses and headed for the hospital with a movie star swagger.

Glen didn't like the ultra-modern building, which had recently opened on the outskirts of the city. He had preferred the old one, a creaking, overgrown mansion taken over by sick people and domineering matrons. He stayed out of hospitals altogether if possible, so he had butterflies in his stomach as he entered the pristine building. This was probably a wild goose chase; he would have to check every floor.

A few gormless types sat in the foyer, waiting their lives away, and no one seemed to notice him as he breezed through a door marked STAFF ONLY. He had to start somewhere, though a stark, empty corridor didn't seem to be the best choice.

Still in John Dance mode, Glen felt invulnerable. He could walk through any door, evade any CCTV, beat any guard while he fantasised about his hero. Spy guys and their brethren could smell danger over the odour of disinfectant or urine or worse. They always knew the right thing to do and say.

His cheap shoes squeaked as he walked. He let his feet land more heavily, then stamped, marvelling at the echoes he made. 'I've found my squeaker!' he said in a sing-song voice, talking to himself and listening to the response. 'I am invincible!' he declared, then clamped a hand over his mouth, remembering where he was. He stopped, listening for signs of life. The corridor was silent.

This is no time to be clowning around, he realised. *I have a mission to complete. I'm here to find Ash, whoever the hell he might be. At least I know how big he is.*

Glen found a nurse's station complete with a glowing PC terminal.

He listened once more for signs of approaching staff as he checked the monitor, looking for employee names. There were a couple of Ashleys, both doctors and both female. If Ash was a false name or a nickname then this really was a goose chase. He was stubborn though, so he kept looking.

'Can I help you, pal?' Glen almost lost his lunch in fright as he turned to face a nurse with dark hair almost as lank as her expression.

'Yeah, I'm looking for a guy named Ash. Large bloke, bad manners.' He was surprised that the nurse hadn't called security already.

'I know who you mean. Friend o' yours?'

'Uh, he's got something that belongs to me,' Glen replied.

'Oh yeah, I never lend stuff to my pals any more. Don't get it back. Leads to bad feelings.'

Glen nodded as he followed the nurse to an area marked RESEARCH & DEVELOPMENT CENTRE. It was stark and quiet, with a couple of swivel chairs and potted plants. She led him into a small room that resembled a traditional doctor's office, complete with table, stethoscopes, BP cuffs and a mirror on the wall.

'Wait right here and I'll get Dr Tozer,' the nurse told him in a tone more suited to the paediatrics ward.

'Is he Ash?'

'You are confused aren't you, you poor dear? Dr Tozer will help you find Ash. Change into the gown while you're waiting, please.'

'I don't need to.'

'You need help?'

'No, no.' Glen was about to tell the nurse that he wasn't a patient, then realised that he would have to explain why he'd been in a restricted area when she'd found him. He was undercover now, playing a role. 'If I put the gown on, he'll help me find Ash?'

'Sure, Mr –?'

'The name's Atone. Tony Atone.'

The nurse raised an eyebrow, leaving the room without another word. Glen stripped off and donned the gown, leaving the ties hanging loose. He sat for a while on the edge of the bed, a sheet of tissue-thin paper rustling under his buttocks. He waggled his bare feet, wiggling his toes. He tapped his fingers on his knee.

After ten minutes of wiggling, tapping and getting bored, Glen hopped down from the bed and caught sight of himself in the mirror. He pouted at his reflection and strutted round the room, pretending he was a girl. Shrugging his shoulders to stop the gown from slipping off, he blew himself a mock Monroe kiss just as Dr Tozer knocked on the door and came in.

'I was, uh, wondering where Ash had got to.'

'So I hear.' The doctor was holding a long thin needle with a wicked glint in its eye. He asked Glen to lie back on the bed, clenched his hand into a fist and rubbed hard on the centre of Glen's chest.

'What do you think you're doing?' Glen found it hard to speak as he yanked the doctor's fist away and started to get dressed. Now his top priority was to get out of the room as quickly as possible.

'Nurse! Get in here!' the doctor shouted. Glen opened the door to find her standing there, barring his escape. Dr Tozer grabbed his wrist, feeling his pulse. 'You've been working too many shifts without breaks,' he told the nurse, 'he's a live one.'

'Are you sure?' the nurse said, in the way people do when they don't want to admit they're wrong. She grabbed Glen's other arm, making him flinch. As he made his way out of the doctor's office it looked as if the two staff members were playing tug of war with him.

'Just did a sternal rub,' said the doctor, 'made him flinch a mile. But I can see how you could make the mistake... the glazed expression, wasted muscles, pale complexion. Hard to spot a diener when you haven't seen one on the move, so to speak.'

Glen couldn't help sniggering at the nurse. 'You thought I was a diener?' he asked her, incredulous.

'I thought you were one of Ash's runaway charges.'

'Easy mistake to make,' the doctor nodded. 'Ash has only got one function to perform and he's rarely here to do it.'

'He's not here now?' Glen looked around the centre. The doctor pointed to a half-open door; staring into the room beyond, Glen could make out a woman lying on a slab. 'Ash is in there?'

'Why all this interest in him anyway?' asked Dr Tozer. 'He owe you money?'

Glen tried to gauge the staff members' feelings towards Ash. 'He stole something from my store. A personal possession, extremely valuable.'

'Sounds like a matter for the police,' the doctor said warily. His beeper diverted his attention. 'Patch this gentleman up will you, nurse?' Before he hurried off, he gave Glen a business card. 'We're always looking for animate male subjects for our research programme. Give me a call if you're ever interested.'

As Glen headed out of the centre he caught another glimpse of the woman on the slab. A porter with bleach blonde hair and a broken nose stood over her body, watching her closely. The scene gave Glen the creeps, salved only when he passed a door marked STAFF ONLY. Unseen, he stepped through the door and started to nose around. Perhaps he could lie in wait for Ash, jump him when he turned up. No, that wasn't very reasonable considering the man's size and violent streak.

He came across a row of battered grey lockers. Name cards were stuck on each, and Glen stopped in his tracks as he saw that was marked ASH NORELL. Now he had to get into the locker without being seen and getting into more trouble.

The lock looked quite flimsy, so he glanced around to make sure he was alone and brought his elbow down on the metal. The strike made a large clatter and numbed his funny bone, but didn't budge the lock.

Ash will come and get me, I know it, Glen thought as he used his shoe for another go. *That guy could crush me like a rotten orange.* The shoe made even more noise, but the lock fell to the floor and the door swung open. There was the reel, property too

hot for Ash to leave at his house (a favourite place for the local
police to play hunt-the-stolen-goods). Glen grabbed the reel and
ran for the exit, vowing never to return to the RHS. From now on
he'd stay close to home, be a good boy, buy his memorabilia from
eBay and lock it up in the garage at night.

Glen didn't often get embarrassed, but this was one of those few
times when he felt himself blush. He had first noticed the stain on
his trouser leg when the speeding lowrider splashed him as he
walked home, but he was sure that he had wiped it off as soon as
he reached the kitchen. Yet there it was, an ugly brown patch on
the left thigh of his moleskins, staring out at his wife in a concert-
ed effort to spoil the evening. The mark would reinforce Misbah's
opinion that he was a dirty slob; Glen knew how powerful false
impressions could be. He tried to hide his annoyance just as he hid
the stain under his napkin.

Chez Andres was a poorly lit restaurant on Broughton Street,
sandwiched between a sports shop and a launderette. The chairs
creaked, the tables listed, but the sophisticated menu and atmosphere made up for anything the furniture lacked in snoot. Glen
liked the place, not because of the food but because of the way that
the waiters occasionally let their French accents slip. He would
suppress a childish giggle as their East Coast dialect resurfaced for
a brief moment. The garcon who had just brought them their
menu, however, was a complete professional, having long ago perfected a surrogate Parisian burr.

Misbah wore a long, black dress, hoping to make herself look
slim; as usual, her hair was bunned back. Her brown eyes glittered
in the restaurant candlelight and she picked at the dripping wax
with tapering fingers. Misbah moved gracefully except when she
was worried. If distracted by a problem, she would become clumsy, bumping into furniture, spilling coffee and dropping plant pots,
her green fingers turning to butter.

Glen was relieved when she ordered a pasta dish; he couldn't really afford anything more expensive. This way he could buy himself something half decent as well.

'Never did like finger buffets. Keep expecting to find fingers in 'em.' Misbah didn't laugh at Glen's gag.

'Nice of Jack and Anna to give us a hand,' she said, still picking. 'We haven't done this for ages.'

'It was either them or Dave. I know who I'd prefer to babysit.' Glen chased his bean sprouts around their plate, his stomach still rumbling. He wished he was at home, reading the paper and relaxing. He didn't understand why he should pay a lot of money for a meal that he could make himself, the way and the size he liked it, at home.

'I don't want our kids hanging round with the neighbours.'

'They're nice people!' Glen protested, wiping his mouth with the back of his hand.

'I don't care how nice they are. Paul and Lucy will pick up bad habits, the wrong kind of values. We've got enough trouble without them turning into kleptomaniacs.'

Glen had visions of his kids falling asleep without a moment's notice, any time of day. Then he remembered what kleptomania meant and relaxed a little.

'My plate's too small,' he grumbled. The secret of good eating, he'd long since decided, was a big plate, preferably one large enough to make the hefty meal look like a starter. Then he could pile on the grub without looking like a pig. The worst party buffets were the ones with tiny plates – if a guest took more than two sausage rolls and a scotch egg he'd be classed as a glutton. Misbah wasn't interested.

'Our children are in a very important stage of their development. They've already got a slob for a Dad and schemies for neighbors.'

'Who's a slob?' Glen asked, sliding his elbows off the table.

'You're useless at making the bed.'

'I'm great at messing it up.'

'Let's just enjoy our meal and get home. Your Mum and Dad will need to get to their beds soon.'

Glen appreciated that his parents liked to sleep in the comfort of their own house. He was happy in his own surroundings, too. That didn't stop him from offering to put them up whenever they visited.

'Mark wants me to come out with him for Hogmanay,' he said plaintively. Misbah's eyes widened accordingly. 'I worry about him,' Glen continued, 'need to keep an eye on him in all those crowds. You know how he's got one of those faces that starts fights – he doesn't need to say a word or spill anyone's pint. He gets bashed anyway.'

'He does have a knack for disturbing the peace. All the more reason for you to stay in with me and the kids.'

'I did that last year. And the year before. And the year before that. C'mon, M.' Glen leaned towards her over the table. 'He's got the tickets and all. Do you want to come?' he added, knowing full well that crowds weren't Misbah's scene.

'All those people crushed up together? Standing in the cold with loud music blasting in my ears?' his wife grimaced. 'Not my idea of a good time. And the fireworks make me jump.'

Glen's toes hurt. Standing in the cold night air for an hour should have numbed them, but they had also been stepped on by innumerable revellers, so they throbbed and stung instead. Thank goodness for Mark's stash of vodka, which the reporter passed to him whenever they could see their way to each other through the throng.

'Shouldn't you have a backstage pass or something?'

'I'm plain old Joe Punter tonight, no work for me. I'm here for pleasure pal, not business.' Mark's nose glowed red, more from the freezing temperature than from the booze. He aimed to remedy that post haste. 'Any luck with your spying?' he asked as he took a swig from a dainty hip flask.

'My espionage days are done. Those hospital guys are a bunch of weirdos.'

'Is that right?' Mark grinned. 'What about the prized possession of yours that guy Ash stole?'

'Whoever he stole it for is the one I really want to talk to.'

'Who might that be?' Mark handed the flask to Glen, his hand shaking slightly.

'I have my suspicions.'

This was the one night of the year – usually the coldest – when people were crazy enough to stand around in the dark and damp in a crowd of strangers for the hell of it. So it was nearly midnight? – an arbitrary division of the day into regimented segments, probably the bright idea of some ancient Roman who thought that sundials were a wheeze. Glen wasn't a huge fan of time keeping or the compunction to be punctual; sand forced to skid through an egg timer when grains were built to sift gradually. In his opinion, sand should be free, on a beach or in the desert, not held captive in a concave cage. His wristwatch was almost as bad a reminder of his responsibilities as his wedding ring. The watch constantly told him that he was late, or that he'd missed the start of *Law and Order*, or that it was time for bed (on a school night). All the same, he couldn't knock a good knees-up. Only on this day of days could he look at those precious minutes ticking away, longing for the big hand to sweep faster, bringing him closer to the new year's birth.

A twinkle up front caught his attention. He and Mark were close to a small stage with two turntables and room for five people at the back. The lights were being checked – spots, strobes, blue and white. An overhead monitor displayed an ad for Radio One, then cut to an image from the camera watching the crowd. The stage had been plonked in the middle of the car park, a bleak place transformed with a wave of Glasgow City Council's magic wand. Fairground rides thundered at the back of the lot, and there was a limbo dancer, and waltzers, and hot food stalls. Next to the main stage, a fantasy mountain/castle had been set up, pumping out neon and dry ice. A band of Greedos jigged to a family-friendly tune.

On the main stage four dancers appeared, one with devil horns, another with a silver wig, the third in red with black shades and the fourth with her mouth painted silver. The warm-up DJ joined them.

'Three hours to go,' Mark beamed. Glen wondered how he could stay on his pulped feet for another three hours – and what happened when midnight came? Did everyone disperse in an instant? He was there for the long haul. Misbah had offered to come and pick him up if he asked – a get-out clause. Maybe she was concerned, or didn't want him to have too much fun. Mark had hired a small room in a nearby B&B, and Glen was welcome to sleep on the floor – if he could walk all the way there. Every step was painful for him, although he managed to hop about to the music when a favourite tune came on.

> We are naughty ladies
> We are naughty ladies
> You are naughty men
> You are naughty men
> Come and kiss me round the back
> I'll be bad again.

In the crowd, youths waved saltires, inflatable hammers, astronauts and space shuttles; a woman in her forties held an 'End is Nigh' placard aloft, hair held neat with deedly-boppers, ready to ring in the new year with both stalks. Her friend wore a T-shirt that said 'I was there when the aliens came.' 35,000 revellers crowded into the car park, wearing leather jackets or long winter coats.

'Getting warmer,' Mark puffed, dancing like a crazy fool. A shower of rain cooled him down. As the dancers became more frenzied and the music increased in volume, the crowd got rowdier. Glen was whipped in the eye with a flag, bonked on the nose by a flying plastic bottle, knocked on the noggin by a flailing elbow. People generally apologised, determined to look after each other, picking up strangers when they fell over – spirits were high, the revellers good-natured. The favorite chant of the night was, 'here we, here we, here we here we go!' followed closely by, 'where's the dopey DJ?'

A new personality got on stage, but this was no disk jockey. The crowd around Glen appeared to slow down, every gyration a sweeping, balletic movement, as he watched Kim Clark sway from side to side. He could see why she was Scottish television's star reporter, with her pigtailed brown hair and blood red lips. He was captivated. *I'm a married spud, I'm a married spud,* he thought, giving himself a mental slap on the wrist.

Kim jumped deftly from the stage and walked up to Mark. Glen forgot about the cold, his snotty nostrils and his sore toes.

'You know her?' he asked his friend.

'Of course he knows me,' Kim smiled. 'Shouldn't you be back-stage, Shiner?'

Mark shook his head. 'Roughin' it tonight, darling. Seeing how the other half live.' He introduced Kim to Glen, who had temporarily lost the power of speech. 'We've covered some of the same stories,' Mark explained.

'Only so many to go round.' Kim raised an eyebrow. 'Got any-thing left in that flask you've been flashing about?'

'No,' Mark lied, then changed his mind and raised the container. 'Maybe a drop.'

Kim snatched it from him and emptied it down her throat. She let out a satisfied gasp and stuffed it in Mark's jeans pocket. 'I'd better do some mingling,' she said, already disappearing into the throng.

'She was... wow.' Glen's jaw was slack.

'She's very dedicated to her job,' Mark chuckled as he watched a couple of girls running around, kissing everybody. By eleven o'clock they were up on the shoulders of two brave lads, and proceeded from one set of shoulders to another. A short girl got talking to an Irish partygoer, making her lesbian partner jealous. They argued. Dave Pierce DJ'd for the last hour, his name flashing away on the monitor. Beams of light criss-crossed the sky like prison search-lights; a helicopter soared overhead, beaming a red light downwards. The funsters were flanked by two clocks that became increasingly hard to see as the stage lights brightened. So far, no scuffles, discrediting Glasgow's rep as the city of hard knocks.

10 Radio One 9 was transmitting live 8 to millions of Scotland's faithful, 7 and the revellers 6 screamed their lungs out 5 as the countdown continued. 4 The buzz transcended the ache 3 in Glen's feet, and the excitement increased as 2 the bells rang out over the disco din. 1 A shower of fireworks heralded midnight, and the *Happy New Year* began with that old standard, 'All You Need is Love.' The dance music started up again and Mark continued to bop. There were hugs and kisses all round, predatory males trying to snog as many girls as possible. Mobiles rang; many of them couldn't receive a signal, or it was too noisy to hear the person on the other end, but wherever possible, friends wished each other a happy new year across the continents. There was nothing stolen, no broken bones or heavy bruising. Everyone was caught up in the moment, drunk on the pageantry, tripping on the stage lights. This was the future and the happiest night of Glen's life.

Saying farewell to his friend, he found a phone booth and called his wife. His feet were too sore to hold him up much longer. He watched the crowd begin to scatter, the fairground lights fade, hoping for a last glimpse of Kim. Misbah's Honda eventually appeared and he hopped over to her, a blast of heat welcoming him into the vehicle.

'No new year's kiss?'

Glen gave Misbah a peck on the cheek. 'Hope it's a good one.'

'Oh, this year's going to be very special for both of us. I can feel it.'

CHAPTER 4

DOA

I knocked on Heaven's door
But they wouldn't let me in
Said I wasn't right
Although I don't know from sin

Made some wrong choices
Chasing rock 'n' roll dreams
Ignored the wrong voices
And I've kept my nose clean

Can't stand all the palaver
I'm just a cool cadaver
And I can't wait
To crash those pearly gates!

From AfterRock: The Ricky Diener Musical

MISBAH KEPT GLEN BUSY on New Year's Day and on the 2nd as well. There were always little things that needed doing round the house but none of them quite as puke-worthy as cleaning Dad's drains. Glen was knackered by the time Sunday evening arrived and the family gathered round their TV set to watch a *Spiderman* DVD borrowed from Video People. The adults sat together on the sofa while their children sprawled on the floor.

'When you gonna get an HD TV?' Paul asked, just as Norman Osborn was about to transform into the Green Goblin for the first time.

'Yeah. We wanna new telly,' Lucy whined.

'Ah, it's just a fad. We'll wait till they get cheaper.'

'The other kids make fun of me 'cos I haven't seen the lush images you can only get with a high definition television,' Paul told him. Glen sighed – he was trying to watch the movie. 'Everyone in my class has got HD. And an x-Box. And a Beyblade doodah.'

'Wait for next Christmas.' Misbah was the diplomat of the family. 'We'll see what Santa brings.'

'Santa Schmanta! We need HD now!'

As the chanting began, Glen placed an arm round Misbah's shoulders. He felt strangely proud of his family.

Glen could have been selling suits, bikes or biscuits. He worked at Video People to earn his monthly paycheck, wasting his life making money for Tony, spending prime days in the store that he would never be able to replace. That scared him.

He'd always known that when he died, it wouldn't be in the company of his loved ones or peacefully in his sleep. It would be at work, in a place he didn't want to be, shunting aside the million useful things he could have been doing with his life to puff up the boss's bank balance. Sure, he was surrounded by charming colleagues, multi-coloured merchandise and cool customers. But when the sun shone outside and he laboured under the flickering glow of the strip lights, Glen's skin looked pallid and he yearned for a tan.

He'd applied for other jobs, even deserting his post a couple of times to try something new – he'd joined the Parks and Recreation Centre, digging borders and mowing lawns; the weather hadn't been kind. Another time, he'd quit the shop in a sulk and trained in a cement factory – too much like hard work. At least he knew Video People, its punters and pitfalls.

Wherever he worked, Glen assumed that he would conk out one day, collapse into a coma, die of boredom. He didn't expect it to happen at age thirty-four.

He was leaning on the counter as usual, sipping his coffee, glancing through a catalogue. His drink tasted terrible and his stomach rumbled – he'd missed breakfast that morning. Vian trotted in, asking about his reel.

'Had a chance to watch it yet?'

'Er, yeah.' Glen wasn't sure how Vian would react if he tried to confront him with his suspicions.

'Quite something, isn't it?'

'How would you know?'

'There'll be people looking for it, you know – rabid collectors, unscrupulous dealers.'

Glen leaned forward to whisper, 'What's so special about it?'

'You don't know?' Vian looked at his friend suspiciously.

'I'm as dumb as they come, mind.'

'You've moved everything around,' Vian said angrily, ignoring Glen's comment, 'again.'

'Tony's orders. See, while you're getting your bearings and looking for your usual comic, you might see something new and buy that as well. I know it's a bit of a mindblower – trying something new. But that's the theory anyway. Works for the supermarkets.'

Paul and Lucy could see through Santa, but Vian apparently still believed that stores based their business decisions on his personal whims. It took all sorts to make a happy shop. All the same, Vian sounded too hostile for Glen's liking. He looked around – Alan was in the staff room, Tony was at a Chamber of Commerce luncheon and Russ was busy opening the day's deliveries, late as usual. Not much back up if things turned messy, then.

'I just do what I'm told.'

Vian turned his back on Glen and found the week's batch of new releases. He hefted them into his hairy arms and carried them across the shop, placing them on their usual rack.

'Don't move them again.' Vian took one of the DVDs, handling it with kid gloves, and placed it on the counter. Glen scanned its barcode and took the fuming consumer's money. As soon as Vian had left the shop, Glen moved the titles back to their new rack.

He returned his attention to the catalogue. It was filled with self-help tapes, bonkbusters and b-movies. Glen wondered how such nonsense got made, while so many worthy films were consigned to development hell. There were a couple of genre productions on this list worth ordering; he left an asterisk next to their titles and a big circle round an ad for an upcoming release. This would be the greatest of all box sets, chock full of special features, Easter eggs and interviews with his favorite stars. The John Dance set would include all the movies, complete with commentaries and behind the scenes documentaries. Getting himself all excited, Glen closed the catalogue.

This simple action took a surprising amount of effort. Glen stumbled back against the counter, bile rising in his throat. He ran to the toilet, chucking up in the sink. He dropped his drawers and sat down on the loo, hoping to relieve the increasing ache in his gut. A good session on the khazi usually helped, and Russ was quite capable of holding the fort in the meantime.

The toilet cubicle was uncommonly small, with dank green walls and a low-wattage lightbulb dangling too low from the ceiling. Damp patches crept from the wainscoting and the cistern lid had gone missing long ago. Glen took another look at the catalogue, still clutched in his hand, but his eyes couldn't focus on the text. Sweat trickled down his face – had he eaten some dodgy meat?

The lightbulb appeared to fail and Glen peered through a thickening gloom. It wasn't the bulb at all; he'd lost the power of sight. His heart thumped in his chest, like a drummer trying to break out of a wooden crate. Then there was nothing.

Russ knew that Glen was fond of toilet breaks, particularly when stock was needing to be shifted. Two hours was excessive even for this loafer. Russ knocked on the toilet door warily.

'You asleep in there?'

Silence.

'Tony's on the rampage. He's not paying you to sit and stink, he says. You can dump in yer own time.' Not as much as a grunt or a chuckle. Russ was anxious now. 'Alright in there buddy?'

Russ ran to fetch Alan, who kicked the door in. Neither of them expected to see their colleague dead on the pan, with only an open copy of the Movie Memory Warehouse catalogue protecting his modesty.

Russ and Alan stood quiet for a while, staring at the body. Glen's skin had started to turn purple. His face was serene, pants round his ankles.

'Used to seeing him sitting about, doing nowt,' mumbled Russ.

'Yeah. He was the quiet sort and all. I'll miss the little bugger.' Alan dialed 999 on his moby and asked for an ambulance.

'We could charge the punters a fiver a gawp. Some of them are into morbid kinda stuff.'

Alan gave Russ a disgruntled look. 'Five quid? I thought this guy was your best pal?'

'You're right. I'm being callous. Not considering Glen's family. I was a child of the Thatcher years, y'know.'

'A tenner. You get what you pay for.'

'Now you're talking.'

The police didn't take long to find the store. The toilet was sectioned off, pictures and measurements were taken, and the catalogue was perused. A blanket covered Glen from head to knees. He had begun to stiffen, knees bent, hands on thighs.

The staff tried to ignore the shock they felt, the it-could-have-been-me fear factor, holding a sweepstake in Glen's honour. Tony favoured an aneurysm, Alan asphyxiation, and Russ went for a long shot, suggesting that Glen had read something so exciting in his catalogue that his heart had stopped. Russ was desperate for the john and went back to say farewell to his pal. He hoped to pee in the sink but one look at the corpse convinced him to hold it in for the rest of the day.

Vian entered, wanted to apologise, was disappointed to hear of Glen's death.

'You're still welcome in here any time,' said Tony, wearing his jolly Meet Joe Public face.

'Wouldn't be the same,' Vian muttered. He moved the new DVDs back onto their old rack and headed out into the sunlight.

Misbah was in the kitchen when the police knocked on the front door. The cops weren't there simply to inform her of her husband's death, but also to ask a few questions – medical history, any recent incidents or accidents, hereditary mentionables or a fondness for booze. They might as well have given her a form to fill in; place an x in the applicable boxes, was your spouse a drug user, bisexual, plain unlucky?

Of course the constables didn't pry quite so deeply, but Misbah felt that her privacy had been violated nonetheless. She already knew about Glen's death thanks to a phone call from her least favorite person. Tony had broken the news to her as gently as he knew how. He confirmed that the store had been held up a few days beforehand, just as Glen had insisted. And now Glen was dead, although there didn't seem to be any obvious connection between the two incidents. That was the word he'd used – incidents. One anonymous staff member had called the local press and now Video People was crowded with rubberneckers, despite the fact that Glen's body was long gone. The punters had to satisfy themselves with a glance at the death scene, nothing more. The store would stay open as a mark of respect for Glen's passing, Tony had concluded with a simper. 'It's the way he would've wanted it.'

Now Misbah was part of due procedure, her husband's approximate time of death a figure on a sheet in a bundle of paperwork. She stayed in the living room after the police were gone, slumped on the sofa, staring at the easy chair. The indents were still there from Glen's back and buttocks. His beloved remote controls sat on the right arm. A curry stain marked the side of the chair and this made Misbah cry. She ran to the kitchen, grabbed a sponge, scrubbed angrily at the stain until it was gone. Fluffed up the cushions, smoothed down the upholstery, until there was no impression left of him. His chair remained, and neither Paul nor Lucy dared to sit in it when they got home from school.

They instinctively knew that something was wrong with Dad. Mum could hardly speak, communicating to them with nods and hand gestures. Jack and Anna were there, offering her endless cups of tea in a silent human chain from the kitchen to the living room. Misbah managed to keep calm until teatime, asking the kids what they wanted and serving what was best for them anyway.

When they were sitting on the sofa, their meals on their laps, Misbah told her children the whole story. 'He's gone. I wasn't sure how to...' She had to be strong. How could she tell her children that their world had been shattered? 'I have to sort everything out.' The tears came at last. 'Make arrangements.'

Perhaps the information hadn't sunk in, or the children were too young to grasp the idea that they'd never see their Dad again. Whatever the reason, Paul and Lucy set their plates down on the coffee table and hugged their mother. For a moment, they were her strength.

The day of the funeral flew in, and the Glass clan gathered on a windy Saturday in Denny. Glen had passed the cemetery occasionally on trips to Stirlingshire, always maintaining that it would be a nice place to end up if he kicked the bucket.

It was set on a small verdant hill, flanked by trees, prominent but unshowy. Bold white tombstones jutted like magazines in a rack, neat and orderly, not too crowded and not too distant from each other.

Russ and Alan stood together. Tony was minding the store, but had agreed to close it at noon as another mark of respect – a proper one this time – even though Saturday was the busiest day of the week for Video People.

'Is he gonna join us for the beer and sandwiches?' Russ enquired out the side of his mouth.

'Who?'

'The boss.'

'How d'you know there'll be sandwiches?'

'I'm an optimist.'

Misbah's children stood either side of her, Lucy clutching her mum's hand tight, Paul's shoulders drooping like his face. Misbah didn't hear the creak of the coffin as it was lowered into its plot. She did not hear Jack crying, complaining it wasn't fair. All she heard was the wind in the air, acheing her ears, numbing her fingers. She was glad to be grieving. After the shock, the overwhelming responsibilities of motherhood and widowdom, it was a great relief to be able to mourn. Glen was lost to her, yet she had Lucy and Paul. They would be enough – they'd have to be.

Jack wiped his eyes then clasped his hands in front of him. Life stank, and he was destined to spend the rest of it without his dear lad. Why couldn't Glen have come back, the same as that guy off the telly? Anna stood still as a figurine, eyes clear, lips thin. Her fellow mourners put her stillness down to the cold, but remaining motionless and quiet was her way of coping.

Flames lick at the cheap leather shoes he wears for work. All the good times and his good deeds come to mind: sticking with Misbah, time spent with the kids, staying in Edinburgh to be close to his parents...

Glen woke to find himself still steeped in darkness, but in a new location. Some kind of wooden box. He knuckled the sleep from his eyes, stretched his legs out and kicked at the panels. Reached up – didn't have to move much – and hammered on the lid. He started to yell.

The priest heard him first. The pallbearers stepped back and Paul screamed. With the coffin lid hastily unscrewed, Glen sprang upright, arms outstretched, hands clawed.

'Who died?' Glen gasped, admiring the motley mob before

him. All his nearest and dearest looking smart, sober, dressed in black. All the people who'd be at his funeral if he was to have such a thing.

As his eyes adjusted to the daylight, he looked around himself and realised that he was in a coffin. He ran his hands along the cheap wooden frame, tried to offer a smile to his father, who promptly fainted. The realisation hit Glen like that first splash of cold water early in the morning, a nip of whisky on an empty stomach, the jolt of pain when you catch your hip on the side-board, lemon juice on a mouth ulcer... he was dead and no pills or parlour tricks would help him.

'Not a bad turnout,' he said once Jack had been lifted to a standing position. Glen wanted to lighten the atmosphere a bit, but this was a tough crowd. Would they have preferred him to stay dead? He climbed out of his coffin and was embraced by his children. Lucy covered her nose with her sleeve.

'Turned you away at the pearly gates?' Russ smirked, clasping Glen's hand warmly. 'They don't take riff-raff, pal. It's great to see you.'

'We missed you buddy,' Alan chipped in. 'Is it time for our beer and sarnies now?'

Computer Games

CHAPTER 5

Home Alone

Unusual Headcases

'These guys are special.' The lieutenant spoke quietly, as if he was afraid the room was bugged.

'As in clandestine ops?' asked Dance.

'Not quite.' The lieutenant scratched his sandy hair. 'They're... unusual cases. See, far as I can tell, the only thing unbalanced about 'em is that they've been driven crazy, stuck in here so long. Heck, half of them're as sane as you or I. Still, the Brass insists on keeping them here. Their only outlet is their training – pretty up-to-date – and that can get fierce, I can tell you.'

'If a lot of them are rational, why am I here?'

'A second opinion, as independent as we can get. I want you to talk to them, assess their mental states and report back to me. No one else. Got that?'

From Cold Soldiers *by Sam Robbins*

GLEN HAD ONLY BEEN home for a few days when his wife began to nag him again. He found it quite reassuring. Glen had been sitting in bed, watching a portable telly and minding his own business, when Misbah had bustled in, drawing the curtains, opening windows and generally fussing about. To complicate matters she'd brought up the subject of his health.

'I know you don't like doctors,' Misbah conceded. 'You can't sit here and fester. I'll make the appointment for you at the clinic.'

'Doctors never do nothing. They take their best guess, prescribe some ineffective drug and never stick their necks out for a patient. Quacks, the lot of them.'

'You're sick, Glen. Sick people with any sense go see the doc. In fact, sick isn't a strong enough word for it. We need to find out what happened to you, and what the future holds.'

'Was there an inquest?'

'No, why?' Misbah folded her arms defensively. 'There were a lot of forms to fill in. Questions asked.'

'It must've been so tough for you, darling. Then the shock of my *Glenus ex machina* performance – the kids seemed to like it, though.'

'Children are good at concealing their feelings, a lot better than most adults. Especially Paul. I hope they don't bottle up their shock like –'

'Like you have?'

'I've been upset and angry, I've cried all I can cry.'

'Sounds like a country and western song.'

'Be serious for a minute. I did all that when you died, I was a cruddy mummy and a worse widow. Now we get on. Somehow, we get on. Go to the clinic. You've got no excuse, it's right across the road.'

Glen put on his jacket, all scuffed leather and loose threads, and went to the doctor's as instructed. He spent a quiet half hour in the waiting room, picking up health tips from *Reader's Digest*. *If laughter's the best medicine,* he thought, *what am I doing here?*

Just as he was about to delve into a tell-all interview with Tom Hanks, he was called into the doctor's office. It was a pokey, low-ceilinged room which didn't look quite as sanitary as it should have.

'Mr – ah – Glass,' said the doctor, 'please take a seat.' Glen had been brought up to stand until otherwise told, but the main reason he dawdled was the woman sitting in a corner of the room. Dr Gibson didn't introduce her; she was there, and that was that. Glen wondered whether she was a patient, or a nurse.

'Haven't seen you before here, have we?'

'No, can't say that we have,' Glen countered.

'Death certificate?'

'Didn't bring it. Don't know where it is, I've never seen it.'

'That's alright, we'll manage.' Richard Gibson had dealt with a few walking corpses in his time. In fact he'd appeared on TV and radio, been interviewed by magazines and papers, all on account of his first dead patient – a young lad by the name of Ricky Diener.

Ricky had been a trainee surveyor who moonlit as a painter and decorator, pinching pennies to make ends meet, until he'd had a stroke of luck – he'd died.

Mr Whyte, his boss, had found him slumped over a laptop, sitting in the kitchen of a ruined farmhouse. Ricky had been surveying it ready for a renovation project, his work cut short by a heavy wooden beam that had fallen on his head. Killed outright, his body had hardly cooled before his eyes snapped open to look at his superior.

'What's going on, chief?'

'I thought you were a goner.' Mr Whyte had insisted on a swift trip to the local hospital, to check for a possible concussion. Ricky was certainly dazed, a sedate expression on his face. The doctor had called his colleagues into the ER, and one of them had called the tabloids. Ricky had no heartbeat, respiration, blood pressure or reflexes – yet he was walking and talking.

The medicos had hailed him as a miracle; to the press he was a phenomenon, and over the ensuing weeks he ran a gauntlet of tests, interviews, photo shoots and attempts to restore him to his former health. Ricky had been fortunate enough to be handsome at the point of his demise, with perfect teeth and neat curly hair.

Although his skin lost its natural shade, Ricky was still presentable enough to become a celebrity. He became a guest on chat shows, charming audiences with his wit and down-to-earth humility. He made public appearances in shopping malls and lecture theatres. He released a cover version of the Motown classic 'There's a Ghost in my House' as a CD single, giving the net profits to a children's charity. A twenty-four hour web cam watched his every move. His second song, 'Dead or Alive,' reached number one in the charts:

> Dead or alive, I'm coming with you
> Our love's impossible to defeat
> Long as you hold me close
> My heart'll never stop its beat

Boys wanted to be him, girls wanted to be with him. Everyone loved him until he started to decay.

He lost his hair. His fingers curled towards his palms. His lips shrank back over his gorgeous teeth. He smelled bad under the hot studio lights, and his TV slots dried up. His album covering various chart hits and ballads of yesteryear bombed. The media lashed back and the public realised that Ricky couldn't sing. Six months after his death, Ricky planned a comeback.

By this time his condition wasn't unique, which made him less phenomenal. Others had kicked the bucket and reappeared to tell the tale. They were dead but still present, vocal, no natural place in the scheme of things.

Boffins remained nonplussed. There was no scientific reason, as far as they could ascertain, why the Scots shouldn't stay dead and buried. Yet they continued to rise from their graves, zombie squatters with emotions and intellect intact. Most of them wanted to go to a better place, preferring heaven to Haddington, paradise to Penicuik. Not everyone was reanimated – the events seemed entirely random. Scientists at the Roslin Institute searched frantically for the appropriate gene to blame.

Ricky had one last contribution to make to the history books: his name. The undead folk were nicknamed dieners, and were even referred to as such by the government when it addressed the situation in a parliamentary debate.

'There are so many implications – medical, scientific, economic, military,' the Prime Minister admitted, 'that we will be funnelling eight million pounds into research specific to this situation.'

But no matter how much money was thrown at it, the puzzle remained unsolved.

'Do you mind if she listens to your chest?' asked Dr Gibson, referring to his mystery assistant.

'Sure,' Glen slurred.

'She's training. She only learns by doing.' Gibson still hadn't given Glen a name to call her by as she pressed the stethoscope against his chest. He couldn't tell whether it was warm or cold. Her nose was wrinkled against his body odour, a general unwashed stench that he couldn't seem to get rid of no matter how hard he scrubbed.

'Nothing,' she declared. A sphygmomanometer registered no blood pressure, and Glen had lost his reflexes too. He felt like a lab rat as the two medics hummed and haaed around him, but he enjoyed the attention of the trainee. She was fascinated – this was her first zombie subject. She handed him a small cup of water.

Along with his vocal cords and brain, it was obvious that some other of his organs worked. He could swallow and excrete food and drink. However, because he didn't get hungry or thirsty and had lost all sense of taste, the process was pointless. He was simply going through the motions. He gulped the water down anyway, encouraged by the assistant's frown.

'Do you feel any stiffness at all, Mr Glass?'

'Yeah. Kind of as if my muscles are all locking together. Slows me down some.'

'High levels of lactic acid.' Dr Gibson talked to his associate as if Glen wasn't in the room. 'This is fascinating. Somehow the cells are still functioning aerobically.'

'Or rigor mortis is taking longer to set in.'

'There's not a lot we can do for you at the moment,' Gibson admitted. 'Monitor your progress, give you a chance to read the leaflets – the government's produced lots of leaflets, you know –

that's about it, really. My main advice is to keep cool, turn the heating off, use ice packs. The hotter you get, the faster you'll decompose.'

'I've got kids, Doc. Can't let them freeze.'

'I appreciate that.' Gibson cleared his throat. 'Let me put this in plain English. There are bacteria inside of us all the time, but after your demise, these internal organisms became more active, multiplying at a great rate. Close contact with your children is inadvisable.'

'Can't you give me antibiotics or something? I can't leave here empty blood streamed, Doc. My wife would never forgive me. I disturb her. Get in her way, y'know, upset her because there's no sign of improvement.'

'There's not a lot we can do about the *escherishia coli*, but –' Gibson turned to his associate, who was busy making notes on a chart. 'Pass me the nikethamide please.' She prepared a jumbo-sized needle.

'You're not going to stick that in my face, are you?'

'This will stimulate your heart, your circulation,' the doctor explained, 'and believe me when I tell you you won't feel a thing.' His eyes as wide as a curious toddler's, Glen watched the needle plunge into his vein.

'Is that me cured, Doc?' Glen didn't feel cured.

'By no means. A pick-me-up at best, at worst a placebo to keep Mrs Glass happy. Who knows? It might revive you. Stranger things have happened.'

Glen was warming to Dr Gibson, who seemed to choose his words less carefully than most medics. He didn't know what a placebo was so he provided the sawbones with an all-purpose smile.

Perhaps it was subconscious, mind over matter, but Glen felt better after his visit to the local surgery. Maybe there was a good side to this condition – when his parents passed away there'd be a chance that they'd come back. If mothers outlived their children it wouldn't necessarily be the end. But no, Glen couldn't wish this existence on anyone.

He recalled all the filmic heroes that had been resurrected over the years – ET, Ellen Ripley, Baloo the bear. Glen was no matinee idol, but he could think of few major movie characters who hadn't cheated death. Now it was his turn.

Sitting in his favourite chair, watching TV, phooing on a cup of coffee, he recalled the conversation he'd had with his son about death and what he thought would happen next. Glen hadn't considered his answer before he spoke it, wished he'd given a more intelligent response – it wasn't often that chats with his son got deep. He'd been right, though. After his death, nothing happened. He'd popped back to the shop but Tony pussy-footed around, coming up with excuses not to take him back – instead of telling him the truth, that he stank and offended the customers.

Glen had asked after the regulars. Vian hadn't been seen since he'd been told about the terminal toilet break, and Alan admitted that the place didn't seem the same without him. No one rallied round, started a campaign or begged Tony to rehire the star staff member. Glen applied for other jobs in vain, spending time with his kids with little to say to them. He blamed the generation gap, but felt guilty as well. Paul and Lucy would come home from school and find their Dad in his chair, watching *Alias*. He felt useless, knew he was wasting time, treading water until a big tidal wave came along to swallow him up. He wasn't living; he was simply existing.

Trying to take control of the situation, he took an interest in the manner of his death. Misbah was unable to produce a death certificate, telling him that she'd burned it, upset; he applied for a copy, knowing that this would take some time. Meanwhile he sorted through his belongings. He alphabetised his CDs, labelled all his DVDs correctly. He put his paperback collection into order and listed all his possessions on his computer. He took a special interest in his Dance collectibles, occasionally digging out the strip of film and holding it up to the light, trying to fathom the blobs. He gave away a lot of junk, distributing items that meant a lot to him but little to the receivers.

As the weeks passed and Glen's eyes grew squarer, Misbah remained supportive and caring towards him. She made him cups of coffee (which he seldom drank) and bought him cigarettes at the local corner shop. She changed his bedclothes every morning and laughed at his jokes. Nevertheless, the strain began to show.

Misbah took it out on her children, not her zombie lover. She nagged her sprogs at the slightest opportunity, barking at them to tidy their rooms, finish their homework, eat their greens and stop wasting all their time playing computer games. Telling Paul and Lucy to do this was like asking a conscientious objector to bayonet a bunny. They had plenty of philosophical reasons why they should hang onto their gamepads: improving hand to eye coordination, reflexes, sharpening intelligence quotients.

It was hard to reinforce Mum's Law when Dad was just as bad as them, sneaking a shot on *Resident Evil* whenever the kids left their console idle. One child always always had to remain on watch while the other took a bathroom break or nipped to the fridge for some Sunny D. Misbah compromised, let them play a Harry Potter game – at least that had some literary associations.

To Glen, a console game could be better than life. You could fly like the North Wind, jump with springs in your heels, zap aliens with aplomb, and if you messed up you got another go, a new life. Game over, back to start as if the slate was wiped clean and nobody knew about it. You could learn from your mistakes instead of moping over them the whole time.

His favourites were the clunking classics of the '90s – *Lotus Esprit Turbo Challenge* II, *Speedball 2*, *Zool* and *Moonstone* (punningly subtitled *A Hard Day's Knight*). He had all the old John Dance tie-ins, and a disk full of Casio keyboard versions of the movie themes. It took a long time for them to load up on his prehistoric

Amiga 500, but that was part of the charm. He could immerse himself in the software and lose track of time.

Misbah became increasingly frustrated with Glen's fanboy obsessions. She didn't understand how a grown man could devote so much time to such inconsequential pursuits, whether there was work to be done around the house or not. She chalked it down to an attempt by her husband to get his mind off his decaying condition, but that didn't stop her from chastising him for getting his priorities all wrong.

Glen justified it as getting in touch with his childish side, enabling him to improve his rapport with Paul and Lucy. What could be more constructive than that? Misbah didn't buy that story, and complained about the mess that the computer console and its cables made. Glen would drape a towel over them if she was on the rampage. Didn't do much good. She would glower at him as she stomped through to the kitchen.

Glen could still be afraid, doubt, lose his temper and get upset, make misjudgments, lie or cheat, keep secrets, suffer bad luck. The only upside to Life #2 was that he'd lost all fear of death. But he wasn't indestructible – he decomposed daily throughout the winter and only had so much flesh to lose. He began to swell up; gases building inside his body and puffing his skin. He smelled bad now, like a steak left out in the sun.

A knock on the door brightened a dull March morning for Glen. He opened up and Mark sauntered into the house.

'How's it going?' Glen asked, trying not to look too pleased. He hadn't seen Mark since the funeral.

'You look like something that fell out of a dog's bottom, pal.' Mark slumped into Glen's chair – there were no complaints. 'Why didn't you call me?'

'You know I can never remember phone numbers. Or names. Or faces.'

Mark flipped a business card in his friend's direction. 'How's your folks?'

'Tired. They look older since – since the new year. They've been a great help. Always bringing food round that I can't eat.'

'Brussels sprouts?'

'I mean I can't eat anything. I can put food in my mouth but I can't taste it. I have the odd drink.'

'Some habits are impossible to break.' Mark couldn't contain himself any longer. 'How does it feel then? To be dead?'

'Christ! You journalists and your half-arsed questions. A boxer loses a fight and you ask him, 'how does it feel?' A housewife's semi burns down and you ask her, 'how does it feel?' It's 'cos you don't know yourself. You don't care, you don't let yourself feel anything. You observe. Sorry mate. You caught me on a bad day.'

Mark cleared his throat. 'So that's how you feel is it? Like a fighter who's lost a bout or –'

'I got a letter today telling me that there's a big backlog for copies of death certificates. Vital statistics forms, they call 'em. Apparently a lot of dead folk are asking for transcripts. How many of me d'you think there are out there? I mean, folks with my condition?'

'*Your* condition? Hundreds now. Thousands even. It's like an epidemic only good, because people are reunited with their loved ones and... well, it's kind of miraculous, isn't it? We don't know how it's happened or how long it'll last.' It was Mark's turn to apologise. He was always getting overexcited, talking too much. He'd get home from an interview, switch his Dictaphone on with a healthy two sides of tape filled, and find that he'd done more chatting than his subject. But Glen knew him well enough to accept his foibles.

'What do you think brought me back?'

'No idea. Fate, accident, the chemical crap they're pumping into the air. God. Maybe you've returned for a purpose.'

'What, like Jesus?'

'Spock. Resurrected to save the whales in *Star Trek* IV. Everything happens for a reason.'

'Even *Star Trek V*?'

'I suppose. What if you weren't meant to die yet?'

'Like if someone murdered me?'

'I was going to say that it was an accident of fate that shouldn't have happened. So you're getting a second chance. But I like the murder angle.'

'I'm not a story! I'm me, your best friend.'

'Everyone's a story, pal.'

'OK. I've got a story for you, maybe.' Glen opened the cupboard under the stairs and dug out his reel of film. He gave it to Mark and asked him to transfer it onto tape.

'You could get this done yourself, you cheapskate. But I can understand you don't want to go out of the house any more than you have to.' Mark shut up before he could say something with even less tact, taking the reel away with him.

After Mark's visit Glen became fixated with his demise, sure that the cause had been unnatural. He interrogated his wife about the inquest, what had been printed on the certificate; he ran over the food he'd eaten, wondering if it had poisoned him. He even drew up a list of suspects in case he'd been murdered.

The more he thought about it, the more he realised that there were several people with motives. Tony, a vindictive son of a sales-man who'd likely kill his own grandmother to sell her rump meat. The thieves whose robbery he'd wanted to foil. Vian, jealous of his car boot purchase. His father, who always seemed so disappointed in him. The government, using Glen in some sinister experiment. Misbah, desperately wanting out of their marriage. No... not Misbah.

The bin men came early that Wednesday morning, the one time Misbah called Glen from her workplace, asked him to put the rubbish out – she'd completely forgotten about it. They never arrived before eleven, usually turning up sometime in the after-noon. This time, when it mattered, when both the bins were full and needing emptied, they let him down. Glen left his orange sacks on the pavement all week; he intended to call the council, slag them off ('what do I pay my taxes for?'), but never got round to it. *The Man from* UNCLE was being repeated every weekday afternoon. Before Glen knew it a week had passed and the rubbish was collected. The bin men rolled up at three.

As the truck whirred and churned outside his living room window, Glen curled up in his easy chair and took the remote between spindled fingers. Now every on-screen shooting, murder and fatal accident took on a new meaning for him. He could empathise with those fictional fates in a way that no live viewer could. The crime dramas and action movies he'd wasted his time watching while alive were the last thing he wanted to see in his present state. But the channels were packed with violence – on the news, in documentaries, even at a time when the kids would be coming home from school. It always amazed him that the stations would dub out every weak and wonderful swear word for fear of offending a viewer, yet show gore and guts at all hours of the day.

Glen finally settled for *The Muppet Show* – some brutal slapstick and more exploding heads than a David Cronenberg scanner scrap, but no actual deaths – and he was still watching the box when Paul and Lucy got home.

'You're looking well, Dad,' smiled Paul. 'Considering.'

'Yeah. You missing work?' Lucy's wee joke.

'I am kinda missing it,' Glen croaked. Misbah hung the car keys up on their designated hook.

'Typical,' she crowed. 'When you worked, you spent all your time complaining about it. Now you're off you're moaning about that.'

Usually Glen would have joined in with the bickering, but he still felt tired and listless. He planned an early night.

'My friends at school are jealous.' Lucy stared wide-eyed at the muppets as a chicken exploded. 'None of them've got a dead Dad.'

'Does that mean we're orphans?' Paul piped up, missing his

mother's glare. Lucy gave him a nudge in the ribs and both kids clammed up. Fozzie Bear cracked a terrible gag, wakka wakka wakka, and Glen wondered how his children had grown up so fast. Where were the two little toddlers who'd sat on his knee watching Jim Henson's finest? Who'd stolen his life?

As the days grew warmer and spring kicked in, Glen spent some time sitting in the garden. He didn't have the energy to cut the grass or weed the skinny flowerbeds. Instead he threw crusts to the birds that visited occasionally. He watched clouds skirt the sun, criss-crossed with jet streams from passing fighters. He listened to hooting trains and police sirens in the distance. Trucks and tractors rumbled up the loan. There seemed to be more midges this year, definitely more ants; he felt itchy as soon as he saw one. The first bee of the year dive-bombed him on 26 April.

A great deal of his attention was spent on fending flies and bugs from his person. Attracted by his smell, they would land on his face and crawl up his legs; without a sense of touch, he didn't always catch them until they'd laid eggs or left larvae on his blackening skin. He took baths and showers several times a day, enjoying the sound of the water gurgling around him.

The itching sensation and clinging heat had disrupted Glen's sleeping patterns in previous years. These days he barely dozed. Sleepers don't tend to smile a lot; they look downright serious if not miserable. No masks are worn and there are no pretensions, something that Glen missed. He could let down his defenses when alone during the day, but he never relaxed totally. There were too many windows, mirrors and other reflective surfaces in the house.

On one idyllic Sunday he sat back in an old blue deckchair, the back door open so that he could hear the kids inside. His eyes closed, he didn't notice as his wedding ring slipped off his bony finger. Though he couldn't sleep, he still dreamed. He was flying up into the air, clouds bursting in his wake, creating rainbows. Laserbeams of warm sunlight were above him, dazzling him.

A passenger plane rumbled past him, en route for Glasgow, somersaulting him with its jet stream. He stalled for a moment, treading air like a coyote off a cliff, thunderclouds gathering around him and clinging, smothering him. Bolts of lightning tethered him and he was choking.

Glen opened his eyes. He could still hear the thunder high above his head – he stood up, peering into the sky. No, it wasn't thunder; it sounded more like boxes being moved, doors slamming, coming from the house.

He wrapped his bogging dressing gown round himself and moved slowly inside, up the stairs towards the bathroom. The thumping and scuffling seemed to follow him – there was something in the attic. The hatch was open and a stepladder gave him access to the loft space.

There were no rats up here, couldn't be, all the rats hung out at the allotments down the road. Was Dave's cat stuck in a crawlspace again? Glen's fear subsided and he immediately missed the sensation – even a bad feeling was preferable to none at all. There *was* movement in the gloom, some organic, restless thing. Not out to get him, though. As his eyes adjusted he saw bare flesh, two legs stretched out, a pair of feet in bright blue sandals. Misbah was searching through an old tea chest in a hurry, making too much noise. She was kneeling on fibreglass insulation, hadn't noticed yet.

Downstairs the kids were shouting. Not arguing, *I'm-gonna-skelp-ya-leave-my-toy-alone-I'm-tellin'-ma* shouting. Today the bairns were excited.

'Where do you think you are – outdoors inside?' Glen yelled down the stairs, then asked Misbah, 'What are you looking for this time in the morning?' He tried to sound helpful; he needed to earn some brownie points.

'A Mary Wesley book,' Misbah replied, breathless. She was making a mess, scattering debris from the chest and not caring where it landed. A car horn beeped rudely out front.

'In the dark?'

'I'm not going to read it up here. Couldn't find the torch.'

'It's in the airing cupboard.' The doorbell rang.

'See who that is, will you? Don't like Lucy answering the door to strangers.'

'Course.' Perplexed, Glen hurried back down the stepladder and made his way to the front door. His children were waiting in the hall with their coats on and rucksacks full.

'Mrs Glass?' asked a taxi driver, standing patiently on the doorstep. He had a new silver Alpha Romeo, all headlights and fancy add-ons. Glen rolled his eyes and turned to shout for his wife. She hurtled down the stairs, handing her hubbie a suitcase.

'Get the nice man to put this in his car, would you?'

Glen passed the case to the cabbie, dumbstruck. Paul and Lucy were already sitting on the back seat of the taxi, cooing at its luxury fittings. What was going on?

Misbah had returned to the loft, still creating a racket. As Glen poked his head up through the hatch, she raised a white object in the air, triumphant.

'*Part of the Furniture*?'

'Excuse me.' The object wasn't a book but an off-white photo album, the kind of colour that's favored at weddings. Pearl or oyster, Glen couldn't decide which. Either way, Misbah had the item tucked under her arm. She muscled past him and went to get her coat from the bedroom closet.

'What's so important?' Glen implored; so much to say but –

'Till death do us part, remember?' Misbah handed him his ring, retrieved from the garden. 'I can deal with your obsession with your stupid spy films – you were a geek while you were alive – but you were never a freak. Now you're scary. Not 'cos of how you look, but because you're unpredictable. Sullen. Paranoid.'

'Because I think someone killed me? What's paranoid about that?'

Misbah let out a sorry sigh. 'I want to remember you when you were full of life,' she explained tenderly; bent forward to kiss him on the cheek but stalled at the last inch. She left the house and jumped into the taxi, which roared away with a puff of black smoke. Not taking the time to change out of his dressing gown, Glen gave chase on his Vespa scooter.

Traffic was quite heavy at this time of day but Glen didn't lose sight of the taxi, couldn't, as the sun illuminated it like the spotlight on a pantomime villain. He weaved in and out of cars, his bare toes curled round the chrome pedal, tyres bumping against the kerb, brakes protesting. He began to gain on his family. They couldn't be running away from him; he hadn't been that much of a pest.

He skidded onto the pavement to avoid a cyclist, took a side street to make up some time. At the far end of the road there was no sign of his prey. Gone. After a moment, glint glint, the flash cab entered his vision and he pulled up alongside it. They were close to the Ferry Road now.

Glen motioned to his wife to roll the window down, indicating that he wanted to talk. The scooter spluttered. *Not now,* he grimaced at his bike, *I take it all back, I don't hate you, you upset me sometimes but I bear you no ill will.* The vehicle conked out and the taxi zoomed off into the distance.

Glen hopped off his ride and took a look at the engine. Nothing out of place for a change. He got back on his seat and tried to fire it up. The petrol gauge was past red.

This never happened in the movies.

CHAPTER 6

Members Only

1   EXT. STREET. NIGHT

A car screeches towards us. Lots of low angles. Maybe it's being pursued. We don't see the driver's face.

2   INT. INTERVIEW ROOM. DAY

DANCE

It's a matter of perception. You look at life from one angle, your boss looks at it from another.

SANDERS

I do what I'm told.

DANCE

Sometimes that isn't enough.

3   EXT. STREET. NIGHT

The car halts outside a tall, imposing building.

4   INT. INTERVIEW ROOM. DAY

DANCE

My job is to see things from your angle, try to help you.

SANDERS

Your job is to get me into more trouble.

5   EXT. STREET. NIGHT

The driver gets out of the car, his back to camera. Cautiously, he heads into an alleyway.

6   INT. INTERVIEW ROOM. DAY

                              DANCE
I know you were trained to think for yourself, use your
own initiative. But you can't disappear –

                              SANDERS
I like my bathroom breaks.

                              DANCE
(picking up folder)
Two weeks is a long time to spend in the john. You need to
explain yourself.

                              SANDERS
I'm not a criminal. I haven't broken any laws.

                              DANCE
Company law. The strictest imaginable.

7   EXT. ALLEYWAY. NIGHT
    Up some steps, though a door – a light blinks in the corner of
    his eye. He's set off a motion detector, holds his breath, looks
    back down the steps so that we see his face in the streetlight –
    it's SANDERS.

           From the Snap Judgement *screenplay by Sam Robbins*

GLEN HAD HEARD NOTHING from Misbah or the kids since their
high-speed getaway several weeks ago. They'd been gone long
enough to punish him, to make him realise how precious they were
to him. The only correspondence he received came from NTL,
Edinburgh City Council and BT. They each wanted a three-figure
sum from the Glasses and they wanted it fast. Glen preferred to
bury his head in his magazines and ignore such demands rather
than fret about keeping cash in the bank to cover every bill. He
pined for a simpler time, before uni, before he'd left home, when
no one felt the urge to bleed him dry. If the bills had been smaller,
the requests reasonable, he would have been able to manage. In the
meantime, Glen tried his best to have fun.

At last he had the peace he'd craved. No more pestering or nagging, brain-crushing homework or jelly-headed reality game shows. He could get up when he wanted to, break wind without fear of reproach, run round in his skivvies, even – oh, how dare you! – leave the toilet seat in the up position. He was cock of the walk, king of the castle, and... silence. He hated it. Tried to breach the sound barrier with noisy music videos, angry rock CDs, jerky computer games. Drank straight from the bottle (less washing up) and tuned into whatever he wanted to watch, no censorship; no kids wandering in. 18 rated all the way. Still he was bored. When he'd worked through all his albums and tapes, reached the highest levels on his best loved shoot-'em-ups, and munched up all the Super Noodles in the cupboard, he was forced to face facts – he would have to step outside his fortress, make a giant leap into the real world.

It was busy and the mass of people scared him. He wasn't used to it. Tried to talk to them but they ignored him. He barely made it to Video People, where none of his colleagues seemed to be present. He kept his head down, eyeing the racks cautiously, looking for a blockbuster he'd yet to see.

This took time.

He lurched to the counter, brandishing a Bruckheimer, found some change, didn't have his membership card, tried to sweet talk the new woman at the cash register.

'I used to work here, y'know,' he told her. Perhaps she pitied him; she certainly recognised him from her multiple excursions to the shop back when he'd been alive. Glen remembered his secret code number; she accepted it and reminded him to bring the DVD back within twenty-four hours.

'Don't worry,' he smiled, 'I won't be leaving town any time soon.'

Back home, Glen settled down in his reekie chair with the DVD nestling in his player. He picked up the relevant remote and pressed play. The lights went out and the TV blinked off. No power. He'd been cut off.

He sat in the dark for a while, contemplating his fate. No electricity meant no heat or hot water; he could handle that. His skin was less sensitive now and an occasional cold bath would do him good. His Amiga and consoles were unusable but he still had a Gameboy tucked in a wardrobe somewhere. He would use the time usually spent watching TV on more worthy pursuits – practicing riffs on his guitar, writing letters to distant family members, clearing out the attic...

He wished he had candles or a friend to call on. Russ was on holiday in Italy. Everybody else would be asleep by now. Glen left the house, glad of the shadows that concealed his features from passers-by. He returned the movie to the shop, dirtied with creamy finger marks, and tried to reclaim his hire fee, but the woman was having none of it, even though he'd retrieved his card. Glen bought a bag of popcorn and headed for a fancy, regentrified part of the docks, alighting at an internet café.

The owner regarded him suspiciously, as if Glen was a swine with a swag bag. Pieces of his skin flaked onto the keyboard as he sat down and began to type. The café was populated with greasy geeks and wan waifs, none sitting close to him, all put off by his odour. An e-mail message was sent to russ69@hotmail.com and it read:

> Now I know how earthquake victims feel. Or flood survivors. My world shaken at its bleeding foundations. I've been cut off, no juice, no fun. Misbah usually handles bills. She's not around at the moment, so they didn't get paid. Haven't heard from Tony – I don't think he wants me back. Weather's dull here, hope you're not wilting in the Roman heat. Sure you're having a lovely time and wish I was there:)

Glen surfed the web for a while, finding several diener sites. He wasn't alone; there were plenty of zombies around with nothing better to do than sit at a PC and maintain a site. A Google search pulled up MARY'S DEAD & LOVING IT SITE, the DEADHEADS UNITE WEBRING, A GOVERNMENT GUIDE TP DEALING WITH LIFE AFTER DEATH and NIKKI'S 'I DESPISED MY LIFE ANYWAY' HOMEPAGE.

As his search intensified, Glen got a shock. An organisation had sprung up as a result of the phenomenon, anti-diener and vocal with it. The group appeared small but it was growing.

> As we go about our daily business, it's easy to forget how precious life is. The deadheads are a constant, disturbing reminder. Only by ridding ourselves of this pestilence can we be sure that our children will survive the coming days.
>
> Posted by J.G.

Glen reckoned that his mission in life could be to bring all the good, deskbound lost souls together against this common foe, link up all the websites and create a virtual world of harmony for the disaffected. But he knew nothing of the mysteries of HTML coding, or putting letters in <p>ointy brackets. So instead he e-mailed the pro-life site with his grand suggestion, simply to piss them off. A note came up on his screen, titled 'Message Delivery Failure.'

> A message that you sent could not be delivered to one or more of its recipients. This is a permanent error. The following address(es) failed:
>
> russ69@hotmail.com
>
> Sorry, this email address does not exist.
>
> Received: by poexchange.jpmail with Internet Mail Service 18:33:34 by cmailg17.svr.pol.com with smtp for russ69@hotmail.com.

So his message hadn't got through. Either Russ had given him the wrong address, or he didn't want to know. Outside, the streets had emptied save for a scattering of blank faced barflies and tramps.

Glen had worn out his welcome at the café; he started to make his way home but then didn't see much point. It would be chilly and unwelcoming there. No life. So he popped into the bowling alley across the road instead, just enough pennies in his pocket to get sozzled.

'Members only, Mr Glass,' the barman explained.

'Never had that problem before. I'm after a quick pint, then –'

'Then forget it. No hard feelings eh?' As far as the barman was concerned, dieners had no feelings. No sense of touch, certainly. If blood didn't flow through this freak's veins, how would he get pissed anyway? The barman didn't wish to consider the matter any further, pointed to the door, and Glen took the hint. As he left the alley a heap of gas escaped from his body, filling the place with a ghastly odour and leaving Glen a few inches thinner.

Azad's Grocery was more welcoming. Glen's money was as good as anyone else's. He bought a bottle of vodka, making a start on it in the local swing park.

It was a balmy evening, overcast but light enough to make out the overgrown grass slopes flanking the area. Glen sat on a round-about, using one foot to spin himself clockwise. The more he drank the giddier he became, and he was unsure whether the ride or the booze was responsible.

Drizzle sent him scurrying under a climbing frame, a slim metal panel acting as shelter. Home was a trap, he decided, a cotton wool coffin of his own making. He wouldn't get anywhere, achieve any-thing, find his family by staying in his house. He took another swig of vodka, found his scooter keys tucked in a jacket pocket, and stag-gered across the road to his beloved vehicle. He fumbled the keys into the ignition and the engine started first time. He would drive over to Mark's – a rock steady shoulder to cry on and a sofa to slump over.

Glen didn't make it across town. A streetlight got in the way. His vision slightly blurred, Glen never saw it coming but he certainly felt the impact. He closed his eyes and didn't want to open them again.

CHAPTER 7

Getting Away From It All

I know you're fooling 'round
I know you're off the rails
Don't know why I love you
You're hard as nails.
But I'm here for you
Unlike those other males
Go on about your bizniz
'Cos dead men tell no tales.

I won't ask for nothing
I won't be unkind
So what if my eyes are dim?
Love is blind.

I'll buy all your bull
Brave the storms and gales
Because I know the truth
That true love never fails.
I will take your hand
Lead you down happy trails
You do what you want
'Cos dead men tell no tales.

'(Dead Men) Tell No Tales'
From the album Ricky D Goes Pop *by Ricky Diener*

GLEN WOKE UP IN a cold, blue-lit room, his vision obscured by a thin white sheet. He was lying on a slab and a tag was tied to his toe. Propping himself up with his elbow, he peered through the cobalt gloom, waiting for his memory to fill in the blanks firing off in his head. He was alone and the room was silent.

I'm in a morgue, he realised. *They found me in the accident, couldn't find a pulse, sent me here. I don't want to be buried again.* He hastily got off the slab, wrapping the sheet around himself, stumbling over to a wallful of drawers that he hoped were unoccupied. He slowly reached out his hands, gripping a metal handle and tugging at it. It was either locked, stuck or jammed with a fat floater.

This is like a nightmare. The whole thing. Like the bad dreams I used to have when I was a kid, watching too many horror films. To make sure that he was alone, Glen banged on the drawers, hoping to attract some attention.

'Hello! Anybody home?' he yelled. The reply came from a live morgue attendant, bursting into the room with his mouth agape.

'Not again,' said the attendant, sounding more fed up than fearful. 'Stay put, will you, until I sort this out?'

Glen nodded, feeling vulnerable in his near-naked state. As the attendant left the room he perched on an empty slab, kicking his heels until he began to imagine who'd taken up his seat before him. The notion didn't appeal to him, so he stood up and leaned against the drawers instead. *I hope they don't stick me in one of these,* he thought. *I don't know if I could take that. Alone in the dark with nothing but my memories for company.*

'Well! Still looking for that friend of yours?' Dr Tozer entered the morgue, his thin lips twisted into a smile.

'He's no friend. There's been a mistake,' Glen replied groggily. 'I'm not – I don't belong here.'

Tozer felt his pulse. 'Well, technically it seems that you do now. My condolences. Would you follow me please?' Tozer sounded unreasonably cheerful, as if he, like the attendant, was used to dealing with the walking dead. He led Glen out of the room, up a flight of concrete steps and into a brightly lit hospital ward, filled with dead bodies. 'Welcome home!' Tozer exclaimed as Glen stood blinking in the doorway. The corpses were reading newspapers, listening to personal stereos and sipping cups of tea. There was paper at the ends of the beds where the dieners put their feet, small sin bins and computerised BP monitors beside them, two ECG machines for the whole ward, plus a sink and a desk by the door.

On the desk was a PC, a slender folder for each patient and two coffee mugs for the staff nurses, along with the buttocks of a skinny little doctor with short blonde hair, brown eyes and a permanently snotty nose, who perched on the edge and gazed across the ward. Glen could tell from his expression that he was overworked and unhappy at pulling the graveyard shift. *Someone should turn off that dripping tap,* thought Glen, watching the doctor sniff. *Maybe he needs a new washer.*

'Dr Jacobs will take care of you,' Tozer assured Glen, leading him into the ward and onto a creaky bed. The rheumy Jacobs was about Glen's age, with a square jaw and straightforward principles. He was running all the usual tests on a diener named Alex – reflexes, pulse, response to mild shocks to the chest and an injection of saline into the eyeball. Only the last of these engendered a response from Alex and Jacobs decided that it was psychologically, not physically, motivated.

'Onset of putrefaction,' Jacobs noted, his nose running furiously, 'exposed tissue is blackened with a creamy consistency... decaying odour is very strong. Dead as a doormat,' was his educated diagnosis. He apologised to his subject for the last test, increasing Glen's respect for the medico. This guy was only following orders after all, and instead of treating the dieners like inanimate corpses he was actually taking the time to explain what he was doing.

This doesn't seem so bad, Glen shrugged, *I can handle it. What are the others so afraid of?*

The ward was lined with cardiac monitors, all in flatline mode with horizontal green lines on every screen, an eerie electronic tone constantly accompanying the everyday sounds of medical bustle. It was as understaffed as any government-run hospital. The charge nurse was trying to do four jobs at once, with a dose of pills in one hand, a thermometer in another, a clipboard tucked underarm and a report sheet in her pocket. Her hair was a medusa mass on top of her head, and the bags under her eyes had taken a great deal of packing. Like all the staff in this part of the hospital, she wore a great deal of warm clothing to combat the low temperatures that she was required to work in. It took some time for her to get to Glen.

Hospitals were top of Glen's list of pet hates, an acid catalogue that included christmas compilation CDs, cinemagoers who sat beside him and breathed loudly through their nostrils for two hours, rude high street shoppers and sassy mall rats, queues, pub quizzes, drunk drivers or sober cyclists, adverts louder than the programmes they interrupted, Sports Personalities of the Year with no personality, comics dumbed down for kids or intellectualised for adults. He disliked being told what to do but when the charge nurse made him lie down in a strange bed in the uncommon microcosm of the hospital he didn't have much choice but to follow orders.

'Turn this way Mr Glass,' bossed Dr Jacobs, 'say "ah", wiggle your toes...' He may have been officious, but at least the doc referred to Glen by his surname as if he was someone important. He wouldn't be here long, Jacobs explained – they didn't have the beds to spare for more than a week. There were some simple routine tests to be carried out before he was relocated. 'I don't know where you're going, so there's no use asking me,' the doctor said matter-of-factly and Glen believed him. In the next bed, Alex introduced himself and offered a friendly thumbs-up.

Glen didn't ask why Dr Jacobs was examining him – he didn't fancy getting a needle in his eye, so he stayed quiet except to say, 'my GP gave me something – some kind of pep-me-up. Have you got any of that?'

'Nikethamide. None of that round here. We need to check your condition without any drugs in your system.'

His tests complete, Jacobs handed his notes over to an RN and moved on to his other patients, giving Glen a chance to talk to Alex properly.

'They're in such a hurry. Guess they don't know how long we'll last before we start falling apart.'

'How long's it been since your...?'

'Since I copped it? Not long. Long enough to start stinking to high heaven. Heart attack, can you believe that? I was only 47.'

'Too much stress?' Glen fluffed up his pillows, trying to get comfortable.

'Too much pizza. And I was a bit naughty with drugs and that. The staff here reckon that might be a reason why I came back to life.'

'I never did drugs, more's the pity. I was always partial to pepperoni, though.'

Alex smiled. He pointed out the young, nervous-looking diener who sat on Glen's opposite side, listening to a fat set of headphones. 'That's Kenny Cartwright, he was brought in with me. Good guy. I'll introduce you to him later.'

'Thanks.' Glen closed his eyes, hoping Alex would understand that he wanted some peace, time to think. Whatever Tozer and Jacobs were playing at, his chance return to the RHS offered a second opportunity to track down Ash. Maybe he'd pluck up the courage to talk to him this time. He would find a phone, call Mark and find out what was on the precious film reel. All the pieces of his puzzled existence would fall into place, all because of a daft traffic accident.

In the ward, none of the patients slept, but they stuck to the nighttime routine, lying in their beds by midnight, lights off or dimmed. Many kept their eyes closed, alone in the dark with kind memories or harsh thoughts. Some read by dull lamplight, westerns or combat magazines, tending towards fantastical thrillers rather than real-life stories – they felt disconnected from the outside world, didn't care for it at that time. To Glen's surprise, even though none of his wardmates slept or breathed, some of them snored – a result of lying on their backs for long periods, perhaps. Snoring seemed to be as much a habit as a physical tic.

Strangest of all, Glen could sometimes make out far-off opera music, occasionally accompanied by a low singing voice. The sounds seemed to come from just outside the ward, along one of the corridors that Glen had glimpsed on his last visit to the RHS. He wondered what the opera was called, and what cultured soul was playing it.

Within the ward, the guys would whisper to each other when they got bored or needed to escape their private mindfields. This was when Glen really got to know his wardmates – many of them had gone through the same pattern as he, trying to cope with death and working out what to do next, how to get even with the unfriendly fates. They'd lost friends or family, too disgusted and despairing to stick around and care for them. They knew that the hospital's findings would go straight to the authorities, to drug companies seeking a cure. Worst-case scenario: this would happen to every dead body, filling the country with a glut of slow-moving couch potatoes with glazed expressions and uncertain futures. At best, the resurrections were a short-term aberration.

Glen tried to find activities to occupy his mind. The hospital radio DJ's drone soon made his headphones a no-no. He picked at the stitching on his sheets and watched his fellow patients lying still, emitting an occasional sigh. With the eerie blue light that shone from the nurse's station, it was like being back in the morgue. *I suppose I am,* Glen thought, *although here they probably do their autopsies in front of anyone who cares to come have a look.*

The mournful opera music gave him something to focus on, floating from away down the wing. He didn't get up to investigate, preferring to work on his own problems instead. Why hadn't he heard from Mark? Whatever was on that reel of film, it had to be important. He cursed himself for letting it out of his sight, hoping that he hadn't placed his best friend in danger.

The atmosphere didn't get much lighter in the daytime. Alex

complained of ghost pains whenever the nurses took a blood sample. All of his nerve endings had atrophied, but he still insisted that his lower arm was more sensitive than his upper. 'Stick me further up, sister,' he'd whine. 'That stings. Leave off the nasty nips.'

In the bed next to Glen lay Kenny, a delicate young man with a permanently frightened look in his eyes. It took a couple of days for Glen to strike up a proper conversation with the youth.

'How did you end up here?' Glen asked.

'Picked a fight with a couple of blokes.' Kenny screwed his face up with the memory. 'I had attitude, they had knives. Surprised them by fighting back.' He proudly showed off the wound that ran across his throat. 'Knocked one of 'em flat, did a runner. Made the mistake of going to the police for help.'

When Glen frowned at this, Kenny told him, 'Deep down the police are just regular folk. Don't like dieners. They tried to finish the job those two thugs started, issued some Borders justice. I was dumped in a Dalkeith gutter, some do-gooder found me... I was shifted around till I ended up in this weird clinic.'

'They messed you up bad.'

'Oh, I was like this before the attack, pretty much. Wasn't a lot handsomer when I was alive. A face only a mother could look at.'

'So you didn't die in the fight?' Glen's eyes were wide.

'Oh, I'm always getting into scrapes. Got the face for it, I reckon.'

'Don't be too tough on yourself,' Alex chipped in, 'there's much worse looking cadavers around here. We're none of us much more than spare parts, really.'

'I got no intention of disintegratin', especially not in a place like this. I got things to do, a family to support. I may've kicked the bucket but I still got responsibilities; I ain't useless and my brain's fighting fit. You know what they say: healthy mind –'

'Good morning, how are you feeling?' the domineering Dr Jacobs entered the ward.

'Nothing,' was Kenny's retort, 'I don't feel nothing at all.'

'I do!' Alex piped up. Kenny glowered at him and Alex seemed to shrink in his bed.

If Glen had only known what Jacobs had in store for him, he would not have been at all pleased to see the doctor.

Glen was wheeled into a small room where he was stripped and wired up to an ECG machine and a fancy-looking computer. Three solemn people in business suits accompanied Dr Jacobs and the nurse. Glen recognised one of them as the assistant from Dr Gibson's clinic, though she didn't seem to recall him. Jacobs explained that they were from a drug company and they were more interested in the computer's readings than Glen, so there was no need to feel embarrassed.

'That's easy for you to say,' hissed Glen, growing weary of the doctor's bedside mannerisms. 'You may be used to parading naked in front of strangers, but I'm not.'

The assistant bade Glen lie still on a cold grey bed while she struggled to insert a tube into a vein on his left arm. The drug that these strangers were so interested in would be pumped into his system, and the computer would register any effects. Glen trusted Dr Jacobs; he wanted to be cured and if experimental medication could help, he would take it.

'Can you feel anything at all at the moment?' asked the doctor.

'A bit depressed, I suppose.'

'No, no. I mean sensations on your skin. Touch. Chills if there's a draught, that sort of thing.'

'Nothing like that.'

'No pain?'

Glen shook his head firmly.

'You're very lucky,' Jacobs murmured.

I don't feel lucky.

'We're using a very expensive catheter today. Much narrower than the standard issue. Only the best for you guys.' Glen didn't watch as the catheter was inserted, but he could imagine it and that was painful enough. The doctor asked him to clench and unclench his bladder, and this produced a reading on the computer. The suits cooed around the monitor.

OK, so the electronic equipment in the room was worth far more than Glen would ever be. But that didn't mean he'd have to enjoy the lack of attention. 'Are you done with me now?' he asked.

One of the suits took out a digital camera and prepared to take a snap. Jacobs held a sheet of paper in front of Glen's face as the flash went off. The picture would include the high-tech hardware and an anonymous body, lying on a cold grey bed.

In the middle of the night, Glen lay still with his eyes closed, desperate to get to sleep. He felt more tired than ever, and blamed it on the drugs and potions he'd been served with. The doctors and drug specialists had seemed most excited about a broth that looked disgusting but imbued its consumer with a burst of energy. Glen didn't know why; all he knew was that after that initial burst, a great fatigue had struck him and he'd had to lie down.

He tossed and turned on his mattress, trying to get comfortable, pondering his limited options, when he heard a 'psst!'

He didn't think anyone really said 'psst' except in *Mad Magazine*, but Alex was crouched beside his bed pssting, loud enough to disturb the whole ward. Glen's fellow patients politely ignored the noise, even though it was about two in the morning.

'What is it?' asked Glen, trying not to sound grumpy.

'I've found him.' Alex sounded hoarse and impatient. 'Come on, follow me.' Reluctantly, Glen peeled off his blanket and swung his feet onto the cold white floor. He wriggled his toes, marvelling at the lack of sole sensation. No more freezing in winter winds or draughty houses; now frostbite meant nothing to him. What was the worst that could happen – hypothermia?

With a long-suffering smile he followed his pal out of the gloomy ward, two ghosts in standard issue gowns fumbling through a maze of dark-lit mauve corridors. Every so often they would tuck themselves into a doorway, out of sight of passing nurses in blue tunics and white trousers. Glen tried to make out the signs on the walls. He was reminded of stories he'd heard about occupied countries in wartime, where the Resistance would mix up or remove signs to confuse the enemy. He almost bumped into his guide as Alex stopped suddenly in front of him. They'd reached a wing full of private rooms.

'Here he is.' Alex knocked on one of the old fashioned wood panelled doors, pushing it open. 'Keep quiet,' he told Glen in a melodramatically hushed tone, leading him into a large single-bed room that was filled with a garden of azaleas, pansies, begonias and blooming cacti. The bright colours were a shock after the gloom of the ward and corridors, and more than anything Glen wished he still had his sense of smell, as he saw a cigar-smoking man sitting in his secret Eden. He had a stubble of white hair on his head and was listening to a CD player, endlessly looping the same opera. Three hefty law books and a copy of the *Financial Times* rested on his bedside cabinet. The reclining gentleman was recognizable to Glen from countless magazine photos and video interviews as *Spyland* director Peter Foothill, in full song no less.

'How on earth did you get in here?' the smoker asked as Glen and Alex pushed their way through the lush foliage.

'We heard you,' Glen replied.

'We've been worried, Mr Foothill,' Alex said humbly, 'about whoever was listening to this music every night. It sounded –'

'Sentimental? You cannot beat a bit of Alfano.'

'I haven't heard it before,' Glen admitted. 'Before I came to this hospital, I mean.'

'And now you're sick of it, I'm sure. Didn't realise I was playing it so loud.' Foothill hit the volume switch, turning the music up, not down. 'This is pretty obscure, I'll admit. 100 years old, forgotten, put into mothballs since then. But back then it was useful. *Resurrection* made a lot of people very happy. It got so close to perfection. We should celebrate the also-rans, the stuff that's almost great. Just for trying.' The CD came to a conclusion, shuffled back to the first track and started to play again. 'You'll have to excuse me. I've been put through the ringer, old son.'

'I think we all have,' Glen said. Although he was jealous of Foothill's cushy private room he still found the man decidedly personable. 'What's with all the fancy trappings?

'I'm a special case, apparently. Smoke?' Foothill offered Glen a cheroot. 'Can't smell it, can't inhale, but I like to sit one in my mouth and feel like a man.'

Glen declined; Alex helped himself.

'I managed to convince the staff that it would be in their best interests,' Foothill continued. 'That I would rouse the public-ward rabble into a frenzy of rebellion.'

'We are the rabble,' Alex pointed out, lighting his cigar with Foothill's Zippo. 'Two of them, at least. And we don't feel very frenzied.'

'I was in my front garden when I had my seizure. They took me straight to the morgue, strapped me to a slab, intending to slice me up and dice me no doubt. But it turns out the hospital administrator and I went to the same college. Small world, eh?'

'What has he told you?' Glen's voice became more insistent. There were footsteps in the corridor. 'Why are we here?'

'You're guinea pigs. An opportunity to try all kinds of drugs –' Foothill stopped talking for a moment, listened for signs of life outside his room.

'To find a cure,' Glen suggested.

'Not quite. To keep you on your feet. Get you working double time. Get you out of this zombie malaise... Young man – take a look outside, will you?'

'I'm Alex, he's Glen. I'll take a quick gander.' Alex cautiously checked for staff. He saw no one.

'You'd better get going, gentlemen. The nurse'll be round for my bed bath any minute now and I don't think she'd take very kindly to you joining me.'

'Neither would we,' Alex said ruefully, fidgeting in the doorway. He never got a bed bath.

'Off you go. Nip back tomorrow, we'll talk more then.' Peter closed his eyes, absorbing his Franco Alfano CD.

Back in their own ward, Glen tried to make sense of their strange meeting. 'Why weren't we told that there were dieners in other parts of the hospital?'

'They don't tell us anything. Maybe they didn't want us to know about him,' suggested Alex.

'That's crazy. Why isn't he in here with us?'

'He has the gift of the gab, that one. A tongue of solid silver. I don't think he'll be joining us anytime soon.'

Soon after his meeting with Foothill, Glen heard the Big News. He was going to be shipped out of the hospital along with several of his wardmates – destination unknown. He didn't really care where he was headed, glad to be getting out of the sterile hospital at last. The buzz of excitement in his ward was palpable. The patients were allowed to listen to the radio for the first time, and they tuned into every news bulletin they could find in the hope that they'd hear some information that had a bearing on them.

Glen almost cried when he saw TV for the first time in a week. It was wheeled into the ward in an attempt to placate the increasingly unruly, inquisitive dieners. Sedatives had no effect and a TV set was cheaper anyway; opium for the carcasses.

The patients watched the ITV news, guest-anchored by Kim Clark, the local reporter. Her long brown hair draped her shoulders and her full red lips were fixed into a warm smiling position. Glen thought she looked beautiful.

'The government announced new legislation today to meet the diener situation head on,' Kim said in a determined tone. 'Experts plan to build a database of citizens most likely to pass away over the next year and return as health-seekers. These specially targeted individuals will be placed in protective areas and monitored carefully for a limited period.'

A shot of Donald Claig, head of Operation Diener, appeared on the screen. 'We want to prevent further outbreaks of this syndrome,' said Claig, his serious expression contrasting with Kim's grin. 'We are doing all we can to cure those afflicted. But our best bet is to nip this in the bud, before it happens.'

Kim finished the story. 'Top scientists believe that by studying terminal subjects, they can divine a way to deal with dieners.'

And in other news: 'The streets of Central Edinburgh were flooded as drains failed to cope with constant rain. Residents found themselves ankle deep in sewage and insurance companies estimate that the incident caused millions of pounds' worth of damage. The Water Board had no comment to make at this time.

'In Inverness, a gang of youths brutally assaulted Colin Brent, a forty-year-old diener. Although the attack took place at noon on a busy main street, no witnesses have come forward. Police are appealing for anyone who saw the attack take place to get in contact.'

'You like her, huh?' Kenny gave Glen a nudge.

'She's alright.'

'You and the entire male population of Scotland. She gets tons of fan mail.'

'You think I should write to her?'

Kenny just smirked in reply.

As if the TV wasn't enough to break the hospital monotony, Glen was visited by an unfamiliar doctor named Wiles.

'Where's Dr Jacobs?' Glen asked her, worried

'Day off. Needed a break.' Glen didn't like this newcomer. Too cold and book-bound. He already knew from the nurses that Wiles was a woman who liked to do everything by the numbers; to her, filling in forms was more important than placating patients.

The examination was unheralded and humiliating. Dr Wiles twisted his limbs every which way, tapping at his joints, jabbing him with needles, probing his anus. Throughout the hour-long process Wiles didn't say a word and worst of all, she hadn't bothered to draw a screen around the bed. Glen's friends looked on with horrified fascination.

'You're next, you know,' croaked Glen to Kenny, who hid under his blanket.

'You're a fascinating subject, Mr Glass,' Dr Wiles admitted, 'so average. Medium height, weight, intelligence. The perfect median. Although deadheads are becoming quite common these days, I'm still frightfully interested. Such a shame they're taking you away.'

There was one last chance to see Peter before the move. Once again, Glen and Alex snuck into his private room in the wee hours. The law books were gone, replaced by a mobile phone and a copy of the Yellow Pages. Glen didn't ask how Peter had gained permission to use a moby in a medical facility – this was obviously a man who could get what he wanted with a click of his fingers; or at least that was what he fooled people into thinking.

'Need to phone a friend?' Glen queried, giving Peter a half-hearted smile.

'This is no matter for mirth.' Peter shook his head slowly. 'You don't know where they're sending you tomorrow.'

'Neither do you.' Alex chipped in. 'All we know is, they're shipping us out.'

'I don't know for sure but it's nowhere nice.' Peter frowned. 'Imagine the best holiday camp you ever visited as a child, with all the fun of the fair.'

'That doesn't sound so bad.'

'This is the opposite.'

'Don't tell me they're sending us to Gourock?' Alex tried to lighten the moment, though Peter was deadly serious.

'If you'll excuse me gentlemen, I have to prepare for my departure. I like to use my time wisely; this sleepless existence is a boon, not a millstone.' Peter picked up the phone book and flicked through it thoughtfully. 'Meet me in the car park out back in about an hour. Don't worry, I'll find you once you're out there and then I'll facilitate your escape.'

Alex and Glen opened the door and peeked down the corridor. All clear. Peter saw them off with a wave.

'Shouldn't we go get Kenny?' Alex whispered as they descended the stairs.

'To be honest if I go back now, I'll change my mind and want to stay. They're probably taking us to a better place and I'll sure miss the routine here. I've got my own reasons for leaving.'

'But I don't have to go with you.' Alex stopped mid-step. 'I getcha. I'm still coming though.' The two men reached the ground floor and cautiously pushed at a fire escape. It wouldn't budge.

'Give it a shove with your shoulder,' was Alex's suggestion.

'I don't want to set off an alarm. We'll have to sneak out through reception.'

'Are you crazy?' Alex followed Glen out of the stairwell. Another murky corridor led to the reception, where the dieners ducked behind a vending machine as a porter passed by.

'Now!' Glen snuck after the porter, Alex staying close behind him, keeping to the gloom. They soon reached the rear exit, which the porter unwittingly shoved open for them.

Once the man had left and the glass doors had almost swung closed behind him, Alex squeezed through. Glen didn't follow.

'What are you playing at now?' Alex asked hoarsely, his sallow palms pressed against the glass.

Glen had seen a familiar figure standing in a small waiting area. Unable to resist, he edged closer so that he could see the man clearly. It was a big guy, clicking on a mouse and staring at a computer screen.

Ash. I've found him. Glen got as close to the brute as he dared without being seen. Ash was playing a video game – it looked like *Grand Theft Auto*, but that might've been Glen jumping to conclusions.

In the dark Glen didn't see a drip stand until he'd bumped up against it, causing a terrible scrap and clatter. Ash turned, startled, worried that he'd been caught mucking around on company time. He lumbered over to the stand, Glen scooting into a shadow just in time.

Satisfied that he was alone, Ash returned to his game while Glen went back to the exit and tried to get it open.

'The porter had a key card,' Alex mouthed from outside, scared. 'The door's locked.'

'Try to force it,' Glen replied, desperately shoogling the door but trying to keep quiet at the same time. Hearing Ash's footsteps heading his way, he urged Alex to hurry.

With a mighty tug, Alex got the door open and Glen rushed through like a drowning man breaking to the surface. The dieners ran down a back path, tucking themselves behind a hedgerow in the car park.

Alex watched as the bulky Ash walked past them, oblivious to their presence. 'What do they feed him on?' he muttered.

'He could be the guy who killed me.'

'Why?'

'He's only a possible suspect.' Glen shrugged. 'There's a lot of people I didn't get on with.'

'Sure,' said Alex a little too quickly, 'but why would this guy want you dead? If you don't mind me saying, you're so –'

'Average?' Glen left his hiding place, aiming for the main road. 'I was going for insignificant.'

'I had a reel of –' Glen shut his mouth. How well did he really know Alex? The man had been uncommonly friendly when Glen had arrived in the ward, and besides, they'd only met a few days ago. He decided to go with his gut and trust him. 'I had a reel of film with Peter Foothill's name on it.'

'That's weird,' Alex told him. 'Maybe you should give it back to him.'

'I don't have it on me right now. When I get it back, it's going straight to him.'

Glen told Alex everything – about Vian, the car boot sale and the stolen film reel. By the time the yarn was spun, the dieners had reached the main road.

'Watch it!' Alex yelled, but it was too late. Ash had spotted them both and was hurtling towards them, his mouth open in a strange smile. He smashed into Glen with his shoulder, knocking the diener to the ground. Alex ran back into the car park leaving Glen to deal with Ash, who towered above him, backlit by a streetlamp.

'I thought I saw someone sneaking around!' Ash yelled as Glen tried to right himself. 'Who do you think you are?'

'You don't know me?'

'Why should I?' Ash couldn't be the murderer if he didn't even recognise Glen. With this insight, all sense of fear left the diener and he launched himself at Ash's midriff, hitting him head-on and propelling him backwards. A taxi cab swerved to avoid them both, horn honking.

'You didn't kill me? Are you sure?'

'Not yet.' Ash swung a fist at Glen but it failed to connect.

'Careful,' said Glen, 'you could hurt someone with that.' He grabbed Ash's meaty arm, leaving a couple of fingernails in the porter's shoulder. Ash kicked him to the ground, raising a heavy boot to stamp on his head. In the distance a train rattled along a rusty set of tracks. Glen closed his eyes tight, steeling himself against the blow. It never came.

'Funny, but I don't miss him as much as I should.' Anna hefted her shopping trolley into the frozen food aisle, wondering why she always got the one with the wobbly wheel.

'That's understandable, what with him still being around.' Misbah was helping Anna with the week's groceries, ticking off items on a lengthy list in her trademark neat fashion

'I just can't bring myself to visit him. Isn't that terrible?'

'He's not the same any more. After he... got the news, he was like a different person. He didn't care about us after that.'

'I'm sure he does. I should have noticed the signs. The trembling hands, the walk, the migraines.' Anna opened a cabinet and picked up some frozen peas.

'It's the doctors' fault, not yours. It's a relief, knowing what's up with Jack.'

'We should tell Glen.' Anna led Misbah to the checkout. 'He has a right to know that his father's not well.'

'Glen hasn't been home for days. We don't know where he is.'

'Then find out for me.' Anna turned and gripped the sleeve of Misbah's jacket. 'Find him and tell him that Jack's dying.'

A hand filled Glen's field of vision. Long goujon fingers reached towards him and he grasped them, rising to a sitting position.

'Are you alright, my friend?'

Funny. He didn't recall having Peter as a friend: a silver-haired, waistcoated Samaritan, dead as a doornail but retaining a twinkle in his eyes.

'Fine,' Glen lied, his head swimming. 'What the hell's going on?'

'Fine,' Glen lied, his head swimming. 'What the hell's going on?' He cussed the air blue as he tried to stand.

'Easy, easy,' said the well-dressed gentleman. 'We're all in this together.'

'In what, and how deep is it?' Two more dieners had joined the Samaritan – a big guy with a beard and Alex, looking suitably meek after his act of cowardice. They all helped Glen off the road, passing a prostrate Ash on the pavement.

'Is he dead?'

'He'll live. I don't think he liked you very much. Follow me.'

'Gladly. But where to?'

'To a train depot, or a warehouse, or whatever they call them these days. Where they keep the engines,' the big man answered, introducing himself as Chris. 'We're going to wait for a train.'

'We're waiting for it to get dark again, actually,' Peter said gently.

'I didn't know you had friends on the outside.' Glen's senses were clearing at last, and he rubbed his forehead to help speed the process.

'Chris was an associate producer on several of my movies, but don't hold that against him. He's been invaluable in helping me to keep track of events outside our cosy hospital. D'you know that half the populace expects us to turn on them at any moment and start munching their brains out?'

'That's ludicrous.'

'Zombie movies and video games are big business these days, especially since Ricky D. arrived on the scene. It's not safe for us around here any more, hence our great escape. We must be cautious.' The dieners had reached their depot, settling in a quiet corner where the moonlight couldn't reach them. 'How are you feeling now?'

'Not too bad actually, considering I was almost run over by a taxi not so long ago. And that was a highlight of my day. How did you get out of the hospital?'

'So many questions,' Peter shook his head, smiling. 'Fire escape,' he added with a wink.

'What about the alarms?' asked Alex.

'No alarms.' Peter kept smiling. 'The sun will be rising in a wee while.'

Glen did have a lot of questions. He wanted to know where the men were heading, how they'd found him and why they were so antsy. Tucked up in his house, Glen had shied away from current affairs, consumed with discovering what or who had killed him, although he knew that he wasn't the only person in Scotland to be resurrected. The phenomenon seemed indiscriminate – he was nothing special.

As the sun rose and oozed amber light across the horizon, the men got up, stretched and prepared to brave the dawn. With nowhere else to go, Glen followed them. They cut a ghoulish figure, silhouetted by the sunrise, lumbering towards a footpath that cut across the main line to Edinburgh. Glen noticed a generous helping of litter – plastic scraps; a small rubber ball; empty soda bottles, mostly green; the inevitable cigarette butts; loose pages of the *Scotsman*; a cornflakes packet.

There was a sharp bend just before the crossing, and it was apparent that oncoming trains would have to slow down at this point. Peter pushed the small wooden gate open with a creak. Beyond the tracks a chorus of electricity pylons sang an eerie aria.

'You're crazy if you think you can hop on a train. I mean, in our state –'

'Done it before,' Chris muttered, 'I'll do it again. There's a goods train due any minute now.'

Right on cue a horn sounded and the surrounding trees and waste ground were illuminated by the cross-country cargo run, all dark brown metal and streaks of grit, its flanks brightened with graffiti. It slowed to a crawl round the bend and Peter reached for an open carriage, Chris at his coat tails, gaining a purchase and climbing aboard as the train sped up again. Glen made it to the next carriage and grabbed a side panel, his arm almost dislocated with the effort. He pulled himself onto the train, trying to open a door.

Wind battered the carriage, Glen fighting every gust. Using all of his strength he managed to yank the door open. As he sat on the edge, his feet dangling, Alex grabbed his ankle and used Glen's tattered trousers to hoist himself to safety. The two men joined the others inside.

'Ever thought of hailing a cab?' Glen enquired, feeling exhausted. 'I hear some of them actually stop for passengers.'

'I hate sitting in traffic,' Alex grinned as the train bucked from side to side. He slammed the carriage door shut and flicked his eyes about. The carriage was empty, with nothing for the group to sit on or fiddle with. It was hot and cramped in their compartment. They attracted flies from the adjacent cars, buzzing round their heads, swatted from one man to another in an aggravating game of bug tennis. Glen peered through a slat in the door, the early light stinging his eyes. He could see countryside flashing by. Alex leaned against him, trying to get comfortable. As Glen surveyed the group around him, he noticed a sound missing. None of the men were breathing.

Alex was chatty, explaining that he had been an ice cream vendor during his lifetime. 'You should have seen the funeral,' he laughed, 'twenty-one vans all playing 'Greensleeves,' and my coffin topped with a 99-cone tribute. Then I had to go and spoil it by waking up.'

'What are we going to do?' whined Glen.

'When?' Chris murmured.

'If we make the journey, put up with each other that long.'

Chris winked at him. 'Don't rip each others' throats out first?'

The rhythm of the train on recently upgraded tracks shoogled its illicit passengers from side to side.

'We're all civilised here and we don't have far to go,' Peter said in his low, reassuring voice, 'we'll have to get off before we reach the next station. The tunnel's our best bet.'

'Are you some kind of suicide squad?' Glen asked. 'That tunnel's full of traffic.'

'This train will slow down again when it reaches the tunnel, waiting for a platform to clear and allow it through Waverley. It may even sit for a few minutes. The perfect opportunity for us to disembark.'

'Why all the subterfuge? You wanted by the police or something?'

'We all are,' Chris moaned, 'including yourself. Every living dead person in the country is being rounded up. Don't know where they want to take us, but I don't want to go there.'

'Probably want to experiment on us,' said Glen, 'find out what doesn't make us tick.'

Peter peeped through a crack in the door. 'This is us. Stay close to me, everybody. We may not have much time.' With Glen's help he shoved the heavy door open and all four men climbed down onto the next set of tracks. Fortunately, although it was pitch black in the tunnel their train had halted at a red light, allowing them to leave at a stately pace. Water dripped onto Glen's bare head, gravel crunched under his feet. He didn't like fumbling around in the dark, and was glad to know that Peter was a few steps ahead of him. Glen found the older man's presence calming; as he stumbled against a rail he grabbed Peter's arm for support.

What's the matter? Glen asked himself. *Scared of the dark?* No, that wasn't it. He liked to know where he was going, that was all.

A second later there was no more darkness. The rails beside him rumbled and the noise of an approaching engine filled the tunnel's empty spaces. Bright beams of light momentarily blinded the stowaways and they scattered, Chris and Alex making for the carriage they'd just left, Peter getting clear of the tracks. Glen stood still, petrified.

'Move it or lose it!' Chris's yell went unheard under the noise of the oncoming train.

Peter grabbed Glen's shoulder and shook him from his stupor; they hopped away over the tracks as fast as they could. Peter stalled, his foot twisting at an awkward angle in the gravel. It was his turn to reach out a hand for help – Glen looked into his eyes, saw energy and ferocity there. He grabbed Peter and pulled hard, yanking him from the train's path with a centimetre to spare. There was a horrible cracking sound as Peter's wrist joint gave way.

'Sorry 'bout that,' Glen mumbled. But Peter was more interested in reaching a refuge and riding the rails in a new direction. One carriage was still open, and Chris was ushering them through the metal shutters. The goods train jolted, ready to rumble.

Peter was bundled into the carriage by Glen and Chris. Alex settled in beside them and the train began to move.

'Looks like we're in for the long haul,' Alex grumbled. 'I don't understand why we're fugitives.'

'Well, we've got a one-armed man here,' smirked Chris, holding up Peter's limp limb.

'Maybe they think we're going to act like movie zombies,' Glen mused. 'I mean, why would they think otherwise? This is a unique situation, after all. Have you never seen that film with rotting naked cadavers filled with a raw lust to wreak havoc?' Alex frowned at him.

'*Calendar Girls*?' asked Chris, his voice hoarse.

'Naw. *Night of the Living Dead*. It's been remade a couple of times.'

'Never liked musicals.' The train rolled into Waverley Station.

'It didn't have songs!' Glen cried, exasperated. 'It was filled with gore.'

'Keep it down, fellas,' Peter shooshed, idly flapping his wrenched hand from side to side in a way that made the others wince. Behind him Alex was pretending to be a monster, arms stretched out before him, chanting 'Brains! Brains!'

'Green folk brought back to life by radiation...' Chris recalled. 'They ate the goodies.'

'They never proved it was radiation,' Glen said.

'What was that?' Peter whispered, tucking his loose hand into a jacket pocket. He was keeping watch through a crack in the shutter. A porter shambled along the platform towards them.

'Just a theory. George Romero never intended that to be taken as the gospel reason.'

'So what, numb nuts?' Chris glared at Alex, who cut his impression short.

'I'm trying to help. You think those filmmakers knew something we don't?'

'Maybe this sort of incident's happened before, and the government covered it up. They're good at that.'

'I think you're thinking of Dan O'Bannon's *Return of the Living Dead*.' Glen smiled, the video clerk portion of his brain taking over. 'It was inspired by a novel by the *Night of the Living Dead*'s producer, John Russo. Came out in '85, the same year as Romero's *Day of the Dead*.'

The others stared at Glen as if being a movie nerd was worse than being a flesh eating corpse.

'You wouldn't eat me, would you?' Alex scratched his right elbow with long fingernails. 'I mean, if you got hungry and there was no food around?'

Glen looked at him thoughtfully. 'You'd be the food, man. Only the brains though. The juicy part...'

'This guy's brains?' chuckled Chris. 'You're talking slim pickings there.'

Glen ignored him. '...Suck them out with a straw.'

'You guys are gross.' Alex turned his back on them.

'Nothing wrong with healthy gallows comedy my friend,' Peter consoled him.

'Where did you say this train was headed?'

'Aberdeen. But we won't be on it much longer if we don't have total silence from all of you right now.' Peter's voice took on a sharp commanding air and his companions shut up. They tucked themselves into the darkest part of the wagon as the door slammed open.

This is it, thought Glen. *We'll be arrested, processed and dissected before the day's out. I know what they do to fare dodgers round here.*

The porter didn't bother to look in the wagon, although he did screw up his face at the musty stench within. A few cardboard boxes were shoved in and the door slammed closed again. Within minutes, the train had left the station and Peter confirmed that it was on its way to Aberdeen.

'Brilliant.' Alex was examining the boxes, wondering if they contained anything useful. 'All the most eligible bachelors are accumulating there, are they?'

'From Aberdeen we can go cross country, on foot,' Chris said with confidence. 'If luck's with us, and it has been so far, we can hitch a lift. So far we've avoided the police.'

The train rattled on towards Aberdeen, where the train slowed, enabling Peter's band to get off without further mishap. Along the way, Glen came clean to his hero.

'I have to admit I'm a John Dance fan.'

It took a moment for Peter to assimilate this nugget. 'That would explain the familiar attitude. Lord, you don't dress up and run around pretending to be a spy, do you?'

'That's the media's kind of image of fans of anything. Much more exciting than the truth. Most of the time we sit around in the pub talking about the books and the movies.'

'Sounds like fun.'

'We have a whale of a time.'

'So I suppose you have some questions for me.'

As a matter of fact Glen did, though humility prevented him from asking more than one. 'Just how did you pack so much action into one little film with a million dollar budget?'

'Ah. *Spyland.* Your favourite film, I trust?'

'It's in a league of its own,' Glen said diplomatically, 'the trendsetting template that everyone else followed. The primo John Dance movie. So how did you do so much on a shoestring?'

'Passion. I cared enough about my story to go out and convince my crew to give their all to help me tell it right. To give up their time, their personal lives, to devote their energies utterly to a movie for six months. And they did it. They sacrificed a lot. Not as much as me, but a lot all the same, for the sake of a celluloid diversion. A flick. Can you believe it?'

'I can believe it.' Glen smiled at his idol. 'That flick means a lot to me and thousands of freaks like me. It's a part of our childhood, a memory we all share. To us, it's a cultural milestone we know and give a shit about in a world where no one gives a tinker's fart about anything much. It makes us belong.'

'Thank you G.G. I think I know what you mean.'

The landscape was less welcoming than they'd hoped, mist falling in narrow strips like pure white paper ribbons, covering the ground. The raucous wind made them shiver despite their lifeless state.

'I hope you know where we're going,' Glen pestered his new friends.

'Sure we do. There's fallow farmland just over that ridge –' Chris pointed at the overcast slope ahead '– a barn where we can hole up, sort ourselves out. I know this area too well. I grew up here – hell, I even died here. Follow me.'

The dieners stumbled across muddy fields, their city boy shoes caught in the muck, cursing the inhospitable terrain. Glen thought that he could hear bagpipes – were they going to land up in Brigadoon? – and red lights flashed in the distance.

'What's that?' asked Alex, peering through the porridge.

'We should take a different route,' Peter told him. 'We can't be seen.'

They reached a rise and squelched to the top, looking out across lush farmland. The red lights mingled with flashes of white.

'No one will see us,' Chris told his friends, heading straight for the source of the gleam.

The field ended at a country road. Tucking himself behind a verge, Chris saw that the glow belonged to a sorry-looking pizza van that had had a bonnet-crunching run-in with a yew. For some reason the van had careened off the road, hitting the tree and spewing pizzas out its back doors. The driver was unbuckling his seat belt slowly, still stunned by the collision. Chris stepped out from his cover.

'What do you think you're doing?' hissed Peter, joining Chris. 'Do you want to jeopardise us all?'

Like a bloody-minded moth, Chris moved towards the vehicle. The pizza man got out of his car, his right hand pressed tight to his head, staunching blood from an open wound.

'Chris! Come back here!' Peter said as the others joined him. 'He's going to get spotted. How could things possibly get any worse?'

'Don't say that,' Glen shooshed. 'When people say that, things invariably get worse.'

Sure enough, a police car pulled up, officers stepped out, and Chris was sighted. The 'pipes' that Glen had heard were police sirens; the cops were responding to a call from a local do-gooder who'd witnessed the crash. The dieners – easy to spot from their poorly-concealed perch – were a bonus for the bored boys in blue.

'No silly business please, gents,' said a silver-moustached officer, approaching them atop the rise. He had rosy cheeks and a fat grin on his face, as if he'd caught four children scrumping apples. 'If you'd like to come with us?'

Nobody (least of all the policemen) expected Peter to walk towards them, hand outstretched for a friendly shake. He even had a placatory smile on his face, mirroring the officer's peek-a-boo grin.

'Is there any tea left, Chief?' Peter asked, pointing to a flask on the police car's dashboard. The officer, who found himself shaking hands with the bemusing fugitive, recognised the question as an attempt to humanise a diener. He still nodded and replied:

'Just a few dregs, I'm afraid.'

'That's a shame. I'm gasping for a cuppa.' Before Peter could build a rapport with the policeman he was brushed aside – Alex and Chris had turned on their heels and were running back across country, hotly pursued by the cop's partner, who until that moment had been collecting pizza boxes off the road. All thoughts of a midnight feast vanished as the fugitives legged it. Peter shrugged and climbed into the back of the car.

'Are you barmy?' Glen yelled. He was rooted to the spot, unable to run with Alex and Chris, too bewildered to move at all. 'Let's get going,' he shouted to Peter.

'Where to, my friend?' The older diener placed his hands behind his head, lacing his fingers together to build a cushion. 'There's nowhere to go. Better to win the trust of these uniformed gentlemen, reason with them, then bugger off later.'

The pizza-loving cop didn't sound very gentle, dragging Alex back over the rise. He'd stumbled in the mud, his chest and knees plastered with dirt. He wasn't very happy.

'Where's Chris?' Glen hissed as he was bundled into the car with Alex. Peter had already settled in, quite the thing.

'He got away.' Chris had pelted across the field, sliding in the mud at an alarming pace, leaving the cop bogged down behind him. He hadn't stopped to help his friend, hadn't looked back. A passing train became his getaway vehicle and his pursuer had satisfied himself with collecting the other runner. Worried that Peter and Glen would disappear in the meantime, he'd dragged Alex back, soggy and sullen.

With an ambulance at the scene of the accident, and the car locked up tight, the dieners were driven to a remote building, dark and unmarked.

'And I thought I'd get chauffeured home,' Glen grinned as he was led into the building. He could hear the sounds of shuffling feet and clanking metal echoing from within. *What happens when all the jails are full?* He thought to himself. *They stick the no-goods in some out-of-the-way warehouse, out of sight out of mindlessness.*

The police shoved Glen, Alex and Peter into the building, its front entrance flanked by armed guards. Glen realised how cold it was when he saw steam escape from the mouths of their captors. Green lights cast an ugly hue on the constables' faces, making them look more ghoulish than the dieners.

'In here,' said one of the cops, pointing to a ramp that led to a raised concrete area. The ramp was decorated with splashes of red, some faded, others vividly fresh. Looking up, Glen saw a scattering of meat hooks dangling from metal beams. He didn't want to climb the ramp any more.

'I have a family,' he protested, 'they'll wonder where I am.'

'We've all got families, son,' said the oldest policeman, giving Glen another shove.

'I've always respected our boys in blue,' said Peter, offering one of his trademark placatory smiles, 'I have no reason to stop now. They have work to do and I'm sure they don't want to be hanging around here longer than they have to.'

'I don't want to be hanging around here at all,' Glen replied, his face grim.

'You won't be here for long,' the elder policeman told them, 'as long as you get a move on.' The dieners ascended the ramp and crossed the concrete platform, with another guard watching them closely from a wide doorway. He unbolted the metal door and they stepped into a room that was apparently even colder than the previous one. A few cow carcasses hung from more hooks, with animated corpses wandering to and fro between them, chatting with each other or leaning dolefully against the frozen meat.

'We should stay pretty fresh in here,' Peter remarked, 'for a while at least.' As the cops left and the door was locked up tight, the new arrivals took in their surroundings.

'No TV,' said Alex, depressed. 'What do people do to amuse themselves in here?'

Some of the dieners checked their mobiles, unable to get a signal. Others played cards, using ears and other loose parts of their bodies as chips. A finger was worth a quid while a nose was considered closer to a tenner. One old radge had smuggled in a copy of the *Record*, nine days old now and still he wouldn't share it. Instead he read it over and over, as if the newsprint would update itself under his scrutiny.

Glen was attracted to a young woman sitting in a corner of the room. She still had thick black curls of hair on her head and most of her teeth. She wore some light make-up to hide her pallor.

'How long've they been keeping you here?' Glen hunkered down to ask her. She looked at him as if he'd just asked her a really dumb question that she'd heard a hundred times before, then relaxed a bit as if deciding that he was an idiot who should be treated very gently.

'My watch froze,' she told him, 'my moby's dead. Your guess is as good as mine.' She shrugged, a smile lighting up her face more than any blusher could.

'Sorry to trouble you.' Glen stood up, about to turn away, when he saw a look on her face that suggested he should stay. He wasn't good at reading signals (his collapsed marriage was a testament to that), but he did try to be receptive to others' needs. 'Anything I can do for you?' he asked, risking another glare.

'You can tell me your name.' She held out her hand, shook Glen's. 'I'm Louise Carmire. From Greenock. I worked for IBM.'

'They know you're here?' Glen sat down beside her.

'I'm not even sure if they know I'm dead yet. I just didn't turn up for work one day. Couldn't. Choked on an apple. The crazy thing is I volunteered myself for this.' Louise pointed one of her remaining fingers at the *Record*. 'It was on the front pages of all the papers, wasn't it? Turn yourself in, don't bring a load of belongings with you. Do your bit for your country, for everyone's peace of mind. I walked into the nearest police station...' Louise faltered, growing quiet.

'What did they do to you?' Glen asked softly.

'They put me in a cell like a criminal. I've kept my nose clean all my life –'

Glen held her tight, crying for her.

'I'm hoping,' she said, 'that they'll take me to the RHS. Find a cure for my problem.' Glen didn't have the heart to tell her where he'd just come from. Instead he kept his arm around her, watching the frozen carcasses swing slowly to and fro.

'Where's my husband?'

Misbah stood at the service window of the RHS reception, her white-knuckled hands pressed against the sill as if she was trying to push the whole wall away from her.

'What was the name again, hen?' The receptionist tapped idly at her keyboard. 'Mr Gass?'

'Glass. G-L-ASS. They told me he was here for some tests.'

'I can't see him.' The receptionist peered at her monitor.

'Why can't he phone his relatives?' Misbah asked, the thought suddenly occurring to her. 'I know they can't go out because of the quarantine, but that shouldn't stop them from calling us.'

The woman didn't reply. Doubtless she was secretly enjoying Misbah's frustration.

'I asked you a question,' Misbah fumed. 'This man has a family who care what happens to him. What's going on in this hospital that's so damned secret?'

'Dunno,' the receptionist looked up from her PC, 'I take people's names and addresses, mostly.' Looking back to the screen, her eyes widened and she got excited. 'Looks like he was moved. He's gone to a better place.'

'Where?'

'They'll probably want to do more tests on him.'

To make sure he's safe to go home, Misbah said to herself.

'Here.' The receptionist gave Misbah an appointment card with a phone number scribbled across it. 'Call this number. They'll be able to help you out.'

'Who?'

'Some civil service department. Good luck.' Misbah took the card, found a quiet corner and dialed the number on her mobile.

CHAPTER 8

Under Pressure

8 INT. INTERVIEW ROOM. DAY

DANCE

I don't care what you were doing while you were AWOL. That's not what I'm here for. The company needs its executives to be reliable. Trustworthy.

9 EXT. ALLEYWAY. NIGHT

SANDERS is attacked by a GUARD who almost knocks him down the steps. SANDERS overpowers him and gets inside the building.

10 INT. INTERVIEW ROOM. DAY

SANDERS

I needed some time to think things through, get my head together. It is together.

11 INT. CORRIDOR. NIGHT

SANDERS moves briskly down the corridor, encounters another, larger SENTRY. They struggle and this time it looks like SANDERS is going to lose. He's knocked to the ground –

12 INT. INTERVIEW ROOM. DAY

DANCE

Then why am I here? Why did your boss set up this interview?

13 INT. CORRIDOR. NIGHT

Using the SENTRY'S weight against him, SANDERS turns the tables and SLAMS his head against a wall. Further down the corridor, he finds a door marked 'PRIVATE' or 'STAFF ONLY.' Opens it, sneaks inside –

14 INT. INTERVIEW ROOM. NIGHT

The room is dark now. SANDERS rifles through a filing cabinet, finds the folder that DANCE was brandishing. Hears a sound, ducks behind the cabinet.

15 INT. INTERVIEW ROOM. DAY

DANCE

You know how much I charge per session? Thousands. Your company paid for a jet to fly me here. They put me up in a nice hotel. I had to do it all under an assumed name – all because of you.

SANDERS

I'm honored.

16 INT. CORRIDOR. NIGHT

SANDERS gets out of the room, the folder tucked under his arm – he's chased by GUARDS 2 & 3.

17 INT. INTERVIEW ROOM. DAY

DANCE

You should be. I'm a plain old psychologist, most of the time. You espionage types I check up on as a favor. Can't have you going crazy mid-mission.

SANDERS

I'm not crazy.

DANCE

That's for me to decide.

DANCE puts the folder, marked with the words 'PSYCHIATRIC REPORT,' in the filing cabinet.

18 EXT. ALLEYWAY. NIGHT

SANDERS is out the side door, BANGING it shut in GUARD 2's face. His car's still parked out front – he's almost home clear. Hurrying down the steps, he DROPS the folder – stops to pick it up – GUARD 1 shoots him. He falls to the ground, mere feet from his car. The folder lies open – we see Sanders' photo and the word 'PASSED.'

From the Snap Judgement *screenplay by Sam Robbins*

A DOZEN OF THE dieners were roused early in the morning, including Glen, Louise and Alex. They were handed some overalls (Alex's fitted perfectly, Glen's were way too large) and ordered to put them on as quickly as possible by the guards. They had got used to following orders from the staff, and they were excited about leaving the abattoir, so they complied.

A few guards herded the selected dieners down the ramp and out into bright sunshine. They slouched around a small car park, hemmed in by three grey walls and a high metal fence.

They waited; Glen was used to that. It was frustrating, knowing that somewhere out there his killer could be lurking, ready to murder some other poor hapless jerk. There was nothing he could do about it, a captive in the car park.

After an hour or so he began to wonder why they'd been uprooted so early in the morning. The officials weren't used to dealing with his kind, he supposed – nobody knew how long it would take to get a bunch of dead guys from one end of the abattoir to the other.

In the interim they were joined by a few acquaintances from the hospital, including Kenny. Peter was ushered into an unmarked police car, his silver tongue bagging him a comfortable vehicle to travel in.

An old bus honked for attention. Beyond the fence a guard pressed a button and a gate slid open, allowing the vehicle to enter the car park. Like preprogrammed sheep the zombies climbed aboard and their long journey began.

The driver was an elderly, dull-headed woman so surly that she would have been perfect for driving kids to school. She occasionally glared at her passengers in the rear view mirror, as if angry at them for contaminating her bus. The hushed excitement of the passengers added to the Friday morning feel, but this was no field trip.

As the jaunt continued, the driver expertly rested a flask between her thighs, unscrewing the cap and pouring coffee into a cup on the dashboard – all without spilling a drip. She drank a lot of coffee but never stopped for a leak.

Glen didn't recognise any of the countryside passing by his window. He saw scarred trees mirrored in a silver river, the empty stores of an abandoned retail park, blurring hedges and miles of roadside verges; a few signs mentioned places he'd never heard of. He didn't dare ask the driver where they were headed.

They were apparently travelling down through the Borders, picking their way carefully to avoid major routes.

'Maybe we're going home now,' Alex hoped.

'I don't think they're quite done with us yet.'

The ride took them towards the mountains, and it was dark by the time they reached their destination. Peering through the window, his own unsightly reflection staring back at him, Glen could make out scattered evidence of construction – diggers, a concrete mixer, shallow foundations.

'We might as well be on the moon,' whispered Alex as the driver told her passengers to disembark. 'Any ideas where they've brought us?'

'Why don't you ask Ms Coffee?'

Alex's eyes met the driver's for an instant. 'No thanks.' Stepping off the bus, Glen glimpsed brick piles and concrete pipes, picked out by torches. A few glowing amber lights helped workers to continue in the darkness and as the bus emptied, the passengers could hear faint, haunting and distinctly annoying mobile tones ringing from builders' back pockets: 'Ride of the Valkyries,' 'The Entertainer.'

The herd headed for a better-lit area down a gravel path where halogen lamps stood. As they crunched down the path it became easier to see the stumps on either side; trees had been cleared and used for timber. Midges gathered in the light patches, busy doing nothing. They homed in on Alex, picking at his hair and back.

Three men awaited the party, icy breath escaping from their mouths, reminding Glen of his arrival in the abattoir. Two of the breathers wore work clothes akin to the dieners', black this time, with sharp tunics. Tweedledum and Tweedledumber flanked a shorter man in a three piece suit, strands of hair plastered across the back of his head, who introduced himself as Donald Claig. It was as if the dead folks' questions and comments had been bottled up all day and Claig uncorked the contents. Responding to his authoritative manner and attire, they bombarded him with sound. Glen shouted above them all, appealing to their common sense, trying to find out where they were.

Claig showed his new guests an old hangar behind him. His two companions opened a door and the dieners filed in, still chattering away.

'Homicides and accidentals to the left,' said Claig's right hand man, the world-weary Morgan. 'Coronary artery diseases on the right. There's the larger bunks if you need 'em. Suicides, you can keep your belts and shoelaces. Gunshot wounds, give the aneurysms a hand, willya? Perforated peptic ulcers'll have to go round the back.'

Much to Glen's disappointment, the interior was similar to the hospital ward – protracted rows of beds, a couple of small dingy windows, and not much else. The only difference was the noise – while the hospital had been fairly quiet at night, this place resounded with the grind of machinery and the bellows of lead bellied labourers.

One diener already sat on a bunk in the corner, tired and dishevelled. Once Claig and his cronies had left, the newcomers naturally crowded round the scruffy old lag, desperate for information. Was this a way station or would they be stuck here for a while?

'Forever. The rest of your existence, however long that may be. Or until they decide what to do with us.' The shabby man introduced himself as Max. Glen noticed the crusted cement on his clothes and the brick dust that gave his long beard a rouge hue. Max also introduced his dog, Randy – a mange-ridden collie cross with eyes too close together. 'Don't worry, he only bites normals.'

Max was pleased with all the attention he was getting, and filled in the blanks for his captivated audience.

'You're stuck here, but the good news is you get to build your own homes. That's right. You'll be set to work in the morning, putting together a dwelling complex strictly for our kind. We're using the cheapest materials, building the blocks too fast, and this is dangerous. But the corporate clowns who came up with this idea are onto a good thing; they have a workforce that doesn't need sleep and if there's an accident – maybe you lose a limb or something – you won't feel it.'

Max's bitter tone scattered the audience early. They found a bunk each and mulled over their fates. Only Glen stayed in the corner, tickling Randy behind the ears.

'We could just leave,' Glen suggested.

'Some big corporations are backing this and the police are backing it up. And the military too; the TA. Even if we could leave we'd be dragged back here before you could say Cool Hand Luke.'

'Why would corporations be interested?'

'Good PR. A high-profile Good Cause.'

'And you don't think this is a good cause?'

'Helping us to help themselves. We'll see.'

Misbah didn't often have dinner at the table with Paul and Lucy. They were usually off at friends' houses or engaged in some after school activity. Even when she did sit down with them, her mother was usually hovering around, fussing enough to give Misbah indigestion. But tonight Mum was at bingo and Misbah had her kids to herself. As good a time as any to discuss their Dad.

'I spoke to a nice man at the Department of Health today,' Misbah said, sounding a wee bit patronising. 'He says that your

Dad's being taken care of, monitored closely, and that he's helping build the new housing estate for dieners.'

'So we can visit him?' Lucy asked, all but jumping up and down in her chair.

'He's going to be around for a long time.' Paul sounded more glum. 'They wouldn't be building these houses if they didn't think that –'

'Nobody knows.' Misbah buttered a slice of bread for her daughter. 'They're just trying to make the dieners as comfortable as possible.' She paused for a moment, knife frozen mid-spread. 'We won't be able to visit your Dad for a while. Not until they're sure it's safe for us.'

Lucy slumped back in her seat. 'I want to see him now!' she whined, cramming the bread into her mouth. 'I miss him.'

'I don't.' Paul folded his arms, appetite gone. 'I hope I never see his stinking, rotten face again.'

'Paul!' The boy didn't hear Misbah. He'd already left the room, slamming the door behind him.

'We will see Dad soon, won't we?' Lucy asked.

'I see him all the time, the way he used to be, in my mind,' Misbah sighed. 'Our memories of your father have got to be enough for me. We've got to hold onto the happy times we had with him. For me, that's enough.' She held Lucy's arm tight. 'It has to be.'

A dishwater dawn marked the return of Donald Claig, escorted by his two aides, Morgan and Truegood. He burst into the hangar with a smile, arms raised. Glen was surprised that there was no accompanying fanfare.

Framed in the doorway, Claig looked formidable. He wasn't especially tall or strong, but his stocky body indicated his stubborn, imposing attitude. He was in charge of the construction project and wanted everyone to know it.

'Welcome to your new world!' Claig declared. 'Of course, these living conditions are temporary, and as soon as your own places are built you'll be free to make them yours!'

'I want to go home,' said Stef, a twenty-year-old Dundonian.

'You are home.' Claig adopted a sincere expression. 'I realise that you've gone through great change recently, suffered through a traumatic rebirth. I feel for you; it'll take a while to adjust. But you must recognise that things are going to be different now that you're back from the dead. Now, there'll be a press conference in one hour so you've got time to smarten yourselves up before the paparazzi appear. Have a nice day.'

Claig breezed off, leaving the dieners shell-shocked in his wake.

They spruced themselves up and those that felt the need (though there was none) took a drink of water from the sole tap in the hangar. Then they were herded out into the bright sunlight by the security guards.

The newcomers blinked, slowed, bumped into each other, taking in their surroundings – the site was vast, with thousands of homes being built or about to be created. On the east side was a lake, its water dark green and deep; on the west, a small woodland area.

A northern slope had been affectionately named Boot Hill by the builders. It led to the foot of the mountains, where guards could get a good view of the whole area. South of the site ran a main road, with new tributaries trickling towards the fresh structures. The entrance to the complex was trapped shut with large metal gates. In the middle of it all was an abandoned church, complete with cemetery.

A group of builders made sure that each diener had a shovel. Before they could use their tools there was a photo opportunity to be seized. A horde of journalists gathered round the bewildered group and there was a loud multiple click as Dictaphones and mikes were switched on; video cameras whirred and the shouting started.

'How grateful are you that this project has been set up for you?' 'Are you happy with the conditions here?' 'How long have you been here?' They were the kind of questions that the press already knew the answers to, but asked anyway. *So this is why they're called the press,* thought Glen, *all this pushing and squeezing and strain.*

In the midst of the chaos was Kim Clarke, delivering a piece to camera, her hair perfect and her suit impeccable. Glen knew that when she saw him, the way he looked at her so intensely – with such adoration – she would instantly fall in love with him. Here was his Christie Cummins, his Heather Hutchinson, his Dance partner.

'How do you feel, sir?' she asked him, her cameraman aiming straight at his wasted face. She didn't recognise him from Hogmanay – he'd changed too much.

'Good. Better than ever.' Kim moved on to Alex, leaving Glen to dream.

It wasn't until the press began to disperse that he recognised another familiar face – an Irish reporter in a threadbare old sports jacket.

'Mark!' The Irishman was within earshot but he didn't acknowledge the cry. 'Mark!' Still no nod to his friend. Mark allowed himself to be ushered off to a waiting van, ready to take him back to Edinburgh.

The greenhorns were set to work, basic hefting and carrying for starters. It was hard to imagine how the complex would look once completed; none of the buildings had roofs or windowpanes as yet. A large cabin housed the administrative offices, including Claig's. One structure was larger than the rest, with easy access from the main road. This would act as show home for visiting press and officials.

While the others went to work on their new homes, Glen lay on his cot, quiet as a cactus. Even Alex couldn't encourage him to join his friends on the site. After several hours of uncooperative behavior, Glen was dragged to his feet by the guards and led to Claig's office.

Glen guessed that the boss hadn't chosen the décor – all cream/grey walls and purple upholstery. Claig still cut a commanding figure sitting behind a vast desk with a green leather surface.

'Mr Glass, isn't it?'

'You got something to say?' Glen folded his arms and widened his stance, making himself comfortable. He was expecting a big spiel, a team-driving talk that would make sense of the situation. Claig said nothing for a while, sizing him up, gauging his intelligence. Glen made a goofy face to put him off.

'Most of the life-challenged people I've met here have been glad to get their hands dirty,' Claig harrumphed. 'They're helping each other, making a contribution to a new society – their own.'

'And what do you do apart from help yourself?'

'I facilitate. Liaise. Above all, it's my job to get you working, to explain why it's so important. This is a pilot project...'

'So if it fails, we can all go home?' Glen slumped in a plastic seat by the door. Claig had to raise his voice to make himself heard across the room.

'This is your home now, or at least it will be when it's finished. A home designed to suit your particular needs.'

'What're they building out there, coffins?'

Claig chuckled politely. He deliberately lowered the volume of his speech so that Glen was forced to draw his chair nearer to hear. 'Why don't you take a look for yourself? When you see the effort your friends are putting in –'

'They're not my friends. We've been lumped together because of our... misfortune.'

'Your acquaintances then. The look in their eyes! They have something to do, a world to create.'

'Who tells you what to do? Who set up this pilot project?'

'I answer to certain corporate concerns. The Prime Minister needs results; the only element that could slow things down is lazy men like you.' Claig's voice was low as a shadow now, with Glen leaning over the desk, head slightly cocked.

'I'm not lazy. Listen, the guys won't take orders from you forever. You're going to have to play smart if you want this whole thing to hold together.'

'You have a solution?'

'They need one of their own to help them think they're one big happy family. A spokesman, to represent them and run things smoothly.'

Claig laced his fingers together, licked his lips and smiled.

The walls of the new domiciles looked so thin, so fragile. Glen remembered the story of the little pig that built its house out of sticks, plain asking for some big bad wolf to come along on a wind-powered demolition job.

Although today's politically correct culture had retooled the fable so that all three protagonists survived, the ending hadn't been so kind to the stick pig back in Glen's childhood days. The flimsy timber he was carrying didn't seem much different from a bundle of branches. He held a finger aloft as a stiff breeze whistled by.

While Glen toiled, Kim Clarke was asking Claig whether she could stay for a while. At first he was doubtful. Although he welcomed some initial, positive media attention, he also had a job to do. It would take a lot of unfriendly persuasion to keep the construction work smooth and swift so that it could be completed within an allotted time and budget. Kim was too intelligent and observant for his liking.

Nevertheless she was eager and persuasive, promising him approval (and a profit percentage) of any book or documentary that might result from her extended stay. An exclusive deal meant that Claig received a fat fee upfront, too.

Kim was given one of the first completed dwellings to live in – the show home – with a spare bedroom for J.C., her cameraman, when he visited. The workers called the fancy home 'the Mausoleum,' because they were told that this was the kind of domicile to expect when their jobs were done. Of course, Kim had heating, carpets, air conditioning and a well-stocked refrigerator; all things that corpses don't require. The dieners would have to make do with bare floors, simple cots for beds and mice for company.

A few days after Glen's arrival a spotless black limousine

arrived at the site, bringing a VIP to stay. Claig gathered everybody in front of the Mausoleum and smiled his official smile.

'I'd like you to meet your new spokesman,' smiled Claig, posing for J.C.'s camera. Out of the limo stepped Peter, looking respectable in a new black suit, a showpiece fit for an undertaker. Glen watched agape as Claig asked Peter to say a few words to the crowd.

'I'm amazed to see so many people with a common goal, working together to help their community.' Peter, photogenic as a phalanx of chubby infants, charmed the crowd along with the camera. 'Our next few months won't be easy. But we will support each other, won't we?' Peter looked from side to side at his fellow dieners, and they hesitantly agreed.

'The tide has turned against us,' Peter boomed. Claig frowned. Was this the right topic for a morale-boosting speech? 'While once we were curiosities, a diverting new phenomenon, we are now reviled. There are too many of us, and the dead continue to rise. The living are uncomfortable. They need to be consoled and so we are here.'

The crowd was still, silent, in a state of mass shock.

'We must prove that we are not a threat, nor disease-ridden, nor uncivilised. We're not going to maraud our way cross-country, sucking the brains from bairns. We're people!' A cheer of agreement. 'We want to be treated nice!' Although there were no tears in his eyes, Peter started to sob, seemingly overcome with emotion. Glen wondered how tearful this crafty crocodile of a man really felt.

Glen wasn't the only one who wanted a strong word with Peter. So he stood in line and waited his turn. When he reached the front of the queue he noticed that Peter's wrist was still stuck at an awkward angle from his accident on the railroad. Any annoyance that Glen felt about Peter's appropriation of his precious 'leader' idea dissipated. If anyone was right for the job, it was Peter.

'Sorry about the, uh, breakage pal.'

'It's nothing. Can't feel a thing. Reminds me of the good times.'

'How'd you hitch a ride on this gravy train?'

'Gift of the gab, lad, gift of the gab. I saw things from Claig's point of view. The hospital administrator was impressed with my social skills, mentioned me to Claig and his cronies. Here I am.'

'It's good to see you. It's getting tough in here.'

'Problems with staff relations?'

'Conditions aren't so hot and the guards are too earnest exercising their muscle, especially with the younger residents. If we don't get out of here soon there's going to be trouble.'

'There's a lot more trouble outside, G.G. Like I said in my pep talk, you're *cadavera non grata* at present. A walking reminder of everyone's mortality? No, thank you very much. The government had to be seen to be taking action, even though they haven't the foggiest idea what to do with you. That's why you're here and why you should stay put.'

'Forever?'

Peter didn't have an answer to that question. His general advice was to make the best of their surroundings. He motivated the workforce with promises of better conditions, a happier atmosphere and greater communication between the living and the dead.

Glen was shown how to use a bulldozer, mesmerised by the flashing amber light above him, finding it awkward at first but speeding up within days, until he was whirling round the complex on his grumbling caterpillar tracks. It only took him a few weeks to master the weaker points of bricklaying, despite his slovenly attitude. He had changed drastically since the hospital sojourn – he'd lost all his hair and his mushy body was drying out, only patches of skin still remaining. He was one of the better-looking corpses on site, although he shared their cheesy stench. He refused to wear his overalls, dressing instead in a grey sweatshirt with black horizontal stripes, Chinos rolled up once at the ankle (so they didn't drag in the mud), and brown suede boots. His stance was awkward, self-conscious, his movement jerky, like a clockwork toy.

Glen didn't have night sight glasses, a bowie knife or a little black book full of numbers from the phone directory. As such he was ill equipped for stalking. Kim was stunning in mind and body, confident, content. She was all the things Glen wasn't – generous, thoughtful, fit and firm, inventive, incisive, not afraid to speak her piece. But none of that really mattered to her. What mattered more than anything else was her job. That was the real grab for Glen.

Kim had the kind of job he couldn't even dream of having, the kind that she found easy as breathing. She was cool about it, didn't make a big thing out of all the money she earned or the famous folk she'd worked for. Interviewing them up close and personal – what a lady!

His attempts to impress Kim worked perfectly; she took a shine to him and appreciated his newborn work ethic. So encouraging was she, in fact, that Glen suspected she was in league with Claig – some trick to get him to toe the line. Well, he didn't care. He hadn't felt this way about a person, so deeply so rightly, since his first few weeks with Misbah. It had been all downhill after that as real life got in the way. This time things would be different; he was older, wiser, and even more willing than before.

'We need more timber in Zone Three,' Claig yelled, and Kenny raced to comply. The site was split into scores of zones, each ready to birth a pack of diener dwellings.

'What d'you think?' Glen asked Alex, who was busy checking a blueprint.

'Of her? You're not wasting your time.'

'I'm a married man, with kids.'

'I don't think that counts now you've passed away and your family's abandoned you.'

'Thanks for reminding me.'

Alex scowled in return. 'It's about time you pulled your weight, mate.'

'What do you think I've been doing, twiddling my knob? This building business doesn't come natural to me, you know. I struggle.'

'I noticed.' The comment was good-natured, as all Alex's were.

'I struggle at the best of times but this – it's futile. You really want to live here in the middle of nowhere?'

'That's a nobody talking.' Alex rolled up the blueprint and used it to prod his friend in the chest. 'I'm somebody. No matter where I live, no one can take that away from me.'

'Whatever.'

Dusk fell. Claig saw the ragged shapes of his navvies hunched over their tasks. He felt good.

'We'll have this done in no time,' he told his aide, Truegood.

'They could collapse at any time,' Truegood pointed out, 'or down tools in protest.'

'They won't. Peter's spread the word, they know what dissent will bring.'

'I don't think they care. They got nothing to lose.'

'Then let's give 'em something. Make 'em care. Tonight I'm Mr Motivator and, by goodness, I'll make 'em motor.'

The guards – or custodians, as Claig preferred to term them – were issued with guns and took strategic positions around the site. A non-so-gentle prompt for the labourers, who worked harder and faster, pleasing Claig even more.

The guards were supposed to be there to protect all the equipment, but there were an awful lot of them and they seemed most concerned with shoving the dieners around, motivating them with pushes and yells. Conditions on the site were grim and brutal, although some of the custodians had a gentle side, or at least a non-threatening scientific detachment.

There was a high fence surrounding the complex, the hangar doors were locked at night, they were far from a town or petrol station, and passing traffic was minimal. So the dieners stayed put, waiting to hear from their families, working to pass the time and do something useful. They'd spent their whole lives working, from school classrooms to office cubicles, and it felt strange to do nothing.

They still hoped for better treatment and a chance to go home – to their real homes – once the project was done with.

There were hundreds of relatives desperate to visit their loved ones, though the majority settled for the new arrangements. Like Misbah, they'd found it difficult to cope with the return of the living dead. When top boffins told them that there was a possible risk of infectious disease as the corpses corrupted, that they should be quarantined just in case, the relatives had to agree.

The dead couldn't vote or claim social security but they still had money, from savings or donations. Some of this was gobbled up in inheritance tax, and more paid for goods brought into the complex; small luxuries like soap, books and beauty products. A warehouse was erected to deal with the import and export of sundry items as well as the influx of building materials.

While the site's suppliers prospered, the outside world was beginning to suffer from the dieners' presence. Stocks and shares sagged in an uncertain market, funeral homes went out of business, and life insurance companies enjoyed an unprecedented demand. For once, people were actually begging insurance agents to visit their homes.

Glen stayed with his friends because he worried about Alex and cared about Peter, but mainly to be close to Kim. She might be able to help him track down his killer, but that paled beside his feelings for the newswoman. The more time they spent together, the more infatuated he became. As far as he could tell she didn't share his feelings. He persevered.

CHAPTER 9

Ghost Pains

Agent Erickson liked to shop for groceries on Sunday mornings. A lot of people were in church that time of day, assuring him of a quiet, clear-aisled trip. Although he was outwardly calm, he lacked patience and nothing tested it more than a long queue at the checkout.

He hopped out of his xterra and grabbed a trolley, his coat flapping in the stiff West Coast wind. On his way across the car park he maintained a firm grip on the trolley, pushing down on the handle to prevent the wheels from wobbling. The supermarket doors shucked open and a bright, sign-happy world of consumable goods welcomed him in.

He aimed straight for the whole roasted chickens. His hectic jetset lifestyle didn't leave time for dilly-dallying with frozen thighs or messy giblets. He only had a few items on his shopping list – fresh bread, Kong bars and Peter Pan peanut butter were the bare essentials – so he hoped to be done shortly after targeting the chicken.

He was reaching into the chill cabinet when a flash of movement caught his eye. He glanced over his shoulder and saw an employee from the bakery department, who greeted him and gave him a polite smile. Erickson didn't smile back.

Placing a plump chicken in his trolley, he tried to fathom what was strange about the baker, who was holding a couple of fresh loaves.

Erickson lashed out with a back kick, catching the baker in the midriff. The loaves fell, scattering crumbs across the floor.

'No gloves, asshole.' Erickson stood beside the trolley, using it to block the baker's attack. The cumbersome shield worked against Erickson as the baker shoved him back against the cabinet. Erickson threw a hefty pack of mincemeat in his opponent's face and lifted the trolley to catch him on the chin.

Out of his depth, the baker ran back towards his own section with Erickson giving chase. This kind of thing really got the agent's goat. He couldn't even get his weekend groceries without some sneaky sleeper popping up to try his luck.

'What are you going to do?' Erickson yelled at the baker. 'Disembowel me with a baguette?' Cornered, the sleeper reached over a basket of Chicago hard rolls and tried to throttle Erickson. The unhappy shopper easily wrenched out of the hold, but the momentum sent him falling against the bread slicer and the baker seized his gruesome opportunity by pressing Erickson's head close to the blades and switching on the machine. The grinding blades spat flecks of bread in the agent's eyes.

'Thin or medium?' the baker sneered. A passing pensioner screamed, clutching her handbag tight to her bosom and running to find the manager. The sound distracted the baker long enough for Erickson to turn the tables on him, grinding an ungloved hand against the blades.

As his opponent collapsed in a quivering heap, Erickson caught his breath and wiped crumbs from his ponytail. A checkout girl ran up to him, staring horrified at her wounded colleague and then at the bread slicer, clogged up with a couple of fingers.

'I guess he has less than ten items,' Erickson admitted, going back to his trolley. 'The mincemeat's off, by the way.'

From Who Ate All The Spies? *by Sam Robbins*

AFTER THE PRESS DEPARTED Glen expected conditions to worsen, with the custodians exercising their power with gusto. Instead, the daily routine of working on the site and spending the rest of the time in the hanger continued. He enjoyed the human contact with his fellow workers. Lunch consisted of the same slop they'd sampled at the hospital – a nutrient that was considered healthy for dieners, a soup akin to embalming fluid. To keep Glen's spirits up, Peter had managed to get hold of a John Dance trivia book and would often interrupt the fan's supping by testing him on his knowledge of the franchise, flinging the names of characters, locations and filmmakers out in an attempt to stump him.

'How did Max Webb die?'

'He was blown up while cuddling surrealist painter Petra Coole in *Dark at the End of the Tunnel*. Too easy.'

'Must've been some cuddle. Who was H-Bomb?'

'A mysterious killer-for-hire who never made mistakes; paid big money to slay John Dance because he knew too much.'

'Yeah, but what was her real name?'

'Turns out H-Bomb was none other than Heather Hutchinson, an avant garde actress and voice over artist from New York. Dance helped her realise that there was more to life than treading the boards and killing people for money.'

Glen's nutrients would often grow cold as he dazzled his pal with his skill for retaining trivia. Glen would argue that knowledge could never be completely purposeless and that such minutiae enriched a dull, grey world like pop art or witty commercials. No one agreed with him.

Glen wasn't so good at building work, spilling cement, directing the diggers incorrectly and bunking off whenever possible. He saw his cack-handedness as deliberate sabotage. Any work that helped the authorities who'd treated him so badly couldn't be good. The others seemed to be sold on the 'all for the good of the community' line; Glen remained sceptical. He did his part though, helping the less able dieners with their tasks, keeping their spirits up by slagging off the boss.

Glen would walk into the forest whenever he could find a long enough break, surrounding himself with life even in the throes of death.

Fluffy bunnies helped, as did the optimistically green leaves of the tallest trees and thickest bushes. Weeping willows didn't turn him on, neither did owls. They looked cute but killed a lot of timorous wee beasties.

He would hold up his hand, palm inward, comparing its lines to the bark of a tree. His fingers were gnarled and tapered like the branches above him. Even though the trees were old and a dark shade of grey, green buds sprouted from their twigs. There was life amongst those complex webs.

Sometimes Glen would lie on his back in the middle of a copse, gazing up at the sky through a verdant canopy. He liked to feel the soil turn beneath him, imagining the worms and bugs tilling there. His body was in decay and so was his brain, but his insight was as vibrant as ever. Perhaps it would be the last thing to go, teasing him with the horrible things that could happen.

His lone rambles ended when two custodians found him one morning, lying on his side with his eyes closed, ear to the ground. He was considering an escape route, past the trees, across the farms and away from the noise and clamour of the site. Nobody could see him, and he would stay well hid – it would be easy. Then back to Edinburgh and the hunt for his murderer.

Glen was yanked to his feet by the two guards, who had been patrolling the natural maze. The black uniforms reminded him of the thieves who'd robbed his store. These chumps wouldn't have seemed out of place in a rogue's gallery, all crumpled features and sly looks.

'Take off his boot,' said one of the custodians. Glen saw the name 'Whitley' labeled on his tunic. The other guard removed Glen's left boot and sock.

'If you guys want to play strip poker,' Glen said nervously, 'I don't have any cards.'

Whitley took a small, wicked hunting knife from his belt and used the point to give Glen's big toe a gentle poke. 'This little piggie went to market,' he said in a singsong voice, making his colleague giggle. 'This little piggie stayed at home.'

Glen didn't dare kick or yank his foot away – one slip and the knife would gouge him.

'This little piggie had roast beef,' Whitley continued, 'this little piggie had none. And this little piggie...' he paused for effect '... went wee wee wee all the way home.' With one deft motion, he sliced off Glen's smallest toe. The other guard handed his boot back to him.

As the guards dragged him back through the trees, he tried to grab at trunks or branches, slowing his persecutors down until they pinned his arms to his sides. A few minutes later they were back in the complex, where Glen was handed over to one of the construction supervisors and set to work on a scaffolding. Glen tried to ignore his injury, but his foot ached a phantom ache, and he felt a profound sense of loss.

The next day, Peter relayed a memo from Claig: no dieners were permitted to enter the forest without express consent from the living, and even then they would have to be accompanied by a guard. The penalty for breaking this rule would be severe – a one-way trip to the clinic for a full autopsy.

When Kim had questioned Glen, she'd noticed something different about him. He looked earnest, positive, more alive than the others around him. A ram amongst sheep. She found out his name from his supervisor, tried to check out his background, but his details were lost in some hospital labyrinth. The air of mystery made her all the more curious, so she sought him out.

He was helping Alex shift some timber when she found him, grousing about his lack of luck in love.

'I'm romantic. Most women I've known would rather have booze than a bouquet for Valentine's. I was prepared to go to the ends of the earth for my wife, only she never asked –'

'You're married?'

Glen flinched. He hadn't seen Kim approach. 'That was a long time ago now. Seems like it.'

'You struck me as a bachelor boy.'

'The single life isn't all it's cracked up to be.' Alex got on with his work, leaving Glen to make puppy dog eyes at his crush.

'Mind if I ask you a few questions?'

'I thought that was what you were doing. Care for a stroll in the compound?'

Picking their way over debris and materials, Kim and Glen traversed the vast site.

'Where are you from, Mr Glass?'

'Edinburgh.'

'And how long were you married?'

'Long enough to raise two adorable kids. Too long. It wasn't her fault; we got stuck in a deep, dirty rut. That's past now.'

'Did you report to the police voluntarily when the... when it was requested?'

'Didn't hear the APB. I was too busy feeling sorry for myself. First time I saw you was on TV a couple of years ago, reading the news no less.'

'Oh, Gene Colby was sick. Tennis elbow. My fifteen minutes of shame.'

'I thought you were brilliant.' Glen had to shout over the roar of a passing bulldozer.

'I had a silly fixed smile on my face.'

'But not one fluffed line,' Glen was gushing now. 'Very professional, and beautiful too, of course.' He shut up and lowered his head, gazing at the fresh tarmac pavement. Instead of impressing his interviewer, he'd embarrassed her. 'You must think I'm some dumb fan.'

'None of my fans are dumb. They have too much good taste. See you around, Mr Glass.'

'Call me Glen!' It was too late; Kim was away to find her next curio.

'How you doin'?'

'Dave! I ain't got nothin' for ya!'

'Saw you on the tube. Had to come visit.' Dave's towering frame cast a dense shadow on Glen and the surrounding area. 'What can I getcha?'

'How did you get by security?' Glen shivered.

'Got a job here, running the warehouse – perfect for some black marketeering. Pilfered a pass and that was me sorted. You should see the lady I'm working with! She's alive and then some.'

'Who's your friend?' asked Peter, strolling over to greet Glen's old neighbour.

'Dave Barr. Likes to refer to himself as a handyman.'

'Oh, not any more pal. I'm an enpreteneur now. Got my own office and everything.' Dave licked his lips. 'OK, it's full of stolen goods but I'm halfway respectable these days. What you needin', anyway?'

'Well, I could do with some merchandise.'

A passing custodian squinted at Dave, trying to place him. Peter didn't approve of Glen's friend, but he held his tongue for the time being.

'I thought you'd packed all that in,' smirked Dave. The guard was heading towards them.

'I may've been fed up with the job, but I miss my memorabilia. The decent stuff, I mean. Not just any old junk with the Dance logo on it.'

'I'll see what I can do, dawg. How about you, mister?'

'Don't think you can waltz in here and corrupt our good citizens. We may be dead but we still have our principles.' The guard, realising that Peter was talking to Dave, assumed that the stranger was a new construction worker; he was under orders to leave the diener spokesman in peace, so he moved off, none the wiser.

'Your principled citizens have ordered an office load of stuff from me. So I guess we'll be seeing a lot of each other over the next few weeks, eh?' Dave winked at the fuming Peter and gave Glen a cheerful hug. 'Good to see you kicking, friend, live or no.'

As Dave left to get on with his work, Glen placated Peter. 'He's got a heart of gold.' The two men walked towards the Mausoleum.

'We've got to keep our noses clean. We're under scrutiny and we have to prove that we're civilised.'

'All we're proving is that we're easy to control. Dave's good people; he just happens to be bending a few laws getting us the goods we need. What could be more civilised than that?'

Dave returned within twenty-four hours with a big batch of books and baubles for Glen. They met in the hangar where Max and Randy always sat. Glen wasn't sure how Max managed to avoid work while the guards constantly harangued the rest of them, but it had something to do with the old man's knack for being late. He had turned up for shifts with increasing tardiness, until eventually he hadn't had to turn up at all. He'd even been late for his own funeral, although that hadn't been his fault – the driver of his hearse had taken a corner too fast, losing his cargo in a ditch. Max had woken up there and stumbled off before the undertaker could complete his task.

'How much do I owe you?' Glen felt embarrassed as he took the merchandise from Dave.

'Nothing. Fell off the back of a truck, as it were.' In amongst some battered Sam Robbins paperbacks, worth a couple of quid apiece, was something special – an empty film can marked *Peter Foothill*.

'Where did you get this?' Glen gasped.

'Told you, fell off the back –'

'No really, where's it from?'

'ok,' Dave sighed, 'I tracked down your old friend Mark and swiped it from him. Simple as that.'

'I don't understand why he didn't get it transferred. There was a time when I was desperate to know what was on this.' Glen flipped open the can, making sure that the film was still inside. 'Now it doesn't seem to matter so much.'

'Mark sold out,' Dave opined. 'Sees you as just another walking corpse now. Sorry.'

'Do you think Mark could be responsible for my murder?'

'Trust me, chum. You weren't murdered. You just aren't important enough, you're too average.' Dave looked suitably apologetic.

'I still have a list of suspects.'

'You never really pissed anybody off in your life. You're

unassuming. Insignificant. Not worth going to jail for in a million years. Not everything is as dramatic as you like to make out, Glen.'

Glen felt the weight of the universe ooze off his shoulders. No matter how paranoid he'd become, he knew that Dave was right. 'Why didn't you sell this thing?' He held up the can, its tarnished metal catching the sun. 'It's still worth something.'

'Well it's not in mint condition, whatever that means. I was waiting till the heat was off it, then I thought of what you'd been through and how much you like this kind of garbage –'

'Thanks Dave. I appreciate it. But please don't go getting guns stuck in my face again.'

'Oh, you mean Ash? He's his own man. Got plonked in Allendale Correctional Institute for GBH, last I heard. Funny how people never change. He still loves guns, y'know.'

'I'm sure he does. I need to know who he was working for, Dave.'

'Well, he swung that hospital porter's job. You know where. But they won't take him back after he's been inside.' Dave gave Glen a cheeky wink. 'I've gotta be going. Anything else you need, give me a shout. I'll be around.'

Later that day, Kim introduced her cameraman to Glen for the first time. 'This is J.C. Conway. He's the gent who makes all my reports look beautiful.' Glen looked the cameraman in the eyes and they seemed to laugh back at him. This man was Australian, super-confident, garrulous, gorgeous, and he knew it.

'Glen Glass. Pleased to meet you.'

Kim was digging under Glen's bunk, finding his pile of books. J.C. led Glen across the hangar until he was sure that Kim couldn't hear them.

'I've heard a lot about you, mate. Kim thinks the sun shines out of your arse.'

'There's only one thing that comes out of my BT and it ain't daylight.'

'Well, whether she's wrong or right, I want you to look after my girl.'

'Your girl?'

'She's fragile, like a petal. Exert too much pressure and >boomph<! She's a gonner.' J.C. flashed a charming grin. 'Like I said, keep her safe.'

'What do you see in all this stuff anyway?' Kim asked, flipping through a tatty *Snap Judgement* photonovel.

'I find it comforting. A reminder of childhood when things were easier, less complex. Careful with that!' Glen gingerly took the photonovel from her dusty fingers. 'These books aren't indestructible, you know. One wrong rustle could decrease their value and –' He noticed the way she was looking at him. 'I'm sorry.' He handed *Snap Judgement* back. She hardly dared to look at it, concentrating on the widening smile on his face.

'I don't think your obsession –'

'My passion. I'm a passionate man.'

'Your *compulsive* obsession stems from childhood. You have a very grown-up approach to collecting these things, collecting trivial information, appraising your merchandise. It's only worth as much as someone's prepared to pay for it, right?'

'I like a woman with a sense of humour.'

'You'd need one.'

He could always rely on her to bring some solid perspective to his day.

Glen occasionally bumped into Louise Carmire, chatting in the hut reserved for mealtimes.

'What do you do when you're not reading thrillers?' she asked, finding Glen with his nose stuck in a Robbins book. There was the trace of a smile on her paper-thin lips.

'Work. A bit. Muck about, chew the fat.'

'I wouldn't call this fat.' The dieners preferred to call their food slop, a cheeky reference to the common slang for freshly poured concrete. Louise glooped a spoonful back into her tray. 'And what did you do before they Shanghaied you here?'

'I worked in a shop.' Glen wasn't trying to be unhelpful; it came naturally.

'Selling...?'

'Renting. DVDs, video games.' Glen left it at that.

'I thought the guys who worked in places like that were all chubby, bald and sarcastic.'

'I was, until I died. Apart from the bald bit.'

'Event like that can change a person.' Despite her reservations, Louise finished her nutrient nosh. Glen asked her what she'd done with her life.

'I skied. Glencoe, Glenshee. Liked my squash, I was pretty good, played for Stirling uni Ran marathons, almost won two years running.'

'Two years... running?'

'Sorry, bad joke. I was into diving, spent all my spare cash on trips to the appropriate resorts. One day I took a deep dive with an inexperienced friend, there was a problem with my oxygen tank and I drowned.'

'Your friend?'

'Oh, he was fine. Felt so guilty he paid for the funeral. Then I didn't need one but they wouldn't give him a refund. Love their red tape, those undertakers.'

'At least my family got their money's worth. Kinda.' *There you go again, talking about yourself,* thought Glen, *your favorite topic of discussion.* 'You must've been fit.' *Brilliant! A real blinding gem of a comment. Any more intelligent insights?*

'I've watched my body wither to a wisp.' Louise replied. 'It's alright for guys, they can look all distinguished when they lose their hair and waste away. We have looks to lose.'

'You could still be active – you work hard on site. You're not immobile or anything.'

'Then I've got nothing to worry about have I? If I tried to ski my arms would go flying off with the poles. It's frustrating. At least I can't say I've spent my life gathering mothballs in some video rental.'

'Hey, I was busy too – martial arts, weight training – but more because I had to, to fight middle age spread, than because I wanted to. I certainly didn't enjoy it.' Glen frowned. 'Are you angry with me?'

'No. Maybe Him Upstairs. The higher power.'

'Donald Claig?'

'Be serious. Whoever – whatever force reanimated me, or select parts of me, my sight, my voice. I don't have much to say. I want to know why, that's all. I guess Dostoevsky was right. It's better to be shivering on a ledge in hell than to not exist at all.'

'Right.' Glen nodded, deciding to cheer Louise up. 'And the Naughty Ladies were right too. "We are naughty ladies, you are naughty men".'

Louise looked embarrassed, moved to another table. She didn't share her mealtimes with Glen much after that.

The Church of Life
After Death

CHAPTER 10

Home

IT WAS A STRANGE year, flowers blooming early, storms arriving late, dawn choruses at high-pitched noon, low temperatures in July. The public was dismayed – those who were allowed fled to sunnier climes for a couple of weeks to warm up and thaw out. Any cows that stopped producing milk were culled as a precaution. The same went for chickens that didn't lay. Everyone believed that life would get back to normal, that this was an aberration.

Over a period of several weeks the structures began to take shape. Once the foundations were dug it became obvious that the dieners were building dwellings with very small rooms, and quite unlike the fancy Mausoleum. They never saw any blueprints – the foremen told them what to do and where to do it and the workers learned on the job. Cheap and flimsy materials allowed even the weakest of the crew to heft them. Machinery was used to shift earth and timber. Despite himself, Glen soon got into a routine and looked forward to seeing the structures completed, with twenty-four flats and two breezeways to each building. The government was keeping the dieners busy, out of mischief, completing what it described as essential construction work.

When completed, the homes and offices that stood on the site may have been rough around the edges but Glen and his crew were proud of them nonetheless. They moved from their hangar to the houses without delay, settling in with a few items of furniture each. Many had brought personal belongings with them, while vagrants like Glen made do with second hand stuff. There were no complaints – anything was better than the soulless hangar.

The roaches enjoyed the close room temperature of the new flats. Without pest control to keep them at bay they thrived, making the walls and ceilings their own. At night they would pick at the flesh of the dead until their hosts noticed them and shooed them away or squished them under heel.

Bugs or no bugs, there was something wrong with Glen's place on the top floor of Building Three, Zone Seven. He realised it as he stepped inside after a hard day's work. It wasn't the lack of furniture; he'd never taken to all of Misbah's futons, cabinets and whatnots. He found it hard to put his finger on the problem. It simply didn't look... lived in enough.

He took off his concrete-crusted boots and dumped them in the middle of the room. That seemed to help. He spilled his cup of soup, staining the floor, then dropped the cup for good measure. He was onto something.

He splayed his precious books out in a corner, removed his overalls and draped them over the crate, scratched the window with his metal watchstrap. He was moving fast now, frenzied almost, scattering his meagre possessions around the flat until he felt at home. Lord of the pigs, living in a sty. Now all he needed was a pizza and a beer.

But he didn't eat, and he couldn't drink for real, not properly, and there was no TV. No TV!

He remembered Louise's words about hell and the ledge and all, and he went to check out his new bed.

Glen's bedspread was pink with light blue and violety stripes. A red-upholstered swivel chair was the only seat in the room. He had a bedside cabinet, where he kept his toothbrush and the Dance books that he read when he got bored at night: *The Morituri Completion*, *Top Priority* and *Remember, Paris*. He often read a few books at a time, reflecting the flighty side of his nature; his short attention span, cultivated through years of watching MTV and Bravo, enabled him to skip from one author to another and back again after a chapter, or even a page. Channel hopping for bibliophiles.

Sometimes he would sit on his bed deep in thought, planning for the future. He would escape from the scheme, become a filmmaker of great acclaim (even though he was inept with the simplest cam-corders). He would be invited to all the biggest award shows and the Dance movie producers would beg him to come direct their next epic. As practical strategies intertwined with far-off dreams, Glen would fall into a kind of light doze. This was a great relief for him, offering respite from the usual worries – paying bills, seeing his kids again, investigating his death, scrambling out of the rut he'd dug for himself.

If he was really lucky, he'd catch dream-flashes that seemed unusually familiar:

The sun is so bright that he's blinded. Still he heads towards it, velocity ever increasing, a waxwinged angel triumphant and scared, not breathing, not daring to look down.

Abruptly, he'd get the sick sensation that he'd been woken from a deep sleep. That feeling would stay with him until the next time he napped.

Glen's haven was the shared courtyard, which caught the sun of an afternoon. It was small and simple but sheltered from the wind, perfect for a clothesline. Two padlocked green doors led to an outhouse where tenants kept their junk. In one of the doors was a cat flap large enough to let in a labrador, cut for a neighbor's giant ginger tom. Soiled salmon slabs paved the ground, with bor-ders displaying seasonal shrubs.

Glen set his rickety stool next to a tall green water butt, catching the best of the daylight. The white sheets hanging on the clothesline bounced the sun's rays straight into his eyes.

A black plastic recycling bin attracted almost as many flies as Glen. A hornet hovered above his head. When he looked up at it the bug would circle him in a halo blur. Behind him was another green door, this one leading to a passageway with access to all the ground floor flats. An A4 photocopied poster had been pinned to it – 'Lost: Black Gerbil. CUDDLESOME' with a nondescript picture of a ball of fluff and the owner's details. A square of MDF covered a hole kicked in the door by some frustrated passer-by. It was the only piece of wood in the yard that hadn't been painted green. Glen suspected that if he sat still long enough, he'd get painted too.

It was in the courtyard that he met his new neighbour, no less than Chris, the man who he'd last seen running from the police across muddy farmland. The big guy didn't look so good now, welcoming Glen with a shy nod.

His skin, now an uncanny shade of dark brown-brown, wasn't in the places it should have been, with his finger bones jutting through what had once been the flesh on the back of his hands. His whole body was covered with a fatty, waxy substance.

'You going to see Peter?' Chris stammered. 'He's doing well for himself.'

'And how about you?'

'Oh, I'm fine.'

Since his arrival, Peter had busied himself organising community events and education, from reading and writing to self-defence. One of the events was a meeting to which all complex residents were invited.

Glen did all he could to spread the word – he owed Peter that much. He used Kim's laptop to run off some copies of his flyers. Nothing fancy; big chunky text announcing a meeting in the ruins of St Jude's church. This large building was currently at Peter's disposal, a place where he could bring the dead community together.

The church didn't look like much from the outside, its mortar crumbling, ramshackle at best. The glass windows were stained right enough, with bird mess, sleet streaks and dirt thrown up by passing trucks. The wide doors had a loose hinge and wouldn't have kept an angry hamster out. The building leaned to one side, recanted over the centuries. There was a blocked drain smell too, lingering in the nostrils; fortunately, the dieners' sense of smell was fading fast.

The fact that the dieners' spokesman would be chairing the

meeting made it important, an event, a highlight on a calendar of drudgery. Some of the younger residents had no idea what the meeting was for or what its outcome would be; they still passed on the news with glee.

In the damp-encrusted hangar, Glen asked Max if he would attend.

'It's bad enough when Claig's stooges force me to listen to that puffed-up poseur. A hand accustomed to taking is far from giving.'

'Hey, you shouldn't always judge a dog by its kennel, Max.'

The old man stabbed a finger at Glen's crumbling ribcage. 'Don't bring dogs into this. You know what Peter reminds me of? A no good evangelical fake. Woe betide any of his disciples.' Randy yelped in agreement.

Apart from Max, everybody was excited. They'd got together before in cliques and little groups, moaning to each other about their lot with few proactive suggestions or solutions. This was the first instance of somebody organising them all, daring to speak up in front of a gathering without Claig's say-so.

Many feared that Claig and his custodians would react harshly, cancelling the meeting before it took place or punishing those who attended with extra work or a reduction in pay. They needn't have worried. As far as Claig was concerned, Peter was in his pocket and posed no threat to the status quo. He assumed that this was one of Peter's attempts to placate the denizens of Bonetown.

They were huddled in a circle, Peter at the centre. The church was small and the dieners stank to high heaven. The remaining stained glass windows were streaked with dust. One of the bulbs was out in the fancy brass light fitting. A flip chart stood by the door, and behind it was a heater that hadn't worked in years. Above the door was a 'Mind Your Head' sign – the group had dutifully stooped on the way in.

Everyone was hunched round the table except Alex, standing at the flipchart, and Kenny, whose neck had gone. He sat with his back to the wall, trying to support his head. Everyone had a pen and paper, and watched Alex fumble with his marker. His numb fingers had a hard time holding the pen, and each member of the group could appreciate his difficulty. When he did manage to scrawl a few words on the pad they were illegible. Alex spelled out the facts anyway.

As Peter commenced his patter, Glen and Chris sat near the door, ready for a fast getaway if the meeting got too uncomfortable or dull. Timbers creaked overhead; the church wasn't used to so much activity, hadn't entertained a congregation for decades. Glen expected the whole place to cave in without warning, so he took care not to scrape his chair or cough too loudly.

'As you all know, I've been working hard to bridge the gap between the residents and the originators of this grand housing scheme. The project is coming along, you're starting to move out of that tatty hangar and into some decent homes.'

'You call them decent?' Kenny fumed. 'I'd like to see you living in one.' It was common knowledge that Peter would be moving into the Mausoleum once Kim had finished her big story.

'Let Peter say what he's got to say,' said Alex, glaring at Kenny. The young diener shrank down into his seat and stayed quiet.

'I've heard your complaints about accommodation, overzealous security staff and the total lack of communication with your relatives. It's unacceptable. What you've got to understand is, we have no rights. We're no longer citizens with a constitution. Most people would like to put us back in our coffins and pretend this whole thing never happened.'

'They're happy to take our taxes,' Glen pointed out.

'And we're expected to obey the law. So there should be some give and take. I've been saying all along that we can prove, in microcosm, that we can be model citizens. Only then can we be incorporated back into society.'

'I've paid my dues,' said Max, late for the meeting. 'I kept my head down and my socks up for sixty years. Took early retirement, which I must've been enjoying too much 'cos bingo! I popped my clogs. Only my dog stuck by me.'

'I'm sure you set a wonderful example throughout your lifetime,' said Peter, wrinkling his nose at the late arrival, 'all the more reason why you should continue to do so.'

Max rolled his eyes and slumped down next to Glen.

'Is he still gabbin'?' the old man whispered. 'Christ man, if they zipped up his mouth he'd find another place to talk from.'

Peter kept talking. 'There's also a question of disease spreading from our... tired old bodies. That's one reason why we've been required to build Bonetown, as some of you fellows have been calling this place. Far better, I'm sure you agree, than being placed in a grubby little housing estate.'

'This way, the drug companies can say they're providing us with employment,' Glen suggested.

'The sponsors of this project felt that we deserved brand new accommodation,' Peter said hastily. 'We're lucky to get anything at all.'

'So what's the next step?' asked Max. 'How long do we have to go on toeing the line, proving ourselves?'

'Our existence will improve with more job opportunities, higher salaries. The construction site is expanding,' said Peter. This was true – part of the forest was being cut down to make room for more blocks of flats, more warehouses, a convenience store and a Starbucks. A few billboards had been erected, some aimed at passing motorists, others facing into the town to tantalise the townspeople. The streets that traversed the zones had gained unofficial names – Infirmary Street, Brokentooth Lane, Death Row. 'We should set our sights higher. Exploit this community's resources to make the most of standards here. It will bring us all together. One last point – it is imperative that we cooperate with the doctors and research scientists at the clinic. Once they prove that we're not carriers of some dread illness, security here will be relaxed.'

'They're still searching for a cure, right?' Kenny piped up. This was a hope that had kept many of the dieners going back to the clinic; human pincushions pored with hypodermic needle holes.

'I believe so.' Glen detected a shaded note of hesitancy. 'We must let the researchers get on with their work, not question their every decision. That will merely slow them down. We don't want that, now do we?'

That evening Glen found his pride and joy sitting outside Building Three, wrapped in plastic to keep it dry. Glen ripped off the covering, all delighted as his scooter was in better condition than ever. A note was attached to the seat:

Found this impounded by the police and I thought of you. This is for all your hard work leading up to our first meeting. My boys gave it a scrub up, hope you don't mind. Looking forward to working with you a great deal in the future.

Peter

Glen didn't mind one bit. He climbed onto the scooter and started it up; he was pleased to find that the gas tank was full. It took a few seconds to warm up and then Glen was zipping through the streets, round cul-de-sacs and over driveways. The wind rippled what remained of his hair as he hunched down over the handlebars, a speed demon look on his face. A childish portion of his brain thought, *I am the Ghost Rider!* While a more adult part made him shout, 'Wahoo!'

One week later, on an overcast, breezeless Friday night, Glen repaid Peter with a movie screening. Dave had managed to dig up a film projector from some disreputable source, along with a rare, collector's print of Peter's directorial debut (the collector wouldn't miss it before it was returned). Glen called Max, Kenny and as many dieners as he could muster to watch the flick, projected on the bright white exterior wall of a storage facility. Midges aimed their specky bodies at the wall, bouncing off its stippled surface.

As the projector purred to itself, simple white titles came up on a black background, reading 'A PETER FOOTHILL FILM.' The audience applauded. Peter had the best seat out the house, front row centre, and smiled good-naturedly as *Spyland* unfurled its boisterous plot.

Guards gathered behind the seated dieners, mesmerised by the action, sharing for once a common bond with their dead captives. When the credits rolled the entire street was filled with whoops and cheers; Peter turned to enjoy a standing ovation.

As quickly as he could, before everyone dispersed, Glen wound the film labelled *Peter Foothill* onto the projector. This one got a different reaction.

The street went dark for a moment, all eyes on a silent black screen. Then there were a few flashes of white, a jumbled series of numbers, and green blobs appeared. The soft round shapes clung together, surrounded by a wide, thin circle. A shaft of white entered the circle, drawing a blob towards it. The film cut to a new circle, which contained a red blob.

'I don't understand,' Kenny's voice broke the eerie silence.

As the green splotch joined it, the red mass began to fade and break up.

'What does it mean?' a devastated Glen asked Peter.

The director could only shrug. 'It's a test title sequence for my old John Dance movie,' he told the audience.

Glen shook his head. 'I don't recognise it.'

'The titles guys wasted quite a bit of our budget,' Peter sighed, 'but they kept promising us a wonderfully abstract opening sequence. We were competing with chaps like Maurice Binder, mind, without his kind of money. We indulged them, let them try several different tacks. Nothing worked. We're talking about a Magic Alex and The Beatles level of results here. You should know this, a fan like you.'

'I should, shouldn't I?' Glen's pride didn't allow him to admit that title sequences and special effects weren't his forte, though Vian had always taken great pleasure in reminding him of the fact back at Video People.

'These little patterns are discarded footage for *Spyland*.' With the weird film done the crowd was parting, leaving Glen to remove the reel from the projector. 'Probably worth quite a bit. You're in the money, G.G.'

'Is it worth enough to rob or kill for?'

'Nothing justifies taking another man's life. We know how precious that gift is now, don't we? You did something very special tonight,' Peter said sincerely, 'you brought these poor souls together. Entertained them, livened things up for two hours. Helped them to forget their troubles. Of course, I'm biased – *Spyland*'s special.'

'The title reel – it belongs to you.'

'I was a movie director, remember.' There was that good-natured smile again. 'I'm rarely responsible for things with my name on. But if it makes you feel better, I'll take care of it for you.'

Glen gave Peter the film, glad to be rid of it once and for all. He hadn't expected to see any rare experimental footage – he'd been looking for an answer to his own woes. He wasn't living in a movie, where some MacGuffin would drive the plot and justify everything that happened to the characters. 'I think it'll be much safer in your hands.'

'Very well.' Peter dug into his jacket pocket. 'For what you've done tonight.' He gave Glen a delicate silver ring. Its band was engraved with the name JOHN DANCE. 'The most expensive prop in the movie – that's why only one of them was ever made.'

'Dance's wedding ring. This is too precious for me to –'

'I think you'll appreciate it even more than I have.'

Glen clutched the ring in his bony right hand. 'You've been so kind to me, Peter, but I have to ask for one more favour. Word will get around that you have this film reel. Be careful.'

'I will.'

'And if anyone comes asking for it… let me know.'

With a nod, Peter left him to pack up the projector. Glen was feeling strangely hollow inside. *Not all mysteries are meant to be solved,* he told himself. But that didn't make him feel any better.

Kim was loathe to leave the town but she had assignments to catch up on, and felt that she was missing out on events in the real world by staying on the self-contained site. Sure, J.C. would trot into Bonetown once a week to give her all the latest gossip, his dark brown moustache always smattered with cracker and corn chip crumbs. But after a couple of months, though her fascination with the undead was undiminished, she needed to spend some time amongst the living. As Claig had tried to tell her on various occasions, the complex was no place for a young, vibrant career girl.

Kim chose Glen as the man to spread the news of her leaving. She found him in his new bedroom, picking the last flakes of skin from his shins. As she expected, he was glad to do her bidding and upset to hear her plans.

'I've got to move on,' she said sadly. 'I've learned all I can here.'

'No, there's lots more. The way that our bodies are changing – our slop seems to be slowing down our rotting rate.'

'I know.'

'And the new dieners that are coming in to help us? There could be some conflict as they join the community. There'll be a lot more youngsters, so I hear.'

'I heard all that too.' She tried to sound disinterested.

'Max has lost an eyeball. We think Randy ate it.'

'Did he?' As usual, Kim was caught up in Glen's enthusiasm.

'Not really, I made that up. It got your attention though, didn't it? You think you know everything, but you didn't know whether I was telling the truth or not, eh?' He stopped picking at his legs. 'When are you leaving us?'

'Now. Packing my things, then going.'

'Will I get a mention in your book?'

'There won't be a book. I've got a feature slot on Channel 4, if I'm lucky. Four minutes tops.'

'Take care out in the real world.'

'I don't think it'll ever seem as real again, after this.' Kim trudged off to the Mausoleum, leaving Glen alone in his flat, blinking, not sure what hit him.

Next morning, with the first phase of construction complete, Glen climbed Boot Hill so that he could overlook the site. The day was misty, fine rain steadily coating his face. He saw a patchwork of red brick and roofs, dotted with black pathways, yellow diggers and bulldozers. Guards patrolled the entire area, with activity focussed on the structures that were half-completed.

He heard a strange cracking sound and saw guards running towards a block of flats in the centre of the site. Smoke billowed from it, mixing with then engulfing the mist, and Glen scrabbled back down the slope. Amber tongues of flame spat from the building – there was an explosion. Glen allowed himself to fall, rolling downwards, but he could see that the flames were spreading to other buildings, including the one he inhabited. Who'd started the fire? Had a bomb been planted – or was this accidental, with so many flammable materials sitting around the place? Would his memorabilia survive?

Worried about his friends as well as his books, Glen got back onto his feet as he reached the bottom of the slope. He ran to Alex's block first; he needed to know that he was alright.

Some of the security guards lay prone on the ground, killed in the explosion. A few of the builders were moving diggers and equipment out of range of the raging fire. The wooden timbers and panels that formed the skeletons of the buildings made great kindling; now a big bad wolf of a blaze had embarked on its wrecking spree.

Alex's building was engulfed; Glen couldn't get anywhere near it and there was no sign of his friend. He saw that the fire would continue to spread until it reached the perimeter fence. Squinting through the smoke, Glen got into a bulldozer and used it to heave some dirt in the path of the blaze. Once he'd piled up a significant amount of soil and rocks, he moved the vehicle away and jumped out, shouting for Alex. He could see Peter and Max throwing water on the burning buildings, their attempts vain at best and bordering on pathetic.

'Have you seen Alex?'

'Sorry, Glen. He was in there,' Max pointed to the Mausoleum, 'when the damn thing blew up. All that work for nothing.'

'Never mind the work!' chided Peter. 'Alex was dead already.' He tried to console Glen. 'This has done that boy a favour.'

Glen shoved Peter backwards, snatching the empty bucket away from him and joining the dieners fighting the conflagration.

'Sorry,' he yelled back at Peter. He realised that he cared more about Alex than he'd ever thought.

By the time it had burnt itself out, six or seven of the makeshift firemen had been lost. The real emergency services had arrived only when the smoke had threatened the forest. With their help, Glen's group began a grim body count. Dozens of people were identified; charred, barely mobile and in deep shock. Some had burned to ash, lost to the world. The only consolation was that they'd gone quickly and were now at peace.

Claig tried to placate the remaining workers and security guards, who were too tired to be angry.

'I know that you've all lost good friends today, and a great deal of your hard toil has been wrecked. I know you have the spirit to rebuild and we'll do it in the name of our lost comrades.'

'You need to find out who did this,' shouted Glen, his face inches from Claig's. 'We want to know how this could happen.'

'And stop it from ever happening again. I understand with all my heart.' Claig clapped his hands together, ensuring that he had everyone's attention. 'No work for the rest of the day. We'll start assessing the damage and issuing you all with new tasks tomorrow.' He turned his back on the assemblage. It was obvious that he wanted them to dissipate but they didn't know where to go or what to do.

Most of them sat around numb, saying nothing to each other.

They communicated through harrowed looks, realizing how shell-shocked troops must feel in a battle's barren aftermath. For a while, they'd considered themselves immortal. They'd begun to deal with the fact that they'd be on earth for a lot longer than expected. None of them had contemplated suicide – how can a dead man kill himself? Yet there would be an end, after all. It might be abrupt, or violent, but the knowledge came as a relief to many of the dieners. They would meet their maker after all.

Mark O'Murchu wrote a small piece about the incident for the local and national newspapers:

> An explosion rocked the deadite accommodation centre at eight a.m. this morning. The centre, nicknamed Bonetown by locals, was ravaged by a fire that spread quickly through the poorly constructed dwellings there. A cause has not been found though police believe no arson is involved. The deadheads were dealing with various flammable chemicals, and their lack of building experience is a likely factor. Project leader Donald Claig has declined to comment at this time.

Over the next two weeks the debris was cleared and building started anew. Glen was informed that there was still a flat free for him if he wanted it. His comics were lost but that was inconsequential to him; Alex's body had not been found, it was either turned to ash or buried beneath a pile of rubble. Glen prayed that Alex was no longer conscious.

CHAPTER 11

Kids

Dance dangled from the narrow ledge, his arms aching, fingers growing numb.

'I've got you right where I want you,' said H-Bomb, training her gun on him from the office window. To the psychologist's great surprise, the killer had long red hair and bright lipstick to match. She gave him a wicked smile. 'What's the matter? Losing your grip?'

'Can't we talk about this?' Dance tried to hoist himself up.

'I'm quite comfortable just watching you dangle. And die.' That way it would look like an accident. As long as H-Bomb had her gun aimed at her quarry, there was nowhere for him to go but down.

A shrill wind whistled in Dance's ears. He was getting tired and it felt like the singing air was trying to suck him downwards. He made one last scrabble back onto the ledge, hefting his body upwards. The hitwoman shook her head, not noticing that Christie Cummins was sneaking up behind her.

'This is your last chance,' said Dance through gritted teeth, 'I'll give you your first session for free.'

H-Bomb's laugh was cut short by a spinning kick from Christie, knocking the killer to the floor. Christie reached out the window and helped Dance in, just as H-Bomb leveled her gun at him and pulled the trigger.

From God Bless America *by Sam Robbins*

GLEN COULD ALWAYS TELL a lot about a neighbourhood by looking at the kids. If they were riding round on shiny bikes, leaving them in driveways and looking both ways before scampering across the road, he had to be in an up-market area. If the kids were in their front gardens playing on their own personal swings and slides, he was on the posh block. Kiddy-sized quad bikes connoted rural communities, and if the moppets had their faces pressed against barred windows, desperate to get out, he'd be passing a primary school.

Long before Glen saw the new youths, he heard their jeers and giggles. There's a type of laugh that spells 'up to no good,' and they all had it. They shouted at the tops of their lungs, knowing that no one would tell them off. The girls squealed, and at first Glen worried that they were under threat. He'd soon learn that the boys were the ones who had to watch out.

His first sight of a child came from an unexpected angle. A six-year-old had shinnied up a lamppost and was teetering on a high stone wall. The lad stuck out his arms and made aeroplane noises.

A half brick thumped against the sidewalk, right next to Glen. He didn't take it personally. It took him a long time to reach his flat on the top floor, a steep climb past green painted doors and dark passageways.

Glen still had to pay rent and utility bills, and the money from his old, pre-death savings account had almost run out. He had nothing left to sell except his body, which he offered to the research clinic that had been set up on the edge of the site. Run by the genial Dr Jacobs, the clinic paid for his time and he used his cheque to teeter on the breadline, with no safety net. Various pharmaceutical companies sought a wonder drug that would prolong life, using the dieners as subjects. Testing usually involved the taking of tissue samples, in conjunction with the adminstering of various drugs, lotions and potions. Glen received enough cash to make the visits worthwhile, but the pay was not extravagant. There were risks involved, of course. Each new test was a shot in the dark, an experiment with unforeseeable consequences. Most of the subjects had little to lose.

Glen didn't see the job as proper work like his labours in the comic store, but he was allowed to lie down and watch TV from time to time. He couldn't knock getting paid to do that. While his fellow subjects were exposed to extreme conditions such as long-term submersion in water, he commonly ended up on cushier details – trying out chemicals that had different effects on lifers, but did little to his ambivalent system.

The number of dieners in the area increased at a rapid pace. This hit home one cool night in March, when Glen left his garret and took a ride round the block on his scooter. He hoped to clear his head, get his thoughts straight. It was so easy to stay indoors, rereading his books, brain stuck in neutral. So now and again he liked to remind himself that there really was a world outside his window, that the grey walls of his tenement had a stark charm of their own.

He couldn't feel the walls, his sense of touch long gone, but he could hear his footsteps echo on the paths between each building. He could imagine (or remember) how the North Wind whipped at his ears and made his flesh goose.

Glen saw four youngsters sitting on a red brick wall near the church, drinking alcopops, chewing gum and tossing a ball around. The lads wore white baseball caps and their female counterparts had braids in their hair. Glen envied the bouncing babies in a way; he hadn't hung out with his pals much in his teens, spending most of his time at home, doing his homework or watching TV. He could appreciate the mall culture of modern times, relaxing with your mates away from brown owl parents' wings. As a youth he'd longed for the kind of camaraderie that these four yobs seemed to have. Now he simply missed his family.

Glen cruised slowly past the church, through a small car park where he kept his scooter. His elliptical route brought him closer to the kids. Their designer clothes beamed out through the darkness, bright white jackets and trainers like beacons on a fog-drenched rock.

The youths sauntered over to him. One of the lads glowered at the adult interloper; this boy's eyes were cold and dark. Probably missing their drugs, Glen surmised. As they closed in on him, he saw the skulls that grimaced from under their caps, strips of muscle and acned skin dangling from temples and cheekbones and chins. This gang of deported undead hadn't caused enough trouble in life; they were set to make far more mischief in death.

'New round here, aintcha?' Glen asked, all friendly. 'I can tell, your flesh is still hanging onto you and your sockets ain't all that sunken.'

'Piss off granddad,' said one of the girls, who had a long greasy ponytail. Her mate hefted the ball in Glen's vague direction and it landed with a thunk on the gas tank of his scooter. He drew their attention to the yellow 'flammable' sign.

'You tellin' us what to do?'

Glen didn't reply.

'Maybe we should play a game with your balls. Mash. Crunch. Shredder.' Glen didn't recognise these pursuits but he didn't fancy participating. He reckoned that the rules would be lacklustre if they weren't made up on the spot. The grim foursome rushed him and he panicked, scrabbling at the ignition.

The kids must have been in a playful mood, giving him time to get the scooter started while they collected a couple of sticks and a length of metal pipe. They battered the scooter with their weapons, hands and feet; a bottle of Buckie smashed against Glen's wing mirror. The pipe gave the windshield a crazy paving glaze. By now the engine was running and the scooter jerked into reverse, leaving the howling hooligans to squabble amongst themselves.

Glen rode to the lake, stopping at the water, empty and starlit. He'd recovered his wits, wondering where he'd park the scooter from now on. Gusts of soil were kicked up across the shore. On the horizon a flock of birds broke the monotony. Glen sat near the water and occupied himself in style, feeling sorry for himself. He refused to raise a hand to a minor, alive or dead; Claig and his guards took a similiar view. But there were other ways to deal with troublemakers.

He skimmed a flat pebble across the lake, watching the ruptured reflection of the star field above. He glimpsed Misbah's face for a second, part of that mirror image, a face that he'd seen every day for so many years and taken for granted. They'd been too mean to each other for too long, husband and wife, for them ever to go back to their old existence. At this point, his scooter battered, paranoia setting in, he would settle for a wishy-washy compromise.

The dead kids soon made a name for themselves in the neighbourhood. They smashed the fascia of the church, unmarred for five hundred years, demolished in an hour. One of them, an unpromising lad named Nail, had an artistic side. He sprayed the local playground with yellow graffiti. His moniker adorned the slide and on the soft ground under the swings he wrote, 'Tamzie J is a mess fae me.' Tamzie was suitably impressed by this gesture, giving Nail a snog in the laundry room.

Glen found out who they were (Nail and Tamzie were accompanied by Colin and Augie) and where they lived. One day he found Nail's cap lying on the stairwell, and posted it through Augie's letterbox with a love letter, purportedly from the gang leader. He bought a can of yellow spray paint and wrote a new message on Colin's door. When Augie saw the words 'Tamzie luvs Col,' she took the hint and made a move on Nail. The gang broke up soon afterwards.

CHAPTER 12

Garbage

THE BOY SUSPECTED SOMETHING. Glen wasn't sure why, but the can in his hand might have had something to do with it. He'd planned one more message, to be sprayed on the stairwell, stirring up the hornet's nest again just to make sure they stung each other.

Nail didn't give him the chance to leave his message. He swung the bat at Glen, catching him on his right temple and sending him tumbling down the concrete steps. Glen recovered immediately, knowing that if he didn't pick himself up, Nail would be on top of him. Glen curled his hands into fists, a don't-mess-with-me snarl on his face, underneath it all *He's only a kid! Not much older than Paul! I can't hurt him.* But he could defend himself, give as good as he got.

Glen didn't feel the knife in his back. He heard Tamzie's happy grunt and the sound of the weapon yanking out again. He spun round to see the rest of the gang blocking the stairs, grabbed Tamzie's wrist, squeezed hard so that she dropped her knife. Nail's approaching footsteps echoed through the stairwell, and Glen dipped his left shoulder to avoid the swinging baseball bat. Sinking to his knees he tried to get up again, couldn't. Tamzie's backstabbing had done its job. As the youths crowded in on him he actually found himself praying for unconsciousness – it would be the first time he'd slept in months. His vision grew dim, reminding him of his demise. This was equally humiliating, equally mysterious. He had no idea where or in what state he'd awake, but he didn't expect any white tunnels or pearly gates.

He plummets to earth too fast, sick in the guts, clouds jetting up past his nosedive body, nimbus smiles sure he'll hit hard. He can make out rivers, trees, houses and rocks as the ground grows closer.

Glen would never have thought that heaven could be found on a rubbish dump. Yet he was so happy to be in one piece that his surroundings didn't matter so much. His sense of smell was almost defunct and the litter around him was nothing offensive: some old toys, a chest of drawers, bin bags, a cot, a few tree branches. He used the debris to hoist himself up to a kneeling position, looking for someone to help him out of the metal pit he'd been thrown into. Dumped by the gang like a worthless piece of garbage, a warning to other residents of the complex to mind their own beeswax, not to meddle in the affairs of the youngsters.

He heard a groaning metallic sound from above and the sky grew dark. An enormous steel claw with three sharp talons swamped him in shadow. The operator – whoever he was – obviously hadn't seen Glen, or had mistaken him for a trash bag. The grabber claimed a clawful of crud, dropping bits and pieces onto Glen. He blinked his dust-ridden eyes and hauled himself upwards again, legs squashed together by the sheer weight of displaced garbage. The claw deposited its catch on a pile at the far side of the pit then returned for more. Glen couldn't move from its path and was scooped into the air. As the device tightened, he slipped between two of the talons and dangled there, one hand clutching the steel claw, the other reaching for the flex from a mangled kitchen appliance. He let go as he closed in on the mound, using the flex to reach the brim of the pit and clamber out into the open.

Nail was in a small orange cab, operating the grabber. Two security guards lay dead nearby, but the rest of Nail's gang was nowhere to be seen. Glen concentrated on the lad's gloating face, determined to get to him and sort him out once and for all. But his cursed body betrayed him and he slumped against a refuse truck. He managed to climb inside and drove across Bonetown.

He would have to rest, maybe ask Max to take a look at his back, recover from the battering he'd taken from the gang. His body wouldn't heal but it could be patched up, and given time he would gain the strength to beat all four of the youths.

He parked the truck near his scooter, hid the keys in a shrubbery. Hearing a rattling in the back of the truck, he wasn't sure whether he should investigate.

The sky was amber, fogged with smoke from the Mausoleum. Some streetlights glowed red as if recently illuminated, others yellow/white. The multicoloured hue gave the street a jazz era neon feel.

Curiosity got the worse of him. He picked up a trashcan lid, just in case, to use as a shield. The gang had followed him home, he was certain. Most likely that vicious little minx Tamzie, sharp object at the ready. Glen stole up to the truck and took a chance, keeking over the gate. The angry weasel face of a freshly dead guard, tunic torn to ribbons, skin in much the same shape, spittle, bared teeth, hateful eyes looked back at him. One of Nail's victims, returned from his own murder, lost and confused. The guard sprang from the truck, a splintered length of wood still jutting from his chest. He leaped on top of Glen and the two men grappled, Glen trying to fend his assailant off and help him to regain his mental balance at the same time.

Glen felt like a midwife at some unholy birth, there to smooth the delivery but wary of getting throttled by the baby. He broke off and moved slowly round the truck, trying to keep it between himself and the oversized infant, who soon tired, tears rolling down his softening face. Despite the callous acts Glen had seen and experienced, he knew the right thing to do.

'It'll be alright, fella. I can help. I think.' Glen held his hand out across the back of the truck, palm uppermost. The murdered man looked at it, weighing his options, realising that he had none. Glen headed for the scheme, leaving the guard to make a decision. Choice made, Glen had a new stray to bring home.

The light switch didn't work first time. Glen gave it a flick and nothing happened; his companion tried, slowly remembering the minutiae of his life, and the light snapped on.

'There's someone here,' Glen whispered, motioning the guard

to hang back. Slipping off his muck-encrusted shoes, Glen crept carefully into the living room.

A mess before, the place was now a wreck. The furniture had been smashed to toothpicks; the TV left screenless; blood and worse was smeared on the walls. Sitting in the midst of it all, cross-legged on the bare floorboards, was Kim, back from her assignments in the real world. Her jaw dropped as she saw the state Glen was in.

'Had a tantrum?' asked Glen, with a joke for every occasion.

'Don't be silly. You've been out making friends, haven't you? Is this one of them?'

Glen turned to see the murder victim, looming behind him.

'This ain't no friend. This is –'

'Reuben. I'm Reuben.' Glen led him to the spare room, where he slumped down on the rug, curled up into a shocked foetal ball and remained for the rest of the night.

In the bedroom, Kim dressed her friend's wounds as best she could and listened to his story.

'You shouldn't have messed with those kids,' she said, wagging a cautionary finger at him. 'There's more of them than you might think. They've got no social conscience. They didn't have much when they were alive, and now – no Christian values, y'see. No parental guidance.'

'Do you know what happened to their folks?'

'They don't want to know. The mums and dads are alive, free; don't want to see their kids atrophy, turn so bad.'

'So Nail and his gang are abandoned.'

'Adopted by the corporations to help, or use, or experiment on. Every child has a right to life, whether it's unborn or evil. But a dead child has no rights.'

'A dead child still has a caring family. Love.'

'That doesn't count for much, statistically speaking. You should know…'

'I'm a statistic myself.'

'Where did you dig Reuben up?' Kim asked quietly, wrinkling her nose.

'The garbage dump. One of Nail's victims.'

'They've taken to killing people now?'

'Like you said, they have no conscience. I want to help Reuben so he can orient himself. Give him the help I never got. Besides, he owes me a toe.'

'Exactly – is this a good idea, the kind of person he is?'

'Was.' Glen's mind was made up.

'Sure, Glen.' Kim couldn't help thinking that he'd just loaded himself with a heavy burden.

'Death ain't the hard part,' Glen told Reuben as they cleared up the flat the next day, 'death is a doddle.' He handed a broom to his roommate, hoping that some simple menial tasks would help the murder victim recover from his shock. Nothing like the mundanities of the old to help cope with something new.

'It's the world around you which changes. The way people see you, point at you, hate you. Even your own family. Got any brothers or sisters?'

Reuben was too flummoxed to answer.

'Kids?' Glen piled up his clothes into one heap.

'Yeah. One.'

'We'll get in touch with your family, let them know what happened.' Reuben didn't look happy at the prospect so Glen added, 'When you're ready.'

'Sometime never.'

'We'll see. Those kids ever hang round the dump before?' That was a mistake. Asking about the kids reminded Reuben of the attack. They'd surrounded him, seven or eight of them. One had punched him in the face, breaking his nose. Another had taken his knife.

When he'd lunged forward to grab it back, the blade had been thrust into his torso, piercing his heart.

He'd
    felt
        it
           stop
               beating.

The end of everything – for a few hours, at least. Reuben gasped instinctively, though he had no breath.

'Sorry. The guards will be sniffing round the area, they'll have found your colleagues. Might be in the papers today. Maybe I can talk to them for you.' Fat chance. The guards couldn't find their arses with both hands cuffed behind their backs. 'It's important you remember. What was your kid called?'

'Caitlin.'

'What's she like?'

'Very pretty.'

'Of course. What's she like?'

'Thick dark curly hair, always getting tangled into knots. Wide brown eyes you can drown in. Sharp teeth. Likes *Totally Spies*.'

'Who doesn't? You see a lot of her?'

'She's four and a half. Into tantrums. She'll snap at the slightest thing. Usually when I get home from work she's snivelling in her mummy's lap. I have to deal with her, it's my turn, my wife's had her all day. So I spend my evenings as a human ounch bag, or bouncy castle, depending on Caitlin's mood of the moment.'

'Punch bag.'

'Ounch bag. One of my little girl's words. I like it.'

'You miss her already.'

'Dreadfully. They'll be wondering what's happened to me.'

'I'll sort it, all in good time.'

Reuben tried to piece together the remnants of a coffee table.

'This isn't a good time. I should be at home, damn it! Or failing that, upstairs.'

'Number 24's already occupied.'

'I mean up there. The afterworld.'

Glen took a look round his flat. It was habitable again.

'Paradise can be found in the strangest of places, pal.'

As Glen told Reuben about his own children and the existence he had experienced since his death, he helped the newlydead come to terms with his circumstances. Unlike Glen, Reuben had harboured aspirations while alive; he wrote poetry, had published a couple of short pieces in magazines.

There was nothing wrong with his day job; he had paid the bills and helped keep the compound secure. However, he'd planned to work his way up the organisation ladder. Reuben had been an ideas man. But not any more; all drive and ambition had left him once he'd died, in a sapping mental drought.

Glen dissuaded him from going straight to his bosses, explaining that he was out of a job – now that he was dead, he certainly wouldn't be allowed to guard other dieners. But if he tried to leave Bonetown and a normal person came face to face with him, he'd be hauled off to a morgue.

Reuben called in sick instead. He told part of the truth – said he'd been mugged, left for dead, was scared that his attackers would try again – he was determined to stay in hiding in the meantime. He did not mention the fact that he could see the unruly gang who'd assaulted him from Glen's window, overlooking the car park. Every time he looked down at them he cursed them for what they'd done to him and planned his revenge.

When Glen was fully mobile again and Reuben felt human, they began to look at ways to combat the cheeky monkeys below. Reuben wanted to use extreme violence; Glen preferred a more subtle approach, worried that hurting the youths would draw the guards to them. When Reuben pointed out that the softly softly approach hadn't caught any monkeys, and that guard involvement might not be such a bad idea at the end of the day, Glen had to acquiesce.

'Right,' he grimaced. 'The clumsy, destructive, noisy way it is then.'

'You bet.'

Nail was bored. He had nothing to do, no money to splurge and he didn't like his friends. They were hangers-on, no ideas of their own, always looking to him to lead them. Colin was the only one with a suggestion that night:

'I've found that Glass geezer's bike. Not far down the street. Let's get it.' The best plan he'd heard all day. The gang trooped past the scheme, collecting makeshift tools as they went, their mission a demolition job. They knew that Glen was still around, hiding in his flat; an attack on his beloved Vespa would flush him out. They'd smash it into tiny pieces then post it through the letterbox. Worth the time and trouble to see the look on the doddering old sod's face. That was the proposal, at least.

Nail laid into the headlight, enjoying the tinkle of glass and plastic as he busted the lamps. Colin slashed the tyres and the others tackled the handlebars; Augie yanked the windshield off, having punched a hole in the centre. She used a crowbar to hook the shield and free it from the frame.

Triumphantly, Nail flicked his lighter on and prepared to throw it onto the back seat. He stopped short when he heard the sound of gears crunching, a large engine rumbling, and was blinded for a moment by the lights of an oncoming vehicle. The gang scattered as a Roly Poly hurtled towards them; the driver slammed on the brakes at the last minute, barely avoiding a collision with the scooter. Only Nail stayed in sight, defiant and curious, as the door of the concrete mixer truck swung open and Glen appeared.

'Taking my little hairdryer out for a spin?' Glen sauntered forward, silhouetted by the truck's high beams.

'Burning some rubber,' Nail flicked his Zippo on and off, 'that's all.'

'Look out!' shouted Tamzie, jumping from her hiding place round the corner. Too late. A small, rat-like man with sharp pointy teeth and tiny eyes had snuck up behind Nail, wrapping a fetid arm round the lad's throat, forcing him to drop his lighter. The hold wouldn't choke him but he still looked uncomfortable.

Their leader threatened, the rest of the gang appeared from their hidey-holes. Before they could help Nail they were cut off by the rat man. In his element, he threw himself at the youths, punching and kicking them with psychopathic fury. For once Glen started to worry about the kids – it looked like the rat man would tear them to pieces. Fortunately for them, they turned tail and scattered into the night.

'Well,' the rat man said, wiping some unidentified mush from his lapels, 'that oughta work.'

'You've done your bit, Reuben. Let's hope that you won't get another opportunity to flex your muscles, eh?'

Glen referred Reuben to Peter, who found him some work on his growing staff, collecting donations for the cause. Reuben got his own apartment in Zone One, Building Three and seemed to settle down, his mood calm and cooperative. But one morning Glen was roused from his bed by a clamour coming from the main road. Grabbing his gear, he ran to the road as fast as his dead legs could carry him. He could make out honking car horns, yelling and banging. A modest crowd of live men and women had gathered at the entrance to Bonetown, with angry faces and clenched fists. The guards were fending them off while Claig attempted to placate them.

'See what we're up against?' asked Peter, standing by the wayside. 'If we had any blood flowing through our veins, they'd be out for it.'

'Why're they here?' Glen had a groggy, first-thing-in-the-morning head.

'Because they hate us. They're stirrers, here to cause trouble. The first of many, to be certain.'

They were formidable: bikers and hooligans, pikies with pit bulls, hotheaded housewives in schemie trappings, screaming youngsters, elderly agitators. All of them hated the residents of Bonetown; they threw sticks and stones at the brand new homes.

Two patrol cars were parked on the opposite side of the road, lights flashing, their drivers waiting for the kickoff.

'Give me a shot!' Reuben appeared from Building Three, hand on the hilt of his knife. He hurtled straight for the lifers and one of the cops, perceiving the consequences, rushed to intercept. The Bonetown guards were too stunned to stop their ugly ex-colleague leaping into the fray like a rabid stage-diver at a rock concert.

'Goddamn deadheads!' shouted one of the bikers, 'get back in your graves where you belong!'

It was the blasphemy that sent Reuben over the edge. His eyes burned with indignation, and despite the guards' attempts to hold him back he hurled himself at the cop.

Constable Jerry Gibbons had been trained for this kind of situation: a sudden attack on his person. But he had also accepted the deadheads as a passive, law-abiding bunch. So he didn't get to his radio or even his baton; he only had time to raise his arms across his face, defending himself from Reuben's sideswipe. The attacker's momentum flung the cop backwards against a postbox, and Reuben gave him no time to recover. All Jerry saw was a pair of flailing fists and the jagged pearly gates that were Reuben's teeth. *Funny*, thought Jerry as tiny lights flashed before his eyes. *Such nice teeth for a corpse.*

Peter turned his back on the melee. 'I think it's time for another meeting,' he told Glen, who watched the chaos open-mouthed. Reuben was about to be torn apart when the crowd suddenly dispersed, walking away from the police.

'I don't get it,' Glen said to Peter, but the older man had gone.

CHAPTER 13

Love and Death

Please Don't Come Home, Daddy

A four-year-old cries in her back yard, grieving for her dead father. Caitlin Whitley, of Lockwood Drive, Aberdeen, knows that her daddy has revived and is in Bonetown, the residential complex built exclusively for deadheads. But she doesn't want him to come home.

'He needs to be quarantined,' says Caitlin's mother, Chastity. 'We need to be safe. I can't risk contaminating my little girl with an unidentified disease. Sorry, Reuben.'

Reuben Whitley, forty, was a security man in Bonetown when he was viciously murdered by a zombie youth. Resurrected in the town, he has requested a visit to his family home on numerous occasions.

'I know he misses us,' Chastity says, 'we love him and miss him so much. This whole thing is frightening.'

Doctor Erland Jacobs has been spearheading research into the rising corpse conundrum. 'We don't know for sure whether these reanimated people pose a health risk. We're playing safe.'

While the scientists battle to find some answers, little Caitlin has a heartfelt request: 'Please don't come home, Daddy. I need you to get better.'

Special to The Times *by Mark O'Murchu*

THEY CAME FROM ALL over Bonetown to hear him. He had clout without striking a blow. No signs promoted him; although the press had been invited, there was no media attention and the only journalist present was Mark. Word of mouth did the job. The very fact that so many dieners wanted to see him was motive enough to bring more along. None of the newcomers expected anything in particular. They would meet a charismatic man, one of their own, with thoughts and experience to share. They had illusions to shatter.

Everything, living and dead, has a voice. The washing machine has its spin and cycle, water its shush, leaves their rustle... the church spoke through a peel of bells, commanding the townsfolk to attend. Peter Foothill brought a lustre to the place, smartly dressed in a spotless smock, going for the black look, his only accessory a silver necklace looped twice round his bullet-shaped head. His hair was greying and his eyes struggled to peer from their sunken sockets. There was still a twinkle in his pupils, a glimmer of life; maybe that was why his congregation flocked about him. Peter also had a commanding voice and an indisputable way with crowd wooing.

Glen had never seen so many dead people flocked together. Some of them were fresh, with their skin still intact and their hair well groomed. Others had really gone to seed, little more than skeletons with maggots for earrings.

Glen had a front row pew this time; close enough to see the scars on Peter's chin. The large man's hair was slicked back, his jowls shaven. He was pleased to note that a hush fell over the congregation as he raised his arms. A wide welcoming smile spanned his face.

'Welcome to Bonetown, a place where the living and dead have been co-existing for the past year. I'm Peter, and I've seen that a lack of understanding about who we are can cause a lot of anxiety and pain. It is misunderstanding – not a plot against us, not hatred of the unknown. The guards greet us and see a reflection of their own mortality. They won't look so good when they die, and they probably won't be happy either. They call us deadheads because of our emaciated state, or perhaps because our flesh is hanging off us half the time.' The comment got a chuckle from the crowd. 'We depress them, we mortify them. Does that mean they don't care about us?' The question was opened out to the audience.

'Some of them pity us,' Louise ventured.

'Pity, mercy are noble concepts. Don't dismiss them. Mercy is a tributary of compassion, and that leads to comprehension. Like many of you here, I've lost my family, been ejected from the world I knew while alive. I was harassed and pursued by the authorities, relocated to a low-rent housing scheme and promptly forgotten.

'The newspapers cajolled lifers into believing that we were being cared for, that there was an answer to our "problem." Is it a problem that we exist, that we are still able to strive and achieve? Don't get me wrong. Lottery funds have been diverted to help us cope with our situation. The government has been sympathetic, most of the time, in its bureaucratic behemoth way.'

A handful of attendees had left by this point. Others stirred in their seats as Peter continued.

'Handouts – cash, pamphlets – aren't the answer, of course. We have to help ourselves first and contribute to society as we did in life. Only in this way can we hold our heads up high and prove that we're worth caring about. We're not some diseased specimens to be placed in jars. We won't fade away, we're here to stay. Everyone will have to get used to that.'

'I have enough trouble getting by, day to day,' said an elderly lady sitting next to Glen. 'How'm I supposed to contribute?'

'You're doing it by being here tonight. I know what a struggle getting here must have been. You can work with me. We can all help each other to succeed.'

'How?' asked Mark, stuck in the back row, scribbling furiously in his notepad. His eyes never left the paper.

'I propose the establishment of a small organisation, dedicated to good works.' An impressive red banner unfurled behind Peter. 'The name of the organisation will be Life After Death, or LAD. The youthful connotations are intentional. We are reborn, you see.'

Peter's eyes twinkled in their magical way. 'We are sentient, we feel heartsick though we have no hearts. Above all, I'm sure that our souls are still deep down inside of us. They skitter about, uncatchable, amorphous. They are there and we can prove that by putting something back into the community.

'St Jude's church has been out of use for years. I will start helping to rebuild the south wall tomorrow. I'll use my bare hands if I have to. Join me! I'm asking you to donate your spare time and use the building skills you've learned to aid your community.'

Peter ended his speech by paraphrasing Ecclesiastes: 'There is an appointed time for everything under Heaven... a time to tear down and a time to build up. A time to weep and a time to laugh; a time to mourn and a time to dance. A time to throw stones and a time to gather stones; a time to tear apart and a time to sew together... a time for war, and a time for peace.'

Satisfied that he'd made his point, Peter didn't give his audience a chance to ask any more questions. He said goodbye to them, shaking hands with the people in the front row, touching everyone with his words. Then he left, allowing what he had said to sink in and the dieners to discuss the details among themselves.

Many of the listeners stayed to talk, to consider, to gossip. Glen caught some of their reactions, all positive. He said hello to Mark, still sitting on the back pew, and got a response this time.

'You still with us?'

'I'm indispensable, you know that.' Glen sat down next to his old friend. 'Not dragged yourself up from the gutter yet?'

'Getting there.'

'Are you still doing stories about us?'

'A few articles in *The Times* and *New Scientist*. Getting to be known as the expert on you ghouls, thanks in no small part to yourself.'

'How d'you mean?' Glen sat down beside his old pal.

'If I hadn't been acquainted with you, I wouldn't have been set down this ugly path.' Mark eyed up a twenty-year-old, still wearing her own hair. 'Anything to do with deadheads, my editors assign me the stories.'

'No hatchet jobs, I hope?'

'Only the subjects. Our readers' fave stories, chum. Murder victims coming back for revenge, like in one of your movies.'

'There aren't any supernatural elements in John Dance films. Fantasy, yes, a little bit of sci-fi maybe, but no EC Comics stuff.'

Mark giggled. 'Same old A-1 geek.'

'The real deal and proud of it.'

'Still, you've got plenty weird tales for me, I'm sure. Next time, eh? Got to dash – deadlines and all, you understand.'

'Wholeheartedly. Off you shoot.'

'Remember – if you hear any rampaging zombie stories, drop me a line!'

Glen was dubious of Peter's intentions, being one of the few people at the meeting who'd known the man since his sorrowful sabbatical in the hospital. Yet even he became less sceptical when the church began to be rebuilt next day. The dieners had managed to organise trucks, bricks and mortar, scaffolding and manpower. No one asked for anything in return, bathing in the glow of their beaming leader. Peter's dream would soon come true.

Kim visited once a week now, and it became obvious that her motives weren't purely professional. She spilled the beans to Glen on a cool evening as they watched the stars, leaning opposite each other in the courtyard outside Glen's building.

How could she possibly be interested in me? Glen thought. *I stink, my fingers have curled into claws and my conversation's mostly gloomy. I'm a wreck. No class act. She still wants to know.*

Kim regarded him with a cool analytical gaze. Weighing up her options, perhaps. Her instincts, her fascination with this man versus the digs she'd receive from the people that knew her. Hanging out with a deadhead, talking to one – caring about one?

Glen wasn't about to make the first move, risk scaring her away. He tried to look nonchalant, not too stiff. But that's what he was. A stiff with all the charisma of a coffin.

Curiosity got the better of Kim. She took a cigarette from her pack and addressed her target.

'Can you light this for me?'

'No match. Sorry.' Glen's voice was small and emotionless.

'Don't need it anyway.' She flicked away the fag with disdain. 'Just checking to see if you're the gentleman you say you are.'

'Oh... You can't go out with me,' Glen grumbled. 'I'm not your type.'

'Worried about what people will say?' Kim smiled.

'I've never bothered about that kind of thing before. But you know what people are like, they jump to the right conclusions and it doesn't take 'em long to do it.'

'You should never second guess the man in the street's ability to second guess you.'

'I guess.'

'We could be like a couple of friends, there's no harm in that. No one would say anything.'

'It's not what they say I'm bothered with. It's what they think and do.'

'They won't do anything. Too busy worrying about their own business to stick their noses into ours.'

'Most folks have enough nosiness to spread around.'

'You'd be surprised how self-obsessed people can be.'

'I don't do surprised, not any more. The way people can treat their fellow man like loose crap, that surprised me. The kids round here, how wild they are, their cheek, that was a bit of a shock at first. Ending up here, stuck with a bunch of bams... losing my family, all the things I took for granted – I've spent the last six months in a state of surprise. Not now. Now I accept everything. The bastards've ground me down and spat me out –'

'You've been stuck in this place for too long.'

'How about unsticking me?'

'Sure.' She held his left hand tight, her hair looking golden and lively in the moonlight. Her earrings sparkled and her mole rode upwards as her mouth curved into a grin, a slim string of saliva bridging her upper and lower lips. Glen wanted to kiss her, was still afraid that he'd repulse her. He'd faced a lot of rejection recently, from strangers and people he loved. He tried to imagine her embracing him, brushing her cheek against his, kissing his shriveled, dry old face. Couldn't. He shook his head slowly, trying to dispel the dread image. She looked at him quizzically.

'I've been having these dreams. Flying, falling, that sort of thing.'

'You don't sleep.'

'Daydreams then. At night. Oh, you know what I mean. Very intense.'

'Do you hit the ground when you fall?'

'Never.'

'Psychologists reckon it's an ancient memory, from when we were apes swinging from tree to tree. The ones that survived their fall passed it down through the generations.'

'The ones that died didn't. These dreams are awful vivid.'

'They could be memories.'

Why would I forget to remember a memory? I've only blacked out once in my – death.'

He plummets to earth too fast, sick in the guts, clouds jetting up past his nosedive body, nimbus smiles sure he'll hit hard. He can make out rivers, trees, houses and rocks as the ground grows closer.

The dieners didn't have many places to go, so they hung around on the building sites that continued to proliferate. As more of the resurrected dead were dragged to Bonetown the place grew, swallowing up the surrounding land. In parallel, the security grew tighter and the walls and fences got bigger. More and more advisers and experts were brought on-site too to study the escalating sideshow. A small school was built for the younger dieners, just to keep them out of mischief. Traffic grew heavier as lucky rubberneckers scored a pass and drove through the town.

If the dieners were soulless then the places they frequented suited them. Glen would watch them as he headed to work, their faces avid and full of expression, battling overtime to compensate for their corrupt bodies. These visages were a direct contrast to the blank facial casts and glazed looks of the living commuters. The dead-heads may not have had any hope but at least their nine to five grind had been interrupted and they were rethinking their existence.

One place they could go was St Jude's. With the roof and walls repaired, the door hinges oiled and a lick of paint inside and out, the Church of Life After Death was ready for business within weeks. By this time several projects had been set in motion, some more ambitious than others – a care service for less mobile dieners, a treasury account set up to receive donations and a neighbour-hood watch-style patrol.

Peter's disciples spread the word for him, explaining that if people helped Peter he would help them in return. Lifers also attended the church out of curiosity or a desire to be part of their adopted community. They came away angry, enthused or con-fused, but at least they felt something. Here was a passionate reli-gion, faith with fire in its nascent belly.

All of the good works and pilot projects were run by the dead voluntarily, in their spare time. They had a fair bit of it, after all, and thanks to Peter's intelligence and charm they fell over back-wards to offer their assistance. A documentary covering Peter's mission was made by a community video group, Fierce Films. Peter introduced the film, took viewers round the neighbourhood and begged for more donations.

Glen didn't get involved with any of the local projects, and he paid little attention to Peter's headline-grabbing antics. His thoughts were filled with Kim, his affection for her still growing, and this made him feel more alive than the performance of any number of good works could. Dave Barr gave him a job picking and packing materials in the main warehouse for a minimum wage. That along with the clinical research enabled him to pay his bills.

For most of the day Glen stood at a conveyor belt, checking items for damage and stowing them in boxes. The boss loved him and the other dieners who worked there; they were cheap, ineligible for sick or holiday pay, and didn't eat or go to the bathroom. Breaks were inconsistent. Glen spent most of them battering Dave's old punch bag, which hung in a corner. The supervisory roles were taken by the two lifers present – Dave and Jenna.

Glen didn't care about the menial job or bad conditions. He spent most of his time looking forward to his next meeting with Kim, recalling previous rendezvous, and regaling his fellow packers with tales of his relationship until they were sick of it. He didn't take the hint.

'She's learning French at the moment,' he told them one day. 'Got friends over there, feels bad when they phone her in perfect English and she can't return the favour. Tried it out on a taxi driver, black cab in Glasgow, he gave her the funniest look –'

'We don't care what she's learning.' Jenna would keep a close eye on her dieners, always checking forms on a clipboard. 'Stop distracting me.'

'Oh yeah, this must really be taxing your mind.' Glen's favourite part of his job involved wrapping boxes with a massive cellophane coating machine. 'Takes some mighty concentration.'

'I think it's sick!' Jenna's outburst surprised everyone. 'You going out with someone who's still alive. I don't mean anything by it, Glen, but she'd suit someone with more... life.'

'Give Glass a break, girl.' It wasn't the first time Dave had stuck up for Glen. 'I used to go out with a fine lady from Stenhousemuir. She had a great imagination, always telling jokes and on for fun. My friends didn't approve, said I could do better.

There was nuffin' wrong with her, they just never took a shine to her. So to keep 'em happy I dumped her. Didn't say anything. I stopped returning her calls and hid when she came to the door. She got the message. I've always regretted the way I treated her and the reasons why. Didn't have another steady relationship for four years, can you believe that?'

'Forget I said anything,' Jenna backed down, 'I'm tired, that's all.'

'I don't mind. I don't know what she sees in me either. We're happy for the moment. No doubt she'll find some young hunk and I won't see her for dust.'

'You go on about her all you like, Glen.' Vern hefted another box as if it was a cantaloupe. 'We need positivity in this place! Optimism moves things on, it stops us all from grinding down and not getting out of bed in the morning. We jump out, or crawl or whatever, because we're hoping something good will happen. Life affirming. Or we're planning what we'll do when we get paid. Whichever way, hope keeps the world turning. Not money, not whether we get these bits and bobs in their boxes and meet our targets and keep our jobs.'

Glen and Kim's first official date took place in the old cemetery, round the back of the church. Not the most romantic of venues, sure, but it reminded the couple that they were better off than the poor buggers still underground. Kim brought Glen a Johnny Depp calendar as a gift.

'I don't really like Johnny Depp all that much,' Glen admitted.

'I do. Hang it up on your wall for me.'

Glen gladly agreed, happy in the knowledge that Depp was slated to appear in the next Dance movie. Kim and Glen read the headstones, garnering what they could from the names, dates and epitaphs carved thereon; they played a game, wondering what these corpses would do if they came back – the purposes they'd serve, the secrets they'd expose, the shocks for their relatives.

A row of urns had been set up to commemorate the demise of

dozens of people in the fire. As Glen passed the vessels, he thought he could hear scraping and rattling from within as if the ashes were trying to escape. It had to be his imagination, sparked by the macabre setting.

The graveyard was crumbling and grey, but it was touched with beauty too. The flowers left to sprout from graves, sculptured angels looking imploringly heavenwards with marble eyes, ancient trees leaning towards the gravestones, branches protecting long lost loved ones while their roots cradled the bodies and used them to build new life. Glen explained to Kim that he felt slightly envious. He wanted to be part of that natural cycle, death and rebirth, but was out of the loop. The rise of the zombies wasn't only unnatural or unholy, it was shattering the status quo.

Despite his misgivings, the world kept turning.

The couple's favourite meeting place was the Oxygen Bar, set up for the live workers – the 'skins,' as the dieners called them – on Infirmary Street, but a haunt of the dead as well. There they could grab a window seat and watch the world whiz past. For Glen and Kim, it was like being in a static bubble isolated from the earth's orbit, the two of them alone. Glen would buy a couple of coffees and Kim would end up drinking both of them, but they weren't really there for the cappuccinos; they were there to spend time together in a relaxed atmosphere.

Gradually the bar would fill with after-work customers, and the management's two-for-one drinks promotion never failed to pack the place. Soft music was replaced with raucous rock and Kim would often go home hoarse after shouting at Glen to make herself heard. They still dug the establishment and went there whenever they could.

'You know what I like best about you?' Kim stirred her drink.

'Tell me, tell me,' Glen replied.

'You listen. Don't go on about how great your job is, or moan about your car. Or the other way round. You sit with me and take in everything I say. I really appreciate that.'

'Appreciate what?' Glen teased, sounding disinterested. Kim gave him a playful slap on the arm, sending his teaspoon clattering onto the next table. 'Sorry,' Glen said to the victims of the spoon attack, a couple of grumbling guards. 'Horseplay,' he added by way of an explanation.

'Stop disrupting the lives of the locals and come back here,' Kim giggled, beckoning her boyfriend back to his seat. 'Speaking of work, how's the dreadful toil going?'

'Flies by, thanks to the people I work with. The only thing they tell me off for is rattling on about how wonderful you are all the time.'

'I'm a hot topic on the workfloor then, am I?'

'The hottest. Apart from what happened on CSI last night.'

'How do you survive with no TV?'

'I suffer in silence, most of the time. Jenna fills me in on all the latest soap goss.'

'What's she like?' Kim sounded suddenly frosty.

'A listener, like me. Plain and plain speaking, wears ankle length frocks and goes to the bathroom to blow her nose. Well brung up, like me again.'

'Maybe I should meet this Jenna.'

'Next time we have a join-up after work I'll give you a bell. You can meet the gang.'

'Can't wait.'

Kim left for a meeting with J.C., arranging to meet Glen back at his apartment at four. Glen stayed longer than expected at the bar. Friends kept offering to buy him drinks, so what could be do? It would have been rude to refuse. Chris popped in for a while and, married by the oxygenated atmosphere, Glen couldn't resist asking him why he was in such a state, covered in a thin, crackling crust.

'I've got your favourite doctor to thank for that.'

'Jacobs did this to you?'

'He wanted to know what would happen to a diener immersed in cold water for a few months. At least I think that's how long it was, I lost track of time. My hands swelled up, my skin became marbly. I know we're not supposed to feel anything but I was cold, Glen, so cold. I bloated, this wax stuff started forming all around me, I was terrified. Then they let me go. Apparently I'd satisfied their scientific curiosity. The experiment was a great success.'

Glen decided never to set foot in the clinic again. He got home late, around six o'clock, and Kim wasn't back. J.C. had so much more going for him – he was alive for starters. He was tall, good-looking and brimming with Aussie confidence. Glen lost his rag, kicking over his DVDs (shades of a beach brat demolishing sandcastles) and ripping the Johnny Depp calendar off the wall, tearing it in half. It wasn't fair, she was his, and although he'd known the relationship couldn't last, he'd still hoped for a few more weeks of happiness before something like this happened.

He tried Kim's mobile, dreading the response, but there was nothing on the other end. Perhaps the phone was switched off or the battery was dead. Glen sat and stewed, too upset to watch a film or read the paper. When Kim finally came home he'd calmed down, despondent, resigned to his lonely fate.

'I tried to call you but you were still at the bar,' Kim explained as she shed her heavy brown overcoat. 'Mickey from the station had tickets for the Twisted Tour when it hit the Fringe. We went backstage, met Jim Rose, it was great.' This news made Glen feel terrible. He loved Jim Rose and hated the idea of anyone having more fun than himself.

'See this?' Glen held a small silver object up to the light. It was the ring that Peter had given him. 'This is my most precious possession.' Once Kim had seen it, Glen closed his hand over it. 'I was going to give it to the woman I loved. But now... I can't go through this kind of torture every time you leave the compound.'

'J.C. was right. You are an idiot.'

'What about J.C.? Aren't the two of you –?'

'The meeting was cancelled. I never saw him tonight.' Kim reassured her boyfriend that she hadn't spent the evening with the Antipodean Atlas. She didn't find Glen's jealousy touching; it seemed childish and petulant. Worst of all, her calendar was missing.

'It's OK,' Glen sulked, 'I can understand you going off with real men. You're wasting your time with me.'

'Only when you get all moody. I don't fancy J.C. He's not my type.' Glen found it hard to believe that *he* could be anybody's type. 'Keep your precious, honey. When you're ready, you'll know what to do with it.'

Kim held him close, reassuring him of her fidelity. She was right. He'd been an idiot. He would trust Kim the next time she went to work, although a tiny part of him was still annoyed that she'd had so much fun without him. How unthinking! How unfeeling! Having a good time in his absence. Wasn't there a cosmic rule somewhere about that?

'We've done it.'

'Done what?' glowered Peter, taking an involuntary step back as Reuben encroached on his personal space. The two men were in Peter's office, sun streaming through the window and highlighting Reuben's excited face.

'Fought back. Used brickbats instead of bouquets. Showed them to think twice before they push us over.' Reuben's eyes were wide with excitement.

'What did you do, exactly?' asked Peter in a sad tone. 'Who did you hurt?'

'All of them. The human race. They'll think twice,' repeated the acolyte, 'in case we retaliate again. He was round the side of Building Eighty-Seven in Zone Fourteen – the primary school. An old guard, fifties maybe, but he'd got a rep in the area for abusing dieners.'

'Physical abuse?' Peter was growing impatient but he remained calm, adopting the posture of a father whose boy has done wrong, but doesn't understand why.

'Verbal. Hurling insults left, right and in the town centre. So we found him behind the church, made sure there were no witnesses and beat eight shades of crap out of him. There was some kind of recital going on at the school, a piano playing, a little choir singing. Beautiful music.'

'You didn't kill the guard?'

'It would've been poetic. If he'd come back, I mean. He would have learned what it's like, how difficult it is *without* all these bad sentiments. We left him mashed up. Tied him to the cross there for all to see. He was screaming, begging to be freed. When the choir came out – you should have seen their angelic little faces! They won't forget.'

'I'm sure they won't,' said Peter gently. 'You're not going to do this again, Reuben. Nor are your brothers.' This was a command, not a request. Reuben looked disappointed.

'We did it for you. We believe so much in what you teach, we want to show -'

'Show the world we're a bunch of irresponsible animals? Acting like brutes who can't be trusted or, heaven help us, negotiated with?'

'You should've heard that music, father. Really pretty. We can go back and finish him off. Keep him quiet.'

'Death isn't as final as it used to be, Reuben.' Peter slumped in his chair, tired.

'He'd see the light, I'm sure of it! Join our cause. Understand why we did what we did to him.'

'Then let nature race its course. You said the man was old and badly beaten. Leave him be, let him die in his own time. I do understand why you did it. But if you wish to pursue this kind of sport in future, don't come running back to tell me about it like a bairn on his first Christmas. Keep it a secret. From me, my congregation and the lifers. Only then will your actions be hale and holy.'

Reuben nodded his assent. Above all else he needed his master's respect; without that, his death seemed meaningless. He left Peter's office and walked downhill to the main street, ignoring the patrolling guards and trotting into the Bottega del Gioiello, a lakeside hangout. Over the next hour or so other dieners filtered in, ordering drinks to keep the living proprietor, Mr Banks, happy.

Once all Reuben's comrades had gathered he explained how his meeting with Peter had progressed. A small candle on his table lit his face with an eerie glow.

'He didn't buy it,' Reuben explained. 'Too soft. Doesn't see the way forward as we do. Don't worry though,' he placated the gathering, 'we'll win him round. Up and at it, lads,' he smiled. The gang rose as one and rounded on Mr Banks.

'Come on gents,' Banks told his customers, his fat jowls creased into a smile. 'I'm warning you, I think you're getting a little overexcited. Why don't you settle down? Otherwise I'll have to give the guards a shout.'

This didn't wash with Reuben and his men. They gently persuaded Banks never to call the guards again.

Peter stood on his balcony, looking out across his town. Receiving Reuben that day, he'd had a glimpse of the future – a dark one for his ilk. Reuben's course of destruction was set, quenching a fire that had been burning in that boy's belly for months. Reuben's prejudice was infinitely greater than the old man's, but he understood that it gave his acolyte a reason to exist. Normals hated him, he could do something about it, so he went out and broke some heads. Spiritually simple. And a not-so-tiny part of him approved of the acolyte's thuggery – it was about time that the living tasted their own medicine.

On the ground below, someone was sweeping dirt from a path that circumvented a rowan tree. Birds flew through its leaves, chirruping happily. The regular sound of the sweeping brush gave Peter comfort, as the rhythmic motion of a rocking cot pleases a baby. The tree's shadow lengthened as the sun dipped behind him.

He did not live in the chaotic future, couldn't control it. He would do what he could with the present.

Reuben's next target was the owner of a launderette who had been overcharging residents. Reuben's group were armed with sticks, bats and bars. They were enough to send the laundry owner fleeing for her life, but she soon returned with an army of her own – her family.

The skirmish was short and decisive. The laundry lads came packing, wielding knives and firing guns at Reuben's rabble. No matter how riddled with bullet holes they became, the zombies kept on coming, surrounding the lifers and quelling them with fists and teeth.

Reuben maintained his strategy of not killing anyone – he didn't fancy being haunted, and living with the memory of that night seemed a bad enough fate. It wasn't yet time to swell his ranks with newcomers and he couldn't have his victims dead and quarantined. He needed them out and about in the world beyond the fence, spreading the word – don't mess with the deceased.

When Peter called his next press conference it was an exclusive one. He wanted to offer his perspective on the squabble in the laundry, but first he thanked Mark and Kim for their help, with Glen and Reuben present as witnesses. Peter's two bodyguards waited outside his office.

'You've both been invaluable to me as allies in this strange new world,' Peter admitted, sitting at his desk. The only other chair in the room was occupied by Kim; the others had to stand.

Mark held a handkerchief to his nose, offended by the smell of rotting skin. Flakes of dust corridored from the window to a sunspot near his feet and he was reminded that a high percentage of house dust was composed of dead skin tissue. He veiled his mouth discreetly.

'These guys have been in your pocket all along?' Glen raised his voice. Reuben took a threatening step towards him while Peter feigned earache.

'Not me.' Kim stood up, indignant. Mark's silence was conspicuous. 'You won't use me the way you've been manipulating this poor schmuck.' Mark fidgeted from side to side like a tot full of beans, anxious to leave. Glen expected him to raise his hand to ask to go to the loo.

'I use no one who does not wish to be used,' Peter replied in a reasonable tone. 'I have access to information, stories, news angles straight from the corpse's mouth. Mark distributes those stories in the papers and he gets paid. Twice.'

'You may find it hard to believe,' said Kim, standing up and grabbing her jacket, 'but I'm impartial. At least I try to be.'

'I'm the spokesman for my minority group. I channel information.'

'The kind you want to channel. Selective tidbits to further your own aims.'

'Isn't that what your media does?' Peter yelled. 'Pick and choose the stories that are told, the slants they're told from, the points of view? I'm a good guy, Ms Impartiality. I have my group's best interests at heart and you can carve that on my headstone, if I ever need one!'

Glen had never seen Peter lose his temper before and he guessed this was for effect, an act to put the point across. Kim stormed out of the Mausoleum that Peter had made his own, leaving Mark chuckling to himself.

'There's no such thing as an unbiased TV reporter,' he smiled. 'As soon as you sign on with a network – or a newspaper publisher, for that matter – you've got to take their interests into account. She'll learn.'

Glen turned on his old friend. 'You've got a lot to learn from her. Get out of here!'

'Sure. Whatever you say, buddy.' With a lingering, pitying look at Glen, Mark did as he was bid.

'Play nice with Kim,' Glen warned Peter. 'She's special to me.'

'I know.'

'Why did you want me here anyway? You want to slap me on the back too?'

'There's a little more to it than that. In my position, delicate information comes my way, some of which I keep to myself. Other news is too important not to share. Do you catch my meaning?'

'No.'

Peter glanced at Reuben, uncomfortable. 'The information I have concerns your death, G.G.'

'I never saw a certificate. Read a news clipping about it, courtesy of Mark. Salesman Snuffs It On The John. What an epitaph!'

'You don't know how you died.'

'Heart attack? Brain haemorrhage? Who can say? All I know is my heart's in the right place and I still got a mind of my own.'

'I can say,' Peter interrupted. 'You were murdered.'

'I knew it! I was way too young to die of natural causes. Who done it? Who killed me?'

'We're not entirely sure.' Another glance at Reuben. 'There are some unusual suspects.'

'You gotta find out for me.'

'We're working on it.'

VOLUME FOUR

Judgement Day

CHAPTER 14

Small Talk

Dead as a doorknob
Turned, twisted
Left with greasy hand marks.
Or a dodo
Stuffed, stuffy and ugly
Peered at in a glass case
Extinking in a dusty museum.
Or a line
Drawn by an editor,
Vexing a journalist.
Or an end
Where you can't go any further
Because there's a wall in the way.
Dead as me.

'Dead End'
A poem by Reuben Whitley

JENNA FELT BAD ABOUT what she'd said to Glen in the factory, not
so much because she'd been rude or spoken her mind, but because
he had politely accepted the comment. No anger or reproach, only
accession. Worst of all, he'd been humble. Like most members of the
general public, Jen didn't know that dieners could feel, and credited
them with limited intelligence. Most of her preconceived knowledge
came from late night Italian zombie movies, now popularised by
the diener phenomenon.

Sure, she'd watched Rick D on TV, but his on-camera persona
had been one of simple, plain-speaking looks-not-brains. And when
the looks had gone, Ricky had faded into obscurity, as documented

by gleeful tabloids, who loved to build celebs up then knock them down again – they had further to fall that way.

As she got to know Glen better and heard him enumerate Kim's virtues – no one could escape from that – she began to realise that he was blessed with some intellect (he used big words from time to time) and cared a great deal for his belle. Caring was a strong emotion, and this scared Jen. It was a lot easier to think of the dieners as automated cadavers; if they were real people, with good and bad thoughts, capable of love or anger, she would have to start considering them in ways she wasn't able to at the moment. She would have to care, too.

Jen cared about the starving children in Africa, but that didn't stop her from eating a double helping of pasta for lunch. She cared about the elderly paraded on TV by Help the Aged, but never called her Gran. And she spared a thought for the dogs and kitties promoted by the RSPCA, but often left her own pets home alone for days at a time.

The dead were different. She worked with them every day, saw them in the street, on the way home. When she started to imagine how she'd feel trapped in a rotting body, gradually losing her beauty, unable to escape and – worst of all – knowing what live people thought when they saw her... the results were revolting. So for the time being, Glen was an underpaid, jabbering robot. As a result, she couldn't approve of his relationship with Kim and resolved to do something about it.

It took her a long time to wheedle Glen's ring from his grasp. He'd gone on and on about it, how Peter had given it to him as a token of friendship, how it was a rare and wonderful item for a fan such as he. She tried convincing him that it might not be the genuine article, that she could have it authenticated for him. She had friends on the outside, after all; as a lifer, she was free to come and go as she pleased. No dice; Glen couldn't accept that Peter was capable of handing him a fake, of lying to him in such a way.

Persistent, she suggested it might help draw out his killer. 'My contacts can put the word about that this piece of... merchandise belongs to you now,' she told him over an Oxygen bagel. 'That's the bait. They come looking and we grab whoever gets too curious. It's obvious to me that whoever topped you did it for that film reel, to make some quick cash, like. The ring'll do the same business. But I'd need to borrow it for just a few days.'

Reluctantly, trustingly, clutching at invisible straws, Glen handed over the ring and promised not to tell anyone about the tentative scheme. The very next day Jen met the fabled heroine of Glen's yarns at a work do. Nothing fancy, just as much as the pickers and packers could afford – a drink at the end of the day at the new bowling alley. Dave insisted that Glen drag Kim along, and she was eager to meet the workmates. With the dieners drinking out of politeness, a boozed-up Jen soon managed to divert Kim into a secluded corner and chat with her.

'Nice that those two are getting on,' Dave commented.

'Kim gets on with everyone,' Glen smiled in return...

'So what's the story with you two?' Jen cut to the chase. 'What do you see in him? He's my work pal an' all. How do you put up with the smell, and the dangling flaps of skin, and his wee thin lips?'

'You've heard the expression, "it's what's inside that counts"? Well, that's what counts with Glen. I've seen what's inside him and it's all good. He worries about me and looks after me, more than any living man ever did. Unlike them he's not possessive.'

'He's grateful. Doesn't think he deserves a lady with a pulse. Have you thought that maybe he'd be better off with his own kind?'

'Is that what he said to you?' Kim watched the game as Dave got a strike.

'He says lots of things, mainly praising you. He won't always be so blinkered though.'

'You think I'll lose him.'

'We all lose the ones we love eventually. I'm alone. Lost my family,' Jen stared at her drink, 'they didn't come back.'

'I'm sorry.' Kim stopped watching the bowlers.

'I broke down once at work, told Glen what had happened. How lonely I was. Glen... consoled me. Said I was the only one who meant anything to him, that we deserved to be happy. But he didn't know how to tell you. I guess he left that up to me.'

'That's terrible.' By the tone of her voice, Kim obviously didn't believe Jen – until she saw the ring.

'Glen's lonely too. He hates that job, thinks it's beneath him. He was in a bad mood that day, and I made the mistake of trusting him. I don't feel like I can do that any more. That's why I wanted to show you this.'

Kim held the ring in the palm of her hand. The metal felt smooth and cold. 'I've noticed his mood swings, they seem to be getting worse.'

'Don't bother talking to him about this. He'll deny everything, of course.'

'This doesn't sound like my Glen. Still –'

'Don't tell me you're just with Glen for his personality,' Jen changed the subject, placing her hand on Kim's knee.

'I've got to admit it, I'm attracted to these dead guys. They're exotic, special. No other girl I know has one. He's introduced me to a different world. That outweighed all the comments from people who saw us together, and the stench and all the other things. Plus being with him pisses my family off, and that's no bad thing.'

'Surely..?'

'I was screwed out of an inheritance. Went to my little brother instead. So I have to keep yabbering away on telly while Corben – my brother – swans off to Greece on his yacht. Don't get me wrong, I'm devoted to what I do, but it gets so bloody hard sometimes.' Kim gave Jen a strange grin. 'They almost choked on their biscuits when I told them I was hanging around with Glen. They're starting to accept him now.' She plucked a snapshot from her purse.

'This is your parents?'

'My siblings. Some of them at least – I've got four brothers, two sisters. You should see us all whoop it up!'

'Your Mum and Dad passed away?'

'Plane crash. They did a Lazarus number on us, we contested the will and it was decided that as they were dead we should have the money anyway. Somehow Corben wheedled it all away from us, and I was left to cover the legal fees.'

'Where are they?'

'Mummy and Daddy? France, with the rest of the outcasts. They escaped before the big round-up. If anything they probably feel sorry for me, having to fend for myself. The acrimony's all burned out, I'm sure. No, it's Corben and the rest of the brood I wanted to annoy.'

'Well, thanks for telling me all this. This whole resurrection business has turned everything topsy-turvy. I know what you must think of me. I should never have –'

'I'm glad you did.'

Glen's team had won the game. With a grin of triumph, he turned towards the two women.

'Seems like all men are the same, alive or dead,' Kim told Jen.

'Please don't cause any trouble. I mean it. I need to keep this affair a secret. If it gets round work... all those people laughing behind my back or worse, trying to console me... You understand?'

'*Absolutement, oui,*' said Kim bitterly, '*bien sur, sans faut.*'

'Another drink?' Glen trotted up to the ladies, feeling flush with success.

'Not for me,' said Jen, 'I gotta go.'

'I think we should head off too,' said Kim in an ambivalent tone, reaching for her bag. 'I've had enough.'

'We've just got started! We're going to have a couple more drinks...'

'Fine. Stay, I'll call a taxi. Make my own way home.'

'No, no, I'll come with you.' Glen sounded like a child told that playtime was over. He bade farewell to his colleagues and drove Kim home. She sat in stony silence all the way.

Max was the rumour mill, spreading gossip and dispelling lies. He did not take great pleasure in his mongering; he did, however, see it as his duty to spread useful news and information amongst his fellow citizens. If knowledge was power then he was the conduit, with some surges of static thrown in.

Max found Glen near the lake, walking home from the warehouse.

'There's talk of giving us all a card,' Max told him. 'It ain't for a local library, I'm afraid.'

'An identity card.'

'You know it. To the researchers we're numbers, statistics. The cards will carry those numbers, our pictures, addresses. It will help the authorities to keep track of us.'

'Who did you hear this from?'

'Oh, everybody.' Max left to spread his news. Glen stood at the lakeside, staring at his ugly reflection. *What do we need cards for? Isn't it easy enough to spot us already?*

The authorities assured the public that plans were at their early stages, and the main purpose of the cards was to cut down on benefit fraud. Peter had already denounced the move in the papers, but Glen couldn't see what the fuss was about. He already had his driving license, which he used as a form of identification. It even had a photo of him on it, along with his signature.

Back at the shop, Tony had once hit upon the idea of giving badges to the staff. This would differentiate the slouchy, laid back shop assistants from the slouchy, laid back customers. Glen had always considered himself opposed to badges until that moment, feeling that it smacked of depersonalisation, pinning everyone down with numbers and allegiances. But he hadn't piped up at the staff meeting, meekly accepting Tony's directive. It was easier to go with the flow, keeping the boat on an even keel instead of rocking it for the sake of your principles.

Tony's idea, like most of his grand schemes, had fallen by the wayside but Glen remembered that meeting vividly. Now he'd carry his card with pride, no danger of hypocrisy, and it would probably make life easier for him. He would not have to engage in conversation at the bank. Instead he would flash his plastic and let it do the talking for him.

Allow me to introduce myself.
My whole life is replicated on this card. You can see what I am at a glance and if I lose it I am nobody, nothing, at least until it's replaced. What do you think of me then? Am I approved?

Peter found him, bodyguards in tow. Glen was surprised when the LAD director invited him for a mocha at Starbucks. Peter was a VIP, with a decreasing amount of time to spend with riffraff like him. Glen didn't drink mocha, either. He accepted the invitation anyway.

Peter led Glen off to the café, where Glen asked for tap water.

'It's very important to me that you understand where I'm coming from,' said Peter, earnest. He was dressed casually for once, in a green sweatshirt over a grey T-shirt, a black baseball cap with a dark blue peak, black trousers, a little too short, and mint and fawn argyle patterned socks.

'Why's that?'

'We make good allies. I need your help for a couple of reasons, my friend. First, we go back a while. You're the missing link between my time as a lost lamb and my newfound role as a shepherd.'

'Baa.'

'Second, you're a normal, everyday dead guy. You represent the apathetic many who don't want to get involved –'

'That's not true!'

'Let me finish. You don't... you're not a trouble maker, you'd rather stay in and watch television and keep your head down. But you don't watch the tube, do you Glen?'

'If I could get ahold of a set, I still wouldn't be able to afford the licence.'

'Excuse me for asking, but what do you do instead?'

'I spend time with my girlfriend. Do crossword puzzles. Think I use my brain.'

'You use your mind. You could be using your body too – to help me! You have no money or prospects. That's what my organisation's all about. Providing men like yourself with a chance, a break away from apathy.'

'I don't know.' Peter had never done Glen any harm, so he didn't mention that the LAD juggernaut made him wary. There was nothing bad about it *per se*, it wasn't a cult or a coven. It just wasn't his bag. 'I've never joined an organisation in my life.'

'There's nothing to join. You help when you can, that's all. You'll have a widescreen television set delivered to your door by the end of the day.' A bribe. This was something that Glen could understand. If every man had his price, Glen belonged in the bargain basement.

'Okay,' he nodded, remembering how his children had bugged him for an HD TV. 'A new telly and you help me find my killer. You are still looking, right?'

'Even Donald Claig is doing everything he can to get some solid information.'

This raised an eyebrow.

'He wants to see justice done, too. He has many influential contacts in the Lothian police.'

'OK, I'll help you. One more thing, Peter. I want to see my wife and kids.'

'I understand.'

'If I notice anything weird going on, anyone getting ripped off or brainwashed, I go straight to Kim. *Comprende*?'

'No funny business.' His fingers all breadcrumbs, Peter took Glen's hand and shook it firmly.

'What d'you want me to do?' asked Glen.

'Something delicate, I know you're good for it. Reuben is a little heavy-handed. People promise money to me and forget, so it's his job to remind them. I would like you to keep an eye on him for me, to see he doesn't get up to any mischief.'

'You've never set me wrong before, Peter.'

'Trust me, my friend.' Peter sucked at his piping hot mocha.

'I should've paid for the drinks.' Glen was concerned.

'Nonsense, I've come into some capital. Call it a bankroll I'm on. I could handle the national debt.' Smiling, Peter led Glen to his limo.

Glen sank into the plush seats and found himself facing Reuben, with a tough-looking lump named Kieron acting as chauffeur. By the time they'd settled down and got comfortable, the limo had reached the Mausoleum. Peter got out of the car, waving as it turned towards Boot Hill.

The first few visits presented no problems, with flat dwellers greeting Reuben cordially and finding a few quid or writing a cheque to cover missed payments. *This isn't so bad,* thought Glen as he cruised round a corner in the whisper-quiet limo. *I could get used to this.*

Kenny was one of the debtors on their list and Glen was curious to see what he'd done to his home. There was a sign on his door that read NO BURGLARS PLEASE I GOT NOTHIN. Inside, scraps cut from magazines decked the walls; models and stars with perfect faces and transparent lives. *Less pricey than Picassos.* Kenny didn't offer an explanation for his décor, but Glen knew that he liked to watch *Trading Spaces.* He said as much to Reuben as they left the building, drawing an 'aha!' from his gruff companion. That made sense of the whole thing.

'Who's giving you all this grief at work?'

'Wow, news travels fast round these parts, doesn't it?' Glen shook his head. 'Not grief really. There's a lifer called Jenna who doesn't like dieners.'

'I could fix her for you.' Glen couldn't believe what he was hearing.

'This next little feller,' Reuben chuckled, 'was captivated with the Chief. He promised all that he owned to the organisation, even signed it over. Then he goes and changes his mind, doesn't he? Won't give us a thing. D'you think that's right?'

'Anyone should be allowed to change their mind.' Glen refused to be bullied.

'We gave him the right to read the small print. I don't think he bothered. He was so happy, you should've seen him. Clapped his hands together he did, couldn't wait to pitch in. Here we go.' Reuben led the way to a newsagent's, graffiti on the wall. His target lived in a small flat above the shop.

A knock on the door gained a rapid response – shuffling footsteps, a throat being cleared, a latch clicking. At the last moment Reuben whispered, 'You stand there,' sidling away so that he was out of sight behind Glen. A wizened diener opened the door, his face expectant. Glen could see that this was a lonely man glad of a visitor.

As Reuben stepped into view the crinkly face transformed. Now the old man was scared, tried to shut the door. It was too late, Reuben barged his way in.

'You know why I'm here, you old gnome.'

'Leave me alone.'

Lost for words, Glen took a look around. There didn't seem much for the occupant to give – a transistor radio, tatty armchair, ceramic Pekinese and a few tarnished medals on the mantelpiece.

'You gave a promise to Mr Foothill,' Reuben growled. 'Now you gotta keep it.'

'I'll deal with him, not the likes of you.'

Reuben picked up the ceramic dog, chucking it aside in disgust. It shattered on the hearth.

'At this moment in time, I am him. I represent him and I'm the one holding this piece of paper.' Reuben held up the document in question, the old man's sheet of shame. Glen told Reuben to go easy.

'He doesn't have a lot to give anyway,' Glen explained in a gentle voice. His partner's tone became increasingly hostile.

'It's principle, innit?' Reuben bellowed in the gnome's face, 'I'm a man of principle! I ain't got a lot but I still got scruples. Without them we'd be nothing.' Under his long black coat was a machete, which he promptly unsheathed. He used it to sever the gnome's right hand. His victim howled, even though he felt no pain – it was a howl of despair.

'You said you wanted to lend a hand. Now you have.' Reuben sheathed his machete, shoved the hand in his jacket pocket and left the flat. Glen stopped behind, trying to placate the old man, who screamed at him to get out. He had to, running downstairs and along the street to catch up with Reuben.

'What the hell do you think you were doing back there?' Reuben yelled at him. 'You were supposed to be backing me up, not getting in the bloody way.'

'Are you a psycho or something?'

Reuben puffed with pride. 'Top of my resume,' he snickered, clambering into the limousine. 'Need a lift home?'

'How can you act so casual?'

'Practice. You know deadheads can't feel no pain.'

'You caused that man psychological pain. You've disabled him.'

'I don't believe in all that Freudian jumbo mumble. I'm Peter's strong arm. I wouldn't be very strong if I acted weak, now would I?' Glen was unable to argue with this flawless logic.

'What've you gotten me into?'

Peter was reading through the rough draft of a speech to the Bonetown Dead But Not Resting Committee when Glen burst into his plush office. Peter had been expecting a visit from Glen in good time, but the indignation on his face made the director sit up and take notice.

'Reuben off the rails again?'

'That's an understatement. You've done a lot of good things for me, made me more comfortable. I could have been happy and hopeful if your court jester hadn't pulled his nasty stunt.' Glen described the events of the previous night. 'I don't think you've ever been frank with me. Tell me everything or I walk out now and to hell with your widescreen TV.'

'You know why we're called dieners?' Peter stopped Glen's rant with this unexpected question.

'There was that big star, Ricky, given a good prod by the fickle finger of fame. Plus it's the name for people who assist pathologists during post mortems and suchlike.'

'Very good. There's a third reason, more sinister. It's German for servant. We're already second class citizens. Many of us have taken on poorly paid manual labor. The Government helps us a little, but not too much. It's in every lifer's interest to keep us in our place, below the poverty line.'

'Your class struggle's got nothing to do with chopping hands off left, right and centre.'

'Reuben is an unstoppable force. You are an unmovable slob. It's up to you to curb his wild streak.'

'Why? Why me? I'm not equipped and I don't have the gumption.'

'There are two polar worlds of understanding, positive and negative, hopeful and hateful. It's up to you which Reuben plugs into. In one, you know something good will survive out of all the dross; in the other, everything rots. You have a conscience and you have intelligence. Use these qualities to reason with Reuben, for the good of us all. We cannot remain the servants of lifers. We have to be strong, show them there's more to us than the horror show they see at first glance. To grow strong, we must use foot soldiers like Reuben. He has a high opinion of you, you know.'

'Why don't you chuck him out of your organisation? I know you like him and all, but what if he does something like this again? What if he turns on me' – the thought Glen hadn't dared to entertain all night – 'or you?'

Peter shook his head. 'Better to keep him close, watch him, use him.'

'Like you're using me?'

'You'll help me voluntarily because you know it's the right thing to do – the only course of action open to you in your present dingy state. Also, like I said you have a conscience. You would be beside yourself if you left Reuben alone to carry out more mayhem.'

'I asked you to tell me what's really going on here.'

'Power, Glen. Only with power – financial, political, spiritual – can we make the world understand how important we are.'

'Tomorrow, if Reuben behaves himself and I'm still in one piece, I'll stay on the team. I won't stand by and see him hurt anyone else, though.'

Glen left the office as noisily as he'd entered, slamming the door shut on his way. Peter looked down at his Dead But Not Resting speech.

> You have consciences and you are intelligent. Use these qual-
> ities for the good of us all. We cannot remain the servants
> of lifers. We have to be strong, show them there's more to
> us than the horror show they see at first glance.

Thanks to Peter's financial assistance, Glen didn't have to go back to the warehouse, but he had no wish to leave his colleagues in the lurch so he did everything properly, giving a week's notice and completing the month's quota as efficiently as he could. He knew he'd miss his colleagues' camaraderie – and the job gave him an excuse to avoid Reuben's company.

'I had a nice long chat with Kim,' Jen told him during their lunch break. 'She doesn't seem so stuck up.'

'I haven't heard from her for days,' Glen admitted, attacking Dave's punch bag with vigor. 'We've both been busy. Maybe it's because I always burn the toast.'

'She doesn't have a high opinion of her family, does she?' Jen chomped on a crusty roll.

'Thinks they've got more money than sense.'

'She'd do anything to piss them off,' Jen continued to wheedle. 'Get in trouble with the police. Embarrass her siblings in public. Bring the wrong kind of man home.' Glen's eyes widened.

'I never had any brothers or sisters. If I did, I'd do my utmost to keep them. You got any?'

'Nope.' They strayed off the subject, but Jen's work was done. Glen began to wonder why his girlfriend hadn't called, whether he was being used again – this time as a shock troop to make her kin feel bad. He would have to ask her – if he ever saw her again.

'I'll miss you, mate,' Dave clapped Glen on the back heartily, 'even if you are rotting. You started a bit slow but once you got the hang of the way we operate round here, you were great.' His voice dropped a notch in volume. 'You ain't been mentioning your missus so much recently. Everything rosy at home?'

Glen hit the punch bag harder than ever. 'I knew you lot were getting fed up with me going on, so I thought I'd better give it a rest before I replaced this tatty old thing.'

'First stage over, is it?'

'Maybe.'

'First stage?' asked Jen innocently.

'Yeah, you know,' Dave smiled, 'that passionate stage when you first meet someone. Might be a week, a month. The days pan out, you're exploring each other's feelings.'

'Ooh. There are more stages?'

'She doesn't know about the five stages.' Dave gave Glen a can't-believe-it look. 'Allow me to elucidate. The next stage is when you enter the comfort zone, you feel safe with your partner but that original spark has lost some of its, well, spark.'

'In the third stage, your eyes start to roam.' Glen gave Jen an exaggerated sideways stare. 'Then in the fourth it's your hands.'

Jen slapped Dave's fingers away from her waist. 'And the fifth stage?'

'Not everybody gets that far.' Dave wore a hurt expression. 'By then, you're doomed. Or married.'

With a special order on, Dave and Jen had elected to work late at the warehouse that evening. They needed the overtime and they wanted to spend some time alone together – they were becoming an item, ribbed mercilessly by their colleagues.

All by themselves in the dark shell of their workspace, they were so busy chatting about their favourite subject – football – and packing up the last-minute order that they hardly heard Reuben enter with the grim-faced Kieron and his other lackeys. He slammed the metal door down, getting the couple's attention.

'Come to pick up the order?' Dave asked cheerily. 'You're a little early. We're nearly done, don't you worry.'

'I'm not worried and we ain't come to collect boxes. We want *her*.' Reuben pointed at Jen. Dave moved his imposing bulk to block her from the interlopers' view as she ran to cower behind the conveyer belt.

'Whatever you want to take out on her, you can discuss with me.' There was nothing to discuss. With a sneer, Reuben signalled his men to outflank Dave and set upon him. Fists flailing, Dave tried to keep them at bay. As he defended himself, Kieron moved around a stack of film-wrapped boxes to reach Jen.

'Who are you? What have I ever done to you?' she cried as Kieron grabbed her arm. In his free hand he held a meat cleaver.

'You don't give a rat's fanny about me,' Kieron answered, 'that's enough.' Dave struggled to get to Jen's side.

'Who sent you?' she asked, watching horrified as Dave was pushed to the ground with a crash.

'Glen sends his regards,' Reuben replied, digging out his trusty hunting knife, 'little piggy.'

'Get your hands away from her or I'll knock your block off,' Dave snarled at Kieron. He leapt to his feet and set about himself, forcing Reuben to retreat with the rest of his crew. Realising he'd been abandoned, Kieron flung his cleaver at Dave and it caught the ex-boxer a glancing blow on the shoulder.

Dave touched the wound with the tip of his index finger and tasted the blood. 'Tomato sauce,' he smiled. 'Betcha can't remember the last time you bled, can you, deadhead?' Dave punched Kieron full in the face, forcing the diener back towards the punch bag and away from Jen. After several blows, there was a loud crack and Kieron's skull left his body. The head flew through the air and landed in a half-full box of preschool books.

'Told you I'd knock your block off,' Dave told the headless corpse before him. With a curious wheeze, it collapsed and lay still.

'Did you hear what he said?' Jen asked breathlessly.

'About Glen? Yeah. We should have a word or two with our gabby workmate, don't you think?'

Dave drove Jen over to her flat in his old Cadillac. He called it the lovemobile because it had been the site of many fondly remembered nights of passion. He'd bought it from his former trainer in Leith for a hundred quid; the codger had been getting too decrepit to drive. He'd passed away soon afterwards and Dave liked to believe that his coach was looking down on him whenever he made a journey, a kind of guardian AAngel. He didn't let the notion put him off those nights of romance, but the car had always been reliable and prang-free, unique in his motoring history.

'Of course, Glen always had it in for you,' Jen was saying. Dave nodded, though he took everything his paramour said with a pinch of potassium. 'You're strong, handsome, full of vitality,' she continued. 'Everything he's not.'

'You make me sound like one of them dogs in a Pedigree Chum ad. You gonna tell me I've got a glossy coat too?'

'He's jealous of you, lover. And jealous men do crazy things.'

'Like setting a bunch of goons on a pal? You've got a funny way with words. Never beat around the bush when you can burn it to the ground. Sure you didn't say anything to raise his ire?'

'His what?'

'Ire. Get his blood up. Piss the poor sod off.'

'I didn't have that much to do with him. We certainly weren't enemies, although I suppose I get on better with Kim than him.'

'Hmm.' Mention of Glen's dark-haired darling got Dave thinking. Kim had met Jen on the night everyone from work had gone bowling. The two ladies had indulged in an intense conversation, after which Kim had stomped off home, Glen following meekly behind. One minute the diener'd been on top form enjoying the evening, the next he'd left with a mope. Glen hadn't seen Kim since that night as far as Dave knew. Was Jen responsible?

This possibility saddened Dave. He'd been very happy for his dead friend, realising that the relationship warmed Glen with a ray of hope for the future. If Jen had shattered that hope for kicks, she deserved a fright from Glen's mates.

'You've got a lot of explaining to do!' Dave bellowed when Glen answered his door. The diener was in his jammies and rubbing his eyes. 'I thought you guys didn't sleep,' he said suspiciously.

'Not very often. Just going through the motions, it makes life seem more natural.'

'Nah, you're supernatural. I'd be proud of it if I was you.' Glen ushered his colleagues into his humble hovel. He'd tried to give the interior a lick of paint, dripping Dulux all over the carpet. In the living room, Dave gave an appreciative whistle when he saw the Dance DVD box set, recently supplied by Peter.

'Went the whole hog, huh? That's a far cry from those tatty paperbacks I brought you.'

'I like those paperbacks best, mate.'

'We got a visit at work the now,' Dave growled, regaining the thread. Glen stuck the kettle on. 'Seemed like you'd sent 'em. Tried to mess with this young lady.'

'God.' Glen buried his face in his hands, guessing at once what had happened. 'I didn't think he'd actually do anything so stupid.'

'Fallen in with a bad crowd?' Dave sounded genuinely concerned.

'The baddest. The power-mad Peter and his band of happy hooligans.'

'The LADdies? I thought they were good guys.'

'All this doesn't mean shit,' Glen exclaimed. 'Did they hurt you?'

'I'm okay,' Jen assured him. 'Shook me up a bit. Scared me. Dave came to the rescue.'

'I'll bet he did. He's a real action hero. Wait here. I'll sort this.'

The kettle whistled. Glen didn't bother keeping any milk in – he didn't have a fridge for that matter – but there was granulated coffee and sugar in the kitchen cupboard. Dave and Jen helped themselves while he wandered out into the night.

Glen passed Death Row and crossed a scraggy lawn. He hadn't ventured out after dark since his last encounter with Nail's gang, but he'd seen neither hide nor hair of them in recent days. He would have heard on the ghouls' grapevine if they'd been relocated or (pigs might fly) arrested by the Bonetown police. They'd probably got bored and drifted off to terrorise another neighborhood.

A dog barked in the distance, its owner yelling at it to shut up. The canine ignored him. Glen heard a creaking sound, one he hadn't heard before, one that stood out from the other night sounds. He had to investigate, a tremble of fear in his belly. He felt like he could handle the gang if he faced them again, but he'd fooled himself into thinking that before. He cast around for a weapon to be on the safe side, couldn't see anything. Eventually he settled for a dustbin lid that he could use as a shield. He could even hit someone with it if the fancy took him.

There was just a shadow first, moving to and fro. As Glen drew closer, shield held in front of him, he saw a dark shape dangling from a lamppost. Dropping his dustbin lid, Glen ran up to the shape, which kicked and jiggled, suspended on a rope noosed round its neck. Nail's neck. He'd been lynched, the rope tight around his throat, though there was no breath to choke from his body. Glen couldn't tell how long the kid had been hanging there – not long, probably, as lynching was a night-time pursuit, with the dusk shadows offering the least chance of being detected – but the kid was still panicking.

Glen wanted to leave Nail there until he saw the look on the boy's face. It was imploring, anguished, struggling, teeth-grinding. Glen shimmied up the lamppost and tried to untie the noose. The lad's weight made this impossible, so Glen took a knife from Nail's belt. He sawed at the rope and winced as Nail collapsed onto the pavement with an echoing whack. Sliding back down the post, Glen loosened the hempen necktie and helped his nemesis into a sitting position.

'Deadheads,' the hanged lad rasped, 'my own kind. I know I've pissed you off –'

'I had nothing to do with this,' said Glen, exasperated. 'Surely even you can see that.'

'I know, I know. I mean, I thought if I got in real trouble it would be with the skins, not your sort. Nowhere's safe these days.'

Glen offered a hand to Nail to get him onto his feet, but he was ignored. The kid wanted to do it himself, the little monster. Fair enough, Glen could appreciate that, especially from an independent sort like Nail. But time was short – the rest of the gang could also be in danger.

'Where did you see them last?'

'Tamzie's pad. Chillin' out there, listening to music. I popped out to get some Buckie… then they jumped me.' Nail had put up a good fight, as expected, but he'd been outnumbered. They'd had the rope ready and had told him what they thought of him – not much. Glen and Nail raced along the street, across the patchy lawn and deserted car park, to the graffiti-grubbed tenement that Nail called home. Inside they began to climb the stairs. Tamzie's severed head stopped them both mid-rush.

She looked peaceful, even pretty. Her eyes were glazed over but that was nothing new. Nail's trademark snarl softened and he gave his girlfriend one last kiss before ascending to the next storey and another head – and another on the third floor.

'We've got to find their remains,' Nail whispered, 'put them back together.' Glen was dubious. He was pretty sure that no one could survive dismemberment – and he was right.

Three bodies lay in Tamzie's flat, one marked 'tramp,' another 'vandal' and the third 'thief.' The gang's crimes had been thoughtless, ruthless, attention-grabbing, and this was their harsh punishment.

'No one deserves this,' he said quietly. 'Not even you creatures.' Nail was collecting up a few items – a walkman, some stolen credit cards, CDs and empty cola bottles.

'It's too late for them,' he huffed. 'Let's get out of here before the pigs come truffling round.'

Glen found Nail's attitude surprisingly callous. He didn't know what kind of reaction he'd been expecting – for the lad to break down, a blubbing mass, or to suddenly convert to devout Christianity, perhaps; these were Nail's friends, one of the bodies belonged to his lover. Glen put the cold attitude down to shock, but not for the last time he found himself wondering whether he'd done the right thing, cutting Nail free from his scaffold. 'If I hadn't, somebody would've,' he told himself as they left the tenement. 'What are you going to do with that stuff?' he asked Nail.

'Sell it.' Nail dissolved into the inky night, leaving Glen to listen to the screams of whoever had just found the heads on the banisters. By the time darkness was dispelled by the flashing lights of two patrol cars, Nail was long gone.

It took time to fill in the appropriate reports and answer the cops' questions. Dawn was approaching when Glen reached Peter's office.

'You're doing a grand job.' Peter was seated at his desk, with Reuben standing at his right hand side.

'I don't know if you're aware of what's going on out there, on your streets...'

'Calm down, my friend.' Peter offered Glen a seat; it was refused.

'You fancy yourself the head of some sect, but this –'

'It sounds like you're the one who's sect obsessed. As far as I'm concerned, the crucifix has been replaced by the television aerial as a symbol of our times. The country is a vast cemetery for audiences dosed on cathodes. We are more alive than any of those telly viewing vegetables. We are not voyeurs, we are voyagers.'

'Attacking the living is bad enough. Now we're fighting each other as well.'

'You knew of the attacks on lifers and you did nothing. You are complicit, G.G. Yet we have more important matters to discuss.'

'What could be more..?' Glen sank into the chair. 'Misbah.'

'No sign of her, G.G. She's not at any of the contact addresses you gave us. Nobody knows where she is.'

'That's just like her, to disappear and start a new life with my children. So what's this latest bombshell you've got for me?' The penny dropped. 'My murder.'

'Your murderer. Vian Lucas.'

The Oxygen Bar offered a rich variety of coffees and, bagels for customers to enjoy. Although the café was seldom quiet and there wasn't much elbow room, Glen and Kim always managed to find a table or space next to the counter to sit at and read the papers. Glen would scan them quickly, looking for a diener story or a byline from Mark; Kim pored over every page. It was in this establishment that Glen met up with his girlfriend for the first time in days.

'I've missed you,' he told her, offering a gentle kiss on the cheek. 'What happened?'

'You happened. I heard some stuff about you – made me think twice about us.'

'Heard stuff from who?'

'I can't say. Sworn to secrecy.'

'I'm the guy who listens, remember? Spill the beans.'

'She didn't give me any great details. Started me thinking, that's all.' Misbah! Glen had known all along. His wife wanted him back and had spun some crap to keep Kim away from him. Now he had the thrill of winning back the TV reporter, the great love of his death, a job that he'd enjoy immensely. Where to start?

'Fancy a bagel? I'm buying.'

'Sorry for the silent treatment. I needed time to work out how to handle this.'

'This?'

'Us. Our strange relationship.' Glen understood – they'd reached the dreaded third stage. 'No more bagels, or Oxygen coffee or anything like that,' said Kim firmly. 'No more walks in the cemetery. No more knocking on the mortician's door then running away shouting, "have you got a stiffy, mister?" And definitely no more roller skating round Pegg Square. My ankles weren't built for that sort of nonsense. I need a normal guy, it's nothing personal.'

'Not even the four pound one with whipped cream and blueberries?'

Kim didn't answer, shaking her head. She dipped her hand into her pocket and gave Glen the silver ring, in a mirror image of Peter's original handover.

'Where did you get this?' Glen slumped against a crumb-covered table, the ring spinning in front of him, catching stray rays of artificial light.

'Jen gave it to me. You said it was for the one person you loved. I guess you made good on the delivery.'

'Jen's crazy.'

'She must be to get mixed up with you. What were you thinking? No, I don't want to know. I just wanted to end it, *finito*.'

Glen knew that he had to say something to stop her from leaving. 'It's you. You're the one this ring is for.' He held up the offending object, showed the engraving inside. The name JOHN DANCE had been replaced with another.

'So much for collectability. This isn't worth so much now,' Kim muttered.

'More to me.'

Kim ran the uppermost tip of her finger across the words. KIM CLARKE. He loved her that much.

'So how did my rival get a hold of this if it's oh-so-precious?' Kim wanted to know.

'Rival? I wanted to find out who killed me. Jen said she'd help – if she could borrow the ring to draw out the murderer. But that doesn't matter now. Peter's discovered the truth.'

Kim put the ring back in her pocket. 'Who killed you?'

'Vian Lucas. An old customer of mine from the video store.'

'How do you know for sure?'

'He always was one burger short of a happy meal. Besides, Peter checked it out. He's put a lot of effort into it.'

'If Peter told you your arse was made of blue cheese would you eat it?'

'I never liked blue cheese,' he said, his expression blank. 'It makes sense, that's all.'

'Why?'

'He fits the profile. The only person I ever knew loony enough to top me.'

'I find that hard to believe. You reckon this Vian guy's the cuprit because Peter says so? I bet you read your horoscope every day, eh?'

'Peter helped me when I was in the deepest trouble I've ever been in.'

'He made you a fugitive.'

'I've made up my mind. I'm sure of it – Vian Lucas must be my murderer.' Glen snatched a menu from its stand, pretending to read it. 'He killed me. Now I'll return the favour.'

'Is that one of your movie lines?' Kim folded her arms. 'You're not a superspy, Glen.'

'Some of my favourite heroes are dead.'

'If you're going on a killing spree you might as well take Reuben with you.' Glen couldn't hold her gaze. 'Reuben's going?' she asked, incredulous.

'He insisted.' Glen shrugged.

'I'll bet he did,' said Kim, tears forming in her eyes.

'When I get back... I'd like to see you again. You could stay over, I'd get a new calendar for you. When you used to sleep in my bed I'd lie beside you, listen to your breathing and it was the most sensual thing I've ever heard.' Glen looked away, hoping that he wasn't scaring Kim. She was fearless.

'I'll be here,' she said, 'as a friend, if nothing else. As long as you get back in one piece.'

'It's a done deal.'

'Did you really lie with me all night long?' Kim smiled.

'Every chance I got. I felt content. Besides, I like to see you nakey.'

'C'mon. My arse is skinny as a wine rack.'

Before he ordered a bagel for himself, Glen told Kim his plan.

'I'm going to see Dave Barr,' he told her solemnly. 'I need something smuggled...'

'How you doin'?' Dave was finishing up some paperwork in his office, a bandage wound round his shoulder.

'I ain't got nothing for ya. But I do need a helping hand.'

'I'm all outta favours. Us businessmen have got to think about our profit margins.'

'You told me to ask if I ever needed anything. You said I could count on you.'

'For a price. Put in a good word for me with your bosom buddy Peter, a real good word this time, and your wish is granted oh master.' Dave folded his arms and nodded his head.

'Alright. I promise.'

'Good enough.'

'Then do this for me: I need you to bust me out.'

CHAPTER 15

The Great Escape

GLEN AND REUBEN WAITED until the last minute before making their farewells. That way there was less chance of arousing suspicion. They met in the church, with Peter, Kenny, Max and Dave among those present.

'I'll miss you all, that goes without saying.'

'Why're you saying it then?'

'Some guys need things spelled out,' said Glen with a good-natured grin. 'I won't forget working with you. Or your mangy old hound.'

Max asked Glen to let everyone outside know what was really going on in the compound. Glen knew that he'd have to keep schtum if he wanted to keep his flat, but he promised to try.

'My friends on the outside have set up a safehouse for you on some old farmland of mine. They're moving your Mum there as we speak,' Peter said. 'Reuben has the address.' He didn't seem too happy that Reuben was accompanying Glen, and Glen appreciated the sentiment.

'My Dad too, right?'

Peter didn't answer the question, but insisted that Glen take his limo.

'For keeps?' Glen frowned. 'It would be way too conspicuous.'

'You need to get as far as the gate without being challenged. My windows are tinted, the guards won't stop you; it's my car or nothing. The tank's full, here are the keys. Trust me!'

'Go on, trust him,' said Reuben. 'We can bust right through the gates!' Glen was tempted.

'I don't know, Peter. That limousine – I've got a problem with it.' This was hard for Glen to admit but as usual, he was taken aback by Peter's generosity. 'It's a status symbol given to you by Claig. It says you're different from anybody else here, better even. The man who has that car –'

'Will be you.' Peter passed him the keys. 'This possession shows that I've bettered myself. That's why I drive it around here, even though I'm forbidden to leave. It gives the inhabitants of this growing town hope. They, too, can improve their lot and achieve great things.'

'Spare the speech.'

'The car's waiting right outside.'

'Great. So I can show off my status.'

'You're not allowed out of here,' Kenny reminded Glen. 'You know what will happen if you're caught?'

'A one way trip to the morgue, hold very tight please, no stopping. Then a tag on one of my few remaining toes and I'm shoved in an icebox for eternity.'

'Wait a minute.' Dave cleared his throat. 'What about my plan?'

'Your plan?' Peter turned away from Dave in an unmistakably dismissive move.

'Yeah, uh, Dave was going to get me out.'

Peter ignored Glen's comment. 'Don't let anyone see these keys.' He wrapped his hand around Glen's. 'And don't tell anyone where you're going.'

'Sure,' Glen nodded, looking round at his friends and making a zip-your-lip sign.

The keys burned a hole in his trouser pocket. He couldn't wait to get out of Bonetown; maybe he would be able to get out into the countryside, amongst the trees, in the fresh air.

'Take care of yourself in that big, wide world,' said Max, all gruff and paternal. 'Stay out of mischief.'

Don't trust any of those living losers,' Kenny warned, 'not even your own folks. They see you as a different person now.'

'Dogs don't like walking corpses as a rule. Except for Randy.

They like bones to sit still so they can fetch 'n' carry them, not move around wrapped in overalls. So take extreme care. They may not be as mean-looking as my hound, but they got a hefty bite and it's all for you.'

'He's right,' Dave nodded, 'I've seen the guards training these mutts. Givin' them diener garb to sniff. And they don't lunge for the polite parts neither.'

'If you value your family jewels, stay out of sight and downwind. Goodbye, Glen Glass. Thanks for it all.'

Nobody said goodbye to Reuben; they were all glad to see the back of him.

Out in the street Glen stopped still, staring at Peter's limo. He still didn't like the idea of driving the fancy automobile, nor did he look forward to smashing it into the main gates. Armed guards, steel and barbed wire would slow him down some.

'You're not really going to drive that jalopy are you?' asked Dave, who had followed Reuben and Glen out of the church. 'It'll be mashed to paper clips when it hits those gates.'

'You think?' Dave's plan did promise to solve Glen's problems. 'Peter's given me a chance to escape. A strong chance.'

'And what happens if you do get out? That limo's ultra conspicuous. I've got my lovemobile sitting right outside the compound for you, ready and waiting. You and Reuben can hop in, no one will say anything.'

'So we drive the limo up to the gates,' said Reuben, 'smash through 'em, wallop, then jump out and take the pash wagon.'

'Too noisy. They'd get you in between vehicles.' Dave folded his arms to signify that his word was final. 'My car's at your disposal, and less conspicuous than Mr Fancy Pants' ride.'

'I'm not so sure about that.'

Reuben shook his head. 'You can't saunter up to the gates with us in tow. No dieners allowed outside, right?'

'Right,' Glen had to agree.

Dave clapped a hand on Glen's shoulder. 'This isn't the first breakout I've helped with, ken? Let's go with my plan.'

Glen looked at his old neighbour, havering.

'Please?'

'What should I do with these?' Glen held up the limo keys on their thick leather fob.

'I'll find a good home for them.' Dave took them and, as soon as Glen wasn't looking, chucked them in the nearest gutter.

The three men made for the forest area. Using the trees as cover, Dave led them towards his lovemobile. Tonight the custodians seemed especially alert and active.

'You'd think they'd have got my note telling them to give me an easy time 'cos I'm smuggling two deadheads out tonight,' smirked Glen's friend, taking the lead through the dense foliage. The wind hissed through the branches, covering the noisy trio as they crunched through the undergrowth. The dawn light caught a spider's tripwire thread, suspended between two trees. Glen stepped gingerly over it; Reuben bust through it, spilling the spinner from its painstakingly constructed house.

'Go low!' Dave ushered Glen and Reuben onto their bellies and they crawled past a trundling digger, the driver half asleep at the controls, headlights spilling onto the edge of the forest. Reuben caught his shirt sleeve on an upstart root.

'I shoulda nabbed some camouflage gear for this gig. Gimme more warning next time, eh pal?' Dave joked.

'I'll take the car next time like a normal person would,' Glen replied. 'Maybe if you weren't wearing that heavy overcoat you might find it easier to move.'

'It's necessary,' barked Dave, 'to conceal stuff in.'

'What *stuff*?'

'You'll see when we get to the fence.'

'Why don't you speak up,' Reuben whispered, 'so the whole place can hear you?'

'I'm a pro. I do this every day, twice on Sundays. Leave it to the –' Dave got up off his hands and knees to greet a guard that had just found him, '– expert.'

Glen stayed out of sight, holding Reuben back with him. If he'd had breath to hold, it would have been held tight. A growling Alsatian was at the custodian's heel, its nose not far from Glen's torn sleeve.

'How's that Tivo doohickey working out?' Dave asked the guard.

'Greaty great. I can pause a live TV show, watch replays... I don't miss anything. Like you promised.'

Apparently, no one was immune to Dave's charms or trinkets.

Half the staff in the complex had well-greased palms, allowing Glen and his friends to reach the perimeter without many more delays. Still, the men remained cautious and quite rightly so – Donald Claig was standing at the main gate, smoking a cigarette, armed guards beside him. Dave ducked behind a skip, dragging Reuben and Glen with him.

'Looks like he's waiting for something,' Glen grumbled. 'How would he know we were coming?'

'I anticipated this. Glen, come with me. Reuben, you hold back till we're sure the coast is clear.'

Honey-coloured daylight was slowly filling the town. Dave and Glen found few shadows to hide in as they ran in parallel to the fence, with only a gravelly open space between themselves and the perimeter. Once they were out of Claig's sight, Dave went straight for the fence, producing a pair of heavy bolt cutters from his overcoat.

'Who tipped him off?' asked Glen, joining him.

'I knew there was something fishy about your friend Peter. I know you worship the old nutter, but I don't think you should put all your faith in him. That's why we went with Plan B.'

'I thought you were just being selfish.'

Dave gave him a mock hurt look. 'Be careful, you great rube. Peter has his own schemes going on, and Reuben's his pitbull. Watch yourself.' With a couple of echoing snaps and twangs Dave tore a hole in the fence. Reuben joined them, having grown impatient, and immediately started criticising Dave.

'Could you not make a bigger hole? I'm not a leprechaun, y'know.'

Glen was already squeezing through, and Reuben soon followed him to the other side.

'Get back here pronto for Kim's sake,' Dave grinned at Glen, sticking his hand through the jagged hole to give him a set of car keys with plastic miniature boobs on the chain. 'That girl'd do anything for you, Lord knows why. You owe me for this, kiddo. You know that don't you?'

'I owe you many times over. So does he.' Glen gave Reuben a nudge. 'Don't you?'

'Sure, whatever.'

They could hear guards approaching and saw lights snapping on in nearby buildings.

'I'll hold 'em off. The lovemobile's parked down past that row of trees. You can't miss it.' Dave disappeared to sweet-talk the sentries. Glen could only feel triumphant as he looked back at the compound. He was leaving friends behind, sure, but a lot of bad memories too. He quickly found the vibrant purple lovemobile tucked away on an overgrown verge, hopped into the driver's seat and strapped on his seat belt, tempted to leave Reuben behind after Dave's words of warning. But he couldn't do that; it wasn't in his nature.

With nobody screeching at him to stop dreaming and start being reasonable, Glen unlocked the passenger door and let Reuben in. Then he turned the keys in the ignition and sped away from Bonetown.

A few miles on, the road to Edinburgh was lined with tents, caravans and trucks. Live people hung about outside, huddled round small stalls dispensing sandwiches and coffee. These folks had been camped out here for some time – their faces had the dark-eyed, drawn look of those who hadn't had a decent night's sleep in days or weeks. Glen put his foot on the brake and opened the car door, looking up at a silver-haired man with a tartan flask.

'What goes on?'

The lifer stared at him, speechless for a moment. Finally, he stammered: 'I'm waiting. We all are.'

'For what?' asked Reuben, sticking his head out of the passenger window. 'A bus?'

'I want to know what's happening with my son,' said the lifer tetchily. 'Any information would do. A glimpse of him, a message, a photo.'

'He's in Bonetown?' Glen was beginning to understand.

'He passed away, a year ago.'

Reuben wanted to move on. The lovemobile was starting to attract attention, with a group of people gathering around it, asking for news about their dead friends and lovers. Glen thanked the silver-haired man and closed his door, pulling away – then slamming his brakes on again. He dashed from the car and into the throng of lifers.

'What do you think you're doing?' Reuben yelled, but Glen was busy hugging a thin woman with fine black hair.

'I missed you, you decrepit old bugger.' Misbah hadn't changed much. Her hair was longer, with a couple of white strands sprouting at one side. She had more rings on her fingers, jewellery with decorative patterns – too busy for Glen's taste. Otherwise she was exactly as he'd remembered her, fancied her, seen her reflected in the lake. Any changes she'd undergone were for the better. In Glen's case, the opposite applied.

Everything was different. His body, his existence, his attitudes. His feelings towards his ex-wife were ambivalent and he didn't know what to say to her.

'Why are you here?' he mustered. Peter had told him that Misbah had disappeared. Was it possible that she'd been untraceable because she was holed up here? How could Peter not have known? 'Looking for alimony? Child support?'

'Told you. I missed you, couldn't put up with not knowing how you were. I was worried about you. I needed to know what had happened – for me, for the family. What will happen to us if we... die an unnatural death.' Maybe altruism wasn't the only reason the lifers had gathered outside Bonetown. 'Everyone was sure I'd give up, go home. But I'm glad I didn't. How are you, Glen?'

'Knackered. Thanks for thinking of me.'

'I haven't come to apologise or anything,' Misbah invited Glen into her tatty tent, which he recognised from camping holidays the family had taken. She lit a cigarette.

'You sure you should be lighting that thing up with all this sagging canvas around here?' Misbah's scowl shut him up.

'I'm here to –'

'– Check up on me. I get it.' Glen passed her an empty can of Irn Bru to use as an ashtray. 'What are the kids up to?'

'Not much,' Misbah sounded guilty. 'Mooching about. Asking after you.'

'They're the real reason you came.'

'They keep bugging me about visiting you, finding out what's happened to you. We've heard so many things... Fights, attacks, bad conditions...'

'You know how the media blows these things out of all proportion. Makes better news that way.'

'But it's hard to explain to the children.' Misbah tapped a length of ash into the juice can. 'They need to see for themselves that you're alright. Before they could do that...'

'You need to vet me. Make sure I'm not a complete headcheese yet. That I'm not in some pisshole unfit for good clean human beings. Take a look, darling. I'm melting fast and I got rats for neighbors. They're big darlings too. This is no place for Paul and Lucy.' Glen didn't want his babies to see him in his skeletal condition. There was nothing here to make them proud, to keep them strong. He desperately wanted to see them, but it would harm them. That was the last thing he wanted to do. 'Maybe I could write to them,' he suggested.

'Sure. Send it care of my parents. In case I get moved on again.'

'Again? How long have you been here?'

'A long while. Since we found out where you were. It was a secret for a long time.'

'They doing OK at school?' Glen had a lot of catching up to do. His wife dutifully told him about the kids' successes and failures, homework and exams, teenage strops, the amusing comments they came out with. She didn't tell him how hard it was to raise them on her own. She hadn't brought pictures of them, knowing that it would be a clincher, convincing Glen to ask to see them again. She could see the desperation in his eyes.

'I would have stuck with you through anything,' Misbah said sadly, 'anything natural. That's part of being in love, even when you want to you can't leave your partner. It would hurt too much. Then when you died I said goodbye.'

'I treated you so badly. I deserved everything that happens to me.'

'No matter what we do the world will keep turning, and certain things are bound to happen. We have to accept this.'

'Consider it accepted.'

'There's something else you'll have to accept.' Misbah doused her cigarette. 'Some bad news about Jack.'

'Is he in trouble? That old duffer, always sticking his nose in where it doesn't concern him.'

'No, no. Passed away in his sleep. I'm sorry. We tried to let you know but, well, you know your lines of communication are practically non-existent.'

'Dad can't be dead. He's indestructible.'

'He's gone and before you ask, he hasn't come back. I only just found out myself, I'm sorry.'

Glen had tried to avoid thinking about his father or caring about him but that was impossible. Despite all the pettiness and sour banter, he loved the curmudgeon and right then he would have done anything to get the chance to tell him so. It was cruel, perhaps, but he wished his Dad was a diener.

'I need to go see Mum. I can take you with me if you like.'

'It's okay,' Misbah shook her head, 'I've got my own transport and some company now.'

'Where is he right now?'

'With the kids. They refuse to call him Daddy, you'll be pleased to know.'

'I'd better go,' Glen said, feeling old. The impromptu meeting over, Misbah opened a flap in the tent and let him out. She held Glen close and kissed him on what was left of his lips. It was the most heartfelt kiss she'd ever given him.

'You're incredible,' he told her. He was sure he could see his children reflected in her eyes.

'Come on, soppy socks!' Reuben yelled as Glen said goodbye to his widow and loped to the lovemobile.

CHAPTER 16

On The Road

Some folks keep their thumbs in jars
Others save their ears
Most will trash the parts they lose
To sweep away all fears.
Some girls use formaldehyde
Pickling their toes
Wise types chuck away their dregs
That's the way it goes.

Curators collect noses
Display them in a box
Set and mounted, ready for
A schooling in hard knocks.
Exhibits for students'
Philanthropic shows
Future lecturers will prove
That's the way it goes.

'Philanthropy'
A poem by Reuben Whitley

A803

TREES RUSHED BY, blurred tints of green, russet and yellow. Looking across the landscape, a blanket of grey roofs reminded Glen of the compound. His route kept him well clear of large, urban areas. He took detours to avoid police vehicles. Along the way he talked to Reuben about a myth that had sprouted up, about dieners who had become scattered around the country, even across the sea. They were wandering pariahs, looking for a home or a reason for being. No wonder so many residents of Bonetown had resigned themselves to their fate, eschewing freedom for a sense of place.

The sun was low in the sky, bathing both men with its rays. Glen looked at the bright patches on his arms, remembering the warmth of that glow. His memories of touch and smell were becoming increasingly faint.

Reuben sat beside Glen, pretending that his hand was a gun, his index finger the muzzle. He took careful aim at every lifer they passed, firing invisible bullets at them.

'Bam! Another one bites the dust.'

'Give it a rest, I'm trying to concentrate.'

'What do you have to concentrate on? You're driving, for Peter's sake. Doesn't exactly take full focus. I can tune in a radio, make a phone call, comb my hair and pilot the limo to work.'

'I guess your work doesn't take much brains either. Beat up some poor fool, take his belongings and toddle off home.'

'I'm not a mugger, I'm a messenger.'

'Listen, if you think you can drive better, you take over. We're headed for Bonnybridge, the safehouse, yeah?'

'Yep. This is the way.' Reuben leaned back in his seat, holstering his imaginary gun. 'Can you roll up the window please?' he said. 'It's getting chilly in here.'

'How can you be cold? Your nerve endings are shot.'

'It's the draught. Never did like it.'

With a sigh, Glen rolled the window up to please his passenger. 'Happy now?'

'I'm stuck with you for hours on a wild goose chase. I *do* have better things to be doing, you know. Think I'm happy? Think again.' Glen looked at Reuben's tight-lipped expression. The thug was sulking, so Glen concentrated on the road ahead. He had to assume his Mum would be OK in Peter's hands, despite the untimely appearance of Claig at the gate. From what little Glen could glean from his surly companion, the safehouse was secluded, tucked away on a patch of farmland far from city hubbub. It had once been an actors' retreat; the cast of *Spyland* had stayed there years ago. That was where his Mum would be waiting.

'I appreciate you coming anyway,' Glen said at last. He'd decided to rise above Reuben's pettiness. Be reasonable, positive.

'I only came 'cos I know Peter wanted me to. A favour, like.'

'You'd do anything for him, wouldn't you?'

'Sure would, the man's a legend, a god.' Glen wasn't sure whether Peter would approve of such a billing. In his present state, maybe he would.

'You sure your friendship is purely platonic?'

'Don't know what you mean.'

'You have any sex dreams about him?'

'Up yours.' Maybe Glen had hit a nerve. He mouthed the words 'ass kisser' and smiled at his companion. Reuben looked daggers at him. 'This is our turn-off, here,' he said in a low growl. Glen took the turn too fast, braking hard as they reached a junction. Heading into dense countryside, losing their bearings, they kept their eyes peeled for signposts.

'It's no good,' Glen said after a long stretch of road. 'We'll have to stop and ask for directions.' Reuben looked at him as if he'd suggested that they take up morris dancing or barbershop singing.

'We can find it ourselves. We just keep heading west.' Reuben returned his gaze to the dog-eared roadmap. 'You're going too slow.'

'Think you can do better?'

'Yeah!' Reuben opened his door, a signal for Glen to stop and change places. 'I'll drive, you navigate.'

'Why do you enjoy it so much?' Glen asked once they were underway.

'What?'

'Inflicting pain and violence. Making people miserable. What does it achieve?' Glen had the map on his lap, trying to smooth out the creases.

'Dunno.'

'What would your little girl think of it all?'

'The one who doesn't want me home, holding her?' Reuben rounded on Glen, angry. 'You know what I think? When I came back my soul didn't come with me. It's lost out there in the ether.'

'You can't justify –'

'I don't have to. I wasn't meant to be here. I might as well have some fun while I am.'

'Don't you have a conscience anymore?'

'A conscience, a soul, doesn't matter what you call it. I never cared much about people either way, except for my family. Chastity and Caitlin. I obeyed the law because I feared the consequences if I put a foot wrong. Now what can they do to me? Chop off my arm and call me Stumpy?' Reuben accentuated his point by giving Glen the finger. 'I can make folks fear me and when I've got a chunk of Peter's power...' he stopped himself, knowing that he'd said too much.

Trying to rejoin the dual carriageway, they hit a heavy jam. Reuben soon got impatient, slamming the car into reverse and scaring a Mini driver behind him. He pulled out, squeezed through the traffic and got onto another road. 'We'll have to take the back route,' he snarled.

'We've got too far to go,' Glen was incredulous, 'it'll take hours.' It annoyed him when Reuben ignored his directions. The weasel didn't trust anyone.

They stopped at a petrol station where the fuel was reasonably priced. They were in a small town in the middle of some benighted nowhere, recovering from the traffic jam. Flower sellers had stood by the roadside, walking up to gridlocked cars and offering them bright yellow posies. Reuben had rejected their proposals with a wilting phrase.

At the services they consulted the map and devised a plan of action to avoid some of the traffic. Desperate to find a familiar route, Glen suggested getting back on the dual carriageway ASAP. Reuben preferred a less predictable route, avoiding busy junctions and scooting through several small towns. Glen compromised in the end, suggesting that they wind their way across the country and rejoin the main road there.

'Fine.' Reuben nodded. 'You go your way, but if the directions Peter gave us aren't good enough for you, I don't know what to think.'

It's as if Peter wants us to be driving round in circles, thought Glen, *buying himself some time.* 'Let's get going,' he told Reuben, crumpling up the map and throwing it on the back seat. Within moments they were off again, like a clueless cavalry to the rescue.

Broughton Road

Where are you? Jen looked up at the night sky through her bedroom window. *Take me away from all this.* Perhaps her psychic wavelengths would be picked up by some merciful aliens, preferably the kind who liked to party. Then the *Scooby Doo* theme popped into her head. *Where are you?*

She felt lonely, tried so hard to make friends, yet they always disappointed her. None of them were as wise as her, though they all thought they were better. It was as if they took one look at her, instantly measured her up and decided she was a worthless ticket. Her mission in life was to prove everybody wrong.

Her first boyfriend Tom had thought he could treat her like dirt. She'd told his employer at the Maclean Garage that he'd been overcharging customers and pocketing the difference, got him fired. Tom had never committed an underhand act but Jen found it shamefully easy to get him out of work and into the dole queue. She dumped him around the same time – what self-respecting girl wants a boyfriend with no job or prospects?

Annabelle, her sister, had rued the day she borrowed Jen's hairbrush without permission. The very next day, a twenty had disappeared from their Mum's purse and popped up in big sister's room, buried in her sock drawer. With her allowance revoked for a month, Jen's sister never trusted her again.

These days the siblings were close, calling each other at least once a week. Jen confided everything to Annabelle, who was a legal secretary in London. She thought that Annabelle secretly made fun of her, shared her secrets with the other secretaries floating round the pool. Jen didn't care. It made her feel superior, because she didn't share Annabelle's confidences with anyone. She didn't really have that option.

Only Jen's generosity redeemed her. She spent little on herself and saved less, preferring to buy gifts for her workmates and send money to her parents.

She was especially generous to Dave, indulging him, feeding his ego and telling him whatever he needed to hear. He did the same for her when he proposed to her, making her cry with happiness. She agreed to marry him on one condition: that she would have a bigger, more spectacular wedding than her sister. Jen wouldn't be lonely for much longer.

Walton Road

It was a two tractor job. One lifted sacks of powder from a trailer, another distributed the chemical across the field. Each sack was twice the size of a man, and two hooks had been fitted to the first machine. The driver deftly manoeuvered his vehicle so that a hook caught the strap on top of the sack then brought it down to earth with a thud. Ten sacks were required to finish the task. As Glen pulled up on a mucky verge, sack number four was being emptied into the second tractor.

A young man with a shaven head vigorously attacked the bottom of the sack with his hoe. The powder poured out, slowly at first then faster until the sack was empty. Glen noted that the men wore no protective clothing, not even gloves, so the powder couldn't have been too toxic.

It was lunchtime and the minor road that ran beside the field was quiet. Not so long ago the area had consisted of wetland, and there were no hills or dips in the road to conceal approaching traffic. You could see clear across the land for half a mile or more, and the place reminded Glen of the exposed belly of rural England.

Between the road and the field was a ditch, designed to drain the land in the event of flooding. A small wooden bridge allowed Glen to cross it and approach the first tractor. It was driven by a man in his fifties, with long white hair and a dirty beard. He looked like a demented Santa Claus.

'I'm looking for Anna Glass,' Glen explained.

'Aye.' Santa kept himself busy, walking to the trailer, where he folded up the empty sacks and packed them all together.

'Is she here?'

'Aye.'

'You work for Peter Foothill?'

'I don't know him.' Santa was appraising Glen, staying an arm's length from him as if his condition was contagious. Glen heard the green tractor pulling up behind him.

'I don't want to interrupt your work or anything, but this is important, I could do with your help. I'm Mrs Glass's son.'

Santa's expression didn't change. Cautious, unblinking. Wondering if he had a job in a department store come Christmas, Glen turned to greet the second farmer, who'd got out of his vehicle again. He was met by the sharp end of the hoe, which struck him on the arm and sent him spinning against one of the sacks.

'Mum?' Glen gasped. The young man bore down with the hoe brandished like a cudgel. Glen ducked behind the sack as the weapon whooshed past.

Reuben stood by the car and watched the struggle, ready to draw his knife if need be. Baldie hacked at Glen with his hoe, striking the sack until it burst, burying the young farmer with its contents.

Glen turned to run and barrelled into Santa, knocking the wind from him. Glen fell on top of him, pinning his flowing white beard to the ground. 'Where is she?' Glen shouted, yanking at the old man's facial hair. 'You want to end up like me? No chin fuzz and not much face either? Course not. Spill it!'

'The farmhouse.' Santa was in a sorry state, flat on his black and gasping for air. 'She's alright. We got nothing against you deadites. We were trying to help Mr Foothill, please don't call the police. We haven't hurt her.'

The farmhouse was falling apart, with the rafters showing and skylights broken; Glen was reminded of Vian's bald patch. With Reuben urging him to be careful, he pushed the front door open (it wasn't locked) and stuck his head inside. Shafts of light from above picked out an unintended atrium, with only a stereo system and a leather chair to suggest that anyone lived there.

'She could be hiding,' Reuben mock-whispered, standing guard at the door. 'Or tied up. Or being tortured in the basement.'

Glen crept up a rickety flight of wooden stairs, cursing every creak.

'Mum?' One upstairs room had been converted into an office, with a computer and fax machine on a pine-effect desk. Anna was sitting on a wooden chair, leafing through some legal documents.

'Oh, hello son.' She was tired, her voice hollow. 'Your friend Mr Foothill told me you might be coming.' Glen moved over to her and crouched down so that his eyes were level with hers.

'Did he set those men on me?'

'Set them on you? They wouldn't hurt a fly, dear. They've been as nice as pie to me.'

'They haven't –?'

'They offered to protect me. I've been getting some rather rude phone calls.' Anna squinted at Glen, her face solemn. You're not some horrid zombie are you? You're still my baby.' She held him tight, arms wrapped round his exposed ribs. 'You'll always be my baby.'

'I'm so sorry I wasn't around when Dad died,' Glen said softly.

'I'm glad he's not coming back. He put up with enough over the years.'

Hours seemed to pass before Anna let go of her son. They sat in the living room with Reuben, the doors locked and windows barred, all drinking tea as if everything was fine and dandy. But although there was no sign of the fighting farmhands, Glen could hardly hold his cup still, and it clinked against the saucer.

'My death wasn't an accident,' he told his Mum. 'Peter probably told you that much.'

'Peter was the one who told you about your murderer, wasn't he?' asked Anna shrewdly. 'What do you really believe?'

'I don't know why he would put you in danger, lure me out here.'

'Maybe you know too much,' snorted Reuben, 'and he wants you out of the way.'

'Why not simply destroy me or lock me up while I was in Bonetown, on his turf? Who's going to miss me?'

'Your TV reporter girlfriend for one.'

'You're seeing someone?' the corners of Anna's lips rose, then fell. 'Does Misbah know?'

'Mum, this isn't the time. I need to sort this mess out, find out who really killed me and why.'

'Some people scheme too much for their own good,' said Anna, slurping at her lukewarm tea, 'and some people watch too many movies.'

Glen caught sight of Anna's copy of the *Scotsman*. A headline read BIG CON, along with the day's date.

'We're going to take you to Auntie Ruth's, Mum. You'll be fine there.' He hauled Anna to her feet. 'Reuben!' he shouted, holding his mother's hand and running for the front door, almost catching his feet in the rotten wood. 'I've got it! I know where he is.'

Leith Walk

It was only when he was sitting in the taxi that Mark noticed that the door locks had been sawn off and there was no driver's ID on display. An illegal cab, and the meter running a marathon.

They were way off course from his intended destination, Chez Andres. He'd been on his way to interview a detective who'd promised some juicy information on a limelight-hungry celeb. He snapped open his mobile to tell the informer he'd be late, but couldn't get a signal.

He hadn't registered the driver's face when he got in. Now he had plenty of time to examine the back of the cabbie's head, a mess of wiry grey hair, boils and sunburnt skin. In the rearview mirror Mark could see a pair of squinting porcine eyes, staring ahead, not acknowledging his presence. The cab careered through alleys, ignoring red lights, carving up trucks and abusing bus lanes. *Funny how the really dangerous drivers never get stopped by the cops,* Glen had once said to him. He wasn't scared by this sudden frantic mystery trip; if anything he was excited. There was a story here, news at the end of the ride. All he had to do was sit it out – the driver didn't seem to be a great candidate for an interview. The reporter chanced a question anyway:

'Where're we going?'

No answer. Instead the cabbie slammed on the brakes, got out of the vehicle and opened Mark's door. He felt a thrill of fear as his kidnapper grabbed his arm and held him firm. This ruffian had been dead for a couple of months by the looks of him, with a greenish hue and his lower lip missing. This gave him a permanent, bottom-heavy smile.

They'd stopped by a cashpoint where two cadavers waited, one carrying a gun, the other a small rucksack. Mark was led up to the machine, where he stood, obstinate. He knew what they wanted but figured it wouldn't hurt to play dumb. He was wrong.

'Your credit card,' the driver growled, 'now.' He punctuated his request with a fist in the reporter's belly, knocking the wind out of him. So he complied with the request, handing over his wallet like a sore Las Vegas loser. With his card in the machine, he was cajoled into punching in his pin code and withdrawing the maximum amount of cash allowed. Looking around the quiet street, the dieners led him off to the next cashpoint. They would continue to take the greatest possible amount out of every machine in the area until Mark's account was drained.

Then what? They've seen my wallet, read my business card. They know what I am. For once in his life, Mark had been saving some money and had a quantity in his account. He'd planned to buy his wife a fancy necklace, a token of his appreciation, because he never bought gifts for her. After this caper he'd be lucky if he could buy her a straw hat. That's if he ever saw her again – these deadheads were stone killers, he was certain.

He didn't think it was anything personal. These guys weren't disgruntled readers, their worlds caught in the wash of some media backlash. They didn't know him, cared less about him. They wanted his cash and if he was lucky, he'd be dumped in a remote neighbourhood when his account ran dry.

The reporter was about a grand down when he bumped into two businessmen out for a night on the tiles. One had a red face, was overweight and still wearing a pinstripe suit from his day's work. His pal, Naus, wore casual gear. He had a pale face and a lopsided bald spot. Red was urging Naus on as they waddled down the street, looking for their next bar.

'C'moan Naus, get a move on! The night's hardly started.' Red didn't notice the three dieners blocking his path. The cabbie looked him up and down, and Mark silently willed the two boozy buddies to clear off before they got into trouble.

'Out the road, pal. You may be dead but I know you're not stupit.' Naus looked like he was about to throw up. The dieners didn't make way; instead the gunman raised his weapon. Naus vomitted all over it, as well as the cabbie's shoes.

'Nice one, Naus!' roared Red. 'Being sick an' all that. Ye need another drink in ye.' Red insisted that the dieners join them in a local bar, never losing his friendly smile. With the gunman dripping puke and the taxi driver fending off the fat drunk, Mark was able to make a break.

The deadhead with the haversack (now containing £500) gave chase, his cries ringing in the journalist's ears. He'd never been part of a news story before and he was surprised to find that his observational skills went out the window. He did manage to see a rickshaw, peddled along by an athletic-looking student. He jumped in and told the youth to ride for it. Despite the weight of the rickshaw, they soon outpaced the diener and left him stomping and cursing.

B4438

It took a while to settle Anna down at her sister Ruth's Falkirk home, but some sherry and scones did the trick. From there, it took a few hours to reach the Birmingham NEC, where Reuben brought the car to a screeching halt. He got out and walked up to two aged ladies standing at a bus stop, who were shocked at his ravaged appearance. They crossed the road hurriedly.

'What's the matter,' Reuben hollered, 'ain't you never seen a dead man walking?' He scowled at his companion. 'This is the reaction we get from lifers. OK, it's more exaggerated down here 'cos they're not used to seeing zombies on the high street. Anywhere you go though, they don't see past the skin and bone. They won't talk to you, nod a good morning. None of them have a smile for me. They're afraid and that disgusts me.'

'Not everyone's afraid.'

'You mean Kim?'

'My wife still cares about me. She didn't flinch.'

'She hated you while you were alive. Why should she change now?'

'You don't know her.'

'Ah, they're all the same.' It was growing dark and Glen made sure he left his car in a pool of lamplight. They'd barely survived a series of speed bumps policing the approach. *We spend decades flattening the landscape then some goodie-goodies come along and decide we should make it bumpy again. No such thing as a smooth ride in this world.* Reuben ushered Glen towards the NEC, a grand building that played host to various events. The two ladies across the road looked on mournfully as their bus hurtled past.

'We've got to find Vian,' said Glen, more determined than ever.

CHAPTER 17

The Big Con

GLEN DIDN'T HAVE A ticket for the Annual John Dance Convention at the Birmingham NEC, so he slipped round the back and in through a fire door, leaving Reuben to try a more conspicuous frontal approach. A narrow grey corridor led Glen straight into the dealers' room, where dozens of stalls lined each side of a long, high-ceilinged hall. Glen passed the tables quickly, keeping his eye out for Vian. Many of the same items kept cropping up – H-Bomb dolls, Christie Cummins T-shirts, *Cyberkill* comics and trade paperback adaptations of Sam Robbins books. The stalls displayed anything Dance-related, expensive escapism for punters desperate to leave their dull world, if only for the fifteen minutes it took to read an issue of *J.D. Magazine*.

As in Video People, this place was awash with primary colours – on posters blu-tacked to the walls, on dealers' sweatshirts, and particularly on the main doors that led from the hall. These bore signs advertising events in the main auditorium – Q&A panels, presentations and a cabaret in the evening, starring writers, artists and publishers with more skill in their professional fields than they would ever have on stage.

A steward walked slowly across the hall, and Glen ducked through a side door to avoid him. The dead man found himself in the screening room, where avid fans could watch film fest fave *Snap Judgment*. On screen, Agent Sanders was sneaking into a naval base, fending off security guards with bone-crushing efficiency. Glen hunkered down in a seat and gave sufficient time for the coast to clear. The viewers around him cheered as Sanders beat another opponent. Shaking his head in bewilderment at these grown-ups getting so excited about a low-budget action movie, Glen left the room and made his way through a crowd of fans into the auditorium.

On the stage, Dance geek Gavin Hughes was talking about his multi-layered space saga, *The Laird of Camster*. Glen scanned the rows of attendees, trying to identify the back of Vian's head. There were lots of families present, with children in their infancy upwards accompanied by adults young and ancient. In the midst of the throng, in the third row, sitting rapt looking up at Hughes, was Vian. Glen recognised his bald patch immediately.

'What was Christina Rhodes like to work with?' the interviewer asked Hughes.

'A joy, a complete joy. She gave the most authentic performance of a Jewish reindeer I've ever seen.'

Glen walked up the middle aisle until he reached the fourth row. Vian was wrapped up in a duffel coat and, despite the heat in the building, the toggles were fastened up to the very top. A black umbrella lay across his lap. Glen couldn't see much of Vian's face, though he imagined that the murderer was intent on the conversation on stage.

Glen managed to get a seat directly behind his killer. He clapped Vian on the shoulder and asked, 'Enjoying the show?'

Vian turned round and Glen jumped. His sickly pallor made Glen wonder if his old customer had become a diener, but then he remembered that Vian had always looked anaemic.

Vian gave Glen a thin-lipped grin. 'You look like crap warmed up, you know that?' A brave spectator shushed them, then wished she hadn't.

'I've been looking for you.'

'Save it for when the stage interview's done.'

Glen grabbed Vian's shoulder again. 'We'll talk now.' More shushes. Like a sullen child, Vian limped out of the auditorium with Glen right behind.

'What's with the umbrella?' Glen noticed that Vian was holding it close, like a greedy girl scout with her last box of cookies. 'Is it authentic?'

'The very one used in *Dark at the End of the Tunnel*, complete with blood groove. They made three, of course. A couple of back-ups in case one was damaged during a fight scene.'

'I know. Only one is supposed to exist now.'

'And this is it.'

'Where did you get it?'

'It's from a mutual friend of ours.' They ended up in a signing room, vacant at present, where con-goers could meet their heroes, get an autograph or have their pictures taken with them – all for a fee.

Vian untoggled his coat. 'You want to know why I killed you?'

'You admit it then?'

'Call it a confession. Good for the soul, right? And with you zombies around, everyone's thinking theological thoughts these days.' It was a long time since Glen had heard Vian being as talkative as this. He reminded the diener of a John Dance villain, explaining a dastardly plan with the hero as his captive audience.

'Why me, Vian? We were friends.'

'Until that incident at the car boot sale. You don't know how badly I wanted that reel of film.'

'You hired Dave and Ash to steal it from me? You could have just borrowed it.'

'I wanted to possess it!' Vian raised his voice and a steward passing the door looked at him, concerned but still moving. There was some kind of commotion at the main entrance.

'Fine, you got it. So why did you have to end my life?'

'I had to. You had the gorgeous wife, your kids, your friends – what wasn't there for me to be jealous of?'

'Thanks to you I lost it all before I could ever appreciate it. My family, my home...'

'I gave you a great gift!' Vian lowered his voice as two more stewards rushed past, heading for the foyer. 'I didn't know you'd come back, of course, but now look at you!'

'This is a curse, not a gift.'

'You don't get it, do you?' Vian sat down under a silver reflector, which created a large hotspot on his pate. Behind him was a 2D background of sand and palm trees, an amalgam of exotic movie locales – perfect for photo ops. 'We only have a finite amount of time to watch the films we love, the books, everything that makes the John Dance saga great.' Vian's eyes shone with wonder. 'There's no point ultimately in collecting anything – what are you going to do with priceless memorabilia in the grave? What good are all those memories, all those scenes we recall, the facts we learn? Sure we can pass on information to younger fans, the next generation, but they don't really appreciate the movies the way we do! You had to be alive when they were first released, in context, to really get them. As a diener, you don't have these worries. You can be a fan forever. And I think that's why people are being resurrected – they're so passionate about... whatever they're passionate about, that they transcend death.'

'They cheat death so they can watch more TV.' Sounds of yelling and tumbling merchandise tables came from the dealers' room.

'If you love something that much,' Vian sighed, 'that love can never die.' He handed Glen the umbrella. It doubled as a kind of sword stick, its tip sliding off to reveal a thin, sharp blade.

'You might not come back,' Glen warned, holding the brolly so that it was pointed at Vian's chest.

'I'm pretty sure I will.'

Glen's hand trembled. After all this time he knew the truth, or enough of it to satisfy him for the moment. His crazy, petty killer stood in front of him. Still, it wasn't in his nature to harm Vian. He sighed, unable to go through with it.

'Fine.' A furious Vian snatched the umbrella from Glen's loosening grip. 'They say that you can kill a diener by cutting up his brain.' He slashed the blade at Glen's head, slicing a slither of skin from his brow. 'Let's see if that's true.'

'Spoiling your plans, am I?' Glen bumped against the reflector. 'I've got nothing to lose, Vian. All thanks to you.'

Reuben burst into the signing room, stewards trying to restrain him. 'Go on, finish 'im,' he shouted, although Glen wasn't sure to whom. The two dieners both tried to grab the weapon, the stewards falling over themselves, some clutching their noses at the unholy bodily stench. Vian collapsed under the weight of Glen and Reuben, taking the idyllic cardboard backdrop with him. As if berserk, Reuben gained possession of the brolly and stabbed it into Vian's torso. Blood seeped from the wound, turning the sandy beach beneath them red.

'Isn't this where you utter a merry, John Dance-style quip?' Reuben asked Glen, snarling at the slack-jawed stewards and convention-goers who'd filled the room. 'Or shall I have a stab at it?'

'The police will be looking for us,' Glen told Reuben as they left the convention centre.

'Big deal. They were looking for us already.' They crossed the car park together.

'Where's the car?'

'What do you mean, where's the car? You were driving.'

The car park was huge, filled with a sea of vehicles at high tide.

'You mean you didn't take a note of what row we were in?'

'We'll start with the first block and go from there.'

'That's smart thinking. Shame you didn't display any back at the convention.'

'I got carried away, that's all.' A queue of pension-aged Dance fans waited patiently for the x63 into central Birmingham. They shuffled forwards to pick up their bags as the bus pulled up, bogging from its last trip. 'Something I done bothered you?' The doors of the x63 stayed resolutely closed. While the elderly line-up grew impatient, the driver munched a sandwich and read the *Sun*.

'Why did Peter insist you came with me?' Glen walked as quickly as his crooked legs could manage, desperately searching for the lovemobile. 'Was it to kill Vian before I could talk to him too much? Or to help Vian finish me off? Why didn't you help me fight off those farmhands back at the safehouse?'

'Wanted to see if you were the sissy I thought you were. I thought wrong.'

'Peter ordered you not to help me – or them, didn't he?' Police car sirens wailed in the distance.

'That too. Is that it over there?'

'That's a beetle,' Glen shook his head. 'The lovemobile's bright purple! How can we lose it?'

'You know, I've been thinking. You've done a lotta good things for me. Helped me get back on my feet after I died, even after I gave your toenails a trim. Kept me company on my debt collectin' rounds, even though you're a whiner.' Reuben turned away for a second, making a decision. 'You know how much I respect Peter. I really would do anything for him. But when he involves your Mum – uses her as bait – in his daft wee schemes, it makes me think twice, that's all. You should too.'

Glen wasn't sure whether to believe Reuben's words or not, but there would more appropriate places and times to figure out his fickle companion.

'You made a right mess of Vian.'

'I enjoyed that one.'

'You're sick.'

'Back when you were livin', did you ever clear your throat of phlegm? Pass water? Breathe? These things were natural to you, to both of us, and we lost 'em. My Dad was a big man, used violence to get his way. It's in my genes to rip spleens and I love it. It's the one thing in my nature that I ain't lost, and I'm not about to give it up.' The dieners had circled half the car park and were back at the bus stop. Reuben walked up to the bus and turned the manual entry switch. The doors shucked open, making the driver twitch with fright. 'See these old duffers?' Reuben growled, his gruesome face dribbling onto the driver's sandwich. 'They don't like standing. Christ knows they've done enough waitin' in their lifetimes. Let 'em in, let 'em get warm, have a seat. Git.'

The driver didn't dare argue with him. He folded up his paper, flung it on the dashboard and switched on his ticket machine.

'That didn't take too much effort, now did it?' Reuben smiled, as good natured a smile as he could muster. He made way for the passengers, too wary and flustered to thank him. 'I'm on your side now, pal. You might hate the thought but you're stuck with me.'

As the bus pulled away they spotted the lovemobile, parked right beside it. Glen stared at Reuben, noticing a fresh blood stain on his t-shirt.

'I think it's time to go home.'

CHAPTER 18

No Future

Reporters are supposed to be impartial. That's what they teach you at journalism school, the fundamentals of your first days on the job. You do the best to tell the facts without your opinion colouring the story. But it does.

Last night I was pursued and had my life threatened by two non-breathing individuals. This doesn't happen to a hack like me every day – a piece landing in my lap, happening to me instead of some other poor smo. It affected me and my opinions. Having your wind and limb threatened does that to a fella.

I wanted to write a hatchet job on the dieners. If a couple of them could leak from the complex and start preying on us, what would happen if they were all released? I hoped to paint them in such a bad light that your attitudes would change, too.

But I realised even as I was writing my piece that these two guys were just that – guys. The dead folk zombieing around Bonetown have individual traits, same as you or me – they can be good or bad, heroic or corrupt, right or wrong.

Some of them admit it when they're wrong, dead people putting me to shame. Don't fear these people and don't pity them either. Instead, look to the living, to the ones that touch your existence.

Don't count on living for another twenty, forty, sixty years. Don't count on being resurrected. Appreciate your friends, family and lovers now. Get to know them better because in an instant everything can cease. We live in a 'me' society and we're blinkered to the people around us, the ones we're linked with. We don't even realise how special they are, what their place is in our lives, until they're no longer here.

Comment by Mark O'Murchu

GETTING BACK INTO THE complex was a lot easier than getting out. As the lovemobile passed the main gates, a crowd of people were keeping the guards busy, making it easy for Glen and Reuben to slip back through the forest. Every resident had heard rumours of their escape, and they weren't happy. They didn't see why they should be cooped up while others roamed free.

While Glen headed for the Mausoleum, Reuben ran back towards the gates shouting, 'I love a good scrap!'

The families camped outside the complex had moved closer, with some of the guards supporting their wish to see the dieners. With a horde of lifers trying to get in and their dead counterparts wanting out, Donald Claig was beginning to realise that he didn't have enough guns to go round.

Reuben's gang had continued their spree, gaining the attention of the press. Anti-dieners also flocked to Bonetown, causing an even greater stir. These were living human beings, proud of it, and holding up placards to say so: 'STAY DEAD AND BURIED,' 'GET BACK TO YOURR GRAVES.'

'When Glen found him in his office, Peter was watching television. A camera caught glimpses of the town's main entrance, jostled by an increasingly hostile crowd. Peter was so glued to the screen that he hardly noticed his new guest. Glen slammed his fist down on Peter's desk.

'It's in the hierarchy's best interests to have people believe that you die and go to heaven.' Peter appeared to be talking to himself. 'Change doesn't seem so important; what you do as a single human being is pretty insignificant. Why revolt in this life when you're going to transcend to the next anyway?'

'While we're around,' Glen replied, 'change is inevitable – whether the authorities like it or not.'

'Not.'

'You can find hope in the most average person, the pettiest action. It was Claig's idea, wasn't it? To send me after Vian?'

'Yes. He wanted to discredit the dieners. But I see the future. A splendid niche for undead killers on the battlefield. I insisted that Reuben went with you in the hope that his bloodthirsty ways would finally influence you.'

'They didn't. I didn't kill Vian.' Glen decided that Peter was being serious, actually meant what he said. 'Why did you drag my mother into this?'

'I had to get you away from your friends here – they care for you more than you realise – and onto the farm.'

'So I could get ambushed.'

'Chose those fellows myself as a matter of fact, sent them down ahead of you. It's amazing what you can find on the internet these days.'

'Am I really so important to you?'

'I thought you were ignorant. Insignificant. Then you went and screened that test footage in front of half the town. I was so disappointed.'

'I did it because… I wanted to please you.'

'Rattle me, more like!' Peter stood up, his voice growing louder, less dignified. This was a side of him that Glen had never seen before. 'You know what that footage really means. How it fell into your hands in the first place I'll never fathom – a misplaced shipment perhaps, or a greedy fan who thought it was something to do with my old ouevre. I tried to befriend you, keep you sweet, but no one could possibly be as stupid as you act and I'm quite sick of your pretence, G.G.' Instead of annunciating the initials in a gentle, friendly manner as usual, Peter spat them at Glen.

'This doesn't make sense. I'm not important. My Mum's not important.'

'Oh, her. Peter started watching the TV again. 'I try never to underestimate the extent of a mother's love, or a son's.'

'Or a wife's? You must have known I'd see Misbah when I left town. Why didn't you tell me she was there?'

'I thought she'd be long gone before you plucked up the courage to leave here.'

'Mum was right – you're too smart for your own good.' Peter had lied to Glen about his mother, so why not Misbah? Or the fire? 'Did you plant that bomb in the complex?'

'Bomb? From what I heard, someone got a hot object too close to a flammable substance. You were quite a hero on that day. In fact, that's one of the reasons why I put up with you for so long.'

'You didn't hire me. I volunteered to stick with you, for the sake of Reuben's victims. Did you cause that fire?'

'Not directly. The incident certainly benefited my cause. Rallied more dieners round to my side. I promised them I'd do my utmost to prevent the occurrence of further tragedies. Of course, the drug companies had a lot to gain.'

'They set up the project.'

'They never approved of it. The accident showed that deadheads were incapable of establishing their own environment without endangering the living. The entire project lost credibility.'

'Surely there was public sympathy for the people lost in the fire?'

'Guards and staff, yes. Remember that as far as the great unwashed are concerned, dieners have no feelings anyway. Nobody cries when a dead man dies.'

'You were wrong about the outside. Most of the lifers out there are so busy with their own goings-on, they hardly batted an eyelid when me and Reuben were around. You and Claig deceived us so that we'd stay in Bonetown willingly, under your control. And look what all your scheming's led to!'

The dieners marched down Death Row, hundreds of shambling forms filling the street. A heavy-set man with missing lips strode beside his wife, who limped on a left foot that had somehow got twisted backwards. A biker with half a helmet fused to his skull was followed by two crispy priests who'd both been struck by lightning while playing golf. Children ran and jumped around the edges of the throng, squealing, full of energy despite their opaque eyes.

Reuben joined the dieners at their head, recognising the potential for a good scrap. One wag held up a hastily scrawled message for the cameras: 'THE END OF THE WORLD IS NICE.' Reuben started chanting:

The dead have risen
To break out of our prison.

His calls were echoed by his followers. A couple of deadheads banged on pots and pans, giving their brethren a steady, driving beat to march to. They clumped down the street to the main gates while onlookers stared or cheered, depending on their disposition. Arguments broke out between the pro- and anti-dieners beyond. The chants and drums acted as a catalyst, giving the dieners a strange thrill – hundreds of men and women shouting as one, following the leader, Reuben Whitley.

'C'mon, let these people see their families,' Reuben implored, and the guards – his old comrades – acquiesced. Opening the gates a tad, a trickle of bereaved family members soon became a flood, the protestors mingling with them.

It was a clumsy ambush, one that Reuben had been expecting somewhere along the line – but not in such force. The protestors apparently outnumbered the dieners. Included among them were PC Jerry Gibbons and several political bigwigs. They weren't baying for blood but they were serious, full of intent. Reuben kept chanting.

The police had made a halfhearted attempt to clear the road. There was only so much a few cops could do. The deadites weren't about to retreat, scurry back to their flats; they wanted to see their kin, go home.

While the police called for back-up and news crews closed in, the two crowds eyed each other up. The dead were defiant, the living hostile or overcome with emotion. Gibbons thought that this was his homeland, that the dieners belonged in the cemetery if they wanted to stay at all; Reuben believed that he had the right to take a stand in his home city.

The two men approached each other. Reuben aimed his loud-hailer at Gibbons and shouted, 'Soup head!' The dead yelled their approval.

Ears ringing, Gibbons didn't stoop to Reuben's level. He took it down a notch, retrieving some dog dirt from the gutter and hefting it at his foe.

'Let us by,' the weasel hissed, addressing the constable. 'You've said your piece.'

'You know the difference between that crap I flung and the man standing in front of me?' Gibbons asked the lifers. They didn't know the answer: 'Nothing.' He smiled a devilish smile at Reuben, who shrugged and recommenced his chanting. He also made a barely perceptible hand signal – a flick of a finger – to one of his boys, who began to sidle towards Gibbons.

'The dead have risen...' The lifers looked at each other, stuck in a bottleneck that had formed at the main entrance. The guards were attempting to close the gates but it was too late. As police sirens wailed in the distance they looked to Gibbons, who opened his mouth and gasped at them. It took them a collective moment to realise that he was in trouble, falling against a government official, a shiv in his kidney. As Gibbons collapsed the dieners shuffled a few steps forward, the assassin absorbed into their ranks.

A shot rang out and a diener fell, a neat hole in his forehead. Someone had brought a rifle along to the party. The dead crowd bayed and surged closer to their living counterparts. Mounted police-men arrived while regular cops tried to shove barriers between the two groups. They were too tightly packed together for that.

Reuben took advantage of the confusion by launching himself at a lifer, knocking over a young man with a 'DEATH TO THE DEAD' placard. He used the heavy wooden sign to batter the lad and encouraged his gang to make similar attacks. The lifers were scared, faced by a pack of indiscriminate zombies. The more responsible members of both flocks wanted to flee now, but they were trapped, with two hardcore factions between them.

Reuben used his appropriated placard to cut a swathe through the living, snarling at anyone who dared to come close. He was in his element, frightful and ferocious, leading his friends into battle. He liked to think that Peter would be proud of him.

There was a lull in the fray when a rumble filled the air. The crowds heard a metallic squeaking and the sound of motors grinding together. Two armed response vehicles appeared, at the fore and rear of a couple of security vans. Reuben's placard had broken into splinters by now, so he used his fists instead. Another shot rang out amongst the stew of lifers and half of Reuben's skull exploded. One of his cohorts sank to their knees, shaking their leader's body – there was no response.

Tear gas dispersed the lifers but the only effect it had on the dead was to obscure their vision a little. Some of them backed off towards the Mausoleum while others stayed and fought the police in a berserker frenzy. The most ferocious kind of combatant is the one with nothing to lose, or scant thought of consequences. In their present hopeless state the dieners became great warriors.

'What've you done?' asked Glen as Peter looked down on the gates from his office window. He could see smoke rising from the entranceway and Glen feared the worst. The reports blurted from the TV didn't help. 'These news reports... people are dying.'

'Too early to tell. Don't believe everything you hear.' Peter turned up the volume on the TV. 'And if a few people die then I'm sure they'll join our ranks.' He continued to watch anxiously through the window while a bright-tied newsreader rambled through celeb stories, a yarn about premature twins, speculation on the economy and a preview of coming attractions at the Edinburgh Festival

Theatre... and finally, the squabble in progress in Bonetown. Kim looked beautiful in full make-up, gas wafting towards her.

'A peaceful protest against a deadite march through Bonetown has ended in chaos. Death head Reuben Whitley sparked a fight as he launched himself at a local youth.' There was a cut to a shaky image of Reuben, arms flailing. 'Police and the army waded in, stirring up this hornets' – 'someone bumped into the camera. Kim let out a yelp and was engulfed in smoke. Glen was already on his way out the door.

By the time he reached the gates the police were mopping up stragglers. Glen found J.C.'s camera shattered, lying on the ground. There was no sign of his beloved.

'Kim!' he cried, his voice hoarse, peering through the last remnants of the tear gas. Broken bottles, torn banners and prostrate bodies were scattered across the road. A fence had been bent inward, as if someone had been pushed or squashed against it with a vast amount of pressure. A couple of cops were examining a rifle, the one that had put paid to Reuben and several of his cohorts. It was empty now, abandoned, with the barrel slightly curved.

Glen saw the ARVs, their drivers sitting expectantly within. Trying to avoid the police, who were still bundling dieners into vans with excessive enthusiasm, he kept looking for Kim. Finally he found her lying in a foetal position near to Reuben's body, and dragged her into Building Four, through to the courtyard, where he felt relatively safe.

No pulse, no breath. She looked so healthy, there was colour in her cheeks, she was calm. Yet the light in her eyes had gone out. That spark that still shone in Glen's every glance no longer existed in her.

'Jen. What are you doing here?' She looked at him, stooped over Kim's body, hands clawed, a grimace on his face.

'I was concerned about Dave. He was in the middle of all that kerfuffle. Always trying to help. She need help?' Jen moved towards Kim but Glen stood in front of the body, blocking her path and spoiling her view.

'She's beyond that, sorry.'

'What are you going to do?'

'I don't know. Give me a sec, will you?'

'Yes. Of course.' Jen trotted out of the building, her pace quickening as she approached Death Row.

Glen had little time to grieve. He heard Jen's footsteps receding then her voice shouting: 'Here's one of them! In here! He's killed a girl.' He had to move fast.

Glen hadn't expected Kim's corpse to feel so heavy as he hoisted it onto his shoulders, barging through a gap in the back fence, out of the courtyard and across to Ketch Terrace. He could hear the police radios squawking not far behind – it wouldn't take them long to locate him. He had to find refuge, somewhere quiet and discreet.

The cellar of the Oxygen Bar provided short-term shelter. The owners were nowhere to be seen – they'd probably been evacuated with the residents. They'd left the cellar doors open and Glen took advantage of this, gently laying Kim's body down beside a large crate. With the doors closed behind him, he listened to the sounds of heavy boots running along the street. He was getting angry with Kim, the police and the demonstrators. Above all he was angry with himself.

How could I have got caught up in all this? I should've stayed at home, done nothing. As soon as I acted, got involved, the pain started. During his life he'd kept his head down, watching the world through his television instead of experiencing it first hand. That world had been so simple, 625 lines and no interference, a cut-off period for watchable programming every night and breakfast with Phil and Fern in the mornings. He pined for the regularity, even the monotony that he'd known. Now nothing was certain, there were no patterns to perceive and he was as likely to turn up on the lunchtime news as to watch it. That safe cathode potion had been the very chalice that had compelled him to save Kim – those immediate images flashed halfway across town.

There was a bang at the door. Glen chose to ignore it – he was pretty sure that no one had seen him enter the cellar. But the thumping continued and it didn't take long for curiosity to get the better of him. He placed his face against a crack in the door and peered out. An equally inquisitive eye stared back. Glen jumped away in fright.

'Let me in, you idiot!' the voice was muffled yet recognisable. It was J.C. Hesitant, Glen opened the door.

'Silly cow,' J.C. mumbled, looking down at the serene form of his colleague. 'Stuck her nose in once too often.' His tone was arrogant but his eyes betrayed his sorrow. He located a crate of beer bottles and cracked one open on the brim of a crate. 'Want one? Nah, you fellers don't really drink, do you?' He bent down, brushed a strand of hair from Kim's face. 'You're supposed to bury them, you know. Not carry them around with you.'

'You saw me?'

'Half the street saw you. They're too busy to deal with you at the moment, that's all.'

'I have to get to my scooter.'

'And you expect me to help?' J.C. took a swig from his bottle of Bud. 'You should leave her here.'

'I couldn't do that.'

'The cops'll find her, take her to the clinic. It's for the best. Sure you don't want a brew for old time's sake?' Glen shook his head, deliberating. Leaving Kim for the police was the right thing to do. But by doing that he'd be losing a last glimmer of hope – that she would be resurrected. He couldn't give up on her yet.

'Will you give me a hand?'

'Is there room on your hairdryer for a couple of crates?'

Under cover of darkness the two men carried Kim's corpse to the Vespa. She was placed carefully on the seat and covered with a blanket.

'Did you see my camera in your travels?' J.C. had an amazing habit of going off on a tangent. Maybe he's trying to take my mind off what's happened, Glen mused.

'It was the worse for wear, I'm afraid. Trodden underfoot by the lifers. Like a piece of scrap now.' J.C. looked more downbeat on hearing this news than he had in the cellar. Then a cheeky grin appeared on his face and he pulled a beta tape from his jacket pocket. 'The camera isn't mine, it's SMG property. And I got most of the footage right here – I'd just changed tapes when judgment day broke loose. Kim fell and she just couldn't get back up again, it was like she was trampled by a stampeding herd. I think her neck got broke.'

Glen wanted the tape. He didn't know whether the dieners would be shown in a bad light – they weren't exactly photogenic – but he wanted to vet the footage before the edit-happy television guys got hold of it. He wasn't sure how to convince J.C. to hand it over.

'This could win me a BAFTA! A Pulitzer! It's got everything – mass chaos, human tragedy, law breaking, political shenanigans (I do like a bit of political shenanigans) –'

'Is it right for Kim's last minutes to be left in the hands of some grubby TV producer?'

'Yeah. It's how she would've liked it. My van's right round here.'

'How do you know?'

'I only parked it there an hour ago.'

'I mean, about Kim. What she would have wanted.'

'I worked close to her for a long time. She was a kind of sister to me – I was an only child, see. She'd tell me everything, she was always happy. Content, sure of herself. Ambitious too. She would have done anything to get a story, make her mark. Even date a dead guy, trying to infiltrate the LADs.'

'I'd like to see that tape.' Glen didn't show it but he was shocked by J.C.'s comment.

'Sure you would, you and your zombie pals. I'll probably sell it for use on a documentary, you can all watch it prime time. I hope it's investigatory style, I like them best.'

'I'd like to view it before your bosses do.'

'I've got a dinky edit suite in my van. We can have a quick spin through the rushes there.'

'Cool.'

The pair soon reached J.C.'s grubby white vehicle and the cameraman helped Glen to carry their cargo inside.

'I must be barmy doing this.' J.C. slotted the tape into a VCR. 'You really loved her, didn't you?'

'I never did understand women very well.'

'You and us all both, mate.' J.C. sat Glen down in front of a battered Mac and left the tape running while he fixed himself a sandwich. Although J.C. was a veteran of TV newscasts, with work for ITN, Sky and STV under his pagbelt, the rushes were a mess. The camera was jostled, people stood directly in front of the lens with the backs of their heads obscuring many shots. The sound was distorted, the balance too high to handle the noise of the protesters.

'Whoa. Can you stop it there? Rewind a few frames?'

J.C. hit a button and, in reverse, the two men watched Jerry Gibbons get shivved.

'That's what started all the violence,' said J.C. sadly.

'Slow it down. Look who's holding the knife.' It was Morgan, Donald Claig's number two.

'The lifers thought the deadheads did it. It drove them crazy.'

'Claig wants to clamp down on us, increase security, ban press coverage and get carte blanche to run this place.'

'A pretty extreme way of doing it.'

'This evidence could save the dieners. You can't give this straight to some news channel.'

'Watch me.'

J.C. drove Glen home and, against his better judgment, allowed the diener to take Kim to his flat. As Glen hefted her up the stairs, J.C. roared off in his van.

Safe in his flat, Glen held Kim's lifeless body in his arms, kissed her eyelids, hugged her close. *Most people don't come back,* he reminded himself. *There's nothing more harmful than false hope.* Glen had never been a lucky man. His children, wife, friendships had been rare strokes. He had always seen his resurrection as a curse, not a gift. Now he realised what a miracle a rebirth could be. Some miracles occurred at a cost, true, but like death itself, another chance – another lease – was a mysterious blessing. Despite all the despair and horror he'd endured, without coming back he would not have got to be with Kim.

He had selfish reasons for wanting her back. But perhaps a second chance would enable her to do all the things she hadn't been able to in existence #1. It might free her.

Glen kissed her cheek tenderly and, like Sleeping Beauty in a twisted version of the fairy tale with Glen cast as Prince Revolting, she began to revive. She looked into his eyes with a gladness that made his cold heart glow. He was transfixed because he knew that she loved him. Picking her up, he lifted her into a chair and brushed her hair from her face.

'You're not an angel. I'm back, aren't I?' she enquired sleepily.

'Yeah,' Glen told her, his voice broken with emotion, 'we're together again.' He made her as comfortable as he could, leaving her on the swivel chair while he made her tea and toast. She wasn't hungry and she wouldn't be able to eat or drink properly, but it would make her feel more at ease – tepid routine in the face of the extraordinary. By the same token, Glen switched on the telly for her and left her to watch Jeremy Kyle while he pottered in the kitchen. She sat motionless in the chair, staring at the screen, barely registered the inane chatter. She could smell the toast burning and that raised a smile. She was home.

CHAPTER 19

Afterlife

PETER WAS SITTING WITH his hands covering his face when Claig entered the office alone, so confident was he that Peter was beat.

'It's time you stepped down,' Claig told Peter, who looked as if he would crumble to dust behind his desk. 'No more swish office. No more fundraising. No more power.'

'I didn't expect this from you,' managed Peter.

'You didn't grant me the intelligence. I've been watching you, Peter. Letting you play your hierarchical games. But I hired you to keep these deadheads in order and now you've failed.'

'*I've* failed? I'm not the one patrolling the area with a gang of thugs, picking on any poor, lifeless soul unlucky enough to pass by.'

'See, once you would have condoned that kind of activity. Now you want to blame this fracas on my methods? You should approve! We're better than them, aren't we? We're strong. We see the big picture, we can use people wisely.' Claig hunched down, leaning over the desk, bringing his head level with Peter's. 'You should practice what you preach.'

'I did misjudge you, Claig. How long has Reuben been answering to you?'

'Longer than you would want to know.'

'It was cunning of you, ordering him to protect Glen Glass on their little road trip, trying to spoil my plans.'

'You didn't want Glass to come back here, did you?'

'It was a surprise. Couldn't deal with Glass on-site, of course – he's popular for a slob. I thought Vian Lucas would get him – I even sent that fanatic a deadly old prop from one of my movies. Then Reuben had to tag along, and he can be unpredictable, we both know that. Who knows what goes on in that psychotic mind of his...'

'I was going to have my guards pick Glass up at the gate,' Claig told Peter candidly. 'His friends would've thought he'd escaped; we'd've put him somewhere very private and given him a good grilling. Reuben had other ideas. He'll get what he deserves.'

'You got Reuben to tag along, deliver Glass to you, but he did his own thing, added his own particular skew to the trip, all with the intention of messing things up for me and toppling me from my perch. I didn't think he'd be willing to set my worthy cause back just to further his own career. You know what they say about false ambition?'

'What do "they" say?' Claig sneered.

'It severs the neck. I do understand, believe me. We all want a moment of glory. We want applause. Who doesn't want to be loved? Some people accept that they don't deserve it. Others will do anything for adoration. Reuben may have heard my sermons but he never listened,' said Peter sadly.

'I know that Glass is important to you, but why? He's Mr Ordinary. I never gave him a second glance until –'

'Until you noticed that I was watching him. Reeling him in.'

'What has that puny fish seen that's so special to you?'

Peter pursed his lips, shaking his head like a boy refusing to eat his vegetables.

'You might as well tell me.'

Peter led Claig into a dark, blank-walled back room, where a projector and screen had been set up. 'When you step out of this room, everything will be different.'

'And everything will make sense, I hope.'

Ten minutes later the two men left the room, Claig blinking slightly as his eyes adjusted to the light. 'This really does raise the stakes, doesn't it?' he said.

'Partners now?' Peter reached a hand out to Claig.

'The project's mine now. Otherwise, no deal.'

'You could make a lot of money from this.'

Claig took Peter's hand, still slightly crooked from the long-past wrench Glen had given it. 'I'm in.'

No more diets, haircuts, trips to the dentist, manicures or pedicures, cosmetic surgery or shopping for messages. Kim would continue to apply make-up and buy cigarettes, although they could only sit in her mouth, balanced on her lower lip. They could hardly harm her health now – she couldn't inhale. Only Glen's presence gave her a reason to carry on, a bolster against despair. He knew the ropes and appreciated the irony of her situation. She'd been hanging round with cadavers for so long, she'd finally become one of them.

From the outset she'd approached Glen with a reporter's curiosity, wondering how different life might be after death, grilling the love-struck Glass for information. He'd obliged, taking her at face value and disarming her with his naivety. What a fool he'd been to think that she could really care for a walking corpse! Yet as the weeks had drawn on and she'd stuck around for longer than she had to, caught up in Glen's wars and woes, she'd discovered that she had a soft spot for him after all. Why else would she have endured his revolting moods, insomnia and fowled-up friends?

She might not have been in love. She didn't really know what that was or what it felt like. But she cared for him deeply and now that she'd passed away, their bond was stronger than ever.

Kim joined Fierce Films, the community video group, adding some investigative spice to its stories. She was out on a shoot when Misbah visited Glen, with a diener in tow.

'He tracked me down, told me everything. You need to hear this,' she said bluntly.

Glen froze. Vian Lucas staggered into his home, his ravaged ribcage bared; a lot of the flesh and muscle had gone and Glen could see some of the rotting organs within. But he didn't flinch. He was used to such gruesome sights by now.

'You're taking a chance, coming into Bonetown.' Glen tried not to sound alarmed. 'They might not let you out again.'

'I think they'll start to let the dieners come and go as they please soon,' Misbah said hopefully. 'We – the real, living people – are beginning to accept what's happened. They let us in no problem.'

'How's Mum?'

'Fine. Always saying she's a burden to your Auntie Ruth, but she's not of course. She's getting by. So kind to the children.' Misbah inspected the flat, running a finger over the dusty surfaces.

'I've missed you.' Glen took Misbah's coat and offered his guests some tea. Vian slumped in a corner, rifling through Glen's memorabilia with a hint of disdain.

'How well do you know this Mr Claig?'

'The guy who runs this rat hole? I don't know him all that well. He doesn't speak to us dieners much anymore, lets his guards do the mingling. He mostly deals with us through Peter Foothill.'

'I'm not surprised.' Vian looked up from the television, which he'd just switched onto the A/V channel. 'I want to come clean,' he explained, 'clue you in. Give you a fighting chance against Foothill and Claig.'

'Listen to him, Glen,' Misbah urged.

'Okay. Spill it, and I don't mean your guts. Not literally, anyway.'

'What was on that reel of film I cadged from you?' Vian asked Glen, who replied with a half-shrug. 'Let me rephrase. What do you *think* was on that film?'

'Blobs.' Glen looked at Misbah as if to confirm this. 'Yeah, blobs.'

'Really.'

'Peter Foothill told me all about them. Test footage. The opening titles for *Spyland*, junked long ago. Rare enough to kill for.'

'Oh, please! I always knew I was a bigger fan than you.' Vian gave Glen a corpse grin. 'You fell for that codswallop. Blinded by your enthusiasm for the Dance saga.'

'Why are you touching my TV?'

Vian was buzzing around Glen's home entertainment system, shoving a disk from his movie box set into the DVD player. 'If you knew your stuff,' Vian whinged, 'you'd know that Peter was gulling you from the start.' The DVD started to play, and Glen instantly recognised the opening credits of the first John Dance movie. A series of circles floated across the scene, with titles appearing over the top.

'Was the footage you saw *anything* like that?'

'No,' Glen looked embarrassed, 'just blobs.'

'What if those blobs were specially treated stem cells? Tests from a lab, not from some movie we're so obsessed about?'

'Then I'd be a fool. Looking so hard at something that I didn't see the obvious.' Glen closed his eyes, partly from sheer exhaustion but also to watch Peter's film again with his mind alone. With a little imagination, the blobs could be cells.

A few flashes of white, a jumbled series of numbers and then the cells appear, bobbing in a Petri dish. One of them is sucked into a tube and the film cuts to a new dish, to which the first cell is added.

The matter in the second dish – a tissue sample? – begins to corrode in contact with the foreign cell.

Next a different blob is added to the same tissue. This time the recipient seems to get fleshier, healthier after the tube's appearance.

'They killed the regular cells, then brought them back to life,' Glen posited. 'But who's they? A drug company? A government R&D department? What's the point?'

'Why do you think you've all been corralled here? You're Foothill's guinea pigs. Extras to be directed wherever he wishes. All in the name of a cure for his disease.'

For the film's big finale, the screen is filled with brightly shining blobs dashing from one side of the frame to another. It creates the sensation of travelling rapidly through a cylinder in a wonderful, frightening rush.

'He wants to bring himself back to life.' Glen opened his eyes. That's why he's been collecting so much money, why he's so secretive.'

'But I'm sure Claig's cottoned on by now.'

'No wonder Peter was mad at me, sent me to mix it up with you. I screened the film in front of a crowd of dieners.'

'Nearly blew his big secret.'

'And then he tried to fob me off with some spiel about an "undead army".'

'Threw you off the scent again.'

The DVD was still playing. Dance was in trouble, dangling from a crane on a busy construction site. 'Now I know why you didn't try to steal the film again, after I got it back. Once you watched it and found out that it wasn't some precious collector's piece, you didn't care about it, did you?'

'Nope. Had to admit Foothill's a crafty filmmaker though. Instead of documenting the process on a computer, he makes a celluloid secret of it and keeps it to himself. Shame it got lost and turned up at a car boot sale; I guess he underestimated the zeal of us fans, eh?'

'But why have you come here, telling me all this now?'

'Because you made me realise something.' Vian watched the TV as he talked; Dance was fending off an insane spy who was trying to throw him from the crane. 'Death isn't all it's cracked up to be. I thought it would give me so much time to pursue my passions – I gave you the whole spiel, remember?'

'I remember. You talked about transcending death.'

'I didn't expect my new existence to be so dispassionate. Everything's lost its lustre. I don't care about all the things I used to care about. I'm not jealous of you and I don't hate you.'

'Well, that's a relief,' said Glen tartly.

'Peter will try to destroy you and the people you love. Burn you, behead you, whatever it takes. He doesn't want to share the cure with anyone.'

John Dance swung himself back up onto the crane, kicking wildly at the spy, who fell to his death on the site far below, the impact throwing up a cloud of cement dust.

'Then you shouldn't be here,' Glen told Misbah. 'You have to go. Thank you for bringing Vian to me. I wish you could stay longer.'

'Oh Glen, you twit.' Misbah locked eyes with her ex-husband. 'I didn't come here just to deliver the rag and bone man.' Vian was glued to *Spyland*. 'You don't know how upset I was having you back in the house, a helpless slob. You seemed more obsessed than ever with your trivia. I didn't believe you'd been murdered. Who'd have thought one of your customers could poison you?'

'The spicy beef soup?' Glen asked Vian, who nodded.

'I'm sorry for running out on you,' said Misbah, 'we do silly things when we're grieving, trying to cope.'

'I think you've just explained why you did what you did. Don't feel ashamed.'

'Oh, I'm not now. So much has happened since then.' Misbah wiped her nose on her sleeve. 'You don't need to go seeking justice any more.'

'All I want is peace and quiet.'

Misbah grabbed her coat and put it on. 'How did we last as long as we did?'

'It was meant to be, at that moment. That's how we lived – moment to moment.' Glen laughed softly. 'I think we enjoyed digging at each other.'

'Dig dig.'

'You were always much better at petty bickering than me.'

'Oh, thank you.' Misbah took it as a compliment. 'They've recalled Easler's Soup in a Box, I believe. They finally cottoned on to Vian's bad deed.'

'I'm a fugitive.' Vian looked up, proud at the mention. 'Misbah got me here in return for this whole exchange of information.'

'I've gone off soup,' Glen told Misbah. 'Tell Mum and the kids I love them.'

'I will.'

Vian stood up, following Misbah to the door.

'Hold up,' Glen told him. 'I think I might know of a job that would suit you.'

'Thank you, Glen.' Misbah have him a peck on the cheek, 'You're going to stay here, aren't you?'

'Haven't really thought about it. I have to protect my friends. And I know you can take care of yourself. If I sort all this craziness out I'd like to check on the kids, but if they don't want to see me...' Glen gave Misbah a sideways look, sounding her out again. Her silence was all the response he required. 'They *will* see me, when we're all ready. The drug companies are still keeping tabs on all the walking dead, as far as I know. I'm stuck here for the time being.' He paused, thinking of lost possibilities.

'If you want help –'

'I can go sling my hook.'

'Seriously, if you get in trouble financially I can drop a cheque in. Post it.'

'We'll burn that bridge when we come to it.' Glen stood in the doorway of his flat, Misbah and Vian out in the hallway. 'I still feel alive,' he told them, 'like an old man still feels like a kid, looking out from the inside. I knew life would be full of disappointment but death –'

'There's hope, too,' Misbah said as she walked towards the stairway, leaving Vian with Glen. 'There's always hope.'

Glen's second visit of the week was from J.C. This time, Kim was also present. 'I owe you an apology,' the cameraman said, before he'd even got through the door.

Kim hesitated before approaching her friend. He dispelled her concerns with a hug. 'You were right,' he told Glen, 'the producers did twist the story around. Said that shot of Morgan that we found was too short for viewers to be able to watch properly. Made it sound as if the deadheads started the whole thing.'

'Deadhead is such a negative term,' Kim said. 'We prefer to be called people. Men and women. Human beings.'

'Sure, I gotcha.' J.C. handed Glen a videotape. 'Here's a copy of some of the footage that I shot. Maybe you can do something with it.' He didn't want to stay. 'Oh, I'm sorry I lied to you, mate. About Kim's feelings for you, why she stuck around.' He avoided the reporter's gaze. 'I was trying to ease your pain.' He changed the subject quickly. 'You going to give evidence against your killer?'

Pro-diener lobbyists were starting to improve legislation, giving the dead more rights – murder victims could name the perpetrators and see justice done. Capital crimes had dropped by ten per cent in the interim.

'There was no killer,' Glen lied, 'I died all by myself, no help from anyone else. A big achievement.'

'I see.' J.C. didn't really, but he liked to give the appearance he knew what was going on.

Once the cameraman had left the flat, Glen shoved the tape in his video player and settled down to watch the contents.

They were candid, jumbled shots of Glen and he looked terrible. He tended to avoid mirrors and the raw honesty of video was a lot to take. The last time he'd seen footage of himself had been in a home movie on the family camcorder, Paul's seventh birthday, a picnic heyday somewhere pretty. He couldn't help comparing that smiling party animal with what he'd become – a grotesque parody of a man. He fast-forwarded through the beta shots, looking for a meaning, a reason why he'd been filmed. There was no story here, no news angle. This was some peculiar brand of voyeurism, not reportage.

'Hey! What is this?' Glen called Kim over.

'That? Oh, um, some shots of a guy I was interested in, once. For my personal viewing purposes.'

The footage cut to an early interview with Glen, when he'd still had some nostril hair and, for that matter, a nose. He'd poured his heart out to Kim in a vain attempt to impress her; she'd listened, nodding, every inch the professional.

'If this is immortality,' the interviewee said, his voice raised over the noise of construction machinery, his wide eyes directed at the camera, 'it comes at a price. I miss tasting chips, beer, chilli con carne. Now if I bite into anything I can't feel it with my teeth, I can't feel my jaw move. Then there's my skin – I could place my hand on a piping hot hob and not feel pain. If I hold you...' he reached forward, grasped the interviewer's fingers, '...no sensation. The memory's still there, like a man who's had his leg amputated and complains that his foot's sore. The strength of my memories have increased to compensate for what I've lost, it's like gaining a new set of emotions. My other senses have intensified too – my hearing's acute, I can see in the dark better'n a bunny and my mind's sharper than ever. Probably got something to do with the lack of TV around here, who knows?'

Kim stopped the tape. 'We've got to go,' she said, dragging Glen from his chair. 'Peter and Claig have an announcement to make.'

CHAPTER 20

The Great Beyond

KIM CLARKE PROFILE

Don't write off stv's Kim Clarke as an ambulance chaser – she's far more than that.

This month she's rebranding herself as an insightful documentary filmmaker, gaining special permission to travel outside Bonetown and interview the husbands of female troops stationed in Middle East hotspots.

'It's the husband's turn to keep the home fires burning,' said Kim. 'I needed to find out what kind of man could stay here and raise the children while their wives are away fighting.'

I asked her how she chose her projects. 'I'm pretty fearless,' she told me. 'I grew up in Greenock, went to a tough school, ran away from home at an early age. But I was always asking questions. A curious child.'

Did she always want to be a reporter? 'When I was 15 I walked into my local TV station and offered to work for free. I was stuck in the mailroom for months, but it was worth it in the end. I invariably get what I want.'

Kim's career continues to skyrocket. Later this year, she'll be presenting her own factual programme focussing on the ramifications of the diener problem. I asked her if the Channel 4 show would draw a large enough audience to make her a national mainstay.

'I'm not the star here,' she said, 'the guests are. We'll cover politics, human issues, economics, sorrow and joy. Something for everyone!'

This one-time News Personality of the Year is set to become an all-time star of the century – whether she likes it or not.

A Remote Magazine profile by Ros McPaul

AT THE CHURCH, SEATED in the front pew, Glen told Kim that his vivid dreams were returning.

'These dreams bother you a lot, don't they?'

'I wish I knew what they were. Fantasies or memories. You know what I think?'

Kim shook her head, indicating Glen to stop talking as Peter entered the church.

'My OBE.'

'Order of the British Empire?'

'Out of Body Experience. When I died, what happened. Little glimpses of what's out there. Maybe that's why we came back, to tell people what we saw or felt...'

'I'm having to announce my resignation from the organisation.' Peter stood at his podium, leaning against it heavily. 'As I will no longer be one of you, it's not fitting that I should represent you. Allow me to explain.' Peter took a hypodermic needle from his pocket and jabbed it into his eye socket. Despite all the ugly sights they saw daily, the dieners still gasped at this.

'Most of you spent your lives striving for nothing, merely existing, easily distracted by media gossip and pop cultural rubbish.' Peter winced. Was that pain that he felt? 'In your deaths, you're no better. But some of us are worthy of greater things. We plan ahead, taking risks, achieving greatness as effortlessly as –' A low, rattling sound came from his throat, like a suffocating man gasping for breath. 'I was one of the first dieners and I've been working on a cure ever since. Now it's perfected, and it will be made available to you at a reasonable price.'

Peter managed a passable salesman's smile. His body felt like it was coming to life again, organs beginning to function, like the sudden switch-on of Christmas tree lights. It was a shock that his system couldn't take. He looked up at Glen.

'Heart skipped a beat... for a while,' he gasped, then slumped over the podium. The magnificent light had vanished from his eyes.

'So there is an end to all this,' Glen whispered, looking at the assembled congregation. 'He's found a cure,' he told them. 'Maybe not the one he was looking for, but a cure all the same. He's dead. I mean, really dead. Officially. No re-release.' The audience was silent for a while, before an excited murmur filled the room. Slowly they trickled out of the hall, never to return. They didn't need Life After Death any more.

'Now what?' asked Kim as Glen closed Peter's eyelids.

'We find Claig. Then we go home.'

This changed everything. There was an end to existence, a heavenly light at the end of the tunnel. Now, just as Glen had found true happiness with Kim, he had learned that his zombie state could end. He could be released from a purgatory he was beginning to love. How many times had he prayed for a grand, bucket-kicking finale? He didn't feel too sorry for Kim, glad that she wouldn't have to exist in her ghastly state forever. As long as they had time to love each other.

By the time medical staff and guards arrived and Peter's body was removed, night had fallen. Glen walked home arm in arm with Kim, stopping only when they saw Claig strolling down Duncan Street, a triumphant swagger to his step.

'Mr Glass! Looks like you saved me the job of coming to get you,' said Claig, as calm and businesslike as ever. He was flanked by two of his favorite lackeys, Truegood and Morgan.

'Someone already beat you to it.'

'A shame what happened to Peter, isn't it?'

'How do you know?' Glen stayed close to Kim. 'You weren't at the meeting.'

'Peter was such a showman. Insisted on demonstrating his cure in front of you all. He was so concerned with his grand rebirth that he forgot to double check what was in his hypo.' Claig held up a vial of dark red liquid. 'I thought you'd appreciate the irony. Now you and I are the only ones who know how to develop the cure.'

'What did you switch it with?' Glen yelled. 'What did Peter jag himself with?'

'Hydrochloric acid. Every schoolboy knows you shouldn't be sticking that in your skull. All the same, what's good for the goose...'

Truegood and Morgan had hypos of their own and seemed eager to jab Glen and Kim with them. As they grabbed the couple, Claig clicked his tongue and took from Truegood's needle from him.

'Let's do this with some élan, shall we?' Claig twirled his wrist back and forth, the needle perilously close to Glen's nose. Duncan Street was quiet, there was no traffic and several lamps were kaput. Perfect for a bit of rough and tumble. Kim broke away, ramming the heel of her hand into Morgan's Roman nose. With Truegood distracted, Glen was able to push him off-balance. The thug fell heavily against a shop window, shattering it with his bulk and landing in a heap amongst a gang of mannequins.

While Kim continued to fend off Morgan, Glen grabbed a large sliver of broken glass and thrust it into Claig's shoulder. Morgan stopped to help his boss and the would-be victims fled to the warehouse, where Dave and Jen were staying late. Abosrbed by each other's wonderfully devious, compatible natures, they weren't getting much work done, canoodling on a pallet, not caring whether they got skelped.

'Dave! It's Claig – he's right behind us.' Dave unlocked his lips from Jen's, stood up and clenched his fists.

'I've had enough of that bozo,' he said, making Jen proud.

Bleeding, half out of his skull with rage, Claig set his henchmen on Dave and Glen. This time Dave wasn't so lucky with his blows; a sideswipe from Morgan knocked him flat on his back, winded. Jen ran from the pallet, pushing herself between Morgan and her lover.

'You won't hurt him,' she cried as Dave got up onto his knees. Morgan grabbed Jen by the throat, starting to squeeze the life out of her.

'Life's a precious thing,' said Reuben Whitley, his voice booming round the warehouse. 'It's like a strong prescription drug.' Though half of Reuben's face had been lost he still retained his weasely air. 'Not to be taken lightly.' He entered with several of his loyal lads, who grabbed Morgan by the arm and forced him to release Jen.

Reuben walked up to Claig, who was attempting to stab a needle into Glen's face. 'I'm not so sure Peter made the right choice,' Claig said, 'for you to be his successor.'

'He didn't make the choice at all,' murmured Glen, 'did he?'

'Get rid of these animals!' Truegood and the guards fired several shots into Reuben's men, knocking them down until they couldn't get up again.

'Why couldn't you have got here sooner?' Dave sobbed over Jen, who coughed and spluttered, barely alive.

'I've been busy,' said Reuben, 'I'm the new head of Life After Death. My followers needed me.' As if to prove the point, dieners filled the warehouse, rapidly surrounding Claig and the guards.

Desperate, Claig thrust his needle into Glen's stomach. Glen crumpled to the floor, Kim grabbing the hypodermic but stopping short of pulling it out.

'Do something, for God's sake!' Kim yelled at Reuben, who loomed behind Claig, wrapped his hands round his throat and steadily choked the life out of him. The last things Glen saw before he passed out were Reuben's half-face, full of glee, and Claig's eyes, bulged and filled with disbelief.

The scuffle over, Reuben ordered his men to take Claig and Glen to the clinic. Glen was still, his mind a daze of memories from the time of his death.

He hears a flushing noise and for a second he's afraid that he'll be sucked down the john. Instead of descending he goes up – that lighter than light sensation you only get in weight loss ads or transcendental meditation seminars, or when you're about to fall asleep at night and it feels as if the bed's levitating. He looks up, doesn't hit his face on the ceiling but floats right through, as transparent as the glass his name suggests, a kind of osmosis; seeping through the roof tiles, into the air like a helium balloon let go by a child, soaring now, at the mercy of the currents of the wind.

The sun is so bright that he's blinded. Still he heads towards it, velocity ever increasing, a waxwinged angel triumphant and scared, not breathing, not daring to look down.

His eyes crushed shut he recalls the heady highlights of his life: Snap Judgement's *twist ending, a Tonka truck he got for his fourth birthday, John Dance in the belly of the Mind Centre, Hogmanay in Glasgow, the death of Webb (in the gritty novel, not the* B-movie *Hollywood rip-off), the honeymoon in Bali with Misbah drinking too much gin, Dance's duel with Chen Sung in a plummeting helicopter, Paul's first bath, the destruction of Notre Dame cathedral in* Remember, Paris, *the hold-up in Video People, a cone-busting car chase in* The Morituri Completion, *an evil Futurist smashing an ice sculpture into hundreds of shiny shards, using the largest as a weapon against Glen's hero... fantasy mixing with reality, making life endurable, a mental escape hatch for a kid who'd never been forced to grow up.*

The realisation brings gravity into play. He plummets to earth too fast, sick in the guts, clouds jetting up past his nosedive body, nimbus smiles sure he'll hit hard. He can make out rivers, trees, houses and rocks as the ground grows closer.

Rather than striking the rocks he slips through a crevice, keeps falling. He's in pitch blackness for a while, the air whistling past him, the nightmare falling sensation that heralds a wake-up to the hell of real life tedium. Anything but that! The world around him fades from black to red and it gets hot. Too hot. Glen remembers the three little pigs, the big bad wolf coming down the chimney into a roaring fireplace, and Glen isn't one of the piggies. Flame licks at him and he's sorry for consorting with his ne'er-do-well neighbour, eating those cereals and not returning his mother's calls.

With a clumsy thump (is there any other kind?) he lands, tries to move, stopping himself before he rolls from a foot-thin ledge into a fiery pit below. Through the blaze he can make out white collar wantons chained to desks in miserable cubicles, overseered by fax machine demons. Knees shaking, brow dripping with the heat he stands, back to the sheer chasm wall, a heat wave rippling the air in front of him.

He doesn't melt. He casts a risky glance from side to side, looking for a way off the ledge, a foothold going up. Instead the mantle curves down around the inside of the crevice – there's no ascent that he can see. Flames lick at the cheap leather shoes he wears for work, frazzling the aglets. For once all the good times and his good deeds come to mind: unblocking Dad's drain, begrudging the sludge, sticking with Misbah when she gets pregnant, moving to Edinburgh to be close to his parents.

Slowly turning to face the wall, he reaches with his sodden hands to find a groove to cling to, hoisting himself up. For a moment he thinks there's a chance to scale the chasm until the sill crumbles beneath his feet. He falls backwards, expecting a pitchfork in the butt.

Instead a hot air current gusts him up through the crevice, bursting him through a sea bed; there's no need to hold his breath as he ascends faster than the air bubbles that are all around him. He geysers into the air and on, heading for the sun again. Its colour changes from yellow to amber. He's tractor beamed by a solar ray, a corridor of light leading to the sun's seething, bubbling surface. The gusting sound of the wind is replaced by the roaring of the inferno high above.

The trip through the corridor (a shaft piercing the darkness of space) seems to last forever, he sees sunspots before his eyes. Finally the roaring stops; there is silence, the bubbling surface of the sun now serene. Glen feels warm, not superheated despite the speed at which he has travelled. White light consumes him, he's surrounded by dead friends and lovers, Dad's there too and he's home.

'Can you hear me now?' Kim's beautiful face faded into view. Glen was back in the real world, the needle removed, his bony body patched up by Dr Jacobs.

'Oh yeah. I can hear you all right. I've got so much to tell you, Kimberley.'

'Please don't call me that. Kimberley Clark – makes me sound like a bathroom product.'

'Sorry.' Glen tried to sit up. 'Where's Claig?'

'They took him downstairs, kicking and complaining.'

'To the morgue?'

'Tethered to a slab, a tag tied to his toe and a gag on his mouth. I actually feel sorry for him.'

'Then I guess the lunatics have taken over the asylum.'

'As one lunatic talking to another, I approve.'

Claig could see and hear, but was unable to move as he was peered at by a prosector wearing a scrub suit, gloves and a clear plastic face shield. Light bounced off the shield, making it hard for Claig to see the man's face.

Claig turned his head to see taps and spigots set into the aluminium table he lay on. The prosector placed a rubber brick under his back so that his chest jutted outwards and his head sagged back, making it even harder for him to see.

The prosector was matter-of-fact, making notes on a checklist before picking up a large scalpel. Claig didn't feel what happened next but he could hear the sound of meat being cut and knew that his tormentor was slicing into him with the blade, then peeling off his skin. A flap from his chest was folded up, over his face. He shook his head from side to side, hardly daring to get a better view. Now the man had what seemed to be a pair of shiny, curved garden shears. A crunching noise and snapping jolts to his body made Claig scream, his gag muffling the sound.

Claig saw a slew of ribs and sternum, yanked away and placed out of sight. The prosector was rummaging inside his chest cavity, removing what was left of his organs. Claig was losing his sense of reality by now, unable to cope with what was happening to him, dimly aware that his torturer had cut his neck open.

The rubber block was taken from beneath Claig's back, his body shoved around like a piece of trash. With the block under his head he was able to see better until the prosector sliced the skin over his crown. His head was shoogled back and forth as the scalp was peeled away, with his eyes veiled again. He heard the buzz of an electric saw and above the noise, before he lost his senses completely, he thought he could hear the laughter of an overgrown boy.

'How'm I doing, Mr Claig?' Vian beemed at him, seeking approval. 'I think I've found a new passion.'

A SECOND OBITUARY

Few of today's business machine-manufactured mainstream idols will find a place in history; far fewer will deserve one.

When Richard Diener died two years ago, he merited a scrawny handful of lines on the obit page of his local paper. Six months later he was front page news, with a higher media profile than Brad Pitt, Schwarzenegger or the King of Pop (whoever wears the crown this week). Diener's singing technique was lax, his intelligence average, yet the nation embraced him as a star and a personality. He handled his handicap – lifelessness – with a charm far greater than that possessed by his songs.

Diener enjoyed the fruits of his success as if there was no tomorrow, and perhaps he was right – his existence was on extended lease and he couldn't be sure when that agreement would be cancelled.

After two eclectic, teen-pleasing albums, paparazzi punch-ups, hotel room hissy fits and a prime time reality TV show, that lease has expired. No warning, no comeback single. Rumours of Diener paying an exorbitant price for a 'cure' for his strange state seem unfounded; unkind critics have opined that his ultimate demise was an act of a merciful God, striking him down before he could inflict another CD on us all.

Diener was not the first star to score a number one hit after death, but he was the only one to date to personally promote that hit after the fact. For the sheer cheek of that, he deserves a funky footnote in the history books.

Editor's Comment
Remote Magazine

'What happens now then?' Glen and Kim sat on Boot Hill, looking down on the complex. Some of the more artistic dieners had painted trees and blue skies on the billboards to create a sense of an unbroken countryside vista. Many of the buildings below were deserted now, their inhabitants back with families or seeking work in the outside world. The flats would soon provide cheap housing for the living. The warm sun took the edge off the wind, blowing in across the lake.

'You deal with your death. I help you. We live as happily ever after as humanly possible.' As soon as Glen had recovered his consciousness, he'd insisted that Kim join him on the hill. Despite her fears that Glen hadn't fully recovered, Kim had helped him up the slope, listening to his description of the out of body experience he'd had at the moment of death.

'Are we still human?' she asked.

'Of course. We have minds, souls and hearts, even if they don't tick like they used to. Think of it as missing a beat for a considerable length of time.'

'I'm glad I woke up with you there.' Kim held Glen's hand tight. 'Not in an ambulance with a sheet over my face, or a morgue with a toe tag.'

'I was being selfish as usual. Wanted to keep you for myself. For a wee while, anyway. How's Jen holding up?'

'Live and needing a good kicking, as usual. She may be a nasty piece of work but what she did was a good, trying to save her boyfriend that way. Funny how people can surprise you – pleasantly, I mean.'

The clouds parted, a small circular opening large enough for the sun to shine through, shading the light around them a burnished orange.

'Any news on the cure?' Glen asked.

'Nothing new. I can tell you that Reuben's still fuming because he wasn't let in on the whole scheme; he's busy trying to keep control of his unruly army.'

'It's hard to maintain control when things are in a state of flux.'

'Reuben can go and flux himself for all I care. I've been keeping a closer eye on Dr Jacobs, actually. He keeps watching Peter's film over and over. That quack's dazzled everyone with his stem cell theories. He's even got Vian Lucas working for him.'

'Gainful employment is exactly what Vian needs.'

'He says this is a fake, by the way.' Kim held out her hand, Glen's *Spyland* ring in her palm.

'I'm sure it is. A ploy to keep me sweet.'

Kim put the ring on her left middle finger; it fit perfectly.

'What do you believe?' Glen asked her. 'Man's been tampering with nature for too long, and we're the side effects?'

'Reuben thinks we were meant to be immortal.'

'We're not gods, Kim. In our heads maybe, not any other way. Isn't that what the ego's all about, rejecting God as the Supreme Being and replacing Him with ourselves? Like it or not, we're mortal.'

'I don't know what to believe.' Kim opened a flask of soup and offered a cup to Glen. 'I know that things happen for a reason, life's a bitch and everyone gets what they deserve.'

'So what you're saying is, my guess is as good as yours.' Glen declined Kim's offer. 'The answer is there is no answer.'

'I can't go to my grave without knowing I've looked behind all those doors, faced the challenges, tried everything I always wanted to do.'

'What do we tell J.C.?'

'Nothing. He'd try to turn my death story into a tacky news item. How much did he sell that footage for?'

'Not much, considering. Five figures at a push.'

'Christ. We're old news now that Ricky Diener's passed on, just like Peter. My death scene'll be turning up on *You've Been Framed* before long, you see if it doesn't.'

'No one should have to watch their own death. It's monstrous.'

There was an uncomfortable silence.

'J.C.'s a fool, not a monster. Probably blow the money on a new camera.'

'Did you go out with him to see Jim Rose that night I trashed the flat?'

'Definitely not,' Kim said to him, her eyes wide, 'he's too rough and ready for me. I'm a good judge of character most of the time.' She held him close. 'That's why I stuck with you. Even when you were acting like an idiot.'

'I ripped up your calendar.'

'I know. I've gone off the Deppster anyway. Got a new idol to pedastalise.' She kissed him and they lay back on the hill, watching the clouds drift high above them, sensing the grass alive beneath them.

Milk Treading

Nick Smith

ISBN 1 84282 037 0 PBK £6.99

Life isn't easy for Julius Kyle, a jaded hack with the Post. When he wakes up on a sand barge with his head full of grit he knows things have to change. But how fast they'll change he doesn't guess until his best friend Mick jumps to his death off a fifty foot bridge outside the Post's window. Worst of all, he's a cat. That means keeping himself scrupulously clean, defending his territory and battling an addiction to milk.

Life isn't easy for a small cat with a big mouth, uttering words that could lead to a riot – or a war. So when the lovely Moira begs Julius for help, Julius is drawn brutally into a life he has only lived in his novels – the life of his hero sleuth Tiger Straight.

For political intrigue, murder, mayhem and milk treading... join Julius as he prowls deeper and deeper into the crooked underworld of Bast.

Smith writes with wit and energy, creating a memorable brood of characters, and skilfully building the sense of unease between sides as the action zeroes in towards its bloodthirsty conclusion.
THE LIST

The Kitty Killer Cult

Nick Smith

ISBN 1 84282039 7 PBK £9.99

In the style of Raymond Chandler, this is hard-boiled detective fiction set in the city of Nub; where cats are king, killer and killed. Tiger Straight, PI, is past his prime, homeless and unemployed until the dame Connie Hant shows up. The PI is back, pawing the mean streets of Nub that he knows so well.

Straight has a new mission – to catch the killers of the broad's brothers. It leads him to the murky, tatty underbelly of Nub, throwing up more kitty deaths and a love for a certain make-up artiste. What are the links between these murders and will Straight and his bug loving side-kick Natasha survive to discover the answers before the edible Inspector Bix Mortis?

For those who know and love Smith's first novel, *Milk Treading*, this is the book feline crime hack Julius Kyle started to write.

...There's a sense of sheer fun to this world that is more than a little infectious...get in on the act and enjoy a well told tale with a smart sense of humour, a fun plot and perhaps just a little to say about the real world as well.

CRIMESCENESCOTLAND.COM

Eye for an Eye

Frank Muir

ISBN 1 905222 56 4 PBK £9.99

One psychopath. One killer. The Stabber.

Six victims. Six wife abusers. Each stabbed to death through their left eye.

The cobbled lanes and back streets of St Andrews provide the setting for these brutal killings. But six unsolved murders and mounting censure from the media force Detective Inspector Andy Gilchrist off the case. Driven by his fear of failure, desperate to redeem his career and reputation, Gilchrist vows to catch The Stabber alone.

What is the significance of the left eye? How does an old photograph of an injured cat link the past to the present? And what exactly is *our little group*? Digging deeper into the world of a psychopath, Gilchrist fears he is up against the worst kind of murderer – a serial killer on the verge of mental collapse.

Can Gilchrist unravel the crazed mind of the killer? With reckless resolve, he risks it all in a heartstopping race to catch The Stabber, knowing that any mistake could be his last.

Everything that I look for in a crime novel.

LOUISE WELSH

Writing in the Sand

Angus Dunn

ISBN 1 905222 47 5 PBK £12.99

At the farthest end of the Dark Isle lies the village of Cromness, where the normal round of domino matches, meetings of the Ladies' Guild and twice-daily netting of salmon continues as it always has done.

Down on the beach, an old man rakes the sand, looking for clues to the future. The patterns show him the harmony of the universe, but they also show that there is something wrong in Cromness. Strange things are beginning to happen.

Because this is no ordinary island. Centuries ago, so it is said, the Celtic gods and godesses took refuge here. Now, behind the walls of the world, there are restless stirring sounds.

Soon everyone is drawn into the struggle against the shadows that threaten the Dark Isle. But is anyone truly aware of the scale of events? And who will prevail?

It is a latter day baggy monster of a novel... a hallucinogenic soap... the humour at first has shades of Last of the Summer Wine, alternating with the Goons before going all out for the Monty Python meets James Bond, and don't-scrimp-on-the-turbo-charger method... You'll have gathered by now that this book is a grand read. It's an entertainment. It alternates between compassionate and skilful observations, elegantly expressed and rollercoaster abandonment to a mad narrative.

NORTHWORDS NOW

Luath Press Limited

committed to publishing well written books worth reading

LUATH PRESS takes its name from Robert Burns, whose little collie Luath (*Gael.*, swift or nimble) tripped up Jean Armour at a wedding and gave him the chance to speak to the woman who was to be his wife and the abiding love of his life. Burns called one of 'The Twa Dogs' Luath after Cuchullin's hunting dog in Ossian's *Fingal*. Luath Press was established in 1981 in the heart of Burns country, and now resides a few steps up the road from Burns' first lodgings on Edinburgh's Royal Mile.
Luath offers you distinctive writing with a hint of unexpected pleasures.

Most bookshops in the UK, the US, Canada, Australia, New Zealand and parts of Europe either carry our books in stock or can order them for you. To order direct from us, please send a £sterling cheque, postal order, international money order or your credit card details (number, address of cardholder and expiry date) to us at the address below. Please add post and packing as follows: UK – £1.00 per delivery address; overseas surface mail – £2.50 per delivery address; overseas airmail – £3.50 for the first book to each delivery address, plus £1.00 for each additional book by airmail to the same address. If your order is a gift, we will happily enclose your card or message at no extra charge.

Luath Press Limited
543/2 Castlehill
The Royal Mile
Edinburgh EH1 2ND
Scotland
Telephone: 0131 225 4326 (24 hours)
Fax: 0131 225 4324
email: sales@luath.co.uk
Website: www.luath.co.uk